DEBBIE MACOMBER

JODI THOMAS

Western Hearts

mira

mira

ISBN-13: 978-0-7783-0835-5

Western Hearts

Recycling programs
for this product may
not exist in your area.

Printed in U.S.A.

Also available from Debbie Macomber and MIRA Books

CONTENTS

MONTANA

Debbie Macomber

Dedicated to Barb Dooley, with thanks
for blessing my life with her wisdom and friendship

One

"I don't know how much longer your grandfather's going to live."

The words hit Molly Cogan with the force of an unexpected blow. Sinking onto a stool beside the kitchen phone, she blocked out the blare of the television and her sons' ongoing argument over whose turn it was to set the table for dinner.

Tom and Clay were at each other's throats, but Molly could only deal with one crisis at a time. "Who is this again, please?"

"Sam Dakota. Listen, I realize this isn't the best time, but I felt I should tell you." He paused, then added, "Walt wouldn't appreciate me calling you, but like I said, you have a right to know his health isn't good."

The unmistakable sound of shattering glass filtered through the television noise as the boys' skirmish escalated.

Placing her hand over the mouthpiece, Molly shouted, "Boys, please! Not now." Something in her voice must have communicated the importance of the call, because both turned and stared at her. A moment later, Tom reached for the broom.

Molly's hand trembled as she lifted the receiver back to her ear. "How do you know my grandfather, Mr. Dakota?"

"I'm his foreman. Been here about six months."

The fact that Gramps had willingly surrendered control of his ranch to a hired hand—a stranger—told her a great deal. For the past few years, he'd sold off portions of the once-huge spread, until all that remained was a couple of thousand acres, small by Montana standards. He'd managed the Broken Arrow Ranch himself as long as she could remember. Hired hands came and went, depending on the size of the herd, but as far as she knew, he'd always maintained tight control of the day-to-day operations. Over the years his letters had been infrequent, but in the last one—which she'd received after Christmas, four and a half months ago— Molly had sensed something wasn't right with Gramps. She'd put aside the feeling, however, consumed by her own problems.

"Tell me again what happened," she said abruptly, struggling to regain her composure. The man's first words had been such a shock, much of what he'd said afterward had escaped her.

"Like I told you, spring's our busy time, and yesterday your grandfather told me he'd be out to help check on the new calves. When he didn't show, I returned to the house and found him unconscious on the kitchen floor. Heart attack, I figured."

Molly pressed her fingers to her lips to hold in a gasp of dismay. Gramps…in pain. Unable to breathe. Losing consciousness. It frightened her to think of it.

With her mother and half brother living in Australia, Gramps was her only family here. Her only connection with her long-dead father.

"I got him to the clinic in town and Doc Shaver confirmed what I thought. It *is* his heart. Walt has a pacemaker, but the walls of his heart are old and brittle, and it isn't working as well as Doc had hoped."

"Gramps has a pacemaker?" Molly cried. "When did this happen?" She raised her hand to the cameo hanging from a gold chain around her neck and clenched it hard. It was the most precious piece of jewelry she owned. Gramps had given it to her the day they buried her grandmother nine years before.

"More than six months ago. First I'd heard of it, too."

"Why didn't he *tell* me?" Molly asked, although she realized Sam Dakota couldn't possibly know. She wished—not for the first time—that San Francisco was closer to Montana. Right now, Sweetgrass seemed a million miles away.

"I can't answer that. I thought you should know Walt's probably not going to live much longer. If you want to see him, I suggest you plan a visit out here soon."

"What exactly is wrong with his heart?" It might have sounded as if she was avoiding the real issue, but she needed to understand Gramps's condition before she could even *begin* to think about anything else. Like her finances. And how she could possibly afford a trip to Montana now.

"Do you know anything about pacemakers?"

"A little." Just enough to understand that they emit an electronic beep, which assists the heart in beating at a steady pace.

"Well, as I said earlier, the walls of your grandfather's heart are brittle and it's difficult to get the pacemaker to function properly. Doc Shaver worked on him a couple of hours, but he couldn't make any guarantees. Said there's nothing more he can do. It's only a matter of time before his heart gives out completely."

Molly clamped her teeth over her lower lip while she tried to take in what this man was telling her. "I…I appreciate the call. Thank you." With each word, she felt herself more overwhelmed by emotion. *Not Gramps, please dear God, not Gramps. Not yet.*

"Sorry to call with such bad news."

"How…how is he now?" She glanced toward the living room and discovered Tom and Clay standing in the doorway, studying her intently. A smile would have reassured them, but even that was beyond her.

"Better. Will you be coming, then?" the foreman asked.

"I'm not sure." Molly didn't see how she could manage it. With the child-support payments cut off and the financial adjustments they'd already been forced to make in the past year, she couldn't imagine squeezing one more expense into her already stretched budget. Even a short trip would require at least a week away from her job—a contract position without paid holidays. Plus, she'd have the cost of airfare or, more likely, gas and lodging for the drive. She'd have to take the boys; Gramps would want to see them, and they deserved to see him.

"When will you know whether you're coming?"

It might have been her imagination, but she detected a note of censure. This man knew nothing about her—

knew nothing about her circumstances or her life. How dared he stand as judge and jury over her decisions?

"If I knew that, I'd have said something sooner!" Leaning the back of her head against the kitchen wall, Molly tried to think clearly, desperate to find a way, a solution—anything that would lighten the burden of her fears. Never one to weep openly, particularly with strangers, she fought the growing constriction in her throat.

"Then I won't keep you any longer," Sam said gruffly.

Molly wanted to shout that he should wait, that she had other questions, but he'd already answered the important ones. What she wanted even more was to hear this stranger tell her Gramps was on the mend.

But he wasn't going to say that.

"Thank you for phoning," she said, feeling guilty about the sharp retort she'd made a moment ago. No one enjoyed delivering bad news, and it was kind of Sam Dakota to make sure she learned of her grandfather's condition. "I'll let you know if we're coming for a visit," she felt obliged to add.

"Fine. Your grandfather should be home in a day or two. I'd consider it a favor if you didn't mention I called."

"I won't. And thank you." Standing up, she replaced the telephone receiver and looked at her sons. Both had their father's deep-set dark brown eyes—and both had been born with the ability to look straight through her. At fourteen Tom was growing by leaps and bounds, a gangly youth with feet too big for his body. He hadn't grown into his height, and had become painfully self-conscious. This was an awkward stage filled with frustrations and raging hormones. They'd once been close, but that had all changed in the past few months. Tom barely talked to her now, no longer sharing confidences the way he used to. Often he was sullen and angry for no apparent reason. His attitude worried Molly; she sensed he was keeping something from her. She tried not to think about it, but every now and then the fear that he was experimenting with drugs or running with the wrong crowd would enter her mind and refuse to go away.

Clay, at eleven, was a younger version of his brother. Neither boy had inherited her auburn hair or clear blue eyes. Both resembled their father's side of the family— dark-haired and dark-eyed. Not that Daniel's family had revealed much interest in her sons. But then, neither had Daniel.

"That was about Dad, wasn't it?" Tom asked, his eyes locked on hers. His shoulders stiffened as though he was bracing himself for her response. The situation with Daniel hadn't been easy on any of them. They'd seen his name in the newspapers and on television night after night for weeks, that whole time the trial was taking place.

"The call wasn't about your father," Molly answered carefully. The kids had been through enough because of Daniel. He'd never been a good father, any more than he'd been a good husband; he had, in fact, left her for another woman. But she'd say one thing for him: until a year ago he'd faithfully paid child support. The payments had stopped when Daniel's troubles had begun. His legal problems had eventually led to financial problems for her and the boys.

"What did Dad do this time?" Tom demanded, his

eyes narrowing suspiciously. It was a look Molly recognized, a look that said Tom, with his newly developed teenage cynicism, wasn't about to believe *any* adult. Especially his mother...

"I told you this has nothing to do with your father!" It bothered Molly that her son would assume she'd lie to him. There was nothing she abhorred more than lying. Daniel had taught her and their children more than enough on *that* subject. "I wouldn't lie to you."

"Then what's wrong?" Clay moved into the kitchen and Molly held out her arms to her youngest son. Clay didn't object to an occasional hug, but Tom had let it be known he was much too old for that sort of thing—and much too cool to display affection toward his mother. She respected his wishes, and at the same time longed for the times when they could share a simple hug.

"It's Gramps," she said. Her throat started to close and she couldn't say more.

Clay wrapped his arms tightly around her waist and pressed his head to her shoulder. Molly sighed deeply.

"Is Gramps sick?" Tom asked, shoving his hands in his pockets. He paced restlessly, back and forth across the kitchen floor. It'd become a habit of his lately, a particularly irritating one. Oh, yes, Molly thought, sighing again. The last twelve months had been hard on all of them. Tom seemed to be having the toughest time coping with everything—the public humiliation of his father's trial for fraud, the lack of any extra money and then the move from a spacious three-bedroom house to a cramped two-bedroom apartment. But this place was the best she could do, and his dissatisfaction underscored her own feelings of inadequacy.

"Gramps's heart is giving him trouble," Molly finally answered. She spoke in a low toneless voice.

"Are we going to go see him?"

Molly brushed the hair from Clay's brow and gazed down on his sweet boyish face. "I don't know yet."

"But, Mom, don't you *want* to?" Tom cried.

That hurt. Of course she did. Desperately. If she had the choice, she'd be on the first plane out. "Oh, Tom, how can you ask me that? I'd give anything to be with Gramps."

"Then let's go. We can leave tonight." Tom headed toward the bedroom he shared with his younger brother, as if the only thing they needed to do was toss a few clothes in a suitcase and walk out the door.

"We can't," she said, shaking her head, disheartened once again by the reality of their situation.

"Why not?" Tom's voice was scornful.

"I don't have enough—"

"Money," her oldest son finished for her. He slammed his fist against the kitchen counter and Molly winced, knowing that the action must have been painful. "I *hate* money! Every time we want to do something or need something, we can't, and all because of money."

Molly pulled out a kitchen chair and sagged into it, her energy gone, her spirits deflated by anger and self-pity.

"It's not Mom's fault," Clay muttered, placing his skinny arm around her shoulders, comforting her.

"I don't know what to do," Molly said, thinking out loud.

"If you wanted to go by yourself," Tom offered with a show of reluctance, "I could baby-sit Clay."

"I don't need a baby-sitter," Clay insisted. "I can take

care of myself." He glared at his older brother, challenging Tom to proclaim otherwise.

"I can't leave now, with or without you boys," Molly told them sadly. She had less than twenty dollars in her checking account. It was the all-too-familiar scenario—too much month at the end of her money.

"I remember Gramps," Tom said suddenly. "At least I think I do."

The last time Molly had visited the ranch was shortly after her divorce almost ten years ago. Her grandmother, who'd already been ill at the time with a fast-spreading cancer, had died shortly afterward. Gramps had asked Molly to come live with him, and for a while she'd seriously considered the invitation. She told herself now that if she'd had any sense, she would have taken him up on his offer. She might actually have done it if she'd managed to find work. Fluent in both French and German, Molly was employed on a contract basis by an import agency. Unfortunately there wasn't much call for her skills in the cattle country of western Montana.

During that visit Tom had been four and Clay still in diapers. Whatever memories Tom had were more likely the stories she'd told him about the ranch. Tucked against the foothills of the Bitterroot Mountains, the Broken Arrow was one of the lonely ranches scattered through the Flathead River valley. Molly often talked about it, especially after a letter arrived from Gramps. There weren't many, only two or three a year. Her grandmother had been the one who'd taken care of family correspondence. Molly had discovered that Gramps hated talking on the phone even more than he hated writing letters; nevertheless, he made the effort to keep in touch with her. Each one of his letters was read countless times and treasured. Losing his lifelong love had devastated him, and even now, nine years after her passing, Gramps mentioned his wife in every single letter, every conversation.

Molly always answered his letters and routinely mailed him pictures of the boys. Over the years they'd talked on the phone a number of times but their conversations had obviously been uncomfortable for him. Gramps never had been much of a talker, nor was he like the stereotypical kindly old characters who populated kids' storybooks. Nope, he was actually a bit of a curmudgeon. He yelled into the telephone as if he thought that was necessary in order to be heard and fretted constantly over what the call was costing.

No small man, he stood a good six-two and weighed at least two hundred pounds. Four-year-old Tom had found his appearance so scary that he'd clung to her leg the first few days of their visit. Clay had buried his face in her shoulder and wailed the instant Gramps came into view. Her grandfather didn't have the slightest idea how intimidating he could be to small boys.

Had it really been nine years since she'd last seen him? It seemed impossible, yet she knew it was true.

"He yelled," Tom murmured, lost in his own thoughts.

That was Gramps, all right. He was gruff and impatient and about as subtle as a gun in your face. To really know him was to love him, but he rarely gave anyone the opportunity to get that close. Never afraid to voice his opinions, Gramps went out of his way to make sure folks around him knew what he thought and why; anyone who dared to disagree was called a "danged fool." Usually to his—or her—face.

When Molly's grandmother was alive, she'd smoothed the waters. Her charm and humor had more than compensated for Walt Wheaton's prickly nature. By now, Gramps had probably alienated just about everyone in Sweetgrass.

The foreman who'd phoned said he'd been around for more than six months. If Gramps had mentioned hiring a foreman in any of his letters, she'd missed it—hard to believe, considering how often she'd read them. But knowing Gramps, he'd rather chew nails than admit he needed help.

Sam Dakota. The name sounded almost familiar. She grinned weakly, allowing herself to be amused for just a moment—maybe she was confusing him with *South* Dakota. Or maybe Gramps had mentioned him, but not in a discussion about hired hands. She was sure of that.

The boys went to bed that evening with a minimum of fuss, for which Molly was grateful. She followed soon after, weary to the bone.

It shouldn't have come as a surprise that she couldn't sleep. Every time she closed her eyes, all she could see was Gramps. All she could think about was the cantankerous old man she loved.

At midnight, Molly gave up the effort and turned on the light. Tossing aside the covers, she went to her desk and sorted through the drawers until she found the last letter she'd received from Gramps. She sat on her bed, legs crossed, and read it slowly.

Dear Molly,
Thanks for the pictures of you and the boys. They sure don't look like they're any relation to us Wheatons, do they? Guess I can't hold it against

them that they resemble their father. They aren't
to blame for that. The picture of you is another
story. Every time I pick it up, it's like seeing my
own sweet Molly at your age. Only she wore her
hair long.

I don't understand what's with women these
days. They cut their hair short like they want to
be men. Ginny Dougherty, the gal who ranches
the spread next to mine, for instance—damn fool
woman thinks she can tend a herd as good as a
man, so she decides to look like one. She might be
a handsome woman if she kept her hair long and
even wore a dress. I tell you, her husband would
turn over in his coffin if he could see what she's
done to herself.

As for the hair business, I'll admit men aren't
much better. Seems a lot of them prefer to wear
it long—like back in the sixties, hippies and all.
But I never thought I'd see grown men—gray-
haired geezers, for Pete's sake!—wearing pony-
tails. Even worse—what do you call them?—those
pigtails. Far as I'm concerned Willie Nelson's got
a lot to answer for.

It isn't just the way people do their hair, either. More and more strange things are going on
in Sweetgrass. A man doesn't know who to trust
any longer. People talk as if the government was
the enemy. I didn't fight in a world war to hear
that kind of crazy talk, but then folks around here
never have been keen for my opinion. I give it to
them, anyway, whether they want to hear it or not.

The weather's been good and bad. Winter
hasn't been too hard so far—only one blizzard.

The chickens are laying more eggs than I can use, which means they're content. There's nothing better than bacon and eggs for breakfast. I hope you're feeding the boys a decent breakfast every morning and not that sugar-coated junk.

Now about you. It sounds like Daniel finally got what he's deserved all along. Imagine cheating those decent folks out of their hard-earned cash! I never did understand why you married that smooth talker. I knew the minute I met him he wasn't any good. If you'd asked me before you were foolish enough to go through with the wedding, you might have saved yourself a lot of trouble. Well, at least you have your boys, so something good came out of the marriage.

You're my only grandchild, Molly, and you're all I have left. You know that. I remember the day you were born and your father called to say Joan had given birth to a girl. Your grandmother wept when she learned your parents decided to name you after her. They must have known something even then, because small as you were, you resembled my Molly, and you do so more every year. She was a beautiful woman, and you are, too.

I wish your marriage had been like ours. It was the best thing in my life, Molly. I'm glad you're rid of that no-good Daniel, but I wish you'd marry again. Though I suppose that subject's best saved for another day.

I want to talk to you about something else. I recently celebrated my seventy-sixth birthday, so I decided it was time I got my affairs in order. I had a new will drawn up. When I was in town last week, I stopped off and talked to Russell Letson. He's an attorney who's been around awhile, and his father and I used to be friends. I like Russell well enough, even though I suspect most attorneys are shysters. Anyway, I brought in my old will, and Russell and I talked a bit and he asked me a bunch of questions that got me to thinking.

There's certain things you should know. First off, I've got a safe-deposit box at the bank. I put some medals in there from the war. When the time is right and they appreciate that sort of thing, you can give those medals to my great-grandsons. I suppose I should put your grandmother's wedding band in there, but I never could bring myself to part with it. I got it on the nightstand next to the bed. Nine years she's been gone, and I still miss her.

The ranch will be yours. I wish you'd moved here after Molly died, but I understood why you decided to return to California. For myself, I don't know how you can breathe that foul air—I've seen what San Francisco's like, on television. It can't be good for the boys to be taking in all that smog. I'm hoping that after I'm gone you'll give Sweetgrass another try. Folks here are hardworking and decent. Most years, the ranch should at least break even. And the house is solid. My father built it in 1909, and after he died, Molly and I added electricity and indoor plumbing. As houses go, it isn't fancy, but it's stood all these years and will stand longer.

That pretty well takes care of what I wanted to tell you.

I love you, Molly girl, and those youngsters of yours, too. I'm sure you know that, although I'm not one to say it often. This letter seemed like a good time to do it.

Remember—don't let Daniel give you any more grief. He's getting what he deserves.
Gramps

Molly read the letter a second time and then a third. It all made sense now.

According to what the foreman had told her, Gramps must have written it two months after he got the pacemaker. Her beloved grandfather hadn't said one word about his health problems, and she knew why.

Daniel.

Gramps hadn't wanted to burden her with more worries while she dealt with the publicity and embarrassment of Daniel's trial.

Gramps was right about Daniel; a prison term was exactly what he deserved. As an investment specialist he'd been regularly stealing retirement income from his elderly clients. He'd been clever about it, concocting schemes and falsifying numbers; it had taken several accountants and finance specialists almost a year to uncover the full extent of his crimes. Throughout his entire so-called career, he'd been cheating the very people he was supposed to be helping. He'd lied to his colleagues and clients, lied to the police and the press. He'd even been caught lying under oath. His trial had lasted for weeks, with mobs of angry senior citizens packing the courtroom demanding justice. They didn't get their money back, but they were there to see Daniel sentenced to twenty years.

Because Molly had been so distressed by what was happening to all these people who, like her, had once trusted Daniel, she hadn't paid enough attention to some of the remarks in Gramps's letter. She'd read and re-read his words for the comfort they gave her, for the way they brought him close, but she hadn't stopped to question his sudden interest in a will and settling his affairs. Hadn't recognized that he was preparing her for his death. It seemed obvious now that he didn't expect to live much longer.

Besides this letter, she could remember only one other time Gramps had told her he loved her—the day they buried her grandmother. She had no doubt of his love; he said it loud and clear, but rarely with words. Open displays of emotion embarrassed him, as they did many other men, particularly men of his generation.

This letter wasn't the first time he'd commented on her marrying again. That theme had been a constant one since the divorce. The ink hadn't dried on the legal papers, and Gramps was already trying to introduce her to the bachelor ranchers in the area.

The thought of another relationship still sent chills up Molly's spine. As she liked to tell her friends, she'd done the marriage thing and wasn't interested in repeating it.

Tucking the letter back in the envelope, she lay down, not expecting to sleep. But she must have drifted off because the next thing she knew, the alarm was buzzing. Gramps's letter was clutched in her hand, held close to her heart.

It was clear to her then. So clear she should've figured it out months ago. The answer had always been there, but she'd been too blind, too stubborn, too willful to see it. It'd taken nearly losing her grandfather to show her what she had to do.

The small conference room off the principal's office was the last place Tom wanted to be. Referred to as "the holding cell" at Ewell Junior High, the room was cold even during the hottest weather, and it had an unpleasant odor that reminded him of a dentist's office.

Eddie Ries sat in the hard wooden chair beside him. Eddie's mother was on her way to the school. Tom hadn't heard when his own mother would arrive. All he knew was that when she did, she wouldn't be happy.

Suspended for three days. That was supposed to be punishment? Tom almost laughed out loud. Time away from classes was practically a *reward* for screwing up! Personally Tom was sick of school. Sick of a lot of things he couldn't change. His no-good dad for one, and the way the kids had looked at him when they learned the guy in the news was his father. He was sick of feeling helpless and frustrated—which was why he'd become involved in something he'd never thought he would.

He wasn't friends with Eddie. Didn't even like him. Eddie went searching for trouble; it made him feel big. Made him look like somebody to the homies. A big man on campus when in reality he'd never fit in. Tom wasn't sure he did anymore, either; maybe that was what had made him do something so stupid.

While he didn't regret the suspension, Tom hated adding to his mother's worries. He could see how this news about his great-grandfather's health had depressed her. All through dinner the night before, she'd barely said a word; she hadn't eaten much, either.

Tom hadn't had much of an appetite himself. He couldn't stop thinking about Gramps. He wasn't sure if he remembered the old man or not, but he let Clay think he did, mainly because he was the oldest and *should* remember. Clay had been a baby that time they were in Montana.

On his twelfth birthday—and the two birthdays after that—Tom had gotten a personal letter from Gramps and a check for twenty bucks. Before that, Gramps had always mailed his mother money and then she'd go shopping and pick something out for him. These last birthdays, the check was made out to him.

In his first letter Gramps had said a boy of twelve was old enough to know what he wanted. Old enough to go out and buy it, too. Tom never forgot the feeling that had come over him with that letter. For the first time in his life he'd felt like a man. He might not remember what Gramps looked like, but Tom loved him the same way his mother did.

His mother was worried. She worried about a lot of things. Tom could always tell when problems got her down. Work, his father, money. Now Gramps. Over the years, he'd come to recognize the symptoms. She'd grow quiet and then three small vertical lines would form in the center of her forehead. It hurt to see those lines and know there wasn't a damn thing he could do to help her. Those were the times he went to his room, put on his earphones and played music so loud his head pounded afterward. The music helped him not to think, because when he did, his stomach ached.

Tom *wanted* to help his mother. When he was a kid, he'd planned to become a magician and make all the bad things in life disappear with one flamboyant wave of a wand. He used to imagine doing that sometimes. With a flick of his wrist every problem would magically disappear.

The door to the conference room burst open, and Tom sat up straighter as his mother stormed in, her eyes blazing with anger.

Tom lowered his own eyes. He toyed with the idea of greeting her, then decided against it. She didn't look like she was all that happy to see him.

"Gang symbols, Tom?" she said through clenched teeth, hands on her hips. "You painted *gang symbols* on the gym wall?"

"Outside wall," he corrected, and regretted it immediately.

"Do you think it matters *which* wall?" she asked in a tone that told him the three-day suspension from school was the least of his worries.

Mr. Boone, the principal, walked briskly into the room, looking far too satisfied with himself—like he'd accomplished what he'd set out to do. Tom had never had strong feelings about the man, but he was inclined to dislike him now—simply for the smug way he smiled, knowing Tom was in major trouble at home.

"As I explained earlier, Mrs. Cogan," the principal said, "this school has a zero-tolerance policy with regard to gang activities. While I don't really believe Tom's involved in a gang, there are plenty of wannabes. I'd like to believe Tom's smarter than that, but after today I'm not sure."

"Get your things, Tom. I'm taking you home," his mother instructed. He could tell from her voice that said she had plenty more to say later.

Nevertheless, Tom nearly leaped off the chair in his

eagerness to escape. He grabbed his jacket and followed his mother outside.

"Of all the stupid brainless things for you to do," she said as they headed out to the parking lot. Her steps were so fast he had trouble keeping up.

Yeah, well, he wasn't especially proud of himself, either.

They climbed in the car and he thought she was going to take rubber off the tires the way she squealed across the lot. She missed the Stop sign and zoomed into the street, almost hitting another car.

"Mom!" Tom shouted, holding on to the edge of the seat as he was thrown against the passenger door. "It's not a good idea for you to drive when you're this mad."

"Mad isn't the half of it."

"Okay, okay, so I made a mistake."

"A *mistake?* Gangs, Tom?"

"I'm not in any gang!"

She tossed him a look that assured him she knew otherwise. "Then why spray-paint their symbols?" Without inhaling she added, "You're going to repaint that wall all by yourself, young man."

"Hey, I wasn't the only one who painted it." Talk about unfair!

"You're going back to school first thing tomorrow morning to do it."

"What about Eddie?"

His mother sent him a sidelong glance sharp enough to cut glass. "I don't have any say over him, but I have all kinds of say over you."

She liked to *think* she did. But this didn't seem the appropriate time to discuss it. "According to what Mr. Boone said, I'm not supposed to be on school property," he told her. One of them had to keep a cool head, and it was obvious his mother had already lost hers.

"Don't concern yourself—I already asked Mr. Boone and he's willing to make an exception."

"That isn't fair! How come I have to come back and paint the wall? Eddie should be there, too." The anger was brewing inside him, and he tightened his jaw, knowing it would do neither of them any good to vent it now.

"Eddie's parents can see to his punishment."

Which meant Eddie was off the hook. Eddie's mother drank too much, and even Eddie didn't know where his father was. Tom certainly knew the whereabouts of his own father—and so did everyone else.

"Can't I paint the wall *after* the suspension?" he asked, thinking he'd prefer to do it during the weekend. Having the entire school watch him suffer such humiliation held little appeal.

"No," came her emphatic reply.

"Why not?" he demanded, clenching his fists.

"Because I need you for other things."

"What things?"

"Packing."

That captured Tom's attention. He waited a moment, then asked, "Are we going somewhere?"

"Montana."

His heart nearly burst with excitement. She'd found a way. His mother was taking them to Montana. This was good news, better than anything he'd anticipated. "We're visiting Gramps?"

She didn't answer him right away. Tom watched

as her hands tensed on the steering wheel. "Not exactly. I handed in my two weeks' notice this morning. We're moving."

Two

Sam Dakota bolted upright out of a sound sleep. His heart slammed against his rib cage with a punch almost powerful enough to hurt. Cold sweat dampened his forehead and clung to his bare chest. One ragged breath followed another as his body heaved in a near-desperate effort to drag oxygen into his burning lungs.

The dream always woke him. Whenever he had it, he would feel that panic again, the fear as vivid and real as the first day the prison door had clanged shut behind him. It had echoed against the concrete walls, reverberating in his ears. Twenty-four months into freedom, and he still heard that terrible sound. It invaded his sleep, tortured him, reminded him constantly that he was a living, breathing failure. Thankfully he didn't have the dream often anymore—not since he'd started working for old man Wheaton.

Closing his eyes, Sam lay back down, his head nestled in the feather pillow. He swallowed and flexed his hands, trying to ease the tension from his body, forcing himself to relax.

It was over. Over.

Prison was behind him, and so was the life he used to live. Yet at one time he'd been a rodeo star, riding bulls, flirting with fame. Fame and women. He'd had his own following, groupies who chased after him. They stroked his ego, cheered for him, drank with him, slept with him and, on more than one occasion, fought over him.

The groupies were gone, the way everything that had once been important to him was gone. In his rodeo career and after his accident, he'd faced danger, injury, death, and he'd done it without a trace of fear.

Riding the wave of success, he'd achieved everything he'd ever wanted. That was at the rodeo championships in Vegas, six years earlier. But the silver buckle that proclaimed him the best of the best had been pawned to help an old man hold on to his ranch. These days Sam stayed out of trouble, kept his nose clean, minded his own business. When the urge hit him, he moved on.

Sam didn't like to dwell on his rodeo days. That was all in the past, finished. The doctors had warned him of the risks of ever competing again. Another fall like the one that had ended his career could cripple him for life. Or kill him. It was that simple. The money, what little of it he'd managed to save, had been swallowed whole by doctor and hospital bills.

Friends had stuck by him for a time, but he'd driven them away with his anger and frustration. Even his parents didn't know his whereabouts, which was just as well. Pride had prevented him from ever letting them know he'd landed in a Washington-state prison for second-degree assault. After two years of silence it hadn't seemed worth his trouble to write and fabricate an account of where he'd been and why he'd stayed away.

It'd been a few years now since his last contact with family, and as the months went on, he thought about them less and less.

Until he ended up at the Broken Arrow Ranch, Sam had drifted across three or four states, depressed, miserable and mad as hell. The restlessness inside him refused to die.

He'd lasted longer here in Sweetgrass than anywhere else.

Mostly because of the old man. Walt was as mean as a grizzly bear and as demanding as a drill sergeant, but that didn't keep Sam from admiring him. Six months earlier Sam had arrived in this backwoods Montana town; six minutes after that he'd crossed the sheriff. He hadn't been looking for trouble, but trouble always seemed to find him. All he'd meant to do was help a lady in a difficult situation, a lady who was being bothered by a drunk, and in the process he'd stepped on the wrong toes. It turned out the drunk was a friend of the sheriff's. Before he knew it, the sheriff had learned about his prison record and Sam was headed for jail, charged with unlawful conduct and disturbing the peace. The other guy—the man who'd been beating up on the woman—had walked away scot-free. Then, for no reason he could understand, Walt Wheaton had stepped in, paid his bail and offered him a job. Eventually the charges were dropped, thanks to some negotiating by Walt's attorney.

Sam could deal with just about anything. Pain, disappointment, the reversal of fortune. But he'd discovered that he was unprepared to handle kindness. It embarrassed him. Made him feel uneasy. Indebted. The only reason he'd agreed to accept the foreman's job was that he owed the old coot. The pay wasn't much, but Walt had given him a small house on the property, rent free. It was the original foreman's place—run-down but livable.

The minute Sam set foot on the ranch, he realized Walt was in dire straits. The Broken Arrow was in deplorable condition. No sooner had Sam started work when a series of mysterious and seemingly unrelated events began to occur. Pranks and vandalism, nothing serious, but a nuisance all the same.

Walt was an exacting employer, but never unreasonable. Sam worked hard and at the end of every day he felt good, better than he had in years. Partly because there was a sense of accomplishment in restoring order to the deteriorating ranch. And partly because the old man needed him. It was as simple as that.

He'd been working for Walt about six weeks when out of the blue the old man invited him to come for dinner one night. That was the first time he'd seen the photograph of Walt's granddaughter, Molly. Set in a gold frame on top of the television, the snapshot had caught her in what he could only describe as a *natural* moment. She stood with an arm around each of her sons; one of them, the younger boy, grinned up at her, while the older one half scowled. The wind tossed her hair as she smiled shyly into the camera. What Sam noticed was her eyes. He didn't think he'd ever seen eyes that blue. He might have suspected she wore colored contacts if not for the photo of Walt and his wife. The other Molly. This Molly's eyes were the identical shade of cobalt blue. Her hair was the same rich shade of auburn. Walt's granddaughter was pretty, in an ordinary sort of way. Attractive but not beautiful. Sam had known plenty of women who could run circles around her in the beauty department, but he liked her picture. There was something about her that appealed to him. And he knew Walt cared deeply for her and his two great-grandsons.

Since his brief conversation with Walt's granddaughter, Sam had found her drifting into his mind at the oddest times. Like now. Actually, it was easy enough to figure out why. He'd been celibate for too long. What he really needed was to drive into town one Friday night and let some sweet young thing take him home. But he couldn't seem to dredge up the necessary enthusiasm.

In his rodeo days he'd enjoyed the occasional one-night stand, but over the years, he'd lost interest in sex for the sake of sex. When he crawled into bed with a woman, he didn't want to worry about remembering her name in the morning. Besides, remembering names was a minor concern these days when it came to one's bed partners. If he chose to self-destruct, Sam preferred to do it on the back of a bad-tempered bull, not in some bed with a lumpy mattress and a faceless woman moaning in his ear.

After that first invitation to share dinner, Walt and Sam began eating all their meals together. The old man routinely plied him with questions. Some he answered. Some he ignored. Walt depended on him, trusted him, and Sam tried to live up to the rancher's faith in him.

The Broken Arrow was a good spread, with plenty of grass and a fine herd. If Sam ever considered settling down, it'd be on a place like this. Not that he could afford it. Some days he struggled against bitterness. If not for the accident, he might have had it all: fame, money, a good life. A demon bull had put an end to those hopes and expectations. But he'd endured.

In the process Sam had learned something about himself. He was a survivor. Fate might sucker-punch him again, only next time he'd be prepared. All he had to do was make sure he didn't give a damn about anything—or anyone. Because if he did, he was vulnerable. It occurred to him that he was already becoming too attached to the old man, and that worried him.

By the time he'd sorted out his thoughts and calmed his raging heart, the alarm was ready to sound.

He climbed out of bed, put on a pot of coffee and dressed as the sun peeked over the Rockies, streaking the sky with translucent shafts of pink and gold. It'd become habit to check on Walt before he headed out for the day. He half expected to arrive some morning and find the old man had died in his sleep. He didn't look forward to that, but as the rancher said, he'd lived a good life and suffered few regrets. That was the way Sam wanted it to be when his own time came.

The kitchen light was on when he stepped onto Walt's back porch. Walt was rarely up this early anymore. With his heart as weak as it was, he spent half the day napping.

"Coffee's ready," Walt said when Sam let himself into the kitchen.

The old man seemed downright chipper, Sam noted, a pleasant contrast to his lethargic manner lately.

Walt gestured toward the coffeepot with his own mug.

"No thanks, I've already had a cup." Sam had never been much for talk in the morning. A grunt now and then usually sufficed.

"I got a call from Molly last night." Walt's crooked grin took up half his face. "Looks like you're going to meet her and the boys, after all."

"She's coming out?" Sam hoped to hell she was smart enough not to mention his phone call. As he'd told her, Walt wouldn't appreciate his interference.

"Better than that." Walt cupped the steaming mug between his callused hands. His eyes fairly glowed with happiness.

"How long is she staying?"

"For good," Walt snapped as if it should have been obvious. "She's finally come to her senses and sold what she could, packed everything else in a U-Haul and she's driving on out. Should be here week after next."

Sam lowered himself slowly into a chair. This was something he hadn't expected. He folded his hands, resting them on the scarred pine table, as the old man's words sank in.

"The ranch is hers," Walt announced cheerfully. "There's no one else. I just pray she'll be strong enough to hold on to the place when I'm gone."

Sam had done some thinking about the ranch and what would become of it after Walt died. He'd always known Molly would inherit the Broken Arrow. He'd even toyed with the idea of forming a partnership with her, running the ranch himself and sharing the profits. He'd make sure the arrangement was lucrative for them both, even if it meant working twenty-four hours a day. Eventually he could, maybe, save up enough to buy the spread himself.

His plans were still vague, but this was the first thought he'd given to the future in a hell of a long time. All that would change now. The last thing Walt's granddaughter would want was an ex-con hanging around the place. In light of this news, it'd be best if he sought other employment. He'd write a letter or two that night, send out a few feelers now his confidence was back. He'd enjoyed working the Broken Arrow Ranch almost as much as he'd enjoyed the feisty old man who'd given him a chance.

"Don't you have something to say?" Walt asked, glaring at him. Then he laughed, and the sound was like a sick calf choking.

This was probably the first time Sam had heard Walt laugh. "What's so funny?"

"You." Walt's mirth died slowly. "I wish you could've seen your face when I said Molly was coming. Just wait till you see her in person. If she's anything like her grandmother—and she is—you'll be walking around with your tongue hangin' out. That photo on the television doesn't do her justice. She's a real beauty."

"Don't get any ideas," Sam warned. Walt had misread the look, but Sam wasn't inclined to correct him. He'd let the old coot have his fun.

"Ideas about what?" Walt was obviously playing dumb.

"Me getting together with your granddaughter."

"You should be so lucky."

Sam didn't want to be rude, but he wasn't up to this conversation. "It isn't going to happen."

Walt's smile faded and he narrowed his pale eyes on Sam with an intensity that would have made a lesser man squirm. "I doubt she'd have you."

Sam couldn't fault him there. "I doubt she would, either," he agreed. Grabbing his hat from the peg on the porch, he headed out the kitchen door.

* * *

The sun broke over the horizon like the golden arm of God, ushering in another perfect California morning. Tom sulked in the bucket seat beside Molly, his arms folded defiantly across his chest. His posture told her that nothing she said or did would placate him for the grave injustice of moving him away from his friends.

Clay, on the other hand, bounced like a rubber ball in the back seat, unable to sit still. His excitement, however, did not appear to be contagious.

Because she wasn't able to see out her rearview mirror, Molly checked the side one to make sure the trailer was all right. She wasn't accustomed to hauling anything and the U-Haul was packed tight. Everything she'd managed to accumulate in the past thirty-four years—everything she hadn't sold, donated to charity or given to friends—was jammed in it.

Although she was deeply concerned about her grandfather, Molly hoped the drive to Sweetgrass would be something the three of them could enjoy. A trip that would "make a memory," as her grandmother used to say. She thought about her childhood summer visits and how her grandmother had let her name the calves and explore the ranch and gather eggs....

The last year had precious few happy memories for her and the boys. This was a new beginning for them all. A challenge, too—building a new life, a new home. Few people were given this kind of opportunity. Molly fully intended to make the best of it.

"Are we there yet?" Clay asked, his head bobbing in the rearview mirror.

"Clay," his brother groaned. "We haven't even left California."

"We haven't?"

"Unfortunately, no," Molly concurred.

Clay's head disappeared as he sank down on the seat. His small shoulders slumped forward. "How long's it going to take?"

"Days," Tom said grimly.

Molly resisted the urge to jab him. From the first, her older son's attitude about the move had been less than enthusiastic—although he'd approved of *visiting* Montana to go and see Gramps. But not to stay there forever, as he'd told her repeatedly this past week. He'd barely uttered a word from the time they started out a couple of hours earlier. As far as she could tell, he continued to blame her for making him repaint the gym wall. Molly didn't know why *she* should feel guilty when he was the one who'd sprayed it with gang symbols.

If she needed confirmation that she'd made the right decision, Tom had provided it. The mere thought of her son involved in a gang turned her blood cold. She was terrified of the attraction a gang might hold for him— for *any* confused angry fatherless boy. Gangs weren't an issue in Sweetgrass. The people were decent and hardworking, and she wouldn't need to worry about big-city influences.

"Did I tell you about the Broken Arrow?" she asked in an attempt at conversation. If she displayed a positive attitude, perhaps Tom would start to think that way himself.

"About a thousand times," he muttered, his face turned away from her as he stared out the side window. The scenery rolled past, huge redwoods and lush green forests, so unlike the fertile river valley of Montana.

"There's horses, too," Molly added. As she recalled,

Gramps always had a number on hand. These were strong sturdy horses, kept for work, not pleasure or show.

Tom yawned. "How many?"

Molly lifted one shoulder, her gaze trained on the road. *Interest.* Even this little bit was more than Tom had shown from the moment she'd announced her plans.

"What about my report card?" Clay asked, launching himself against the front seat, thrusting his head between Molly and Tom.

"The school promised to mail it." Molly decided not to remind her son that she'd answered the same question no less than ten times. They'd miss the last couple of weeks of school, but had finished all their assignments beforehand. Molly had feared even a two-week delay might be too long, considering her grandfather's condition.

"You could've asked if I wanted to move." Tom leaned his head against the back of the seat and glared at her. Apparently holding his head up demanded more energy than he could muster.

"Yes," Molly admitted reluctantly, "you're right, I should have." This was a sore point with Tom. A transgression he seemed unwilling to forgive.

"But you *didn't* ask me."

"No, I didn't. Gramps needs us right now and I didn't feel we could refuse." Perhaps she'd made a mistake; it wasn't her first one and certainly wouldn't be her last. Molly felt she'd had few options. Besides removing Tom from involvement in a gang, she had to get to Gramps as soon as possible, to be with him during his remaining days. And since she would inherit the ranch, the more she learned about the management of it now, the better.

"You're taking us away from our friends."

"Like Eddie Ries?"

It was clear to Molly that Tom needed a better class of companions. She worried incessantly about her son and wondered what had happened to the good-natured helpful boy he used to be. The transformation had come virtually overnight. He'd grown sullen, ill-tempered and moody.

In the beginning she feared he might have started using drugs. She'd gone so far as to call a drug hot-line. She'd learned that the best way to figure out if her son was experimenting with illegal drugs wasn't to dig through his backpack or his room for evidence. Kids were experts at hiding paraphernalia, and even better at convincing family they were innocent of anything so dangerous or devious. She suspected that was because parents didn't want to believe their children were caught up in something so destructive and therefore chose to believe whatever the kids told them. Facing the truth was far too painful—and would demand action.

The true test, according to the pamphlet she'd read, was knowing your children's friends. One look at the type of friends your son or daughter associated with was usually enough.

Until last fall Tom's friends had been good kids, from good homes, who made good grades. She felt relatively reassured until he started hanging around with Eddie Ries. Even then it was difficult to gauge the truth.

According to Mr. Boone, the school principal, Tom's friendship with Eddie had been a recent development. Molly hoped that was true.

"Will Gramps teach me to ride?" Clay asked, straining forward in his seat.

"Probably not," Molly said with a renewed sense of sadness. "Remember, he isn't well. I don't think he rides anymore."

"This is gonna be a bust," Clay said, slumping against the window.

Molly shook her head in wonder. "What in heaven's name is the matter with you two?"

"We don't have any friends in Montana," Tom said sulkily.

"You'll make new ones." That was one thing she could say about her boys. Not more than a week after moving into the apartment they'd met every kid within a five-block radius. Neither Tom nor Clay had any problem forming new friendships. The ranch kids would be eager to learn what they could about the big city, and before long Tom and Clay would be heroes.

"Let me tell you about the ranch," she tried again.

"Yeah!" Clay said eagerly.

"I'm not interested," Tom muttered.

One yes. One no. "What's it to be?" she asked cheerfully. "Do I get the deciding vote?"

"No fair!" Tom cried.

"Plug your ears," Clay said, snickering.

Tom grumbled and looked away, wearing the mask of a tormented martyr. He had brooding down to an art form, one he practiced often. Molly couldn't remember her own adolescence being nearly this traumatic, and Tom was only fourteen. She hated to think of all the high-scale drama the coming years held in store.

"Originally the Broken Arrow was over 15,000 acres," Molly began. She said this with pride, knowing how difficult it had been for Gramps to sell off portions of his land. All that remained of the original homestead was 2,500 acres.

"How come the ranch is named the Broken Arrow?" Clay asked.

"Because they found a broken arrow on it, stupid."

"Tom!"

"Well, it's true, isn't it?"

"Yes, but it wasn't a stupid question. If I remember correctly, Tom, you asked me the same one."

"Yeah, but that was when I was a little kid."

"About Clay's age, as I recall." She recalled no such thing, but it served him right for belittling his younger brother.

"What about his foreman?" Clay asked next.

Gramps's foreman. Molly had nothing to tell. All she knew about him was his name and the fact that he was apparently devoted to Gramps. Devoted enough to make sure she knew of Gramps's ill health.

She'd reviewed their short conversation a number of times in the two weeks since his phone call, afraid she might have missed something important. She wondered if there'd been something else he'd wanted to tell her, a hidden message beneath his words. She'd sensed his urgency, accepted the gravity of the situation. Yet when she'd phoned Gramps the next night, he'd sounded quite healthy. He'd been thrilled with her news, and she'd hung up equally excited.

Molly's thoughts turned from Sam Dakota to employment possibilities. Eventually she'd need to find a job in Sweetgrass. While there might not be much demand for a translator, she wondered if the high school needed a French or German teacher. If all else failed, she could try getting long-distance freelance assignments. Perhaps she could tutor or give private lessons. Several of the upmarket preschools in San Francisco were beginning to offer foreign-language lessons to their three- and four-year-old clients. Hey—she could start a trend in Montana!

Molly sighed. She didn't want to think about the dismal state of her finances. She'd sold everything she could—furniture, dishes, household appliances. She wasn't carting away fistfuls of dollars from her moving sale, but with her meager savings and her last paycheck, she'd have funds enough to see her through the next couple of months. After that—"Mom," Clay said, breaking into her thoughts, "I asked you about Gramps's foreman."

"What about him?"

"Do you think he'll teach me to ride?"

"I...I don't know, sweetheart."

"Why should he?" Tom asked, and rolled his eyes as if he could barely stand being in the same car with anyone so stupid.

"I can ask, can't I?" Clay whined.

"Of course," Molly answered, attempting to divert a shouting match.

After repeated warnings, Clay finally secured his seat belt and fell asleep, his head cocked to one side. Because the car's air conditioner didn't work, Molly had hoped to avoid the heat as much as possible by leaving before six that morning. Already both boys were tired and cranky. Not long after Clay dozed off, Tom braced his head against the window and closed his eyes.

The silence was a blessed relief after two hours of almost continual bickering. Molly was grateful for the quiet, grateful for her grandfather—and grateful to Sam Dakota for calling her when he had.

She hadn't met the man and already he'd changed her life.

A cooling breeze came from the north. Walter Wheaton sat on his rocker on the front porch and enjoyed the fresh sweet morning air. He was weak, but even his bad heart couldn't curtail his excitement.

Molly and the boys were on their way. They'd been on the road two days and by his best estimate would arrive around noon. He was already imagining how they'd turn from the highway and onto the meandering dirt road that led to the ranch. When they did, he wanted to be sitting right here on the porch waiting for them. Damn, but it'd be good to see Molly again. Good to see those young ones of hers, too. She hadn't said so, but he knew she worried about being a good mother. The world was a different place now, compared to when he'd grown up, but love and discipline still worked wonders.

The older boy had a sassy mouth; Walt had heard it himself when he'd talked to her on the phone. And the younger one was like a puppy, making a mess wherever he went. In time they'd learn, though. Tom might require a little help adjusting his attitude, but Walt felt up to the task. What that boy needed was a man's influence, a man's guiding hand. That and a switch taken to his backside when he deserved it!

In the big city someone was liable to report him for suggesting the rod. Child abuse they'd call it and probably toss him in the clink. Walt believed that child abuse was ignoring your children, neglecting them, not giving them guidance or a good example. Those things hurt kids far more than an occasional smack on the rear. What was the matter with people these days? he wondered.

A plume of dust showed at the end of the driveway. Molly. He hadn't expected her quite this early. His Molly and her boys.

Walter stood carefully, taking his time so as not to overtax his heart. My, oh my, he was looking forward to seeing his family. Thank goodness Molly had mailed all those pictures! Without them, he wouldn't recognize the boys.

His eyes weren't what they used to be and it took Walt far longer than it should have to realize it was a truck that barreled toward him and not a car pulling a trailer. Another minute passed before he recognized his neighbor, Ginny Dougherty. The woman didn't have the sense God gave a rock chuck.

Walt grunted in annoyance. Ginny was a damn fool. The widow simply didn't know her limitations; she was crazy trying to run a ranch on her own. Fred, her bachelor cousin—aged at least sixty—lived with her and helped out on the place. In Walt's opinion, the two of them were like the blind leading the blind. And he'd told her so, too. Frequently.

Ginny's truck squealed to a halt, kicking up dust. The door opened and she leaped out so fast you'd think the seat was on fire.

"Before you start shouting," she began, "I suggest you hear me out."

Walt didn't have the strength to yell much these days, but he wasn't letting Ginny know that. "What do you want this time?" he demanded. He wrapped his arm around the post and casually leaned against it, so she wouldn't realize how weak he was.

Ginny stood with her hands on her hips. Walt looked her up and down, then shook his head. A woman her age had no business wearing dungarees; he was firm on that.

"Someone knocked down your mailbox," she told him, her chin angled stubbornly toward him. "The way the tire tracks went, it looks deliberate."

Vandals had been wreaking havoc the past few months. Walt didn't understand it. "Who'd do such a thing?"

"Anyone who knows you, Walt Wheaton. You've gone out of your way to make yourself the most unpopular man in town."

"Are you going to stand on my property and insult me, woman?" He forgot about conserving his strength. Ginny always did have a way of getting his dander up. He suspected she did it on purpose, and if the truth be known, he often enjoyed their verbal skirmishes.

"I'm not insulting you. I'm telling you the truth."

"I don't...have to...take this," he said, then slowly lowered himself into the rocker.

Ginny frowned. "Are you okay?"

"Of course I'm okay." He closed his eyes, and his breath came in shallow gasps. It always happened like this; without warning, he'd be unable to catch his breath. No feeling on earth could be worse. It felt as though someone's hands had closed around his throat.

"Walt?"

He dismissed her with a flick of his hand.

"Walt?" She sounded much closer now.

"Pills," he managed between gasps. He patted his

shirt pocket. His head slumped to one side and he felt Ginny's hand searching around for the small brown bottle. The entire time, she was talking. Leave it to a woman to chatter at a time like this. If his heart didn't kill him, Ginny's tongue would.

An eternity passed before she managed to get the pill under his tongue. A couple of minutes later, it took effect. Walt managed to remain conscious, but only by sheer force of will. He refused to pass out; otherwise Sam was sure to haul him back to the medical clinic. If a man wasn't sick when he walked in there, he would be by the time he walked out.

Dr. Shaver had damn near killed him while Sam sat there watching. Walt had fired Sam three times in the next few days, but Sam had ignored his orders. The problem was, his foreman could be as stubborn as Walt himself.

"Drink this." Ginny thrust a glass under his nose.

"What's in it? Arsenic?"

"Water, you old fool."

When he didn't obey her fast enough, Ginny grabbed it back and gulped it down herself.

"I thought you said that was for me," he grumbled.

"I needed it more than you."

Ginny collapsed in the rocker next to his own. Molly's rocker. For forty years she'd sat on the front porch with him each night. She'd darned socks, crocheted, knitted. His wife hadn't believed in idle hands. Every now and again he'd find a way to steal a kiss. It had never ceased to amaze him that a woman as beautiful and talented as Molly MacDougal would marry the likes of him. Her one regret was that she'd only been able to give him one son.

Now they were both gone. Adam killed by a drunk

driver while still in his twenties and then, later, his
Molly. He'd be joining them soon. But not right away.
There was work that had to be done. Affairs settled.
Arrangements made. He wanted time with Molly and
her boys first. God would grant him that much, Walt
was sure. The good Lord had seen fit to take Adam and
Molly early in life, and as far as Walt was concerned
God owed him this additional time.

"You gave me the scare of my life!" Ginny cried.
She was rocking so fast she damn near stirred up a
dust devil.

"What'd you do with my mail?" he demanded, hoping to change the subject.

Ginny glared at him, her dark eyes burning holes
straight through him. "I saved your life and all you care
about is your stupid mail?"

"You've got it, haven't you? Suppose you read it,
too."

"I most certainly did not."

He snorted in disbelief.

"How about thanking me?" Ginny muttered. "If it
wasn't for me, you could be dead by now."

Walt made a disgusted sound. "If I'd known you were
going to nag like this, death would've been a blessing."

Three

"It's probably the biggest, most beautiful home I've ever seen," Molly told her boys wistfully as they sped along the two-lane highway. Eager to reach Sweetgrass, she drove fifteen miles above the speed limit. They hadn't seen another car in more than half an hour, and she figured the state patrol had better things to do than worry about an old country road.

"How many rooms does it have?" Clay asked.

"More than I could count," Molly said, smiling to herself. As a child, she'd considered her grandparents' home a mansion. It had taken her two entire summers to explore all three floors. The original house had been built just after the turn of the century, a grand home for its time, with a turret dominating the right-hand side of the wooden structure. There was a wide sweeping porch along the front of the house, added in later years; it looked out over the rolling green paddock where the horses grazed. A narrow dirt drive snaked in from a marked entry off the highway.

"I can have my own room, then?" Tom asked, showing some life for the first time since lunch.

"There must be four, possibly five bedrooms not in use now."

"I'd sleep in the attic without electricity if it meant I wouldn't have to share a room with Clay."

For Tom, that had been the most difficult aspect of their move into the apartment. He'd been tolerant about it for a while, but living in such close proximity to his younger brother had quickly become a problem.

"My grandmother kept the house in meticulous condition," Molly said. During her last visit, the month following her grandmother's death, she'd marveled at how clean and neatly organized the house still was. Molly Wheaton had regularly waxed the wooden floors and washed the walls. She'd line-dried all the clothes, ironed and crisply folded almost everything. Even the dish towels.

Out of respect for his wife, Gramps had removed his shoes before stepping into the house, to avoid tracking mud across the spotless floors. Every room had smelled of sunshine, with the faint underlying scent of lemon or pine. Molly could almost smell it now.

"How big's the barn?"

"Huge."

"That's what you said about the house."

"I named you right, son," she said, reaching over and mussing his hair. "Doubting Thomas."

Tom slapped at her hand, and she laughed, in too good a mood to let his surly attitude distress her.

They were within an hour of Sweetgrass, and Molly felt a keen sense of homecoming. It was an excitement that reminded her of childhood and warm summer days, a joy that wanted to burst forth. After the long hard months of Daniel's trial, months of struggle and embarrassment while their names were dragged through the media, this was a new beginning for them all. At last they could set aside the troubles of the past and move forward.

"There's a weeping willow beside the house," Molly said. "When I was a girl, I used to hide behind its branches. Gramps would come looking for me and pretend he couldn't find me." The remembrance made her laugh softly. Her grandfather might be crusty on the outside, but inside he was as kind and loving as a man could be. While her grandmother fussed over her only grandchild, coddled and pampered her, Gramps had growled and snorted about sparing the rod and spoiling the child.

But it had been her grandfather who'd built her a dollhouse and hand-carved each small piece of furniture. It'd taken him a whole winter to complete the project. Instead of giving it to her, he'd placed it in the attic for her to find, letting her think it'd been there for years.

Her grandmother had never allowed any of the dogs or cats in the house, but it was her grandfather who'd smuggled in a kitten to sleep with her the first night she was away from her parents, when she was six. Molly wasn't supposed to have known, but she'd seen him tiptoe up the stairs, carting the kitten in a woven basket.

All the memories wrapped themselves around her like the sun's warmth, comforting and lovely beyond description.

"Does Gramps have a dog?" Clay asked excitedly.

"Three or four, I imagine." Gramps had named his dogs after cartoon characters. Molly remembered Mr. McGoo and Mighty Mouse. Yogi and Boo Boo had been two of her favorites. She wondered if he'd continued the practice with more recent dogs.

"That's it!" she said, pointing at two tall timbers. A board with BROKEN ARROW RANCH burned in large capital letters swung from a chain between them. The brand was seared on either side of the ranch name.

"I don't see the house," Clay muttered.

"You will soon," she promised. Molly took a deep breath. They'd been on the road for two days and it felt ten times that long. Her heart was ready for the sight of the house, ready to absorb the wealth of emotion that stirred her whenever she remembered those child-hood summers.

Her ten-year-old Taurus crested the first hill, and she gazed intently ahead, knowing it was here that the house came into view for the first time. She could hardly wait for her sons' reaction. Could hardly wait for them to suck in their breaths with awe and appre-ciation. Could hardly wait to show them the home that would now be theirs.

It wasn't Tom or Clay who gasped, but Molly her-self. The house, at least the outside, was nothing like she remembered. It sat forlornly, revealing years of ne-glect and abuse. Most of the shutters were gone, and those that remained hung askew, dangling by a couple of nails. The paint had blistered and peeled, leaving behind large patches of sun-parched wood. Two of the posts along the porch had rotted away, and the railing around the front showed gaping holes as unsightly as missing teeth. A turquoise tarp was spread across the roof over what had once been her bedroom, presum-ably to stop a leak.

"Are you sure this is the same house?" The question came from Tom.

"This isn't it…is it?" Clay's words seemed to stick in his throat.

"The Addams family would love this place," Tom said sarcastically.

Molly felt her sons' scrutiny, but was speechless, not knowing what to say.

"Are we just going to stay parked here?" Clay asked.

Molly hadn't realized she'd stopped. She squared her shoulders and forced herself to swallow the disappointment. All right, so the house wasn't exactly the way she'd recalled it. She'd personally see to the repairs and the upkeep; it was her responsibility now. Her hands squeezed the steering wheel as a new thought struck her. If the outside was this bad, she could only imagine what had happened to the inside.

"We need to remember Gramps is ill," she said more for her own benefit than her children's. "He hasn't been able to take care of things. That's why we're here, remember?"

"This place is a dump."

"Thomas, stop!" She would hear none of this. None of it! "This is our home."

"We were better off in the apartment."

Molly's fingers ached from her death grip on the steering wheel. "It'll be just as beautiful as ever in no time," she said forcefully, defying the boys to contradict her.

Either they recognized the determination in her voice or were too tired to argue.

Molly had half expected Gramps to be on the porch waiting for her when she arrived and was disappointed when he wasn't. She pulled the car around to the back of the house, close to the barn where Gramps generally parked his vehicles. Two dogs, one of them hugely pregnant, began barking furiously.

She turned off the engine and a man stepped out of the shadows from inside the barn. He removed his hat and wiped his forearm across his brow, then paused to study her.

This could only be Sam Dakota. Her grandfather's foreman. The boys scrambled out of the car, eager to escape its confines. They were obviously anxious to explore, but stayed close to the Taurus, waiting for her. The instant he was out the door, Clay squatted down and petted the pregnant dog, lavishing her with affection. The other dog continued his high-pitched barking.

Molly worried when she still didn't see Gramps. Her immediate fear was that she'd arrived too late and her grandfather was already dead. Sam would've had no way of contacting her while she was on the road. It'd been foolish not to phone from the hotel, just in case… As quickly as the idea entered her head, she pushed it away, refusing to believe anything could have happened to Gramps. Not yet! She opened her car door and stepped into the early-afternoon sunshine.

Sam walked toward her, which gave Molly ample opportunity to evaluate his looks. After that first glimpse, when he'd briefly removed his Stetson, she couldn't see much of his facial features, which were hidden beneath the shadowed rim of his hat. The impression of starkly etched features lingered in her mind, his face strong and defined. He was tall and whipcord-lean.

If his clothes were any indication, he didn't shy away from hard work. His jeans were old, faded by repeated washings. The brightly colored shirt with the sleeves rolled past his elbows had seen better days. He pulled off his right glove, and even from a distance Molly could see that those gloves had been broken in long ago.

"You must be Sam Dakota," she said, taking the initiative. She walked forward and offered him her hand; he shook it firmly—and released it quickly. "I'm Molly Cogan and these are my boys, Tom and Clay. Where's Gramps?"

"Resting. He thought you'd arrive earlier. He waited half the morning for you." The censure in his gruff voice was unmistakable.

Involuntarily Molly stiffened. Clay moved next to her and she slid her arm around his neck, pressing him close. "How's Gramps feeling?" she asked, choosing to ignore the foreman's tone.

"Not good. He had another bad spell this morning."

Molly frowned in concern. "Did you take him to the clinic? Shouldn't he be in the hospital?"

"That'd be my guess, but Walt won't hear of it. It would've taken twenty mules to budge that stubborn butt of his."

Molly smiled faintly. "My grandmother was the only person who could get him to change his mind, and that was only because he loved her so much."

An answering smile flashed from his eyes. "Unfortunately he holds no such tenderness for me," he murmured, then turned his attention to Tom and Clay. "Are you boys thirsty? There's a pitcher of lemonade in the fridge." Without waiting for a response, he led the way into the house.

With a mixture of joy and dread, Molly followed. She paused as she stepped into the kitchen—it was even worse than she'd feared. The once-spotless room was cluttered and dirty. A week's worth of dirty dishes was stacked in the sink. The countertops, at least what was visible beneath the stacks of old newspapers, mail and just about everything else, looked as if they hadn't been cleared in weeks. The windows were filthy—Molly could tell they hadn't been washed in years—and the sun-bleached curtains were as thin as tissue paper.

Molly wasn't nearly as meticulous a housekeeper as her grandmother had been; as a working mother, she didn't have the time for more than once-a-week cleaning. Nevertheless she had her standards and this house fell far short of them.

"Is lemonade all you got?" Tom asked when Sam took three glasses from the cupboard. Molly was surprised there were any clean dishes left. "What about a Pepsi? A Coke? Anything?" Tom whined.

"Water," Sam suggested, then winked at Clay, who had no problem accepting the homemade offering.

Tom tossed his mother a look of disgust and snatched up the glass of lemonade as if he was doing them all a favor.

"Your grandfather's asleep in the living room," Sam said, motioning toward it.

Molly didn't need directions, but she said nothing. Not wanting to startle Gramps, she tiptoed into the room. She stood there for a moment watching him. He leaned back in his recliner, feet up, snoring softly. Even asleep, he looked old and frail, nothing like the robust man he'd been only ten years ago.

It demanded both determination and pride to keep her eyes from filling with tears. Her heart swelled with love for this man who was her last link to the father she barely remembered. She'd been so young when her father died. A child of six. Her entire world had fallen apart that day of the car accident; she missed him still. Her mother had remarried less than a year later, and Molly had a baby brother the year after that. And the summer she graduated from high school, her mother, stepfather and half brother had immigrated to Australia.

Kneeling beside the recliner, Molly gently brushed the white hair from Gramps's brow. Needing to touch him, needing to feel a physical connection, she let her hand linger.

"Gramps," she whispered, so softly she could hardly hear her own voice.

No response.

Tenderly Molly placed her hand over his. "We're here, Gramps."

His eyes flickered open. "Molly girl," he whispered, reaching out to caress the side of her face. "You're here at last. To stay?"

"I'm here to stay," she assured him.

His smile made it to his eyes long before it reached his mouth. "What kept you so damn long?" he asked in his familiar brusque tone.

"Stubbornness. Pride," she said, and kissed his weathered cheek. "I can't imagine where I got that."

Gramps chuckled, looking past her. "Where are those young'uns of yours? I've been waitin' all day for this, and none too patiently, either."

Tom and Clay stepped into the room. Tom had his arms folded and a scowl on his face. He lagged behind Clay, who was grinning and energetic, unable to hold still. "Hi, Gramps!" Clay's exuberant greeting was echoed by Tom's reluctant "Hi."

Gramps studied her sons for what seemed like minutes before he nodded. It was then that Molly saw the sheen of tears in his tired eyes. He sat up and braced both hands on his knees.

"You've done a fine job raising these boys of yours, Molly. A fine, fine job."

"That her?" Lance whispered, staring out from the alley between the café and hardware store. He motioned with his head toward Molly Cogan.

She walked out of the Sweetgrass bank, glancing up at the man beside her. He wore a Stetson and walked like a cowboy.

Monroe's gaze followed his fellow Loyalist's to the other side of the street. It surprised him that a cantankerous old guy like Wheaton would have a granddaughter this attractive. From what he understood, she'd been divorced a number of years. A woman who'd been that long without a husband might appreciate some attention from the right kind of man. He'd heard redheads could be real wild women in the sack.

He quickly banished the thought from his mind. It'd be a mistake to mix business with pleasure. And it could end up being a costly mistake. Once this matter of getting hold of the ranch was settled, he'd show her the difference between a Montana man and a city boy.

Oh, yeah. Monroe had heard all about those men in California, especially in the San Francisco area. Those gay boys sure didn't know what to do with a woman. Seemed they were stuck on each other, if you could imagine that! The whole damn country was going to hell in a handbasket—but not if he could help it. That's what the Loyalists were all about. They were a militia group—been around for ten years or so. At their last meeting, more than a hundred men had crammed the secret meeting place to show their support for the changes he and the other Loyalists were planning to bring about. Of course some folks who didn't know any better took exception to the cause. Walt Wheaton, for one. The old cuss was as stubborn as they came. Monroe had done everything in his power to convince the rancher to sell out. Subtly of course. Guarding his own identity and his position of power in the organization was crucial. Only Loyalists knew him as Monroe, and although he'd attended the last meeting, no one in Sweetgrass had any idea how deeply involved he was with the militia. His cover was useful and too important for Loyalist purposes to break.

After a careful study of possible sites for their training grounds, the group had decided old man Wheaton's property was the ideal location. But Walt Wheaton had remained inflexible. As his banker, Dave Burns was in a position to put the pinch on him, but it hadn't worked. When things hadn't fallen into place, the head of the Loyalists had sent Lance to help them along. Monroe didn't think much of Lance, but he kept his opinions to himself.

In a last-ditch effort to keep violence out of the picture—not that he was opposed to using force, if necessary—he'd convinced the powers-that-be to give him one last chance to reason with the old rancher. He hated like hell to see a hothead like that fool Lance get credit for obtaining the property when he might finesse the deal himself—with a little assistance.

That was when he put the pressure on a third cousin of his to make the old man an offer he couldn't refuse.

Now that Walt's granddaughter was in town, they might finally make some headway. The ranch was on its last legs, Burns had seen to that, refusing Wheaton any more loans and calling in the ones he already had.

"How much longer is the old guy gonna live?" Lance asked, cutting into his thoughts.

"Not long," Monroe said under his breath. If necessary he'd let Lance give Wheaton a good shove into the hereafter, but he'd prefer to avoid that. Too messy. And the last thing the Loyalists needed was a passel of state cops and reporters looking in their direction.

"Who's that with her?"

"Sam Dakota." Monroe snickered softly, disliking the protective stance the foreman took with the woman. He could see the lay of the land with those two. Sam wanted her for himself, but Monroe wasn't going to let that happen. Dakota was a jailbird and once old man Wheaton found out, he'd send the foreman packing. Right quick, too, if he knew Walt Wheaton.

"Will he make trouble?"

"Unlikely." Dakota wouldn't know the meaning of the word "trouble" until he tangled with the Loyalists. The foreman was admittedly a problem, but Monroe didn't expect Sam to stay around much longer.

"I thought you said we'd have the Wheaton land soon," Lance grumbled.

Monroe frowned. "Takes time."

"You're sure the old man doesn't know?"

"I'm sure." Monroe's patience was growing thin. It wasn't the younger man's place to question him, and he let it be known he didn't appreciate it by glaring at him fiercely.

"I could convince him to sell in a week if you'd let me," Lance muttered.

"We'll do this my way," Monroe said from between clenched teeth. The necessity of maintaining a low profile was key to the group's survival. The government, especially the FBI, would go to great lengths to stop the militia movement. All you had to do was look at Ruby Ridge and Waco and you'd realize just how corrupt the feds had become. Well, that was all about to change.

"I'm not going to do anything stupid," Lance assured him.

"Good." Against his better judgment, Monroe found himself staring at Molly Cogan again. Her jeans stretched nicely across her butt. Not so tight as to invite a look and not so loose that they disguised the fact she was a woman. And just the way she walked proved she was a Wheaton, all right. Proud as the day was long, and if she was anything like her grandfather, stubborn, too.

"She's pretty, I'll say that for her."

"Don't get any ideas," Monroe said, struggling to hold on to his temper. "We've already got more complications than we need."

"All right, all right, but let me visit one of the girls soon. I'm a growing boy, if you catch my drift."

The kid might think he was clever, but Monroe failed to be amused. A large part of the Loyalists' financial support came from a prostitution ring that covered the entire state. The money they brought in was the lifeblood of the organization, but there wouldn't be enough with young bucks like Lance and his friend Travis helping themselves to the goods. He was guilty of taking advantage himself, but then he considered Pearl and a couple of the others his fringe benefits. He figured *he* was a hell of a lot more entitled to them than Lance.

"Stay out of town unless I tell you different," Monroe instructed the other man.

Lance frowned.

"You heard what I said, didn't you?" He knew Lance had been sneaking into town behind his back. That boy better realize he had ways of learning about whatever went on here.

"I said I would," Lance mumbled.

"Good." Monroe sent Lance off and waited long enough to be sure he'd taken the road out of Sweetgrass. Then he climbed into his car; it was as hot as a brick oven. He was hot in other ways, too, and blamed the Wheaton woman for that. It was time to pay Pearl a visit—she'd probably missed him. He drove down several streets and stopped next to the community park. No need to announce where he was headed by leaving his car in front of her house.

He cut through the alley and walked across Pearl's backyard, then let himself in by the door off the kitchen. He didn't bother to knock.

Still in her housecoat, Pearl stepped out of the hallway. She looked shocked to see him. Noon, and she wasn't dressed yet. Not that he was complaining. It saved time.

"What are you doing here?" she demanded, placing her hands on her hips. The action tugged open the front of her robe and offered him a tantalizing peek at her breasts.

"Guess," he said with a snicker. He loosened his belt buckle, in no mood to play games.

Her bravado quickly disappeared and she backed away from him. "Our agreement was once a month."

"That's not the way I remember it."

Pearl might have been pretty at one time, but too many years of making her living on her back had spoiled whatever had been attractive about her. Her makeup was applied with a heavy hand—not like Molly Cogan's. Monroe frowned as he thought about the old bastard's granddaughter.

"I...I don't want you to tie me up this time." Pearl's voice trembled a little. He liked that. Just the right amount of fear, enough to make her willing to do things she might not do for her other customers. But then he wasn't like the others. The Loyalists owned Pearl, and she did what he damn well pleased, whether she wanted to or not.

Gramps had insisted Sam accompany Molly into Sweetgrass, and although she couldn't see the sense of it, she hadn't made a fuss. The boys were far too interested in exploring the house and unpacking their belongings to be bothered with errands. So Molly had left them with Gramps.

Actually she'd hoped to use the time alone with Sam to find out what she could about her grandfather's health. The old man seemed pale and listless this morning, although he'd tried to hide it from her.

Gramps's old pickup had to be at least twenty-five years old. Molly could remember it from when she was a child. The floorboard on the passenger side had rusted through, and she had to be careful where she set her feet.

The ride started off in a companionable enough silence. Every now and then she'd look at Sam, but he kept his gaze carefully trained on the road ahead.

She'd spoken first. "Are you from around here?"

"No."

"Montana?"

"Nope."

"Where else have you been a foreman?" she'd asked, trying a different tack.

"I haven't been."

"Never?" she asked.

"Never," he repeated.

That was how their entire conversation had gone. In the forty minutes it took to drive into Sweetgrass, Sam didn't respond once in words of more than two syllables. Stringing together more than a couple of words appeared to be beyond his capabilities.

Molly had hoped to ease into her conversation, get to know him before she dug for answers concerning her grandfather's condition. But no matter how she approached him, Sam Dakota remained tight-lipped and uncooperative.

Molly gave up the effort when the town came into view.

"Oh, my," she whispered.

If the Broken Arrow Ranch had changed in nine years, Sweetgrass hadn't. Main Street seemed trapped in a time warp. Foley's Five and Dime with its faded red sign still sat on the corner of Main and Maple. Her grandmother had often taken Molly there as a child so she could watch the tropical fish swim in the big aquarium. The hamsters, racing about in their cages, had intrigued her, as well. In addition to pets, the store sold knickknacks and tacky souvenirs to any unsuspecting tourist who had the misfortune of dropping by. Not that there'd ever been many tourists. In retrospect, Molly decided it must be the bulk candy displayed behind the glass counter that kept Foley's in business.

The bank's reader board, which alternately flashed the time and the temperature, was directly across the street from Foley's. Sweetgrass Pharmacy and the barbershop were next to the bank. Molly wondered if the singing barber had retired. As she recalled, he'd done a fairly good imitation of Elvis.

The ice-cream parlor with its white wire chairs was exactly as she remembered.

Sam glanced at her.

"Everything's the same," she told him.

"Everything changes," he said without emotion. "Looks can be deceiving, so don't be fooled." He eased the truck into an empty parking space and turned off the engine.

"I need to stop at the bank," she said, looking over at the large redbrick structure. From there she'd go to the Safeway and buy groceries. The Safeway was at the other end of town, about six blocks away. A stoplight swayed gently in the breeze at Main and Chestnut. For a while it had been the only one in the entire county. But five years ago Jordanville, forty miles east, had its first traffic light installed, stealing Sweetgrass's claim to distinction. Gramps had taken the news hard; he'd written her a letter complaining bitterly about the changes in Montana. Too damn many people, he'd grumbled.

Without looking at her, Sam added, "I've got some supplies to pick up."

Sam wasn't unfriendly, but he hadn't gone out of his way to make her feel welcome, either. Molly had no idea what she'd done or hadn't done to create such...coolness in his attitude. This morning he'd seemed neutral, but neutral had definitely become cool.

"I'll meet you at the bank when I'm finished," he said.

Molly climbed down from the truck and hooked the strap of her purse over her shoulder. Sam walked close beside her until they reached the bank, then he crossed the street. As she opened the heavy glass doors, she caught a glimpse of him studying her. It was an uncomfortable feeling.

While the outside of the bank was relatively unchanged, the inside had been updated. The polished wood counters were gone, and except for the lobby with its marble tiles, the floor was now carpeted.

Molly moved toward the desk with a sign that stated: New Accounts.

"Hello," she said, and slipped into the chair.

"Hi." The woman, whose nameplate read Cheryl Ripple, greeted her with a cordial smile.

"I'm Molly Cogan," she said, introducing herself. "Walter Wheaton's my grandfather."

Cheryl's smile faded and she stood up abruptly. Almost as if she couldn't get away fast enough, Molly thought.

"Excuse me a moment, please," the woman said. She hurried toward the branch manager's office, and a moment later, a distinguished-looking middle-aged man appeared.

"Ms. Cogan?" he said, coming over to her, hands tightly clenched. "I'm David Burns. Is there a problem?"

Molly blinked at him, taking in his well-tailored suit and polished shoes. "No, should there be?"

David Burns's laugh held a nervous edge. "Not exactly. It's just that your grandfather has...shall we say, challenged the integrity of this banking institution on a number of occasions. I came to be sure there wasn't any problem with his account. Again."

"None that I know of," Molly said, wondering what her grandfather had said or done to raise such concern. On second thought she didn't want to know. "Actually I came to open my own account."

"Your own?" His relief was evident. "That's great."

"I'm moving in with my grandfather."

"I see. Welcome to Sweetgrass. Cheryl will be more than happy to assist you." He took a couple of steps backward before turning toward his office.

Within ten minutes Molly had signed the necessary documents and chosen a check design. As she got ready to leave, she noticed a tall attractive man standing in the lobby, watching her. When he saw Molly, he smiled and nodded as if she should know him. She didn't. A moment later he approached her.

"Molly Cogan?"

She nodded, frowning, certain she didn't recognize him. His was a face she would have remembered, too. Appealing, boyish, blue-eyed. His blond hair was tousled as if he'd forgotten to comb it. He stood well over six feet.

"I'm Russell Letson," he said, stepping toward her, his hand extended. No wedding ring, she automatically noticed. His eyes darted away from her and she realized he was actually rather shy. This was something she didn't expect from the rough, tough cowboy types she generally associated with Montana.

They exchanged handshakes as Molly mulled over where she'd heard the name before.

"I'm your grandfather's attorney," he added.

Gramps's letter. That was why the name was familiar. Her grandfather had mentioned him when he'd told her about having his will updated.

"Would you have time for a cup of coffee?" he asked, glancing at his watch. "I've got an hour before my next appointment and there's a matter I'd like to discuss with you." He seemed slightly ill at ease about this.

Molly wondered what he could possibly have to say to her; she couldn't help being curious and, to her surprise, tempted. Russell Letson was one of the best-looking men she'd seen in a while, and what amazed her was that he didn't seem to know it.

Russell added, "It won't take long."

Just when Molly was about to agree, Sam walked into the bank, and she experienced a twinge of disappointment. "I'm afraid I can't today."

"Dinner then?" he suggested. "Tomorrow night, if that's agreeable?"

"I…" Too stunned to respond, Molly stood in the middle of the bank with her mouth hanging half-open while she struggled for an answer. A date. She couldn't remember the last time a man—an attractive single man—had asked her to dinner.

"I don't know if Walter's told you, but there's a decent steak house in Sweetgrass now. We could talk there."

"Sure," she said, before she could find a convenient excuse. "That'd be great."

He set a time for dinner and promised to pick her up at the ranch, although it was well out of his way. Handsome and a gentleman, besides. She could grow to like Russell Letson, Molly decided. He was a pleasant contrast to the surly foreman who'd driven her into town.

"I'll see you tomorrow evening, then," Russell said, giving her a small salute before walking out of the bank.

It had happened so fast Molly's head was spinning. She walked over to Sam, who leaned against the lobby wall, waiting for her.

"What was that about?" he asked with a scowl.

After the silent treatment he'd given her all the way into town, she wasn't inclined to answer him. "Nothing much."

"You're letting Letson take you to dinner."

If he already knew, why had he asked her? "As a matter of fact, I am," she returned, and enjoyed the rush of satisfaction she felt at letting him know she had a date.

Four

It felt good sitting on the porch, rocking and whittling, Walt Wheaton mused. Molly's boys sat on the top step, sanding a couple of carvings he'd fashioned from canary wood. The yellowish wood was one of his favorites. He hadn't worked on his carvings for at least six months. Molly and the boys had renewed his energy. Gladdened his heart. He might not always remember what day of the week it was anymore, but that didn't matter. Not now, with Molly and the boys here where they belonged.

It wouldn't take much to imagine it was his own Adam sitting on that step, forty or so years back, with a school friend. Or to imagine his Molly in the kitchen getting dinner ready to put on the table.

Walt's fingers skillfully moved the sharp knife over the wood, removing a sliver at a time, cutting away everything that wasn't the bear. He'd chosen oak for this piece, and the black bear would stand about ten inches high on his hind legs. He'd give it to Tom. The boy reminded him of a young bear, struggling to prove his manhood, all legs and arms and feet. He remembered himself at that age, when his voice had danced between two octaves. He'd been tall and thin like Tom, with legs like beanpoles and no chest to speak of.

Walt toyed with the idea of saying something to his great-grandson. He wanted to assure Tom he'd fill out soon enough, but he didn't want to embarrass the boy.

The three worked in comfortable silence. Walt yearned to share stories of his youth with the two brothers, but talking drained his energy. The hell with it, he decided. God had given him the opportunity to spend time with these young ones and he was going to use it.

"Bears eat trees, you know," he stated matter-of-factly.

Tom glanced up. "Trees? Are you sure, Gramps?"

The older of Molly's two boys had a skeptical nature; Walt approved. He didn't like the idea of his kin accepting anyone or anything at face value. He suspected his granddaughter might be more easily swayed, but her son wouldn't be. It reassured him that the boy revealed some good old-fashioned common sense, a virtue in shockingly short supply these days. Take that local militia group, for example. He'd butted heads with them more than once in the past few years. While Walt didn't necessarily agree with everything the government did, he sure didn't believe the militia's wild claims of foreign troops planning to invade the country with the assistance of the federal government. That was as ludicrous as their other ideas, like computer chips surgically implanted in people's brains so the government could control their activities. He'd never heard such nonsense in all his days and cringed every time he thought about decent folks believing such craziness.

"Gramps?"

Tom's voice shook him out of his thoughts. He had trouble keeping his mind on track these days.

"What is it, son?"

"Is that true?"

He frowned. What was the boy talking about? The militia's paranoid ideas, he guessed. Wasn't that what they'd been discussing? "Of course it's not true," he barked. This computer-chip nonsense was as asinine as the supposed sightings of black helicopters swooping down and spraying bullets from the sky. "Question everything, son, you hear me?"

Tom nodded and returned to his sanding.

With his heart as weak as it was, Walt didn't know how much longer he'd be around on this earth. He liked to think there'd be time to tell Tom and Clay about life during the Great Depression. And the war. Children these days didn't know the meaning of hardship, not like his generation.

"Gramps?" Clay stared at him expectantly. "But you *said* bears ate trees. So don't they really?"

Oh, yeah. That was it—*that* was what he'd said. About bears. "They eat the bark," he explained, his mind traveling the winding twisting byways of time long since passed. He shelved the Depression stories in order to explain what he knew of bears. "They scrape off the bark with their claws. Without the bark, the tree dies. So, yeah, you could say bears eat trees. Next time you're in the forest, take a gander at a dying tree. If it isn't some disease, my guess is that a bear's been clawing on it."

"Is that why you're carving a bear?" the older boy asked. "Because they eat trees?" He ran the sandpaper lightly over the carving of the owl. Watching him reminded Walt that he didn't see many of the northern saw-whet owls these days. The saw-whet was small as owls went, only seven inches high, and weighed less than four ounces.

He didn't get much opportunity to study nature the way he once had. He missed his walks, missed a lot of things, but that was all part of growing old.

"Gramps?" It was Tom again.

"What is it, son?"

"Clay asked you about the bear. Why you're carving it."

"Oh, yes…the bear. It nearly got me, it did at that."

Both boys stared up at him, and he grinned, recalling the adventures of his youth. "I happened upon her clawing up a conifer. I was just a kid at the time, but old enough to know better than to do something stupid—like get too close to a bear," he added, muttering to himself. "Neither my horse nor I saw her until it was too late. The mama bear had two cubs and she was in no mood for company. She reared onto her hind legs and scared my horse so badly he tossed me clean off. I thought I was a goner for sure."

Both boys listened intently. "What happened next?" Tom asked.

"Happened?" Walt chuckled, remembering the incident as vividly now as that day almost seventy years ago. He smiled and continued whittling as his mind filled with the details of that fateful afternoon. "Once I recovered enough to stand, I took off running, screaming at the top of my lungs." He shook his head, grinning again.

"How old were you, Gramps?"

"Ten or so," Walt answered. "My legs were good and strong."

"So you ran?" Clay's hands went idle.

"I didn't figure on hanging around there and letting that bear eat me for dinner." This reminded him of another lesson Molly's boys needed, a lesson only a man would think to teach them. Women didn't take to fighting much; they didn't understand a man's need for confrontation. What was important, however, was knowing when to fight and why. Knowing what was worth fighting for. And yet there were times when all the questions might have the right answers and still the best thing to do was walk away. He'd turned his back on a fight or two, and it had taken far more courage to back down than it had to stand his ground.

"She didn't catch you, did she?" Clay asked.

"Damn near, but my pappy saved me." To this day Walt remembered the surge of relief he'd experienced when his father burst into the clearing, his horse at full gallop. He'd raced toward Walt and it was hard to figure who'd reach him first, his father or the bear.

"My pappy saved me," he said again. "He galloped up, grabbed me by the arm and swung me over his horse's back."

Even with his eyes so tired and faded, Walt saw the awe in the boys' faces. He nodded slowly. It did his heart good to spend time with Adam's grandsons. They needed a man in their lives, someone to take the place of their useless father. He *wanted* to teach these boys, but he didn't have much time left....

The screen door creaked and Molly stepped onto the porch, holding the door open. "Dinner'll be ready in ten minutes," she announced. "Time to put your tools away and wash your hands."

Almost from the minute they'd arrived, Molly had been scrubbing and cleaning that kitchen. It comforted him, somehow, to see her put the house to rights. His own sweet Molly would've thoroughly disapproved of his housekeeping methods. He probably should have hired one of the women from town to take a scrub brush to the place, at least before his granddaughter arrived to find such a mess.

He'd always intended to hire a housekeeper, but had yet to meet anyone he wanted in his home for longer than five minutes. Nor did he like the idea of a stranger touching his Molly's things. Maybe Ginny, but she didn't keep her own house too well, and he'd wager she'd be insulted if he suggested she clean his, even if he was willing to pay her.

Tom and Clay didn't need to be told twice about dinner. They were inside the house quicker than two jackrabbits. Walt wasn't as fast on his feet. He heaved himself up, grateful that the boys had put away his carvings and tools. That Tom might have a smart mouth on him, but at heart he was a considerate kid. Walt took a deep breath, inhaling the aroma of something delectable. He didn't know what his granddaughter had cooked, but the tantalizing smells wafting from the kitchen told him he was in for a treat. Preparing meals had become an onerous chore; more and more of late Sam had been seeing to his dinner.

Walt trusted Sam, and that trust hadn't been given lightly. It was why he'd asked his foreman to drive Molly into town earlier in the day. When they returned, Sam had silently carried in the groceries and left immediately afterward. Walt smiled to himself, amused at the way Sam was keeping his distance since Molly's arrival.

Walt headed for the kitchen, moving at his own pace. Although Sam hadn't said anything, he probably wasn't too keen on Molly dating Russell Letson. It surprised Walt that she'd agreed to have dinner with that puppy of an attorney. The boy hadn't let any moss grow under his feet, that was for sure.

Letson was a good man, shy and kind of quiet. Nothing like his father, who'd been outspoken and opinionated. His son seemed to keep to himself. He wondered why Russell hadn't married. Of course there weren't a lot of marriageable women around Sweetgrass.

Now that Molly was here, Walt suspected plenty of young men would be dropping by the ranch. Once they got a good look at his granddaughter they'd find excuses to visit. Pretty as a picture, Molly was. Smart, too, and a fine cook. Given time, she'd make a good rancher's wife.

He believed that Molly needed a man, although he was sure she'd disagree with him. He'd like to see her get married again. She was still young and if she remarried, she'd probably have more children. It saddened him to realize he wouldn't be around to know and love them, but he refused to think about that. He was determined to enjoy what time he had with her and the boys and let the future take care of itself.

He paused in the doorway leading to the kitchen. He barely recognized the room. The walls shone because Molly had washed them, the floorboards gleamed with wax, and the windows sparkled behind new gingham curtains Molly had sewn on her grandmother's old Singer. She'd found a length of cotton up in the attic;

his Molly must have bought it shortly before her death. As the boys hurried about setting serving dishes on the table, Walt marveled at the change in the room. So it took him longer than it should have to realize the table was only set for four.

"What about Sam?" he asked, surprised that Molly had excluded the foreman.

Molly's chin came up slightly, as if she was affronted by the question. "I invited him over, but he said he had other plans."

That was interesting. Walt watched his granddaughter as she brought a platter of chicken from the counter to the table. Her lips had thinned slightly when she mentioned Sam. Now that Walt thought about it, he'd sensed a bit of tension between the two.

"What other plans?" Walt pressed.

"He didn't say."

And Walt figured she hadn't asked, either. Grinning, he glanced out the kitchen window to the small foreman's house where Sam lived. Beyond that stood the old bunkhouse; the run-down structure was a reminder of the Broken Arrow's glory days, when the spread had been large enough to justify hiring on several hands. Now there was only Sam. His battered truck was parked the same place as before, which meant he hadn't left the ranch.

"Isn't he hungry?" Walt demanded. The man had too much pride for his own good. His stubbornness was cheating him out of the best damn meal he was likely to get. Not that there was any point in telling him. Might as well argue with a tree stump.

Clay put a green salad on the table with a bottle of no-fat dressing.

Walt frowned. He preferred his own brand and he didn't care if it was loaded down with fat. A man could only be asked to sacrifice so much. As it was, he already had one foot in the grave. His cholesterol count was the least of his worries.

"Do you want me to invite Sam again?" Molly asked, standing stiffly behind the kitchen chair.

Although she'd made the offer, Walt could see she had no desire to do so.

"If he doesn't want to eat with us, fine. The choice is his."

She nodded. "My thought exactly."

Sam hardly knew Russell Letson, and he wasn't sure why he was so angry with the guy. Except for that incident his first day in Sweetgrass, he and Russell had very little to do with each other. Which was fine with Sam. It occurred to him, as he pitched a forkful of hay into Sinbad's stall, that he couldn't think of a single reason to dislike the man—other than the fact that Letson had invited Molly to dinner. True, Sam had an innate distrust of lawyers, but he had no personal reason to feel wary of Russell Letson. And, of course, what Molly chose to do was none of his business.

Then why did it bother him so much?

The muscles across Sam's shoulders tightened. He'd mucked out the stalls and put down fresh straw—although it wasn't really necessary—simply because he felt the need to keep moving. If he worked hard enough and long enough, maybe his thoughts would leave him alone.

Not only did Sam dislike Letson, he wasn't sure he

liked Molly Cogan, either. Not that anyone was asking his opinion. Nor was he offering it.

An endless series of questions buzzed around his head like pesky flies. But Sam decided he wasn't going to concern himself with the answers. He wasn't willing to waste time analyzing his feelings about Molly. First and foremost, why should *he* care who she dated? He didn't, dammit!

Perhaps he should think about moving on. He'd worked on the Broken Arrow Ranch longer than anywhere, and he wasn't the kind of man who was comfortable staying in any one place. When he was in town that afternoon, he'd gotten the addresses of a number of large ranches in the state. This was as good a time as any to inquire about jobs. He'd been here too long, and he'd grown restless. At least that was what he told himself.

But he realized almost immediately that it was a lie.

Working for Walt Wheaton had given him a sense of satisfaction. The old man had needed him, and Sam had definitely needed a job. And more. He'd needed a home, needed some respect, needed to be *useful*. He was willing to admit that now, although it wasn't easy. The last six months had given him perspective.

The bitter taste of his anger was gone and he was able to look back on his time in prison with a sort of… acceptance. He'd been drunk and stupid, raging over the loss of his career and every dime he'd saved. He'd been looking for trouble that night—almost four years ago now. The fight had been his fault, and he'd paid the price for his stupidity.

Sam had *thought* he'd learned his lesson, but he hadn't been in Sweetgrass more than a few minutes when he made the same mistake. He'd gone into Willie's for a beer; all he'd wanted was to quench his thirst. Everyone in the bar had been content to ignore the quarrelling couple. Sam, too. Until the drunk started slapping the woman around. That was when he'd stepped in. The fight had spilled into the street, where Walt Wheaton was standing, talking with a couple of old cronies. Before long, the sheriff was on the scene and Sam had been hauled away. Walt had seen the whole thing....

Sam was grateful to Walt for hiring him without asking endless questions about his past. He didn't understand what had prompted the old man to bail him out. All the rancher cared about was Sam's skill in running the ranch, and once assured he knew his way around a herd, Walt had offered him the job.

Unless someone else had told him, Walt didn't know Sam had served a two-year sentence in a Washington-state prison. Sam didn't figure it was relevant; besides, being an ex-con wasn't something he was proud of. And it wasn't something he liked to talk about.

Sam still wondered why this sick old man had trusted him. It'd been a long time since anyone had willingly placed faith in him. That was why Sam had stayed, why he'd worked himself to the point of exhaustion, month after month. Sam would rather have died than disappoint Walt Wheaton.

It'd been a long time, too, since he'd allowed himself to care about anyone. Feelings were a luxury a man on the move couldn't afford. They'd always made Sam uncomfortable, for more reasons than he wanted to examine.

Over the weeks and months he'd worked the Broken Arrow, he'd become fond of the crotchety old man. On some level they'd connected. He owed Walt, in a way he'd never owed anyone before. He also saw Walt's despair over the deterioration of his ranch, and he was determined to salvage as much as he could. In an effort to prove himself worthy of Walt's faith, Sam had struggled to build up the herd. He'd ridden the land so often he was familiar with damn near every square inch of it.

And he'd made a mistake. A big mistake. He'd started to dream.

Once in a while he'd find an excuse to ride up to the crest of the hill that overlooked the valley and dream that this land was his.

He supposed it was because he carried the sole responsibility for this ranch now. He'd started to feel he *belonged* here. And that was dangerous.

At night, it had become his habit to walk among the outbuildings and check everything one last time before he turned in. All too often his thoughts grew fanciful and he'd pretend that inside the house a woman was waiting for him. His wife. He'd pretend that his children slept upstairs, tucked securely in their beds, loved beyond measure.

It was never meant to be. When Walt died, the Broken Arrow would pass to Molly and her two boys. Then she'd find herself a new husband, who'd send him on his way.

He grimaced. His dreams were downright laughable, and the sooner he put them out of his mind, the easier it would be to pack his bags and move on. With this experience under his belt, he'd apply elsewhere and await the replies. No point in lingering when he could read the writing on the wall. He'd be out of a job by the end of the year.

All of a sudden Sam realized he was no longer alone. He turned and found Tom, the older of Molly's two sons, standing just inside the barn. The boy looked hesitant, glancing about as if he wasn't sure he should be there.

"Do you need something?" Sam asked gruffly, sounding more unfriendly than he'd intended. Actually he liked Tom. The boy reminded him a little of what he'd been like at that age.

"No. I...thought I'd feed the horses."

Sam noticed the boy had one hand behind his back. "And what do you think you'll feed them?"

Tom brought his arm forward and revealed a handful of carrots.

"Have you been around horses much?"

Tom shook his head.

"Then let me give you a few guidelines." The last thing the old man needed was the shock of having one of his great-grandkids bitten by a horse. Or kicked in the gut.

Hearing voices, Sinbad arched his sleek black neck over the edge of the stall. The gelding was friendly, just right for a boy about Tom's age. Gus, Walt's Morgan horse, wasn't opposed to a bit of attention himself, but Sam would rather steer the kid toward the more reliable Sinbad.

"You like to ride?" Sam asked, while he showed Tom the proper way to hold a carrot without risking the loss of a couple of fingers.

"I never have," the boy admitted.

"You're going to have to learn, then, aren't you?" If his mother decided to keep the ranch, Tom would probably be riding the herd himself, taking on some serious responsibilities.

"I'd like to know how to ride." Tom shot a look at Sam, as if to suggest he'd need someone to teach him, and Sam was the obvious choice.

"You feel you're man enough?" Sam asked bluntly.

"Yes." The boy's voice sounded confident.

Sam grinned. "That's what I thought." Opening the bottom half of Sinbad's stall door, Sam grasped the horse's halter and led him out. "He's about fifteen hands high," Sam explained, running his palm down the gelding's neck. "Which means you'll be about four feet off the ground." He glanced at the boy to gauge his interest. "I gotta tell you, the air's just a little bit sweeter when you're sitting tall in the saddle."

Tom's grin stretched all the way across his face.

"I always feel everything in life is much clearer when I'm on a horse. There's a good feeling in my gut. When I'm riding, I'm happy and it's the type of happiness I've never found anywhere else."

Tom was mesmerized and, with such a willing audience, Sam could have talked all night. Riding was more than just a means of getting from one place to another. It involved a relationship with another creature. You depended on your horse; you and your horse had to trust and respect each other. This inner wisdom was as important as any technique Sam could share with the boy.

"If you ask me, spring's about the best time of year for riding. Especially after a downpour, when the wind's in your face and the scent of sweetgrass floats up to meet you. It's even better when you're riding a horse with heart." Nothing was more exhilarating than a smooth steady gallop across acres of grassland. But it was the silence Sam loved best, a silence broken only by the rhythm of the horse's hooves.

"Sinbad's a working horse," Sam went on to say, in case Tom believed that any one of these animals was bred for fun and games. Gramps and Sam shared the same opinion when it came to animals. They worked for their keep. The dogs, too. Gramps might have given them cutesy names, but every last one of them worked as long and hard as he did himself.

"What do you mean by 'working horse'?"

The question was sincere and Sam answered it the same way. "He's a cow pony. He's been cutting cows, trailing cattle and rounding up steers all his life. A cowboy is only as good as his horse, and Sinbad's a damn good horse."

Tom tentatively raised his hand to the gelding's neck. Sam could tell he didn't want to show he was intimidated by the large animal. He didn't blame the kid for feeling a bit scared. In an effort to put him at ease, distract him from his nervousness, Sam continued to speak.

"Sinbad's a quarter horse, which is an American breed. All that means is they were used at one time to compete in quarter-mile races. Far as I'm concerned, a quarter horse is the perfect horse for ranch work."

Tom's interest sharpened and he moved closer. His stroking of the horse's neck was more confident now, and it seemed he'd forgotten his fears. "Is that one a quarter horse?" the boy asked, looking at Gus, who'd stuck his head over the stall door.

"Gus is a Morgan," Sam explained. "It's an excellent breed, as well, especially for a ranch. They can outwalk or outrun every other kind of horse around. Did you know that the only survivor of the Battle of the Little Big Horn was a Morgan? Go ahead and touch him. He's pretty gentle."

"Hi, Gus," Tom said. He smiled broadly and walked over to rub the Morgan's velvety nose.

"When can I start learning to ride?" Tom's voice was filled with eagerness. "How about right now? I've got time."

"Hadn't you better talk to your mother first?" Sam resisted the temptation to discreetly inquire about the boy's father. He knew Molly was divorced, but little else.

At the mention of his mother, the excitement slowly drained from Tom's dark brown eyes. "She won't care."

"You'd better ask her first."

"Ask me what?" Molly said. She had just entered the barn. The open door spilled sunlight into the dim interior. Bathed as she was in the light, wreathed in the soft glow of early evening, Molly Cogan was breathtakingly beautiful.

No wonder Russell Letson had asked her out to dinner. It demanded every bit of concentration Sam could muster to drag his eyes away from her.

"Sam's going to teach me to ride!" Tom burst out excitedly. "He's been telling me all kinds of things about horses. Did you know—" He would've chattered on endlessly, Sam felt, if Molly hadn't interrupted him.

"Teach you to ride a *horse?*" Molly asked.

"Duh! What did you think? It isn't like I could hop on the back of a rooster!" The boy's enthusiasm cut away his sarcasm. "Sam says we can start tonight. We can, can't we?"

Molly's gaze pinned Sam to the wall. "I'll need to discuss it with Mr. Dakota first."

Mr. Dakota. Sam nearly laughed out loud. The last time anyone had called him that, he'd been flat on his back in a hospital emergency room in pain so bad even morphine couldn't kill it.

"Mom…" Tom sensed trouble and it showed in the nervous glance he sent Sam.

"I didn't come outside to argue with you," Molly said, her voice cool. "I need you to go back in the house. Upstairs."

"Upstairs?" Tom cried indignantly. "You're treating me like a little kid. It's still daylight out! You aren't sending me to bed, are you?"

"No. Your grandfather has some things he wants you to get for him, and they're upstairs. He can't make the climb any longer."

"I'll get them," Sam offered. If Tom didn't recognize an escape when he heard one, Sam did. With Tom out of earshot, Molly was sure to lay into him for what he'd done—agreeing to teach her son to ride.

"Tom can do it," Molly said pointedly.

So he wasn't going to be able to dodge that bullet. Taking Sinbad's halter, Sam led the gelding back into his stall and closed the gate.

"I can come back, can't I?" Tom asked his mother.

"If…if Sam agrees."

Tom swiveled to look at Sam, his heart in his eyes. Sam couldn't disappoint him. "Sure. We'll start by learning about the tack, then once you're familiar with that, I'll show you how to saddle Sinbad and we'll go from there."

"You're doing all of this tonight?" The question came from Molly.

"I'll stick with the tack lesson for now," he assured her.

Taking small steps backward, Tom was clearly reluctant to leave.

"It'll be fine," Sam said, hoping the boy understood his message.

Tom nodded once, gravely, then turned and raced out of the barn.

The moment they were alone, Molly let him have it.

"Tom is my son and I'm responsible for his safety," she began. "I'd appreciate if you'd discuss this sort of thing with me first."

Sam removed his hat. If he was going to apologize, might as well do a good job of it. "You're right. This won't happen again."

His apology apparently disarmed her because she fell silent. Still, she lingered. Walking over to Sinbad's stall, she stroked his neck, weaving her fingers through his long coarse mane. "Was there something I said earlier that offended you?" she said unexpectedly. Her voice was softer now, unsure. "Perhaps this afternoon while we were in town?"

"You think I was offended?" he asked, surprised.

She slowly turned and looked at him. Sam had never seen a woman with more striking blue eyes; it was all he could do to avert his gaze.

"Gramps was concerned when you didn't join us for dinner."

He wasn't sure how to put his feelings into words. The simplest way, he decided, was to tell her the truth. "You're family. I'm not."

"It's silly for you to cook for yourself when I've already made dinner."

"I don't mind."

"I do," she insisted, her voice flaring with anger. She

tamed it quickly by inhaling and holding her breath. "Both Gramps and I would like you to join us for meals." She paused. "It'd mean a lot to Gramps."

"What about you? Would it mean anything to you?" Sam had no idea what had prompted the question. He was practically inviting her to stomp all over his ego!

"It just makes more sense," she said. "But—" she took another breath "—whether you come or not is up to you."

So that was it, Sam reasoned. She'd done her duty. No doubt Walt had asked her to issue the invitation.

"Will you?" she asked, then added, "I need to know how much to cook."

"I haven't decided yet."

"Don't do me any favors, all right?"

What Sam did next was born of pure instinct. It was what he'd been thinking of doing from the moment he first set eyes on her. What he'd wanted to do the instant he heard Russell Letson invite her to dinner.

Without judging the wisdom—or the reasons—he stepped forward, clasped her shoulders and lowered his mouth to hers.

Their lips met briefly, the contact so light Sam wasn't sure they'd actually touched until he felt her stiffen. Taking advantage of her shock, he parted his lips and was about to wrap his arms around her when she pressed her hands against his chest and pushed him away.

"Don't ever do that again!" She wiped the back of her hand across her mouth. "How dare you!"

Sam wondered the same thing.

"Gramps would fire you in a heartbeat if I told him about this."

"Tell him," Sam urged. He didn't know why he'd done anything so stupid, and he wasn't proud of himself for giving in to the impulse. But he'd be selling snow cones in hell before he'd let her know that.

"I *should* tell him—it'd serve you right!"

"Then by all means mention it." What Sam should do was apologize—again—and let it go at that, but the same craziness that had induced him to kiss Molly goaded him now. He might have continued with his flippant responses if not for the pain and uncertainty he read in her eyes.

"I'd like your word of honor that it won't happen again."

Without meaning to, he laughed outright. Honor? Ex-cons weren't exactly known for their *honor*.

"You find this humorous, Mr. Dakota?" Her eyes narrowed and her voice rose in a quavery crescendo.

If he hadn't riled her earlier, he sure had now. Unintentionally. She whirled around and marched out of the barn. Sam sighed, leaned against the center post and rubbed one hand over his face, still wondering why he'd kissed her.

Then again, maybe he knew. He didn't like the idea of her dating Letson. His dislike of lawyers was instinctive, following the less than fair treatment he'd received from his own defense attorney. Which, to be honest, wasn't Letson's fault. In any case, it was more than that.

Sam had seen the way Letson looked at Molly—like a little boy in a candy store, his mouth watering for lemon drops. Letson would take Molly to dinner and afterward he'd kiss her. And when he did, Sam wanted Molly's thoughts to be clouded with the memory of *his* kiss. The memory of *his* touch.

Why, though? He reminded himself that he didn't even *like* Molly all that much. So why was he competing with Letson?

Damned if he knew.

And which kiss would Molly prefer—his or Letson's? Sam groaned at the thought.

If he were a betting man, he'd wager it wouldn't be his.

Five

Russell Letson was by far the most attractive man Molly had ever dated. When it came to looks, Sam Dakota took a distant second. Actually, she told herself, he wasn't even in the running. Nowhere close.

If she was interested in remarrying—which she wasn't—Molly wanted a man like her grandfather. While Gramps was no Mr. Personality, he was solid and strong in all the ways that mattered. The world needed more men like him. His body had deteriorated with age, but in his prime he'd been a man who inspired others. He was honest and good and fair, and he'd loved her grandmother to distraction. Just as her grandmother had loved him.

From her conversation with the bank manager and from the infrequent letters Gramps had sent her, Molly realized that over the past few years, he'd alienated a number of people. When her grandmother was alive, she'd smoothed over quarrels and difficulties, but with her gone, Gramps had turned cantankerous and unfriendly. Molly hoped all that would change now that she'd moved in with him. And while he had his faults,

Gramps was her knight, her compass, her guiding light. Molly couldn't imagine life without him.

At least Gramps seemed to approve of Russell—and Russell had gone out of his way to make this a special evening.

The restaurant was everything he'd claimed. The interior was elegant, the booths upholstered in a plush rust red velvet, and the lights low. There was a small dance floor and a live band every Friday and Saturday night, according to the sign outside. Molly was surprised a town the size of Sweetgrass could support an upscale restaurant like The Cattle Baron.

"I'm delighted you could see me on such short notice," Russell said as he closed his menu. His smile was cordial and Molly smiled back.

She'd gone to some lengths with her appearance. Even Gramps had noticed how long she spent fixing her hair and applying her makeup.

The move to Montana offered a long-overdue opportunity for a social life. Molly was ready to set aside the mistakes of the past and look to the future. As a member of the Sweetgrass community, she wanted to meet and mingle with other adults, and this dinner date was a step in that direction. Marriage didn't interest her, but a social life did.

When she lived in San Francisco, she'd rarely dated. She wasn't opposed to meeting men and never had been. But it was difficult to find a man who understood the responsibilities of single parenthood and shared her values. Even if she'd actually met someone interesting, squeezing in time for a relationship between her family and her job—well, there just weren't enough hours in the day.

Excuses. All excuses.

She hadn't been ready then, but she was now. The difference was her willingness to take a risk. Maybe it was because, with Gramps close at hand, she felt safer, more secure. He obviously liked and trusted Russell. And Sam…

"I hear you've created quite a stir among the fellows in town," Russell said, looking at her and blushing slightly.

"Me? I caused a stir?"

"There aren't many single women your age in Sweetgrass. There's been plenty of talk—you know, interest." Russell seemed a bit flustered as if he'd said more than he should. Not a trait she would have expected in a lawyer, but it made him all the more endearing. She liked him already.

"I'm sure you've had plenty of phone calls." This sounded more like a question.

"Some." A lady from the local Baptist church and a return call from the school-district office, but that was it. Men weren't exactly pounding down her door, but it didn't hurt her ego any that Russell assumed otherwise.

The waiter, a staid older man, delivered their wine, and after Russell had tasted it, filled their goblets. Russell had chosen well, Molly determined after her first sip. The California merlot was excellent.

She finished her glass and allowed Russell to refill it. A relaxing evening out was just what Molly needed, especially after the long week she'd endured. She'd driven from California to Montana, carting all her worldly belongings. She'd refereed her sons' battles across several states, dealt with the realities of Gramps's health and had begun to improve the appalling condition of the ranch house. It was a week to remember.

After ordering dinner, they chatted amicably. Russell had charming manners and Molly was soon enjoying herself. She couldn't remember the last time she'd spent a quiet evening in the company of an attractive man.

The band arrived, and around nine o'clock, the music started. Not the country-and-western tunes Molly expected, but the mellow sound of light rock. The music was an accompaniment, not an intrusion into their conversation. A few couples got up to dance, and Molly glanced enviously toward the small hardwood floor.

"Would you like to take a spin?" Russell asked, and held out his hand. His eyes twinkled as if he'd been waiting for her cue. A woman could get used to a man this sensitive, she mused.

Not until Russell had placed his arms around her waist and brought her close did she experience a sense of disappointment. It took her a couple of anxious moments to understand what was happening.

The last man to hold her close was Sam Dakota. His hands on her shoulders had been strong and forceful; his touch had rocked her, but his kiss had been gentle. The contrast had been…shocking. Memorable. Twenty-four hours later, and that memory was still potent.

Molly closed her eyes in an effort to banish Sam Dakota from her mind. Russell was handsome and well educated. Polite. Successful. Exactly the type of man she'd hoped to meet. Sam, though, was hard and lean and rough as rawhide. A hired hand. She knew almost nothing about his past, nothing about his future.

It exasperated her that she could be in the arms of

a perfectly good dinner date and her mind was full of another man. The *wrong* man!

Despite her determination to put Sam out of her thoughts, Molly found it difficult. She was grateful when their meal arrived and she could sit across from Russell and talk.

"You might remember there was something I needed to discuss with you," Russell said. He smoothed the napkin onto his lap and sipped his wine.

Molly had the impression he wanted to get this matter, whatever it was, settled now. Immediately. From the way he nervously toyed with his wineglass, she guessed this wasn't a discussion he'd been looking forward to.

"I imagine you're curious as to what I wanted to ask you," he began, gripping his goblet with both hands.

Until he'd mentioned it, Molly had actually forgotten the reason behind this dinner invitation. "Naturally," she responded, pretending she'd been breathlessly awaiting their discussion.

"I realize this is a bit premature," he said. "Personally I'd prefer to wait, but my client is anxious, which is understandable." His eyes darkened with sincerity. "Forgive me, Molly, if this offends you."

"Offends me?" Client. He was talking to her on behalf of a client? None of this made sense. She'd assumed they'd gone out primarily to get to know each other and enjoy each other's company—and perhaps to discuss some trivial matter in regard to her grandfather's will.

"This has to do with the Broken Arrow Ranch," Russell continued.

She tensed. "What about the ranch?"

He frowned as if this was distasteful to him, something he'd prefer not to do. "My client wants to know your intentions after your grandfather dies."

Molly put down her knife and fork, and clenched her hands in her lap. "My intentions to *what?*" she asked, her voice low. The evening was ruined, her illusions shattered. This was no dinner date; this was some kind of business negotiation.

"I've been asked to approach you with the idea of selling out. Naturally my client is prepared to wait until the appropriate time."

Until Gramps is dead and buried, that is. But not long enough for his body to grow cold. For an instant her anger was blinding. Her chest tightened and her breathing went shallow.

"This is a sick joke, right?" It wasn't, deep down she knew that, but she had to ask.

Russell's apology was instantaneous. "I'm sorry, Molly, really I am. Like I told you, I felt the timing with this was wrong, but my client insisted. I didn't want to approach you about it now, not so soon, but my client's afraid someone else is going to contact you first. I'm sure once you think all this through, you'll recognize his request as reasonable."

Her grandfather wasn't dead yet, and already the vultures were circling overhead. "You can tell your... client, whoever he is, that I won't be selling the ranch."

"You're not serious, are you?" Russell's eyes widened. "What do you plan to do with it?"

Molly hadn't made any decisions yet. Her one overwhelming concern had been to reach her grandfather before the unthinkable happened. The move from California to Montana had absorbed all her time and energy, dominated every waking moment. She wasn't prepared to answer Russell, nor did she feel any obligation to do so.

"Who hired you?" she demanded. "Who would be so cold and unfeeling—offering to buy the ranch before Gramps is gone? And doing it like this—through a lawyer. Who would do such a thing?"

Russell avoided her eyes. She knew he'd dreaded this and understood now why he'd invited her to dinner. He'd been hoping to smooth the way—and soften the blow.

"I can't answer that, Molly. My client has requested anonymity."

She laughed shortly. "That's understandable, isn't it?" She sighed and glanced at the ceiling while she collected her thoughts. "If you must know, I'll be working the ranch myself."

"You," Russell said slowly. He'd begun to frown again.

"You make it sound as if you don't think I'm capable of doing it."

"How much experience have you had?" he asked matter-of-factly.

"Experience," she repeated, feigning a laugh. "I'll learn as I go."

Russell's frown deepened. "Molly, I realize this whole subject is…unpleasant. Trust me, I wasn't looking forward to broaching it with you so soon. If it'd been up to me—well, never mind, that isn't important. The fact is, a woman alone with two school-age boys isn't going to be able to manage a ranch on her own. Not in these times. Not in this current market."

"Why not? According to Gramps, Sam Dakota is an excellent foreman."

Russell crumpled the linen napkin and set it on the

table beside his plate, his appetite apparently gone. Molly's had vanished, too. "The foreman's another question. How well do you know this man?"

Molly mulled over her response, but no ready answer came to mind. "Gramps hired Sam and that's good enough for me," she said. There simply hadn't been enough time to find out much about him or assess his character. She knew she found him somewhat disturbing. But she also knew that Sam cared about her grandfather, and had, in fact, saved Gramps's life. If for nothing else, his devotion to Gramps had earned him her gratitude. And her loyalty.

Once again Russell appeared hesitant. "If Dakota does agree to stay on as foreman, will you be able to continue paying his wages?"

"Wages?" Something else that had never occurred to her.

"You'll remember I was the one who drew up Walter's will, so I'm well aware of the state of his financial affairs. Molly, I have to be honest with you. They're dismal. Even if you were able to strike some kind of financial agreement with Dakota, there's no guarantee you'd be able to make a go of ranching.

"Cattle prices are down. Many long-established ranches are experiencing financial difficulties. There are fewer and fewer independent ranches left. Fewer and fewer true cowboys. Conglomerates are moving in and buying financially strapped spreads at prices well below market value. Ranchers often have no option but to sell, and they're left with nothing to show after a lifetime of effort. I don't want to see you lose your inheritance like that."

"Thanks for your vote of confidence."

"It isn't easy saying these things to you," Russell murmured. "But I feel it's my duty. In six months, when the ranch is on the auction block, I don't want you to look at me and ask why I didn't warn you."

Molly inhaled a deep stabilizing breath. In time she knew she'd need to make these decisions, but she hadn't expected to be confronted with them her first week in Montana. On a dinner date, yet.

"Molly," he said, and stretched his hand across the table to grip hers firmly. "I realize this is upsetting— hell, it would distress anyone. But you need to give the matter of selling your consideration *now*. When Walter does die, it'll be the worst time emotionally for you to make this type of decision. All I want you to do is think ahead a few weeks or months, or however long Walt lives."

Molly knew Russell was right, but she didn't want to face this question yet. She propped her elbows on the table and leaned her head on her hands. "The land has been in the family for four generations." Gramps and her own father had been born in the very house in which she and her sons now lived.

For all those years the family had stuck together. Survived. During two world wars, the Wheatons had held on to the land; they'd struggled through the long lean years of the Great Depression. Through it all, cattle prices had plummeted and then risen, over and over, like a wild roller-coaster ride, and through it all, the Wheatons had managed. They would again, God willing.

The ranch was Molly's heritage from her grandfather and from the father she barely remembered. One day it would belong to her sons. Briefly she closed her eyes. As angry as the offer made her, Russell had done her a favor by forcing her to acknowledge her responsibilities to her grandfather and the ranch.

"This is very difficult," she whispered, "but…"

Russell relaxed and smiled as if to say he knew he could count on her to be reasonable. "Then you'll consider the offer?"

Molly stared at him dumbfounded. He'd misunderstood completely.

"Let me assure you right now the money is good," he told her warmly. "Damn good. You won't need to worry about finances for a very long time."

"I'm not selling, Russell," she announced flatly. "Not while I live and draw breath. I'll do whatever needs to be done in order to hold on to the ranch."

Russell was right about one thing—she would definitely need help. If that meant swallowing her pride and asking Sam Dakota for his expertise, then she'd do it. Pride, even female pride, had its limits.

"How are you planning to do this? Who's going to help you?" Russell demanded. His face had contorted slightly, masking his striking good looks.

"Sam Dakota, for one." There'd be others, too, Molly knew. Gramps had lived in this community all his life. She didn't doubt for an instant that, when the time came and she needed help, someone would step forward and lend a willing hand.

Russell settled back in the booth and held her eyes for a long moment. He seemed to be carefully gauging his words. "I wasn't going to say anything, but now I realize I must. Molly, exactly how well do you know Sam Dakota?" he asked.

"This is the second time you've mentioned Sam. Gramps hired him and he's—"

"Don't let your judgment be clouded by your grand-father's relationship with him. You need to form your own opinion."

"I only met him a few days ago." Molly was begin-ning to wonder if she *should* trust her instincts regard-ing Sam. They'd been muddled, confused by his kiss. Confused by a lot of things that had nothing to do with her grandfather or how good a foreman Sam was.

Russell nodded thoughtfully. "Sam Dakota is a stranger, a drifter. No one knows exactly where he came from or anything about him. He showed up in town one day, down on his luck."

"There's nothing wrong with that."

"True enough, but it's what happened afterward that's cause for concern."

"What?" she asked, not entirely certain she wanted to hear this.

"Trouble, Molly, lots of trouble. He wasn't in town more than an hour before he became involved in a…an altercation at Willie's tavern and—" He stopped. "I'll leave it at that."

"What do you mean?"

"I think it would be best if you asked Sam yourself."

She hesitated, watching Russell intently.

"Molly, listen to me, please. I'm not sure you should trust him."

"Don't be ridiculous!"

"You think that's what I'm being?" The attorney was obviously uncomfortable. "All I ask is that you be damned careful, understand?" His face was somber, concerned—as if it was all he could do not to divulge further information.

"Oh, no, you don't." Molly wasn't about to let it go

at that. If Russell knew something she didn't, she had every intention of getting the facts, even if it took half the night. "Tell me what you know, Russell. I have a right to know the truth."

"I can't, Molly. I'm stepping out of line as it is." He looked away before slowly releasing his breath. "Let me put it this way. Wherever Dakota goes, trouble follows. There've been a number of unexplained incidents around the area recently. Strange incidents. Has Walt mentioned them?"

Molly shook her head.

"None of this started until after Sam Dakota arrived."

"What are these incidents?"

"Ask your grandfather. I'm not a distrustful person, but I'd find it mighty coincidental if Sam wasn't involved."

"Involved in *what?*" Her immediate concern was for her children. With Gramps at the ranch they were probably safe, but he was feeble and in ill health. She couldn't imagine what Russell was trying to tell her.

"I can't say, Molly. I probably shouldn't have said anything at all, but I felt it was my duty to warn you."

"Strange, you said. What is it? You're blaming Sam for some mysterious alien sightings?" The suggestion was enough to make her laugh.

"It isn't that kind of strange," Russell was quick to inform her. "Ginny Dougherty and her cousin were in town not more than two days ago and reported a case of vandalism. Apparently someone knocked over Walter's mailbox. It's the third time this month. She's had trouble herself."

Molly could vaguely recall Gramps saying something about the box being vandalized.

"That isn't all."

"What else has happened?"

"Ask Ginny Dougherty," he said.

"Ginny?"

"I've said more than I should have already." He pinched his lips together and Molly could see it would take a crowbar to pry any more information out of him.

That evening Tom sat on the front porch with a dog by his side. Natasha, the pregnant collie. Sighing, he stroked her silky ears. He'd heard about people experiencing withdrawal, but he never thought he'd have to deal with it himself. Only he wasn't on drugs. No way— he wasn't *that* dumb. What he missed to the point of wanting to scream was television. Good old-fashioned color television with a remote control and a twenty-three-inch screen.

Gramps got one channel on an old black-and-white set. Tom was surprised to learn there were still black-and-white televisions left in the United States. What irked him most was that Gramps refused to buy a dish or bring in cable, and the only station his tinfoil-wrapped rabbit ears delivered was from somewhere up in Canada. An educational channel! If he wanted to learn something, he'd go to school. Even sadder was that Gramps didn't have a clue what he was missing. The old man didn't know what MTV was, and furthermore he didn't care.

Gramps was asleep on the recliner now, with the television on Mute, the picture fuzzy. What Tom could make out convinced him he wouldn't want to watch it even if the picture came in clear.

Sweetgrass's lone radio station was just as bad. Every morning at ten-thirty the entire town apparently went into a frenzy for radio bingo. Tom knew certain people enjoyed playing bingo. In San Francisco the Catholic church down the street had bingo nights twice a week, but he'd never heard of anyone playing it over the *radio.*

And if that wasn't enough, Tom had been subjected to a litany of farm prices from about noon on. He hated to disappoint Gramps, but he didn't really care about the price of pork bellies. Then the extension agent would come on and talk about the fall fair and something called 4-H. Mostly his little discussions had to do with how to grow vegetables and groom cows. Tom didn't know what an extension agent was or what he did, other than talk about animal grooming. And when the radio station actually played some music, it was this horrible stuff from the 1940s and 1950s. Stuff that was around before his mother was even born!

Now she was off on some hot date. His mother dating? Tom wasn't sure he liked that idea, but had decided he'd be mature about it. Still, he thought, if she was interested in an evening on the town, she should check out Sam.

Tom liked Sam. Clay did, too. Neither of them knew anything about Russell Letson. They'd met him when he'd come to pick Mom up, and Tom didn't have feelings toward him one way or the other. Letson was all right, he guessed. Sam, however, was terrific.

Okay, so the foreman wasn't as good-looking as the lawyer, but Sam had the advantage of knowing everything there was to know about horses. The attorney looked clueless, on *that* subject, anyway.

For the past two nights, Sam had spent time with Tom after dinner, teaching him about horses. He'd seemed distracted this evening, though. Maybe it was Clay's fault. Clay had been a pest, but Tom was used to his younger brother making a nuisance of himself. Sam wasn't.

He would say one thing about Gramps's foreman— Sam hadn't once talked down to either him or Clay. He spoke to them both as if they were regular guys.

Clay was sound asleep, but Tom had come downstairs and sat in the dark, waiting for his mother's return. He'd heard about mothers waiting up for their kids to come home from a date. He'd never thought *he'd* be the one sitting there killing time until *she* showed up. But with Gramps asleep, someone needed to keep an eye on the clock.

Headlights appeared in the distance. Tom knew the car could be miles away. He'd never known anyplace to get darker than Montana. In California in the middle of the night, no matter where he was, Tom could look out the window and find a light. Somewhere.

Not in Montana. When night came, it settled over the land like…like black ink. It covered everything. Except for the moon and the stars, he couldn't see a thing. The first night when he looked out the window, he'd been astounded. At the darkness. And the quiet. It was enough to unnerve anyone.

The headlights missed him as the car took a sharp turn and followed the road around the back by the outbuildings. Tom almost made the mistake of walking into the house, but he didn't want to stumble on his mother and her lawyer friend kissing. That would embarrass everyone. Besides, Tom wasn't sure how he'd feel if he saw the attorney with a lip lock on his mother. He might do something stupid, like punch him out.

Tom returned his gaze to the heavens. Away from the city lights, the night sky was ablaze with stars. He'd had no idea there were that many. Suddenly he noticed that the car was leaving, its lights stretching out toward the highway. Well. That hadn't taken long.

"Gramps, are you awake?" Tom heard his mother ask from inside the house.

He stiffened. His mother's voice was agitated. Letson had tried something and she was telling Gramps. Damn. Tom knew he should have gone inside, but it was too late now.

"Gramps, I hate to wake you, but I have a few questions."

The urgency in his mother's voice brought Tom up short. Letson would be sorry by the time Tom was finished with him. No one messed with his mother!

"Molly, darlin'," Gramps said and Tom heard the old man yawn. "Did you enjoy yourself?"

"Gramps, we need to talk."

"Talk?"

From his position on the porch, Tom could look into the living room through the screen door and not be seen. Gramps was on the recliner and his mother sat on the ottoman in front of him. She leaned forward and folded her arms around her knees.

"What do you know about Sam Dakota?" she asked abruptly.

"Sam?" Gramps scratched the side of his head. "You went to dinner with Letson and discussed Sam?"

"Tell me what you know about him."

"Why?" The word was a challenge.

"Because…I need to know if we should trust him."

Tom wasn't sure he liked the tone of his mother's voice or her questions, but he wanted to hear what she said even more than he wanted to run in and defend Sam.

"Why are you asking me such a thing?"

His mother threw back her head and stared at the ceiling as if counting to ten. She did that sometimes when she wanted to keep her cool.

"Did you check his references?" she asked quietly.

Gramps rubbed the sleep from his face. "I don't recall that he provided any."

"Then why'd you hire him?" Her voice rose slightly.

"'Cause I needed help."

Gramps seemed to think that was all the explaining necessary. But Tom knew his mother wasn't about to let it drop. No, she'd hang on until she got what she wanted. All mothers weren't like that, but his was. Stubborn, and she wouldn't let you get away with changing the subject.

"Sam Dakota is a good man, Molly."

"But you don't know that for sure, do you?"

"I didn't need a piece of paper with a bunch of people's names to tell me what two hours on the range said a whole lot better."

"Okay, so Sam's good on the back of a horse." She made that sound like a small thing.

"He handles cattle like a pro," Gramps added. "He's one of the best cattlemen I've worked with in years. Now tell me why all the questions. You're not makin' a lick of sense, girl."

She hesitated, then shrugged. "Russell Letson said

there were a number of unexplained incidents that've happened since Sam arrived. He said people in town talk about him." Her voice rose again and she leaned forward.

"I'm not a man who listens to rumors. You disappoint me, Molly, if you do."

"But, Gramps, Sam spends time with my boys."

"You've been taken in by that silver-tongued devil of an attorney."

"But I thought you liked him! He's your attorney!"

"I should fire him, that's what I should do! I don't want him filling your head with doubts."

"How do you know he's not telling the truth?" Molly demanded. "What did Russell mean by 'incidents'? Why didn't you tell me? Is it true, Gramps?"

"Fiddlesticks."

"Gramps, please. Listen to reason. Everything is fine and then Sam Dakota arrives and stirs up the town…"

"It needed a little stirring up. Whole damn place has gone to seed. I don't know how it happened, but overnight the population of Sweetgrass has turned into a bunch of fanatics. I'm telling you right now that fight wasn't Sam's fault. I saw it happen. I'd have done the same damn thing myself."

"Tell me about this fight. Russell mentioned it, too, but he didn't give me any details."

Apparently his mother didn't know everything. Tom was interested in the particulars himself. Sam might not be as big as some, but he was strong. And Tom knew he wasn't a man inclined to walk away from a challenge, either.

"There's nothing you need to know about it, other than what I already told you."

"Gramps, I'd rather—"

"You're forgetting something, Molly girl," Gramps interrupted. "If it wasn't for Sam Dakota, I'd be a dead man now."

A moment of silence followed his words.

"Oh, Gramps…"

Tom watched as his mother took one of Gramps's hands and pressed it to her cheek. She closed her eyes and Tom knew how grateful she felt that he was alive. He had to admit he felt pretty grateful, too.

"One more thing I'm gonna tell you," Gramps said gruffly. "Sam was a champion rodeo rider—one of the best till he had a bad accident. He knows about hard work, and the value of a dream. Not only that, he's managed to keep this ranch going. So if you've got anything to say to the man, I suggest you start with a thank-you."

Six

It was more out of habit than necessity that Sam stopped by the house each morning. With family around Walt didn't need Sam checking up on him. His visits had become courtesy calls—first he would inquire about the old man's health, then he'd list his plans for the day.

Although Sam's title was foreman, he'd taken on just about all the responsibilities of what bigger ranches would call a general manager. He did the paperwork, ordered supplies, hired and fired temporary hands when they needed extra help and organized the work. And he dealt with any problems that arose, of which there never appeared to be a shortage.

Toward the end of Molly's second week at the ranch, he walked into the kitchen one morning and found her in her bathrobe, standing barefoot in front of the coffeepot. His reaction at the sight of her—looking warm and sleepy, her hair tousled—surprised even him. It felt as if…as if someone had kicked him in the stomach.

"Mornin'," he said, aware that he sounded flustered. In a gesture of respect he touched the tip of his hat.

"Sam…hi." Seeing him had obviously unnerved her,

too. Sam watched as she tugged the robe more securely about her waist and rubbed one bare foot against the other.

They'd been avoiding each other for almost a week. Kissing her that night hadn't been one of his most brilliant moves, but try as he might Sam couldn't make himself regret it. Seeing her now, her hair mussed and her face bare of makeup, he thought Molly Cogan was lovely—much lovelier than he'd realized before. It was difficult not to stare. He pulled his gaze away and wondered if her appeal had something to do with getting to know her and the boys. He enjoyed Molly, the small things she did to make every day special. Not a night went by without her adding an extra little touch to the evening meal. Sometimes it was a bouquet of wildflowers placed in the center of the table; other times a low-fat dessert made especially for her grandfather. Without further discussion, Sam had joined the family for supper on Sunday night and every night since.

He and Molly didn't speak or meet each other's eyes, but he found himself listening for the contagious sound of her laughter. It always made him smile, no matter what his mood. The gentleness she displayed toward her grandfather touched him. And he sensed that she was a good mother, too. Not only that, he was impressed with the improvements she'd made around the place. Molly and her boys had already done a number of small repairs that he'd been putting off for lack of time. Fixing the porch steps. Painting the front door. Things like that.

"Do you want coffee?" she asked, breaking into his thoughts. She opened the cupboard and reached for an extra mug.

"Thanks, but no, I've already had my fill." He'd been

working the better part of two hours and had downed half a pot before sunup. Sam's routine was to rise around four in order to sort through an accumulation of paperwork, then head out to the barn.

Last week he'd hired two hands, high-school kids who worked cheap and were grateful for the jobs. They arrived early in the morning and returned home at the end of the day. Pete could shoe horses, mend fences and fix machinery. Charlie would work half the time as a hand and the other half as a wrangler; his particular responsibility was caring for the horses.

Some ranchers used all-terrain vehicles, instead of horses, but Walt would have none of that. A horse was the original ATV, he said, and while his opinion might be outdated, Sam tended to agree with him. He wasn't opposed to taking the pickup onto the range and often did, but nothing beat riding. Nothing compared to the feeling of exhilaration and freedom he experienced on horseback. During his darkest days in prison, this was what he'd thought about, how he'd escaped the hell he was trapped in.

Sam forced his mind back to the matters at hand. Charlie worked well with the horses, but Sam guessed that by this time next year Tom would be knowledgeable enough to tackle the job.

Molly's older son possessed horse sense. It was something you either had or you didn't. For Tom, it seemed to come naturally. The boy had a real affinity for animals, especially horses, and he was a fast learner. He frequently reminded Sam of what *he'd* been like at that age—eager to prove himself, looking for ways to establish his manhood. Nothing better than ranch work for doing that.

Both Molly's boys were good kids. Sam would have liked to tell her, but hesitated because the tension between them remained so strong. Probably because of that damn kiss.

Sam started into the living room where Walt was resting. He knew it was hell on the old man to sit idle, something he had to do more and more lately. That was one reason Sam made a point of visiting Walt every morning, consulting with him and seeking his advice, although he rarely needed it.

"Sam." Molly stopped him as he left to find Walt. He turned around.

"I—there's a question I'd like to ask if you don't mind," she said without meeting his eyes.

Ever since Saturday night, when she'd gone to dinner with Letson, he'd noticed a change in her attitude. He'd assumed it had something to do with the kiss; now he wasn't sure.

"Gramps said you didn't offer any references when he hired you," she said, holding her coffee mug with both hands. "Why was that?"

"He didn't want any." He squared his shoulders in challenge. "Are you asking for them now?"

"Gramps doesn't seem to feel he needs them." A dubious quality in her voice told him she didn't agree.

If he hadn't demonstrated his ability and his commitment by this time, Sam doubted he ever would. He was about to tell her exactly that when she asked another question.

"I've heard there've been a number of…unexplained incidents around the ranch since you started here."

"Unexplained incidents?" There had been, but they'd begun *before* he was hired; Walt had told him that.

He wondered who'd mentioned it to Molly. Letson, no doubt. Any problems Sam encountered he'd dealt with promptly and efficiently. For the most part he didn't see any need to worry Walt, so he hadn't brought up any of the recent incidents. The old man knew about the mailbox being knocked over three times, but only because Ginny Dougherty had said something. The damaged fence posts, strewn garbage and rotten eggs thrown against the side of the barn were more a nuisance than a hazard.

The most dangerous incident had happened earlier in the week. A windmill used to pump drinking water for the cattle had been toppled. At first Sam suspected that wind and time had been the culprits, but on closer inspection, he'd discovered the damage was deliberate. It'd taken half a day for two men to repair it.

Molly's right hand clasped the front of her robe. "Gramps suggested if I was concerned about any of this, I should ask you. He's right—you should have the opportunity to defend yourself."

Sam's hackles instantly went up. "Defend myself?" His narrowed gaze locked onto hers as his anger simmered just beneath the surface. "Are you suggesting *I'm* the one responsible?"

"That's not what I said." The hesitation before she answered implied something else. "What I want is the truth. I can deal with anything but lies. If there's some hidden agenda here, then I'd rather you told me about it now."

"Hidden agenda?" He worked his fingers, clenching and unclenching his hands. "In other words you're asking me if I'm causing these problems. That doesn't make much sense to me. Why would I bite the hand that feeds me?"

"To prove how valuable you are."

She'd apparently given the matter some thought. "I don't have to make more work for myself to prove how much I'm needed around this place. Look around you— the ranch is in terrible shape! I can't keep up with everything that needs to be done as it is. Trust me, the last thing I'd do is add to my own workload."

She studied him as if to gauge the truth of his words. After a moment she nodded. "Thank you, Sam. I apologize if I offended you."

"No problem." She *had* angered him, but he admired her for having the courage to confront him directly. Most folks wouldn't, and he'd be dismissed without ever knowing why. "Now if you don't mind, I'm going to talk to your grandfather for a while."

Walt looked pale and drawn when Sam finally entered the living room. Just sitting up seemed to drain him of strength. "Mornin', Sam."

"Walt." Sam removed his hat and took the seat across from the old man.

"My granddaughter givin' you trouble?"

Sam laughed softly. "None that I can't handle."

"Good." Walt let his head fall back against the sofa cushion and closed his eyes. "Were you able to get the Stetson?"

"Yeah, I picked one up in town yesterday." He didn't mention that it had cost almost a hundred dollars—or that he'd paid for it himself.

Walt's smile was full, rare even at the best of times. "Tom will be surprised, won't he?"

"I expect he will." Delighted, too.

"Good."

It was time to get on with the business of the day. "I'm sending Pete and Charlie out to Lonesome Valley and I'll have them check the—"

"Fine, fine, whatever you think." Walt cut him off with a flick of his hand. "How are Tom and Clay doing? Molly told me they follow you around like shadows."

The boys had taken up the role of sidekicks, asking questions and trailing after him, but Sam didn't mind. Much of the time they were actually a help— Tom especially—doing small chores like cleaning tack and sweeping out stalls. He could always use a couple of extra hands.

"Tom's doing well with his riding lessons," Sam said. "I'd like to take him out on the range."

Walt's mouth quivered with a half smile. "Whatever you think," he said again. "What about the younger boy?"

"Not yet. He's too nervous. Needs his confidence built up first."

Walt showed his agreement with an abrupt nod. "Didn't you tell me Natasha recently delivered her pups?"

"A couple of days ago now." Sam grinned. "Clay's been spending his days baby-sitting them—when his mom hasn't got him painting shutters or nailing down steps."

"Good. Let the boy choose one of those pups for his own."

The old man was wise; giving the younger boy a puppy was the perfect thing. "I'll see to it."

"And—" A clamor arose outside, followed by a shout. Sam recognized Ginny's frantic voice and knew it meant trouble. He leaped to his feet and raced through the kitchen, nearly colliding with Molly in his rush.

Stepping away to avoid him, she lost her balance. Sam instinctively reached for her shoulders to steady her. He wasn't sure how it happened, but his hand grazed her breast. The briefest of contacts, completely unintentional, and yet he felt a jolt of desire so potent it was as if someone had pounded a stake right through him.

Molly felt it, too, light as the touch had been, and her startled gaze flew to his.

He opened his mouth to apologize, but she shook her head, wordlessly conveying that an apology wasn't necessary. She understood. He had more important matters to attend to.

"Sam." Ginny's Appaloosa pranced about the yard, his neck lathered from the long gallop. "I was out checking my herd and saw that your fence is down. You've got a hundred head or more making straight for the river."

Sam slapped his hat against his thigh and swore. He'd already sent Pete and Charlie out for the day. First he'd need to find them, and then the cattle. He just prayed none of the herd was injured or managed to get lost before he found them. That wasn't all he had to worry about, either. He'd recently planted seventy-five acres of alfalfa; those cattle could destroy the entire crop in ten minutes.

"Thanks for letting me know, Ginny." He was already running toward the truck.

"What is it, woman?" Walt hollered from the doorway, his eyes flashing with more life than Sam had seen in a week.

Sam stopped abruptly and turned toward them. "There's a fence down," he explained.

Walt's reaction was identical to his own.

"That's not the worst of it," Ginny muttered.

"There's more?" Walt cried. "Dammit, woman, can't you bring any news except bad?"

"It isn't my fault, old man! If you'd gone out of your way to create friends instead of enemies, you might not be in this predicament."

"Would you two stop bickering?" Sam shouted. He didn't have time to stand around while they exchanged insults. If there was more trouble, he needed to hear what it was so he could deal with it as quickly as possible.

Ginny's gaze traveled from Walt to him. "It was deliberate, Sam. Someone cut the wires."

This time Walt and Sam swore in two-part harmony.

Molly didn't understand the full significance of what had happened; all she knew was that she didn't see Sam for three days.

She'd phoned the sheriff's office to report the damage but heard nothing back. She wondered if this kind of thing was considered a routine crime in Montana—the way police in San Francisco viewed car break-ins.

Meals were hurried affairs during those days of crisis. Either Charlie or Pete would take something out to Sam, but he never showed up himself. Molly wasn't sure when he slept. Almost against her will, as she worked on the garden she'd begun to plant, she caught herself watching for him, worrying about him. She was constantly aware of his absence.

Gramps was anxious, too, grilling her with questions, repeating the same ones over and over until her patience was gone. He fretted and stewed, and Molly knew it couldn't be good for his heart. She worried about leaving him even for a short time, but Gramps hated her fussing over him. The atmosphere in the house seemed to crackle with tension. Molly gardened obsessively to escape it.

The boys were nervous and at loose ends, and Molly didn't object when they started spending most of their time hanging around the barn. That was their way of coping with anxiety, as gardening was hers.

Saturday evening, the third day, just as the sun was about to sink into the horizon, Tom spotted Sam riding slowly toward the house.

"Mom! Mom!" Tom raced over to her, his thin legs kicking up dust. Molly set aside the hoe and rubbed her arm across her sweat-dampened forehead. She still wasn't accustomed to seeing Tom in a cowboy hat. Not a cheap imitation, either, but a felt one that must have cost the earth. He'd found it on his bed the day they learned the fence had been cut. The only person who could've put it there was Sam. Why, she couldn't guess. Not that it mattered to Tom. He'd placed it on his head and hadn't removed it since, except to sleep.

"I see him, honey," Molly said, looking out at the horse and rider. Their shape was silhouetted against the pink sky of sunset.

Despite herself, Molly felt her breath catch. The scene was classically, beautifully Western. *Return of the Cowboy.*

But this cowboy had barely slept for two nights. He'd eaten on the run. And he'd worked long back-breaking days.

Molly's hand crept to her throat. Sam was slouched over the saddle; it looked as if he barely had the strength to stay on his horse. As he drew near the yard and saw Molly and the boys, he straightened.

Tom and Clay gathered around her. Sam rode still closer, and she searched his face for signs of trouble, fearing he'd come with more bad news.

Unsure what she intended to say, Molly hurried toward him when he stopped. There'd been so many things she wanted to tell him, had thought about over the past three days. Not a single one came to mind now.

"Hi." That sounded incredibly stupid. Juvenile. She wanted to grab the word back the instant she'd said it.

"Hi, yourself," he said. He grinned. It was the lazy tired smile of a man who'd been too long away from home. A man who'd finally returned and found someone waiting for him there. His gaze held hers an extra moment, then moved to her oldest son. His grin broadened. "Nice-looking Stetson, son."

Son. The word slipped effortlessly from his lips, and Molly watched Tom's reaction. It seemed he stood a little straighter, a little taller.

The tension between Molly's shoulder blades eased. "Did you find all the cattle?"

"Think so. The last two were trapped in a bog hole, up to their knees in mud. I had a hell of a time freeing them. Are Pete and Charlie back?"

Tom answered. "Came back about an hour ago."

"Good."

For the first time Molly noticed that Sam was wearing some of the bog hole. His clothes were caked with dried mud. The hem of his jeans was thick with it, as were his sleeves. His face was splattered. Funny she hadn't realized it earlier.

"I'll take Thunder for you," Tom offered. "I'll give him a good rubdown and some extra oats—he deserves it."

"Charlie should do that. It's what we're paying him for."

"Charlie and Pete have gone home now," Molly said.

Sam's eyes flared briefly before he sighed. "Can't say I blame them. I don't think they figured they'd be working this hard on a summer job."

"I don't think *anyone* figured they would," Molly added.

Holding on to the saddle horn, Sam slid heavily from Thunder's back. The leather creaked and for a moment he braced himself against the horse. "I need a shower, something to eat and my bed, in that order."

"There's plenty of leftovers from dinner," Molly assured him.

Tom took the gelding's reins and led him into the barn. "Don't worry about Thunder," he said, not hiding his pleasure at helping Sam.

"I'm sure Gramps is going to want to talk to you, too," Molly said. She hated to burden Sam with any more demands, but with the state Gramps had been in these past few days...

"I'll give him a report as soon as I've finished eating," Sam promised.

Molly wondered if Gramps would be able to wait that long.

Tom and Clay were still in the barn tending to Thunder when Sam entered the kitchen fresh from his shower. In a clean set of clothes, his hair wet and just combed, he made a striking figure. Trying hard not to stare, Molly turned the thick slice of ham sizzling in the pan while she warmed mashed potatoes and peas in another skillet.

Sam closed his eyes and for a wild moment Molly feared he was about to collapse. It turned out he was just inhaling the aroma of a home-cooked meal. "I swear I could eat a horse."

"Don't let Thunder hear you say that," she joked.

Sam pulled out a kitchen chair and sat at the table. "Or Tom," he muttered with a laugh.

Molly brought him his meal, along with a letter that had arrived for him. He glanced up expectantly when she set the envelope on the table, then stuck it inside his shirt pocket, unopened. Not without a sense of guilt, Molly had studied that envelope long and hard. The return address was a well-known ranch on the other side of the state.

He was halfway through his meal when Gramps wandered into the kitchen. "So you're back."

"I'm back," Sam agreed.

"Didn't hear you come in," Gramps said. "Fell asleep." He pulled out a chair and sat across the table from Sam, who didn't so much as pause in his appreciation of the meal. He reached for a second buttermilk biscuit and slathered butter across the warm top.

"You've had a few rough days."

Sam nodded, biting into his biscuit with a look of pure contentment.

Molly brought Gramps a cup of coffee, then sat down beside him.

"Molly's been hard at work herself," Gramps said next. "She's put in a garden. Exactly the same place my

Molly used to have hers. That woman had a way with plants." He shook his head wonderingly. "My guess is her granddaughter has the same green thumb."

Only days ago, the spot where her grandmother had cultivated one of the finest gardens Molly had ever seen was covered with blackberry vines and weeds. With the boys' help, she'd cleared the space, roto-tilled and enriched the earth, then planted vegetables and—she couldn't resist—flowers. Low-maintenance flowers, like nasturtiums and impatiens. The work had been physically demanding and her body ached everywhere.

"We'll have to wait and see about that green thumb, Gramps." He embarrassed her with his praise. She'd weeded her grandmother's garden during her childhood summers, but she'd never created one of her own. It would be an experience, especially planting as late as she had.

Gramps frowned. "I had to stop Molly from climbing up on the roof, though. Fool woman seems to think she can patch a leak, too." He shook his head. "She's beginning to act like Ginny—thinks she can do everything herself."

"I've been meaning to get to that roof myself," Sam said, and his face darkened briefly. "It's just one of those things I've put off."

"You have enough to do as it is," Molly protested. She wasn't entirely helpless, and she wanted both her grandfather and Sam to know that she intended to do her part. While she didn't relish the thought of maneuvering her way across the steeply pitched roof, it had to be fixed before the fall rains started.

"Your grandfather's right—you shouldn't be on that roof," Sam told her. "If I don't get to the repairs within the next week, I'll have someone else work on it." He looked straight at her until she met his eyes. "Understand?"

"Yes," she grumbled, but she had to admit it felt good to hand the responsibility over to him. Other than during the first few years of Tom's life, there hadn't been a man around to help her with things like that. She'd had to learn to handle small repairs and fix what needed fixing—knowledge that came in handy now.

A short silence followed. "There was a call for you this afternoon," Gramps muttered.

Something about her grandfather's voice told her this was more than a casual comment.

"For me?" Sam's head jerked up.

"Curly Q Ranch outside of Laramie. Ever heard of it?"

His expression decidedly uncomfortable, Sam shifted in the chair. "What'd they want?"

Molly glanced from one man to the other, puzzled by the undercurrent of tension. Now that she thought about it, Gramps had been agitated since answering the phone, muttering under his breath and asking about Sam again and again.

"The foreman said he'd gotten a job inquiry from you. Is it true?" Walt demanded.

Sam slapped the biscuit down on the edge of his plate. "Yeah, it's true."

"I'm not dead yet!" Gramps barked, his voice shaking.

"Maybe not, but Molly's going to sell out. All I'm doing is protecting my interests." Sam pushed his plate aside, his appetite apparently satisfied—or ruined, she didn't know which.

"I'm not selling the ranch," she insisted, wanting that clearly understood.

Sam's expression said otherwise.

"You may not think so now, but when the offers—"

"I've already turned down one offer," she interrupted. Her anger seared each word. Sam was like everyone else. He could see the vultures circling overhead and he was going to bail out at his earliest convenience. What struck Molly hardest was the thought of running the ranch without him. She was a novice at this, a greenhorn, and without his help and guidance she'd be at a terrible loss. If Sam left, she might not have any choice but to sell.

Both Gramps and Sam were staring at her.

Molly blinked. "What?"

"You've already had an offer for the ranch?" Gramps asked. "Who from?"

"I'm not exactly sure who Russell's client is. He never said."

"Letson brought you the offer?" To Molly's alarm, Gramps's face turned a deep red, and he let loose a string of swearwords—some of which she'd never heard before.

"Gramps!" She was grateful the boys weren't around.

"That son of a bitch is not to be trusted." Closing his eyes, Gramps took several deep breaths, apparently hoping to calm himself.

"I'm not selling the Broken Arrow," Molly repeated, directing the comment at Sam. It felt as if the foundation of everything she'd planned was cracking. Without Sam to manage the ranch for her, to sell off cattle and teach her what she needed to know, she'd be hopelessly in trouble within days. There was no one else she could ask. The hands he'd hired were only high-school boys, and they'd be back in school soon.

"I apologize if I disappointed you, Walt," Sam said, and he did sound contrite, "but I've got to look out for myself. You and I both know that I'll stay as long as *you* need me."

Molly didn't miss the emphasis. He was saying his loyalty belonged to Gramps and not to her or the boys. The foundation of her future had not only cracked, the entire structure was about to crumble at her feet. But pride had carried her a long way, and she wasn't about to let this…this fickle foreman know how badly he'd let her down.

"He's right, Gramps," she stated breezily, as if Sam's defection was of little concern. "It would be unreasonable to expect Sam to stay on any longer than necessary. He's got his own life to worry about." Even as she spoke, her blood heated at the thought that this man she'd chosen to trust—against her better judgment, dammit!—would do anything so underhanded. It'd been a mistake to put her faith in him, to believe he'd care enough about the ranch, care enough about anyone here other than Gramps, to want to stay on.

She'd begun to lower her guard with Sam and so had her boys, who admired and trusted him implicitly. That had been a mistake, all right.

She stood abruptly and grabbed the dirty dishes from the table, clattering cutlery onto the plate.

"Molly."

"It's all right, Gramps." Thankfully something in her voice revealed that she was in no mood to discuss this further. With her back to the two men, she slammed the plate into the sinkful of hot water and scrubbed it force-fully enough to remove the floral pattern.

She heard Sam leave and her grandfather shuffle into the living room again. She closed her eyes in gratitude that they'd both left her in peace. Bracing her hands on the edge of the sink, she inhaled a deep breath and continued washing the pans, fighting back the emotion that threatened to choke her.

Men were not to be trusted; Molly had learned that painful lesson years earlier. But Sam Dakota, with his gruff gentleness toward her grandfather and his patient encouragement to her sons, had somehow worked his way into her stubborn heart. She hadn't wanted that to happen! Then there was that kiss in the barn.... It mor-tified her to remember how she'd worried about him the past three days, waited for him, even missed him.

Sam wasn't the problem, she decided, as she banged the frying pan onto the drainer. *She* was. Her hand trem-bled, and she paused, closing her eyes once again.

After cleaning up the kitchen, Molly headed back outside to work. It was already dark, but the yard light was turned on. Hard physical labor might help her deal with her anger.

In all honesty, she had to acknowledge that Sam had no reason to continue working on the ranch without Gramps. She'd *assumed* he'd be willing to stay on—but then, that was the way of assumptions.

The hoe was where she'd left it, and she picked it up and started hacking away at the base of the wild black-berry vines that had tangled in the lower limbs of the apple trees. Her grandmother's six-tree orchard sported two each of plum, pear and apple. The orchard was as badly run-down as the garden had been.

Venting her frustration as she chopped at the stubborn vines and yanked them away with gloved hands, Molly realized that the letter addressed to Sam must have been a response to a job inquiry.

Not that it mattered. Not really. Why should Sam Dakota be any different from Daniel or any other man she'd ever known? With the exception of Gramps, of course. She ignored the small faint voice that said maybe she wasn't being fair. This was her reward for giving a damn, she raged. This was her reward for allowing herself to hope and care! What hurt most was that she'd actually started to *like* Sam. He'd shown more interest in her boys in the past two weeks than their father had their whole lives.

He'd made friends with her children, and all the while he'd been planning to leave, to walk out on them. It was heartless and cruel. Dammit, he'd made her believe he cared—cared not only about Gramps but about the ranch...and the boys. Despite Russell Letson's warnings, she'd given him her trust.

"Mom! Mom!" Clay came racing out of the barn, screeching with excitement.

Molly leaned against the hoe.

Clay carried a small bundle in his arms. "Look!" he cried, holding out the puppy for her to examine.

The brown-and-black collie was so young his eyes had yet to open.

"Remember I told you Natasha had her litter? Well, guess what?" Clay could barely contain himself. "Sam says I can pick one of them as my own! I've never had a dog before, and now I can choose one myself. Sam says I'll need to train him and take care of him and everything. Sam says—"

One more *Sam says* and Molly swore she was going to explode. "He gave you the puppy?" she cut in sharply.

Clay nodded. The excitement emptied from her son's dark eyes, replaced with the sober look of a child knowing he was about to hear something disappointing. He held the tiny newborn pup tight against his middle, as though he feared she was about to jerk it from his arms.

Molly threw down the hoe and with quick steps headed toward the barn. She wanted to confront Sam now. She wouldn't rest, wouldn't sleep, until she'd settled this.

"Mom...Mom, what are you gonna do?" Clay asked, catching up with her. "I'm old enough to take care of a puppy, honest I am! I'll do everything, I promise. I'll feed him and brush his coat and train him to work with the cattle the same way Natasha does."

Of all the nerve. Sam had given Clay the puppy without asking her first. He'd promised he wouldn't do things like that! Not only was he abandoning her and the children, he was complicating her life before he left. She'd had enough.

Tired though he was, Sam hadn't gone directly to bed the way he probably should have. He met her outside the barn, and his posture, his very stance, spoke of defiance.

"I warned you about this sort of thing before," she snapped.

"Warned me?"

"I specifically asked you to check with me first before doing anything like this again."

Sam stared at her as if he didn't know what she was talking about. "Listen, Molly, if you're talking about the puppy—"

"What else could it be?" Even as she spoke, she realized her reaction was out of all proportion, but she couldn't help herself. Anger and resentment fused in her mind.

"Mom, I'm old enough. I am!" Clay insisted, close to tears. "I'll take good care of him, I promise." His pleas were breaking her heart.

"This isn't about the puppy, and you know it," Sam said quietly.

He was right.

"This is about the phone call Walt took for me, isn't it? And that letter." He wiped his hand across his brow. "A man needs to eat, Molly."

"You might have asked me what I plan to do with the ranch first!"

He frowned. "Perhaps, but at the time the situation didn't look all that promising."

"Mom, Mom." Clay tugged at her shirttail in an effort to get her attention.

She glanced guiltily down at her son. "You can keep him," she said softly, feeling wretched for the way she'd treated him. Before she could say another word, she heard Gramps calling her and Sam. She turned to see him standing on the top step leading from the house.

Thinking something might be wrong, Molly raced toward her grandfather. Sam was right behind her.

Gramps leaned weakly against the doorjamb. "I need to talk to you both," he said.

"Now might not be the best time," Molly advised. Sam was exhausted, and she…so was she. Emotionally and physically exhausted.

"Now seems as good a time as any," Gramps said.

Without waiting for an argument, he led the way back to the kitchen, giving them no choice but to follow.

"I've come up with a solution," Gramps announced, grinning broadly.

"Solution to *what*?" Sam asked. He sounded as impatient as Molly felt.

"You two and the ranch," Gramps explained. His smile grew even wider as he gazed first at his granddaughter and then at Sam. He chuckled in real amusement. "You two already squabble like you're married. What I figure is, you should make it official."

Seven

Pearl was tired. It'd been a busy night and her regular clients had been more demanding than usual. She found it increasingly difficult to dredge up enthusiasm—or the pretense of it—for her trade. She was good. One of the best. Guys had been telling her that since she was sixteen years old. She'd never had a chance to be like normal teenagers. Her uncle had stolen her virginity when she was barely old enough to know what had happened, and later he'd introduced her to his friends. By the time she was in high school she'd learned how to use her body to get anything she wanted. Every emotion was expressed through sex. Happiness. Grief. Pain. Anger. It was all she knew. The ever-present need to be needed, loved. Used.

She'd never intended to become a prostitute, but pleasing men in bed was the only talent she possessed that earned her a decent wage. In the beginning, when she was young and still pretty enough to attract a lot of attention, it'd actually been fun. It hadn't been just sex back then. There were restaurant dinners and bottles of champagne, and for a few hours she could make believe she was on a date. The pretending had come a lot easier, too. The soft sighs and shallow pants had been effortless, and when her john was finished, she clung to him and smiled secretly to herself. Each one laid claim to her body, which she gave for a fee, but no one had ever touched her heart.

Until Russell.

With him it was different. It'd always been different. The first time he'd visited her he'd been nervous and even a little shy. Surprisingly, a lot of men were. Some sought her out because they had certain "problems" and felt she might help. Others were nervous because they feared discovery—although the fear often heightened their pleasure.

Pearl controlled these eager but reluctant lovers, tempted them and teased them and encouraged their fears. Just when they were ready to turn tail and run, she'd calm them, satisfying their every need. Inevitably they returned. The fear brought them back. The fear and the pleasure.

Then Russell had walked into her life. She was his birthday gift, and the instructions Monroe gave her had been specific. She was Russell's reward for doing a favor and she was to keep him happy all night. In exchange for her services she would be handsomely reimbursed. Pearl had willingly accepted the offer. Keep one man content for the night and she'd earn more than she normally would with five or six.

When he'd first arrived, Pearl had been surprised. She'd anticipated a man who had trouble attracting women, but that clearly wasn't the case. Russell was good-looking enough to have any woman he wanted. He certainly didn't need her when plenty of women would eagerly have slept with him for free.

Because he was nervous and struggling not to show it, and because she had plenty of time to fill, Pearl had suggested they have a glass of wine first. Russell had started talking to fill the awkward silence. He spoke to her as if she were a friend, as if she were a real date. Not a hooker. More importantly he treated her with respect.

They quickly learned they enjoyed the same movies and listened to the same kind of music, New Orleans–style jazz. Normally she was the one responsible for putting a client at ease, but it was Russell who'd gotten her to lower her guard and relax.

Soon she was laughing and joking with him as though she'd known him all her life. Russell was wonderful, with his interesting conversation and dry sense of humor. After a while he'd removed his shoes and propped his feet on her coffee table. Next he loosened his tie. He hadn't eaten dinner and suggested they order pizza. It was the first time a customer had dinner delivered to her house.

While they ate, he'd found the listing for a favorite movie and asked if he could turn on the television. They'd cuddled on the sofa like high-school sweethearts, and Pearl had rested her head against his shoulder.

She'd never experienced this kind of tenderness as a teenager. She'd never sat on a sofa with a man and not had his hands crawling all over her. Not until that first night with Russell.

The ironic thing was that she'd been paid more to entertain him than to service a bachelor party, and in the end all they'd done was kiss. Gently. Slowly. And with such sweetness it brought tears to her eyes every time she thought about it. He could have taken her at any time and she would have welcomed his body. But he hadn't.

If she'd told anyone what had happened that night— or more precisely, *hadn't* happened—she knew people would get the wrong idea about him. Some would suggest he was gay. Or that he was impotent. Or asexual. But he wasn't any of those. Pearl had a sixth sense about such things, and she knew better. He was all man, but more than that, Russell Letson was a gentleman.

Sweetgrass being a small town, it didn't take her long to inadvertently run into him again. She'd been in the grocery store, and her heart, the one she'd assumed had shriveled up and died, had nearly leaped out of her chest when she saw him. A hooker, however, knew her place, and one thing she never did was greet a customer in public.

Avoiding eye contact, she'd walked past him without a word. It was one of the hardest things she'd ever done. By the time she was in the parking lot she wanted to cry. But whores didn't cry. It was the first rule. Never care. Never reveal any genuine feeling. The mind was hollow, and the body was…something to be used.

Russell had followed her out of the Safeway store, and she'd explained that it wasn't a good idea for him to be seen with her. People would talk. He insisted he didn't care. He wanted to see her again, even if it meant paying for her services. For the first time in her life Pearl turned down a paying customer.

But Russell wouldn't leave it at that. Because she was afraid of hurting his reputation, she refused to let him visit her. It was then that Russell told her about his cabin on Lake Giles, fifty miles outside town. He simply set a time on Sunday afternoon and gave her directions.

Pearl couldn't have stayed away to save her soul. When she arrived, he'd stepped onto the porch and smiled as if her coming meant more to him than anything in the world. After that she drove out to Russell's cabin every Sunday, and with each visit Pearl changed a little more. When she was with him, she didn't need makeup or sexy clothes. He loved her best with her hair pulled back in a ponytail, wearing tight jeans and a loose cotton shirt.

Eventually, because she trusted him, Pearl told him her most shameful secret—that she'd never learned to read. Pearl had never written a check, never become engrossed in a good book or followed a recipe. She'd wept and hidden her face after he learned the truth. Unlike others who'd snickered and called her stupid, Russell had kissed away her tears and said he'd teach her himself. That was the day her entire world changed.

They had become lovers, but not right away. Not for several weeks. He was a considerate lover, passionate and caring. It was with him that Pearl *made love* for the first time in her life. Afterward she wept in his arms and he'd held her against him and wept with her.

They never talked about what she did at night. The subject was as taboo as the future.

Pearl didn't know if this was love. All she knew was that she felt something for Russell she'd never felt for anyone else. She lived for Sundays, for their time together. Although she'd never been much of a housekeeper, she discovered how much she enjoyed cooking. Each week she tried out new recipes, cooking and serving him gourmet meals. Pearl liked to pretend this was her real life, these few stolen hours away from Sweet-grass, and everything else a bad dream from which she would eventually awake.

Two a.m. Friday, after she'd finished for the night, Pearl heard the back door open. Adrenaline shot through her blood, and she stiffened. Only one person had a key to her back door; only one person would dare to come to her this late. The man she hated. Monroe, Russell's cousin. How could any two men be less alike? Monroe controlled her and a dozen other women in a number of small towns across northwestern Montana. He kept her customers in line, supplied her with condoms at a discount and made frequent use of her body himself.

"Pearl." He slurred her name, his voice demanding and impatient.

She closed her eyes and cringed. He'd been drinking. Sometimes he was a mean drunk, and it often took a week for the bruises to fade. Other times he was like a child. A few months earlier, when he'd been drunk, he'd tied her to the bed, and by the time he'd finished with her, she'd been frantic, certain he intended to kill her.

"Pearl." He called for her again, sounding now like a little boy who'd had his toy taken away. A little boy in need of his mother. Pearl's shoulders sagged with relief. The little boy she could handle; the mean drunk frightened her.

"I'm here, baby," she replied softly, slipping into character.

She heard him make his way down the dark hall-way and forced herself to smile when he stood in her doorway looking lost and forlorn in the soft haze of her bedside lamp.

"Do you want Mama to make it all better for you?" she murmured sympathetically.

He unhitched his belt buckle and nodded.

"I've been waiting all night for you." She said the well-practiced line as she untied the sash to her silk robe. "You know how very special you are to me. Come to Mama, and let me make it all better for you."

"That's why I'm here. Make it better, Pearl. Make it better."

She managed a smile—more of a grimace—as he crossed the room and fell on top of her, crushing her with his weight. He smelled of hard liquor and cigarettes. She barely had time to fit him with a condom before he was gasping and moaning, his head thrown back and his teeth clenched.

Pearl closed her eyes and turned her head away, praying he'd finish soon. With her eyes shut she could dream of the day she'd be free of him and all the other men like him.

Walt smiled slightly at the identical looks of shock on Molly's face and Sam's. If he hadn't been serious, he might have laughed outright. But the suggestion that they get married made sense to him. A lot of sense. To be fair it had only occurred to him recently, so he couldn't blame Molly or Sam for overlooking the obvious when the idea was almost as new to him as it was to them.

Sam stared at Walt in a way that implied there was more wrong with him than a bum heart. Molly's eyes were the most telling; they snapped like fire on wood too green to burn properly.

"Gramps."

"Walt."

"Let's sit on the porch a spell," Walt said. He'd always loved the peacefulness of a summer evening. He liked to imagine his Molly rocking at his side, and in a spiritual way he believed she'd never really left him. He felt her presence far more than her absence these days, and suspected that was because he'd be joining her soon. No doctor needed to tell him his days were numbered. Walt felt it himself, and difficult as it was to leave his granddaughter and her boys, he was ready to go.

Easing himself into the rocking chair, he waited for one or the other of the pair to raise the first objection. He chuckled softly when he realized they were still too dumbfounded to speak.

"You think this is funny, old man?" Sam asked in a hard voice.

His foreman generally didn't use that tone with him, but Walt forgave him, considering that Sam had spent most of the past three days in the saddle, chasing cattle.

"Gramps, I don't think you understand what you're saying," Molly offered next in gentler tones.

"You think I'm senile, girl, is that what you mean? I realize this is something of a shock, but let's be realistic. I'm not going to be around much longer and—"

"Don't say that," Molly interrupted, more comfortable with her denials than facing her fears.

A sigh rumbled through Sam's chest. "You're talking nonsense, old man."

Walt's amusement didn't fade. He hadn't expected either of them to take to his idea right off. The first time it had popped into his mind he'd immediately assumed it wouldn't work, either; on closer examination, however, the wisdom of it became apparent. He sincerely hoped these two had enough common sense to recognize that. To see the advantages.

"You takin' that job offer?" Walt asked, pinning Sam with narrowed eyes.

"I already explained. I don't hand out charity and I don't expect any, either." Sam's expression was as unyielding as his voice.

"Molly can't manage this place on her own," Walt continued. "What I'm asking you, Sam, is this: are you planning on walking out on her and the boys the minute I'm six feet under?"

Sam didn't respond, not that Walt blamed him.

"I don't need him," Molly said defiantly.

"That pride of yours is going to get you into nothing but trouble, girl," Walt said. "Without the right kind of help you'd lose the ranch inside a month. Are you ready to wipe out four generations of history because you're too damn proud to admit you need Sam?"

"I need someone to manage the place, I'll admit that, but a *husband* I can live without."

"I'm not looking for a wife, either," Sam snarled. He crossed his arms, leaned against the porch railing and stared down at the newly painted wood-plank floor.

"It wouldn't be a *real* marriage," Gramps said. He'd mulled this part over, and he figured that if they weren't interested in a normal marriage, a business arrangement might be the best solution. Although he suspected that this marriage of convenience wouldn't remain merely a convenience for long....

In the months since Sam had come to work for him, Walt had grown fond of him. His own son was long dead, and because he loved Molly, he worried about her future and that of his great-grandsons. In his view, she needed a man, and he could think of no better man for her than Sam Dakota.

"You're talking about a marriage of convenience?" Molly asked, folding her arms. "You mean to say people actually agree to that sort of thing in this day and age?"

"It makes sense," Gramps said mildly.

"Not to me, it doesn't," Sam muttered. "When and if I marry, it isn't going to be any business arrangement. My wife will share my life *and* my bed."

Molly's chin rose a defiant notch at the mention of his bed. "This entire thing is out of the question."

"If you'd both quit being so damn stubborn and hear me out, then maybe you'd learn something." Walt knew his strength was limited, and he didn't want to waste it arguing with two stubborn fools. He inhaled deeply and started again. "First of all, Sam, you should be able to appreciate Molly's concern. For all either one of us knows, you'll hire out somewhere else. You've already started looking."

"Exactly." Molly glared at Sam as if to say she doubted she'd ever be able to trust him; Sam frowned back at her. Walt shook his head, but he understood their need for defenses far better than they realized.

Sam's mouth thinned. "Walt, what makes you think marrying Molly would help?"

"Because you'd have a vested interest in keeping this ranch in the black."

"Are you suggesting I'm not giving one hundred per-cent right now?"

The fact that he was nearly dead on his feet said more about his commitment to the ranch than any statement he could have made. "It's because you *have* worked hard that I'm prepared to make you this offer," Gramps replied quietly.

"Offer?" Molly exclaimed. "Exactly what is it you're suggesting?"

Walt liked how she drove straight to the point. His own Molly had been like that, but her ways were more subtle. The hard edge around his granddaughter's heart was because of the divorce. She'd made one mistake in judgment and intended to punish herself for the rest of her life. Yes, the more he thought about it, this marriage would be good for her. Good for Sam, too.

Walt loved Molly, loved Tom and Clay. His blood flowed in their veins. They were all he had left in this world, other than the land his father had handed down to him. Persuading them to go along with this marriage might be the last thing he could do for her. The last way he had of protecting her future. And dammit, that was important.

"I was thinking..." Gramps's voice was almost a whisper, so depleted was his energy. It was a task to find the right words. "I'd feel better leaving your care in the hands of someone I trust."

"I already told you, Gramps—I don't need someone to take care of me! And I don't need a husband." She glanced at him sharply. "Gramps, you're tired!" When he shook his head, she sighed. "Look," she began, "let's say we were to agree to this preposterous idea. There's nothing to prevent Sam from walking out on me after we're married."

"Not if he's got something of value at stake."

"Like what?" Sam asked. He uncrossed his arms and rested his hands on the railing, leaning forward slightly.

"Five hundred acres and fifty head of cattle."

Molly gasped and her face turned a deep shade of red. "You're offering him land and cattle to marry me? A dowry? Now, I *know* they don't still do *that*."

"I'm offering Sam what he's always wanted," Gramps explained. No use wrapping it up in a silk bow. It was the truth, as plain and simple as he could make it. "A man will fight to the death for land and cattle."

"And dump a wife and family in a heartbeat!"

"You appear to hold a low opinion of men," Sam stated matter-of-factly, revealing none of the emotion Walt knew simmered below the surface. Molly was at a disadvantage; she hadn't known Sam nearly as long as he had. The adage "still waters run deep" had been coined for men like him.

Sam hadn't said much about his background, but Walt trusted him. Completely. He'd handed over the management of his ranch, and when it would have been easy to steal from him or cheat him, Sam hadn't. Not by so much as a penny. He worked hard, and Walt couldn't ask for more than that.

Only, he *was* asking. He wanted Sam to marry Molly. To be a father to Molly's sons. Walt yearned to know that when they carried him to his grave his family and his land would be in the hands of a man who'd take care of them.

"What you make of the marriage is up to you," Gramps said, glancing from one to the other. Weary now, he closed his eyes. He almost wished he could be around to see the battle. Molly would put up a good fight and so would Sam, but he'd wager a year's income that it wouldn't be long before they fell in love.

His biggest regret was that he wouldn't know their children or hold them close to his heart.

"Walt?" Sam's voice caused his eyes to flutter open.

"You *are* tired." Molly spoke softly. She sounded so much like his Molly that Walt was confused for a second.

"Let's help him inside," Sam was saying.

Molly must have agreed, because the next thing Walt knew the two of them had escorted him into his bedroom. It was the only one on the main floor; the other five were upstairs. "Get out of here," he said, using the small reservoir of strength that remained. "I can undress myself. You two go talk." He aimed his look in Molly's direction. He felt that of the two, she was the one who needed convincing most.

"Talk some sense into her, boy," Walt advised.

"I think you're both crazy!" Molly cried. "Get this straight right now, Sam Dakota. I'm not marrying you. I'd be a fool to agree to anything so...so..."

"Ridiculous," Sam supplied.

Molly's mouth sagged open and she nodded. "That's exactly the word I was searching for. It *is* ridiculous. That my own flesh and blood would suggest such a thing..."

"Perhaps we should let Walt rest now," Sam said as if fed up with the subject.

It would take an extraordinary man—a strong and honest man—to handle his granddaughter, Walt decided. He was convinced Sam was that man.

Now all he had to do was convince Molly.

If he hadn't heard it with his own ears, Sam would never have believed that Walt had actually suggested he and Molly get married.

Molly appeared none too pleased with the idea, either. "I want you to know up front that nothing you say is going to change my mind," she said the minute she walked out of her grandfather's bedroom.

"I didn't say I was interested in marrying you," Sam returned.

"You didn't have to." She marched into the kitchen, grabbed the kettle and stuck it under the faucet. "It's nothing personal, but I have no desire to marry again."

"Fine." He wasn't in any mood to argue with her, although in all honesty the sound of those five hundred acres and fifty head of cattle appealed to him. He'd be a liar if he claimed otherwise.

But if he'd wanted to get married, he'd have done so long before now. Still might. But like he'd told Walt, he wouldn't enter into any marriage of convenience; he and his wife would sleep in the same bed.

He had to admit it, though—for a moment insanity had taken hold and he'd been tempted. Damn tempted. Land and cattle were a hell of an incentive.

Feeling wearier than he'd ever been in his life, he headed out the door. It banged shut behind him, the sound echoing in the silence of the night. Tom met him halfway across the yard, followed by Boris, the father of Natasha's litter. The Stetson was a good fit, shading his youthful face. Tom hitched his thumbs in the waistband of his jeans the way Sam did and walked with a stride that suggested a swagger. A cowboy stride.

"What'd Gramps have to say?" the boy asked.

"He, uh, had an idea."

"For what?"

Sam grinned, wondering what Tom would say if he knew. Well, damned if *he* was going to be the one to tell him. "Ask your mother."

"I know she won't tell me, but I was thinking you might."

"Really?"

"Yeah." Tom walked up to the corral and braced his right foot on the bottom rail.

Sam stood beside him and experienced a sort of twinge. A strange feeling. One he had difficulty defining. The tiredness had seeped into his bones, and he was ready to call it a night. But he lingered, looking out over the property. He could see it clearly, despite the darkness and the wan moonlight. And he knew that without him, without someone like him, it would all come to nothing.

A coyote cried in the distance, and Sam's gaze returned to the boy at his side.

Sam had wasted a lot of years on the rodeo circuit, chasing an empty dream. Killing himself one bull ride at a time. In the end all he had to show for it was a bad back, a pretty belt buckle and a broken-down truck. It wasn't long before he'd added a prison sentence to his list of accomplishments.

Tom looked up at him and grinned. "It doesn't get any better than this, does it?"

Sam laughed. "You've been watching too much television, kid."

Tom's face fell, and Sam could see he'd offended him. He cut his laughter short and patted Tom's shoulder. "It's late. I'll see you in the morning."

"Okay." The boy's eagerness was undisguised, and Sam was relieved his thoughtless amusement hadn't damaged their relationship. As Tom loped off, Sam glanced over his shoulder and grinned at him.

"I would've been proud to call you son," he murmured.

The light on the porch behind him suddenly came on, and he turned to see Molly standing there, watching him. She was a fine-looking woman, too stubborn for her own good, but then he was far from perfect himself.

In time he suspected she'd remarry. Probably someone like that attorney. Well, no denying it, Russell Letson would make her a hell of a better husband than *he* ever would.

For the life of her Molly couldn't sleep. She'd tossed and turned so many times that the sheet had wrapped itself around her legs, binding her at the knees.

Groaning, she reached for the lamp on the nightstand and switched it on. Light flooded the room, and Molly squinted until her eyes adjusted, then glanced at the clock radio.

Three a.m.

She wouldn't do it. That was all there was to it. Marriage was never intended to be a business arrangement. It still irked her, the way Sam's eyes had lit up at the mention of land and cattle. Gramps hadn't a clue how badly he'd insulted her! He would never intentionally hurt her, of that Molly was certain. But his suggestion had opened her eyes to the truth.

Gramps was right to worry about her, she thought wryly. Sam was no solution; he'd stick around the Broken Arrow until he had a better offer. Because of his fondness for Gramps, she doubted he'd leave until after her grandfather was dead and buried.

She could hardly breathe when she realized where her thoughts had taken her. Gramps was dying. Much as she wanted to reject the evidence, it was unmistakable. In the few weeks she'd been in Montana, she'd witnessed his physical and mental decline. Each day he seemed a little weaker, a little frailer. Even his memory was going. Twice now he'd thought she was his Molly.

Gramps tried, but he couldn't hide how ill he was. As an adult, she needed to face the reality of the situation; she knew that, but it didn't make things easier. She owed it to Gramps to provide some reassurance, to show him she could look after herself and her boys. And the ranch. That was what all the marriage-of-convenience nonsense had been about.

Right after breakfast, she'd call the local newspaper and place an ad for a foreman. Naturally she'd talk it over with Gramps first, get his approval. Sam was already seeking greener pastures, so to speak. Not that she blamed him—at least, not entirely. But she had to accept that he'd eventually be leaving, which meant it was time she took control.

That decided, Molly leaned over and turned off the lamp. Gazing up, she watched the moonlight make patterns on the ceiling.

She wasn't sure what time she fell asleep; it must have been close to dawn, but even then her sleep had been fitful.

She awoke at six, hearing sounds in the kitchen. Bolting upright, she reached for her robe and raced down the stairs to discover Gramps sitting at the table. Tom and Clay were busy fixing him breakfast. Dry cereal littered the tabletop and there was a small puddle of milk beside an empty bowl.

Standing in her bare feet, Molly yawned.

"We think you should do it," Tom said eagerly, his eyes bright and happy.

Molly blinked, afraid to ask what he was talking about. Gramps *wouldn't* have. He couldn't have. If he'd mentioned anything about her marrying Sam to the boys, she didn't know *how* she'd respond.

"Do what?" she asked uneasily. Her gaze slowly traveled to Gramps, who looked far too pleased.

"Learn to ride," Clay answered. "Sam can teach you."

"I could teach you, too," Tom said confidently.

She hoped her relief wasn't evident. "I...I think that's a good idea," she said.

The back door opened and Sam walked in. His eyes immediately went to her, and self-conscious, Molly gripped the lapels of her robe together. This was the second time he'd come upon her in her nightclothes. She didn't imagine herself as any beauty, not with her hair plastered to the side of her head and her eyes red from sleeplessness.

"Morning, Sam," Tom greeted him.

"Mornin'." He removed his hat and set it carefully on the counter. "I've got a list of supplies I need," he said, unfolding the sheet. "But I don't have time to run into town."

"I'll go," Molly offered before he had the opportunity to ask.

His smile told her he appreciated it. Nodding once, he handed her the list. Molly read it over and it might as well have been Greek for all the sense it made. Sam must have noticed her confusion because he took the time to explain each item to her, making small notes in the margins.

When he'd finished, Molly realized they were alone. She'd heard Gramps and the boys leave but she'd been busy concentrating on what Sam was telling her, and had paid it no mind. The supply list was important if she intended to learn how to manage a ranch.

"Did you sleep well?" Sam asked, the question catching her unprepared.

"Like a log," she lied, brushing the hair away from her face. She didn't want him to know how restless her night had been. Or how often she'd reviewed the conversation they'd had after taking Gramps to his room.

Sam hadn't appeared too eager to marry her, either. Although if he *had* revealed any enthusiasm, she'd have to credit it to the offer of cattle and land.

Judging by his smile, he knew she'd lied about sleeping well.

"I was awake most of the night," she admitted, lifting her hand to her forehead and running it through her uncombed curls. "What about you?"

"I certainly didn't have any trouble falling asleep," he said, "but I woke up early."

"I slept late."

"So I see," he said, eyeing her robe and bare feet.

Turning away, he helped himself to a cup of coffee, took his first sip and grimaced. "I take it you didn't brew this?"

She smiled and shook her head. He offered her some, but she declined. "I've tasted Tom's efforts before. He can't seem to understand it's only one scoop of grounds and not five." Molly wasn't sure when Sam moved closer, but suddenly he had. Scant inches separated them. His gaze burned into hers as he set the coffee aside.

Molly held her breath. She knew what he wanted and realized she wanted it, too. She was tempted to close her eyes and offer him her lips—but that would be wrong. They'd made their decision, both of them. Marriage was marriage and not to be mocked. Neither one of them was interested in a business arrangement; he'd assured her he wasn't, and she'd told him the same thing.

Sam didn't move. Nor did she. Molly began to wonder if they'd both stopped breathing.

"I…I did a lot of thinking last night," she whispered, lowering her gaze. He deserved her honesty if nothing else. "I can't see it working with you and me." She seemed to have difficulty shaping the words. "Following through with Gramps's idea, I mean."

His face moved a fraction of an inch closer to hers.

Hardly aware of what she was doing, Molly let her tongue moisten her lips. A quick movement—but that was all it took for Sam to accept her unspoken invitation. His warm moist mouth settled over hers.

The kiss was gentle, unhurried. Pleasurable. Even more than that first kiss, in the barn. Not satisfied to keep it simple, Sam stroked her lips with the tip of his tongue, sweetening the contact. She shivered and grabbed hold of his upper arms.

She wasn't sure which of them moaned. Then Sam wrapped his arms around her waist and pressed her body to his as he devoured her mouth with his own.

Her mind screamed that this had to stop, while her body responded to him totally, almost involuntarily. The kiss went on, slow and soft, until he trapped her bottom lip between his teeth and introduced his tongue, coaxing and enticing her own.

A sharp discordant sound shattered the moment.

They broke apart like teenagers caught necking in the school hallway.

Molly reeled back, her chest heaving. The sound, whatever it was, was gone. It took her a moment to register that Gramps had turned on the radio in the living room.

Sam moved behind her and nuzzled the side of her neck. "You okay?"

She couldn't have spoken to save her life, so she nodded.

"Good."

Still he lingered, his warm breath fanning her neck. "I'm glad we got that settled," he murmured.

"Settled? What…"

"I've got to get back to Pete and Charlie." His reluctance to leave her was as apparent as her unwillingness to let him go.

"Sam!" she cried, stopping him before he walked out the door.

He turned back, his eyes darker and more intense than she could ever remember seeing them. "What… what did we settle?"

He placed the hat back on his head. His gaze held hers for a long moment. "You figure it out."

Eight

"Bingo!" Clay yelled. He leaped up and danced a triumphant jig about the living room. The puppy, who'd been asleep on the couch, barely raised his head at the commotion.

"Hurry and phone in before someone claims your three bucks," Gramps said, pointing to the telephone. Radio bingo was one of the few pleasures he could still enjoy. Molly had agreed to collect the bingo sheets every week from the sponsoring merchants in town, and Walt listened at eight and ten-thirty each weekday morning for the announcer to read off the numbers. The big jackpot was up to 385, but to win that, you had to bingo within the first five numbers. He'd come close several times. Close but no cigar.

"The line's busy," Clay said, beginning to pout.

"Then someone beat you to the punch, boy," he said. This was one of life's lessons, Walt believed, and Clay would be wise to learn it now while he was young. Act fast. Don't delay. Take a risk once in a while. Walt wished Molly had learned that lesson a little more thoroughly, that she was more of a risk-taker. Then this marriage business might be resolved. As things stood, his granddaughter stubbornly refused to marry Sam.

"But I had a bingo," Clay argued. "I should be able to get my prize."

"You need to be the first one to phone in with the correct numbers," Gramps said. "I told you that when we started. Someone else got bingo, too, and they beat you to the phone."

The three-dollar prize money wasn't much, but Clay would have had bragging rights. Walt had an inkling that was what concerned him most.

Molly strolled into the living room, holding Sam's shirt. Walt seemed to remember that she'd offered to mend it for him. "What's all the commotion?" she asked.

"I had a bingo, but I didn't call in fast enough." Clay's shoulders sagged, as if this were a tragedy of biblical proportions.

"I haven't had bingo in three weeks," Walt complained. If he didn't know better, he'd think the game was rigged. He placed the bingo sheets inside an old greeting-card box and set it down beside him on the end table. Normally he kept the sheets on his desk, but it was crowded with bills and invoices and bank statements, a lot of them in unopened envelopes. He felt a surge of guilt every time he thought about adding the paperwork to Sam's already heavy workload.

Working all hours of the day and night, Sam had no time for dealing with the piles of business-related documents and correspondence, so Molly had recently taken it on. She'd just begun to study the books, to get a grasp of the situation. Walt tried to answer her questions, but his mind wasn't always clear. He was afraid he might be doing more harm than good, confusing her rather than explaining things properly.

Their finances weren't in good shape, he knew. Cattle prices were down and had been for a number of years, dipping lower and lower each season. To say money was tight was an understatement. Walt had barely scraped by the past few years. Paying bills only depressed him, so it was a task he tended to avoid. Molly hadn't said anything yet, and he wondered if she was aware how poorly the ranch was doing.

"The Millers are having a moving sale Friday, Saturday and Sunday at 204 Walnut from eight to five all three days," the radio announcer said.

Molly looked astonished. "They're advertising a garage sale on the radio?"

Gramps reached over and turned the knob. "They do every weekday. It's part of the community programming."

"I remember the Millers," Molly said thoughtfully. "They ran one of the service stations."

"They've been around here nearly as long as the Wheatons," Walt told her, shaking his head sadly. "They sold out." It bothered him that Brady Miller had given in to outside pressures. Brady said it was because of financial problems, that the business wasn't making a profit, but Walt was convinced those damn fanatics had something to do with it. They wanted *his* land, too, but Walt had refused to sell.

"I never heard a radio station that plays hardly any music until we moved to Montana," Clay said. He cradled the puppy against his shoulder like a mother carrying her newborn babe.

Walt figured the dog had been one of his better ideas.

Clay was learning about responsibility, about caring for another creature. And when Bullwinkle was about four months old, they'd start his training. The dog would earn his keep, the same way Boris and Natasha did.

"This is a small-town radio station," Gramps heard Molly explain.

"But all they do is talk," Clay said. "The bingo's fun, but the rest of it's all about how much alfalfa costs and stuff like that. What about rap? What about grunge?"

"They play that for a couple of hours at night," Walt explained. "Kid stuff." It wasn't real music, in his opinion. Tom had been listening to some hideous tape one night recently, and it sounded more like a barnful of sick calves crying for their mothers than anything associated with musical instruments. It'd bothered Walt so much that he'd wadded up tissue and stuck it in both ears. Molly had taken one look at him and burst out laughing, but hell, a man needed to protect his hearing.

Walt hadn't appreciated being the source of Molly's amusement. Dammit, a man could go deaf listening to what his great-grandsons considered music. He'd told them both exactly what he thought of it, too.

"You're going into town later?" he asked Molly, "'Cause I need razor blades."

"I'll make sure I pick some up while I'm there."

He nodded and raised his hand to his jaw. His Molly had asked one thing of him shortly after their marriage, and it was that he shave every night. It seemed a small thing, so he'd complied, willing to do whatever it took to make his sweetheart happy. A lifetime habit was hard to break. Even now, all these years after her death, he rarely went to bed without shaving.

"I've got a list going," she said. "Do you need anything else?"

Walt shook his head. He watched her as she returned to the kitchen and the sewing machine she'd set up on the table. He'd been worried about her and Sam. A week had come and gone since he'd made his suggestion, with no result. Walt studied the two of them every chance he got, hoping to read their thoughts, but it was impossible to decipher what either one of them was thinking.

Especially when they worked so hard at avoiding each other. Sam rarely joined the family for supper these days, although Molly always set out a plate for him. Generally, he reheated what she'd left and ate alone, often out on the porch, surrounded by dogs. Some nights he didn't get to the ranch house until well after dark. Walt didn't know if he purposely stayed away or if he was doing the work of two men. Probably both.

"You napping, Gramps?" Clay asked softly.

"Just resting my eyes, boy." Walt's afternoon naps came earlier and earlier these days. He'd only been awake a couple of hours and already he was so tired he couldn't keep his eyes open. The doc had wanted him to make another appointment, but Walt couldn't see where it would do any good. It cost money he couldn't spare. Not only that, the price of medicine these days was outrageous. Highway robbery. No government handouts for him, either. Walt Wheaton paid his own way or he went without. True, he'd let the government help him with the cost of his pacemaker, but that was as far as it went. That was all the charity he was willing to accept.

"Sam's taking us to the Fourth of July parade," Clay said, sitting down on the ottoman with the puppy. The kid would be the ruin of that dog yet, but Walt was secretly delighted that there was such a strong bond between those two. A boy needed a dog—and vice versa.

"Good." He liked the idea of Sam spending time with Molly and the kids. Walt himself couldn't handle standing in the hot sun to watch a bunch of youngsters walking down the street pulling little red wagons. He'd never been fond of parades, although he'd attended plenty in his time because his wife had enjoyed them. He'd have done anything for his Molly. *A man does that when he's in love.*

"Sam…said he wanted to come along?" This news appeared to surprise Molly.

Walt peeked at his granddaughter who'd come to stand in the doorway. He saw that this information had flustered her considerably. Good. Maybe, just maybe, the idea of marriage wasn't a lost cause, after all. Holding back a grin was damn near impossible as Walt leaned his head against the recliner and dreamed of Molly's future with Sam.

In all her life Molly had never washed clothes this dirty. Mud crusted the knees of her boys' jeans, dirt they'd accumulated following Sam around the ranch. Tom spent the majority of his time with him. That wasn't all; her son was beginning to sound like him and to walk like him, and even to imitate his gestures.

If that wasn't bad enough, Tom constantly talked about him, too. It was *Sam this* and *Sam that* until Molly felt like covering her ears and demanding he stop.

She stuffed three pairs of jeans into the washer. As the water churned, a thick layer of mud and scum formed on the surface. She'd have to run this load through the wash cycle twice, which meant keeping a close eye on the timer.

Sam. The harder she tried to push him from her mind, the more difficult it became. Twice he'd kissed her and twice he'd left her...confused.

I'm glad we got that settled.

He'd said that to her after the most recent kiss, almost a week ago, and when she'd asked what he meant, he'd told her to figure it out herself. Molly was still so angry she could barely look at the man.

Her only conclusion—and it didn't settle anything—was that she was a woman with normal needs and desires. It'd been years since a man had kissed her the way Sam had. Years since her dormant senses had been stirred awake. Well, she didn't like the feeling. Didn't enjoy being vulnerable. His kisses embarrassed her, and consequently she'd avoided him all week.

And he'd avoided her, too. Why, she could only speculate. Perhaps he regretted the kissing incident as much as she did. Somehow, though, she knew that wasn't the real reason he'd kept his distance.

He was giving her space. Enough space to flounder in. She wanted to hate him, but she couldn't. Not when he was so good to Gramps and her boys.

That was what made everything so damned difficult. Gramps didn't need to tell her how pleased Tom and Clay would be if she married Sam and how devastated they'd be when he left. Especially Tom, who worshiped the ground Sam Dakota walked on.

That hurt a little. No, actually it hurt quite a bit. Not for a second did Molly begrudge her son a mentor, but she missed the closeness she and Tom used to have—until a year ago, when he'd become so moody and difficult.

She should be thrilled that Tom's attitude had completely changed. And she was. What she found hard to take was the fact that the positive influence on her son had been Sam's. Not hers. Only Sam's. She supposed it was natural enough, but...

The tears that brimmed in her eyes came as a surprise. She blinked several times, trying to keep them at bay.

Sam would marry her, she thought grimly. All she had to do was say the word. He'd be a fool not to, seeing that Gramps had offered him what amounted to a dowry. The memory of that conversation—five hundred acres and fifty head of cattle—was enough to make her want to stomp her foot with outrage. Gramps had actually tried to bribe his foreman to marry her! It was absolutely mortifying.

More than once in the past week she'd felt Sam watching her. His eyes were like a warm caress and left her all too aware of what he wanted. What she wanted, too. What distressed Molly the most was her own response. Idiot that she was, she'd have welcomed his touch—and he knew it.

When she'd restarted the wash cycle, she picked up the shirt she'd mended for him. Folding it, she left the laundry room to return it to Sam's place.

Still angry with herself, she crossed the yard to the small house where he lived. She knew so little about him; he revealed so little of himself. Russell Letson had suggested Sam wasn't trustworthy and implied that he had information he couldn't or wouldn't share. Gramps had been furious that she'd listened to such gossip and had defended Sam as if he were his own flesh and blood.

While her instincts told her Sam *was* trustworthy, Molly reminded herself she'd once had complete faith in Daniel, too. By the time she'd discovered the truth, it was too late. To be fair, she'd been younger then, less experienced, more naive. Nevertheless, she didn't want to repeat her mistake.

Molly had been in Sam's living quarters, mostly to drop off laundry, a number of times. His bedroom was small and cramped. But although the accommodations were modest, he kept them in decent order.

She placed the mended shirt on his bed and turned to leave, then paused in the doorway and looked around, seeing the room with fresh eyes. Sam had slept in this room for more than seven months. Not a single picture was displayed. No family photographs. Nothing to indicate there was anyone important in his life.

The letter that had arrived a week or so earlier—the letter from the other ranch—was the only piece of personal mail he'd received in all the time she'd been here. Suddenly she saw the ticket, tucked in the corner of his mirror. She shouldn't have read it, should simply have walked away, but she couldn't seem to stop herself from crossing the room and looking.

The ticket was from the Sweetgrass Pawnshop. Sam's name was printed on it, along with the article he'd pawned. A silver buckle. Sam had pawned a silver buckle and going by the amount of cash given him, this wasn't any ordinary buckle. A rodeo buckle? She couldn't imagine why he'd pawn it, since it must have held real significance for him.

She knew from Gramps that Sam had been a rodeo

cowboy, a successful one, and that he'd had an accident of some kind. She found herself wondering what had happened and how he'd felt, seeing his career come to an end like that. And pawning the buckle… He'd obviously needed the money.

Stepping away from the mirror, she decided to put the matter out of her mind. This was Sam's business, not hers, but it made her suspicious. Once again she recognized that he was a man who had nothing to lose and everything to gain should she agree to marry him.

With her hand on the doorknob, she glanced around one last time. Her thoughts skittered crazily about— from rodeos and prize money to the ranch and its bills. Every evening this past week had been spent going over the financial records. Gramps's bookkeeping left much to be desired. The books were a mess; despite that, she could tell almost immediately that the Broken Arrow's finances were in dismal shape. She'd been paying for groceries and supplies from her own limited savings, but with no money coming in, those dollars would quickly disappear. Then what? Molly didn't want to think about the answer.

Of one thing she was sure: when the money ran out, so would Sam. He'd as much as said it himself. Unless he had a reason to stay, a reason like five hundred acres and fifty head of cattle, Sam would be moving on. The reality of their situation terrified her. There had been no response to her ad for a new foreman, and the hands would be gone by the end of the summer.

Completely lost in thought, Molly closed his door, turned around—and walked smack into Sam.

"What are you doing sneaking up on me like that?"

she demanded, furious that she'd been caught gazing into his bedroom.

"I came to tell you there's been a small accident—Tom cut his hand on a piece of wire. I couldn't find you at the house, so…"

Molly sucked in her breath. It must be serious if Sam had brought her son in from the range. "Does he need stitches?" she asked, her heart pounding in her ears. "Should I drive him into town?"

"He's fine," Sam assured her, gripping one of her shoulders. His touch calmed her immediately. Calmed and somehow reassured her. "The cut's nasty, but he's going to be fine."

"Stitches?" she repeated.

"No."

"What about a bandage?"

"I already did that."

"Oh." She'd always looked after things like this. Cuts and bruises. Hugs and healing. She was Tom's mother, after all, and Sam was the mentor. Couldn't he at least keep their roles straight? She knew she was being petulant, but she couldn't help it. "I would've preferred to do it myself," she said in a tight voice.

"I'm sure you'll want to clean it and rewrap it," he said. His hands, free of gloves, stroked her upper arms. A warm sensation settled in the pit of her stomach and refused to go away.

He understood what she felt. His eyes told her so. Told her that, and more. Without words he said he'd been watching her the same way she'd been watching him.

He wanted her. His longing was unconcealed. He tensed, and she knew he was fighting back the sharp pungent taste of desire. Then abruptly he removed his hands.

"Where's...where's my son?" she asked.

"In the house."

"I'd...I'd better find him."

Sam nodded and stepped aside.

Molly raced toward the house, grateful to be away from Sam's influence. It was growing stronger every minute of every day. She began to feel panicky. Soon it would be impossible to escape him. Soon she'd be just like her boys, completely in his power. Unless she took measures to keep it from happening, she'd risk trusting another man. Risk saying yes to Sam Dakota.

The cut was on the fleshy part of Tom's palm. Although it looked mean, it wasn't terribly deep. Her son was more angry than hurt.

"Sam hasn't left yet, has he?" he asked, squirming as she reapplied the bandage.

"I wouldn't know," she said, gritting her teeth at his eagerness to get back to the foreman.

"He didn't need to bring me here. I would've been all right."

"Maybe he was worried about blood on the saddle," she said frivolously.

"Sam sees blood all the time," Tom argued, frowning at her for suggesting anything so silly. "He didn't want you to be mad at him."

"Me?"

"Yeah," her son explained patiently. "You're a mother. He said mothers worry and that you'd be furious with him if he let me work all day without taking care of this stupid cut first."

"Well, he was right about that. You could've ended

up with an infection if you'd waited until you were done for the day."

"Mo-om," he groaned, rolling his eyes. "Hurry up, please. Sam's waiting for me!"

She finished with the bandage and Tom roared to his feet like a roped calf suddenly set free. He was out the door before she could stop him.

Molly followed, but by the time she got outside, Tom and Sam were both back in the saddle and headed south. Standing on the top step, she watched them ride off, like John Wayne and his sidekick in some dumb Western.

When she returned to the kitchen, Molly found Gramps sitting at the table. "Sheriff Maynard phoned while you were out," he announced.

Molly flicked a stray hair from her face, hoping Gramps could read none of her frustration. "What'd he say?" She'd called the sheriff shortly after the fence had been purposely cut, and the man had taken his own sweet time responding.

"Not much. Just that there's been a series of such things happening the past few months." A scowl darkened Gramps's face, telling Molly he hadn't revealed all of the conversation.

"What is it?" she asked.

Looking disgruntled, Gramps shook his head.

"I'll need to hear it sooner or later." She pulled out a chair and sat across the table from him.

"Damn fool sheriff suggested we ask Sam about it."

"Sam? That's ridiculous." She might have had her suspicions about him earlier, but no longer. Sam had spent almost seventy-two hours rounding up the lost cattle. No one in his right mind would create that kind of work for himself.

"That's what I said." Gramps's gaze held hers; the approval in his eyes made it clear that he was pleased by her quick defense of Sam.

"What reason did the sheriff give for suggesting it?"

"All he'd say was that Sam's a stranger." Gramps's voice was gruff. "Far as I'm concerned, he's more than proved himself. I don't consider him a stranger. And I trust him enough to hope he'll marry my only grandchild."

Molly froze; she didn't want to discuss this with Gramps.

"Are you going to do it, girl?" he asked.

Inhaling deeply, she mulled over her answer, knowing Gramps would argue with her. "Probably not."

Gramps went quiet, then muttered, "That's a shame."

"It's my life, Gramps. I make my own decisions."

"And your own mistakes."

"Those, too." She couldn't argue with him there.

"Molly girl," he said softly, his disappointment obvious, "you need a man. For lots of reasons. Especially living on this ranch. If not Sam, who?"

"Gramps, you're way behind the times." It was difficult for Molly not to laugh. Or cry. Her heart ached just thinking about what would happen to Tom and Clay when Sam walked out on them.

As if reading her mind, Gramps added, "All right, you insist you don't want a husband. But what about the boys? Look at the change in them since you got here. You might not want to marry Sam, and that's your choice, but both Tom and Clay have made him a substitute father."

Molly swallowed tightly, unable to deny it. She'd been thinking about this very thing.

"They're desperate for—whaddaya call it?—a role model," Gramps went on. "It would have been an easy thing to ignore them, but Sam didn't do that. I'll tell you what, Molly girl, he's been more father to them than Daniel ever was or ever will be."

"I'm leaving for town now," she said, reaching for the list Sam had given her that morning. Talking to Gramps was impossible, she decided. Just impossible.

It was well past the supper hour—and just before the storm broke—when Sam and Tom arrived back at the ranch. Pete and Charlie had already returned and left for the day. Thick gray clouds had followed them in from the range, and the scent of rain was heavy in the air. The day had been busy but productive. They'd moved the herd from one pasture to another, the second such move that summer. Each time, they brought the herd closer to the house and the road, so when it came time to sell the cattle, they'd be nearby and easier to transport. Rotating pastures was good for the land, as well.

Boris had put in a hard day's work. When Sam dismounted, he stopped to pet the dog. For every mile he went, Boris had gone two. Later on, Bullwinkle would be good with the cattle, too, especially with his father to learn from.

Thunder crashed close enough to shake the barn roof. "We beat the storm," Tom said proudly as he opened the door and led Sinbad toward his stall.

The boy didn't understand that storms came and went; they struck when they damn well pleased and left without rhyme or reason, often just as quickly.

Rain beat against the barn roof, echoing through the building. Tom looked up. "Wow, that's some storm."

He slipped the saddle from Sinbad's back and carried it to the tack room. "I wonder what Mom's cooking for supper. I'm hungry."

"Me, too."

"I bet she made chili. It's one of my favorite dinners, with corn bread hot from the oven so the butter melts as soon as you put it on. Yum."

The kid was making Sam hungry just talking about it. Sam had been staying away from the house at suppertime, preferring to give Molly a chance to think, consider her options. He didn't want to influence her one way or the other. In a matter as serious as marriage, he wanted her to be sure. He'd marry her, if she agreed, but not for love—and he'd be honest about that. He intended to be a good husband, though, and a father to her boys. What interested him was the promise of that land and the herd. It represented a second chance, and second chances didn't come along every day.

"You go on in and wash up," Sam told the boy. "I'll finish out here."

Tom hesitated. "You mean it?"

"I always mean what I say." Sam didn't want Tom ever to question that. A hundred times in the past week he'd stopped himself from talking to Molly. He wanted to assure her that given the chance, he'd prove himself to her and the boys. Even though it wouldn't be a love match, he *liked* her, dammit. And he was attracted to her. Another thing—if they got married, they'd be man and wife, and none of this sleeping-apart business. The couple of times they'd kissed should tell her they were compatible sexually. A lot of marriages started out with less.

Tom set his hat lower on his head as he opened the

barn door and raced across the yard. Sam saw a jagged flash of lightning cut across the sky. As his stepfather used to say, the night wasn't fit for man or beast. That memory brought with it an unexpected ache, a desire to reconnect with his own family. Someday, he would, he promised himself. Later. When he was ready.

Taking the brush, he rubbed down his gelding, hands working at a steady pace while he thought about marriage. Marriage to Molly. He knew next to nothing about her ex-husband. The boys hardly ever mentioned their father. From what he'd gathered, Daniel Cogan hadn't spent much time with his sons. His loss, Sam decided. Walt hadn't said much about Molly's ex-husband, either, only that he was a damn fool, and without even having met the man, Sam agreed. Anyone who'd walk away from a woman like Molly and those boys didn't have a lick of sense. As for Molly herself, it was plain the breakup of her marriage had soured her.

Sam let his mind drift back to his own family. He'd learned—from a hometown newspaper—that his stepfather had died a couple of years earlier. Sam's heart ached each time he realized he'd never had the chance to thank Michael Dakota for being a father to him. His mother had been a teenager when she'd gotten pregnant with Sam. Three years had passed before she married Michael, who'd adopted Sam as his own son, loved him and raised him. When he'd reached his teens, Sam had rebelled and brought nothing but trouble and grief to the family. Michael had reacted with patience, but it was Sam who'd rejected him. Sam had allowed his stubborn immature pride to hurt his family.

At the time all he'd wanted, needed, was the opportunity to compete in the rodeo. He found it painful to admit now, but those years had been a waste. A selfish indulgence that had cost him more than he wanted to think about.

The barn door flew open and, assuming it was the wind, Sam hurried over to close it.

"Mom isn't back!" Rain pouring off the brim of his hat, his eyes filled with panic, Tom burst into the barn. "She left for town a little after twelve and she isn't back. Gramps expected her home around three."

Sam checked his watch. Seven-fifteen.

"I thought she might've decided to wait out the storm, but she would've phoned. I know she would." The boy was trying to stay calm, but it was an obvious struggle.

"Which vehicle did she take?"

"Gramps's truck."

Sam handed Tom his brush and headed outside. Walt's vehicle was on its last legs. She shouldn't be driving it at all! Then he realized that she was probably picking up the shingles and drainage pipe he'd ordered—which would never have fit in her car.

"Where are you going?" Tom asked, racing after him.

"Where else, boy? After your mother."

"But she could be anywhere."

"True." But it made no difference. "You won't see me again until I've found her, understand?" No one would rest easy until Molly was back, safe and sound. He'd find her, and he wouldn't return until he had.

Five minutes later Sam was on the road that led to town. The windshield wipers slapped the rain from side to side, and visibility was practically zero. The rain streamed down in torrents that quickly filled the gullies and washed across the roadway. Driving was hazardous and it took Sam's full concentration to keep his truck on the road.

Wherever Molly was, Sam prayed she'd be smart enough to seek shelter. If the truck had broken down, the worst thing she could do would be to leave it. Anyone from the country would know that, but Molly was a city girl.

As he carefully steered down the highway, going no faster than ten miles an hour, he shuddered, trying not to think beyond the moment. If anything had happened to Molly, it'd kill the old man. She was the only thing that kept him alive. She and her boys. And what about Tom and Clay? What if they lost their mother?

What if *he* lost Molly? Without ever really knowing her. Without ever having the chance to see if they could build a life together.

Sam saw a vehicle in the distance parked by the side of the road. He squinted through the furious beating of the windshield wipers and tried to make out the type and color.

It didn't take him long to recognize the vehicle as Walt's run-down truck. The Chevy was in about the same shape as the old man's heart.

He pulled over and left the headlights on, facing the other vehicle. Through the pounding rain it was impossible to tell if she was inside the cab or not.

He opened his door and leaped out. Hunching his shoulders against the storm, he ran, slipping and sliding, to the other truck. With both hands, he shielded his face and peered through the passenger window.

She wasn't there.

He cursed and turned around, looking frantically

up and down the road. His biggest fear was that she'd decided to walk to the ranch, fallen into a gully and drowned.

"Molly!" he shouted.

Nothing.

He'd told Tom he wouldn't return without her, and he'd meant it. He tried to think where she'd go, what she might have been thinking. Logic would've told anyone with half a brain to stay in the truck, dammit.

Lightning briefly lit up the sky, and in that second he saw a flash of color huddled against the trunk of a massive oak tree. It stood across a field planted with alfalfa.

"Molly?" He couldn't understand why she'd be sitting next to a tree with the rain pouring down on her when she could be warm and dry inside the truck.

It wasn't until he drew closer that he realized Molly wasn't sitting.

She was lying facedown in the mud.

Nine

"Molly! Molly!"

Her name seemed to echo, ringing in her ears. It was giving her a headache. No, she already had a headache. She struggled to sit up but couldn't. When she tried to raise her arm and investigate what was wrong, she found herself unable to move.

The sound of her name was clearer now. Sam? What was he doing here? For that matter, where the hell *was* she? Molly moved her hand and black mud oozed between her fingers. Slowly, painfully, she used what strength she possessed to raise her head.

"Molly." The relief in Sam's voice was unmistakable.

She felt herself being lifted and turned, and all she could see was Sam Dakota against a backdrop of dark sky. Rain hit her face and she blinked. There was a blinding streak of lightning, and she squinted at the brightness and the instant pain it produced.

"Are you all right?" Sam demanded fiercely. He sounded worried—and angry. He was rubbing a cloth across her face, smearing the mud.

Molly shook her head in order to avoid this punishment, but it did little good and only served to make the pain worse. "Don't, please...don't...don't." But he ignored her pleas.

"What happened?" He brushed the hair from her brow, and when he drew his hand away she thought she saw blood. She hoped it wasn't hers.

"Is that blood?" she asked. "And is it mine or yours?" Her mouth felt so dry she had trouble speaking.

Apparently he didn't hear her or more likely didn't want to answer. His attention seemed to focus on her forehead. "What are you looking for now?" she asked irritably, her voice gaining strength. "The mark of the beast?"

The merest hint of a smile flashed in his eyes, but his mouth remained drawn. "You must have fallen and hit your head."

His words prompted Molly's memory. On her way back from town, the truck had suddenly died. Although she'd never been mechanically inclined, she could certainly read a gauge. Gas wasn't the problem, and the battery had been fine earlier. Nonetheless, the truck had sputtered and stalled, and after a few gasping coughs stopped altogether. Not knowing what else to do, she'd waited for help.

After several hours, with no other vehicles on that road, the storm had come. The rain had pounded the truck, vicious and unrelenting. Any hope she'd had of rescue disappeared. She realized she'd have to wait out the storm. But after thirty minutes, when it showed no sign of lessening, she'd ventured from the safety of the cab to be sure she wasn't in danger of floating away.

"While I was out there, I saw a light," she told him. "So I was sure there must be a farmhouse close by."

She avoided meeting his eyes, knowing he thought her every kind of fool, and she didn't blame him. It had been stupid to leave the truck in a storm, but the light hadn't seemed far away, and she'd assumed she could walk there.

"Didn't you stop and think about...?" Sam didn't bother to finish his question.

"Crossing the field didn't look all that daunting, and I figured I'd rather deal with a little mud than leave Gramps and the boys worrying. It seemed like the right thing to do at the time."

"What happened then?"

"I'd only gone a short ways and the mud was up to my ankles. I...tripped and the next thing I remember was you bending over me."

"Hasn't anyone ever told you that..." With what appeared to be considerable effort, he bit off whatever else he intended to say. Molly was grateful; she wasn't up to hearing a lecture right now.

"Don't scold me—I know what I did was stupid." She was drenched to the bone, her temple throbbed something fierce, and she was covered head to toe in black ooze. Worse, she'd made a world-class fool of herself—and naturally Sam had been the one to find her.

At least the rain had slowed to a drizzle.

Sliding his arm around her waist, he helped her stand. Rainwater ran from her hair down her neck and back. Once she was upright, the alfalfa field began to spin and she had to lean against Sam. He tightened his arm while she struggled to regain her equilibrium.

After a moment, in which the world still reeled, Sam cursed under his breath and hoisted her into his arms.

"Put me down," she insisted, closing her eyes at the

sudden jarring pain. "I can walk—just give me a couple of minutes and I'll be as good as new."

"The hell with it! You can't even stand." He started toward the truck, taking slow careful steps. He was having as much difficulty as she'd had earlier, with the mud pulling his boots deeper and deeper. Each time he lifted his foot the ground made a sucking sound of protest.

"How much do you weigh, anyhow?" he growled when they'd covered about half the distance.

"I'll have you know I've lost five pounds since June."

"Right now, I wish it'd been ten."

Feeling as wretched as she did, she could do without the insults. "Put me down this instant." Molly figured he'd welcome the opportunity to dump her right then and there; she steeled herself to being dropped butt-first in the muck. But he ignored her and continued the long arduous trek back to the road.

Every couple of steps he'd mutter something she was glad she couldn't understand. Her head hurt, throbbing in unison with her pulse. After the first few minutes she closed her eyes and pressed her temple against his shoulder. She was cold and miserable, yet she felt secure in Sam's arms, secure enough to be thankful he'd found her—despite his anger. And her embarrassment. Soon they'd be home....

"Molly, wake up."

Her eyes flew open. "What?"

"Don't go to sleep. You've probably got a concussion."

"Okay." But despite her efforts, her eyelids drooped.

"Dammit, Molly," he said, "this is difficult enough."

It was so hard to keep her eyes open. So very hard. "I...I'm sorry. I never meant for this to happen."

Sam's labored breathing slowed once he reached the road. He carried her to his truck, opened the passenger door and helped her inside, settling her on the seat with surprising gentleness. She glanced at her reflection in the side mirror and gasped. Her wet hair was plastered to her head, and the stringy tendrils trickled water against her shoulders. A large bump protruded from her forehead, along with a nasty-looking gash at her hairline. It didn't seem too deep or in need of stitches. Mud was smeared across her cheeks. Her clothes dripped with thick black muck.

"I've seen cattle with more sense than you," Sam said between clenched teeth as he climbed into the driver's seat.

Molly turned and stared out the side window, shaking with cold and feeling more wretched by the moment. The brief illusion of security she'd felt in Sam's arms was gone. Perhaps the best thing would be to contact Russell Letson and tell him she'd had a change of heart and she'd sell the ranch, after all. No. She couldn't do that to Gramps. It was just her misery talking.

Silently she waited, expecting Sam to turn on the ignition. Nothing happened for so long that curiosity got the better of her. She looked over to find him sitting with his arms outstretched, hands clutching the steering wheel. He seemed to be staring at something directly in front of them.

He must have sensed her scrutiny because he gave a deep sigh. "I apologize, Molly. I shouldn't have said that."

"I…I don't blame you. I deserved it—and your other insults, too. It was stupid to leave the truck." Even wearier now than before, she laid her head against the window and managed a weak smile. "Can we go home now? All I want is a hot bath and about a hundred tablets of extra-strength aspirin."

"Home." He repeated the word as though it was some kind of magical incantation, and in that instant she realized that the Broken Arrow Ranch *was* home. Hers—and his? Somehow she'd find a way to keep this property. He'd be welcome to stay. But with or without Sam Dakota, she was going to do her damnedest to hold on to her heritage.

Tom had pretended he had no real interest in participating in the Fourth of July celebrations. But in truth he was excited about it. He just didn't want anyone to know. Back in San Francisco his friends bought illegal firecrackers and set them off to annoy people. Stupid. This was going to be different. He couldn't remember the last time his family had gone on a real picnic or watched a parade.

To admit he was looking forward to the holiday might give his mother the wrong impression, though. He wasn't a kid anymore, but a man. Or almost one. He worked alongside Sam, who'd assured him he was a real help. Tom felt good about that. He'd never expected to like Montana, but found he enjoyed life on the ranch and the challenge of each new day.

And his little brother—well, Clay was as excited about this picnic as that silly puppy of his. He ran back and forth from the house, loading up the car with stuff from the kitchen. His mother sure knew how to pack a picnic basket. There was enough food to last them a week—which suited Tom just fine. He kind of wondered if she'd gone to so much effort to impress Sam.

The foreman was driving into town with them. Ever since they'd come here, Tom hadn't seen Sam take a single day off. Not a whole day, anyway. Man, if anyone deserved a holiday, it was Sam! Better yet, Sam would be with his mother. Not that this was a real date or anything, but close enough to maybe get them talking. Tom wished they *would* talk.

Ever since Sam had gone looking for his mother in the storm, things had been better between them. Before that, he'd noticed how stiff and polite they were, as if they were afraid to say what they really meant. Like everything was on the surface, not from their hearts. Tom had his own suspicions—his own hopes—about what their hearts might want to say.

The goose egg on his mother's forehead wasn't as big anymore, and with that powder stuff she put on her face, the bruise was barely noticeable. She'd been in bad shape when Sam brought her home. Although he was cold and wet himself, he'd insisted she take a hot shower right away, and while she was doing that, he'd reassured Gramps there was nothing to worry about. He'd phoned Doc Shaver, telling Gramps it was just a precaution. Then he'd called a garage in town to arrange a tow for the truck. Sam's clothes had dried before he ever got a chance to shower.

The afternoon his mother had gone missing hadn't been an easy one for Tom. He hadn't wanted to say anything to Clay, but he'd been worried. Real worried. His stomach had cramped, and every time he thought about what might have happened, he felt like he had to go to the bathroom. What had helped most was remembering Sam's words about not coming back without her.

Every few minutes he'd looked out the window, hoping to see headlights, but it'd been hours before Sam finally pulled into the yard.

Gramps was relieved, too. He'd been just as concerned, but kept it hidden, the way Tom had. They'd exchanged worried glances, but neither of them had said anything.

"You ready, cowboy?" His mother stood at the foot of the stairs and called up to him.

"I guess." Although his voice didn't reveal any enthusiasm, he raced downstairs and nearly collided with Clay.

"I'm taking my pillow," his brother said as he slipped past Tom and bounded up the stairs.

"I didn't know you still took naps," Tom said. He enjoyed riling his little brother.

"I don't," protested Clay as he ran downstairs clutching his pillow. "But when the fireworks start, I want to lie back and watch them."

"Sweetgrass isn't going to have any fireworks," Tom muttered, amazed at how disappointed he felt. A town only big enough for a weekly newspaper wasn't going to come up with the money to afford real fireworks.

Either Clay didn't hear him or wasn't in the mood to argue, because his little brother let the comment slide.

"What car we taking?" Tom asked, slouching in the kitchen chair as if this was all too much effort.

"Ours," his mother answered, tucking a jar of pickles into a cardboard box.

"Your mother trusts me enough to drive," Sam said, and held up the car keys. "Before long you'll be doing the honors."

"He's only fourteen," Molly said, adding a can of insect repellant to the box.

"He'll be at the wheel before you know it," Sam told her. He caught Tom's eye and winked.

Tom hid a smile. What his mother didn't know wouldn't hurt her. Sam had been giving him lessons for a couple of weeks now. His legs were just long enough to reach the clutch and the gas pedal. At first he was sure he'd never be able to do it, but Sam had assured him everyone had trouble in the beginning. Before long he'd gotten the hang of it and was confident enough to drive Sam's truck for short distances.

Molly ran her fingers through her hair. "Gramps," she said, "are you sure we can't talk you into coming with us?"

Gramps shook his head and grumbled something about a parade being a waste of taxpayers' money. He left it at that.

"Guess that means he's not interested," Sam said, picking up the cardboard box. "It's your loss, old man."

Gramps stood in the doorway, as they piled into the car. Tom climbed into the back seat with his brother, although he almost always sat next to his mother up front. He didn't mind—but only because it was Sam who sat beside her. With anyone else, he might not have been so generous. On the way into town his mother sang. Little kids' songs, for crying out loud—they were the only ones she knew all the words to.

She only did that when she was happy.

They arrived in Sweetgrass early enough to get prime seats for viewing the parade. They found a vacant bench at the edge of the park, and the four of them sat facing the street, eating flavored snow cones while they waited.

Sam teased Tom and Clay, telling silly jokes that

made them both laugh. Tom noticed when Sam stretched his arm across the back of the bench and placed it around his mother's shoulders. He encouraged the foreman with a wink, but if Sam saw it, he didn't respond.

Just as the parade was about to begin, something happened. Tom didn't understand exactly what it meant—only that it changed the course of their day. Sam had been laughing when all at once he went quiet.

Tom looked up to find Sheriff Maynard standing directly in front of Sam, blocking his view of the street. The sheriff was a big man with a belly that hung over his belt. But he wasn't soft, Tom could see that. He stood with his feet apart and glared down at the four of them. The way he scowled at Sam made Tom angry. And it really bugged him that the sheriff was checking out his mother like...like she was some bimbo in a bikini.

"Dakota," the sheriff drawled.

"Sheriff."

"Come to enjoy the festivities?"

Although the words were friendly enough, Tom had the impression the sheriff would have welcomed a reason to ask Sam to leave or, better yet, arrest him. Tom glanced from one man to the other.

"I understand there's been some trouble at the Broken Arrow," the sheriff remarked next. Just the way he said it irked Tom. He knew Sam was angry, too, because he saw a small muscle jumping in his jaw.

"Nothing I can't handle," Sam returned after a moment, and there seemed to be a hidden meaning in his words. His eyes had narrowed and there was a hardness in his face.

Tom studied the lawman and decided Sheriff Maynard looked like he ate too many doughnuts. His hands were huge, too. Tom wondered what Sam had done to get on the bad side of the authorities. It didn't take much; he'd learned that himself back in San Francisco.

The sheriff left as soon as the parade started, but he might as well have stayed, because all the fun had vanished. Both his mother and Sam were subdued. They tried, everyone did, but to little avail.

Later, when they ate at a picnic table in the park, Tom wondered why everything had changed. He watched his mother and Sam. In the past the idea of his mother remarrying had bothered him. It wasn't that he didn't want her to be happy, but things were good with just the three of them. She didn't need anyone else. Every now and then she'd dated when they lived in California, but there'd never been anyone Tom would want for a stepfather.

He wouldn't mind if Sam married his mother. That might be cool. And he wouldn't have to worry about Sam moving away, either.

Russell had given up counting the number of excuses he'd invented to get out of attending the town's Fourth of July celebration.

Carrying a tall glass of iced tea onto the cabin's deck, he gazed out at the valley below. He'd bought the place a couple of years earlier as an investment. He wasn't really the outdoor type. He'd always figured he'd leave the adventures of back-to-the-wilderness living to those who appreciated that sort of thing.

He'd never guessed the cabin would become his love nest. *Love nest.* Silly term. Kind of old-fashioned. It made him smile. Sitting down, he arranged the chess pieces on the board and waited for Pearl to join him. She wasn't long.

"I'm after revenge," he announced, grinning up at her. Pearl claimed she hadn't known how to play chess until he'd taught her. After the first few games he found that hard to believe. Her skill was amazing. It wasn't only chess that she was good at, either. She had an incisive logical mind and grasped ideas quickly. Because of her reading difficulties, she'd assumed she was stupid when in reality the opposite was true. He marveled at her almost photographic memory. That, together with her wit, made an intriguing combination. She fascinated and challenged him. The Sundays he spent with her had become the highlight of his week.

He'd asked her about IQ tests in high school, and she had told him she'd dropped out before ever taking any. Then, when she confessed she couldn't read, he'd decided to teach her. She picked it up with astonishing ease. He loved her reaction, the excitement and giddiness she didn't try to hide. She was never without a book these days, and he was impressed by her insights into character and theme.

Ironic. Pearl had been his birthday present. An evening with a prostitute. He'd felt sordid, at first, going to her—as sordid as he'd always considered his older cousin. But what his cousin didn't understand was that knowing her, loving her, was perhaps the greatest gift he'd ever received.

The one question that had hounded him for months was how she'd become involved in this life. Despite his curiosity, he'd never questioned her. Fear was the main reason for keeping his questions to himself. He'd recognized immediately that the subject of her career, for lack of a better word, was strictly off-limits. The one time he'd mentioned it, she'd refused to speak and had nearly run away. He couldn't, wouldn't, risk it again.

What most concerned him was the question of her pimp. She had one. Almost every hooker did. But Russell had never had the courage to ask who it was. So he had to pretend things were different. Pretend they had a normal relationship.

Either he was the biggest fool who'd ever lived or her love for him was as real as his law degree. As real as she said it was. He chose to believe her. It was as if there were two Pearls. One of them was the brazen cold-eyed hooker he'd met on his birthday. The woman who was a consummate actress, using soft baby talk with him and behaving in an almost subservient way as she offered tantalizing glimpses of her wares.

Then there was the other Pearl. The real Pearl.

He wasn't sure why he'd suggested they talk first that night. Probably because he'd been nervous and on edge. His cousin had made a big deal of this evening, and while it had embarrassed and even disgusted Russell, he'd reluctantly gone along.

He'd never intended to go to bed with her, never intended to visit her again. But their first evening together had been…so wonderful. So unexpected. He discovered he could be himself with her, whereas with other women he felt self-conscious and shy. He knew women considered him attractive; nevertheless he'd never found it easy to talk with them.

Later his cousin had interrogated him about his gift. Pried him with questions. Russell had lied, saying as little as possible. His cousin had given him a congratulatory slap on the back, then lowered his voice and asked if he'd sampled Pearl's specialty. It was all Russell could do not to slam his fist down the other man's throat as he relayed in profane detail what kept Pearl's customers coming back again and again.

Then Russell had stumbled on her in the grocery store, and they'd started meeting at his cabin. He was fairly sure no one knew, which was undoubtedly for the best. Their secrecy protected his reputation and, she'd once implied, her safety. And there was the fact that she wasn't exactly the type of woman a man introduced to his mother. Yet Russell would gladly have married her. He'd asked her to be his wife a dozen times; he'd stopped only because he could see how much it hurt her to turn him down. Tears would fill her eyes and she'd whisper that he didn't know what he was asking. Russell *did* know. But he'd let the matter rest and went about proving how much he loved her, even when it meant turning a blind eye to how she made her living.

Looking at her now, no one would ever guess her occupation. Her hair was tied back in pigtails and her baggy T-shirt disguised the fullness of her breasts and just about every other feminine attribute.

"Your move," she said, glancing up and beaming him a wide triumphant smile.

It was difficult to stop gazing at her long enough to examine the chessboard. Once he did, he frowned. The obvious move would put him in check; any other move would place his queen in jeopardy. He reconstructed her moves and saw that there was no hope for it. She'd won. They could play to the end, if she insisted, but the outcome was inevitable. She'd outsmarted him again.

He looked at her and grinned. "Come here," he whispered.

"Russell?"

He held out his hand to her. She knew what he wanted and blushed. The first time he'd seen that tinge of color on her cheeks he was convinced it was a trick. This woman knew everything there was to know about sex. But over time Russell had come to trust that everything between them was as new and fresh for her as it was for him. Like him, she was in love for the first time in her life.

"You can get out of that," she said, pointing at the chessboard.

But Russell already had his next move planned, and it didn't involve chess.

Pearl giggled, sounding like a teenager. She exhaled the softest of sighs, then gently placed her hand in his. Russell pulled her close.

Out here he could forget that this never should have happened. That he'd fallen head over heels in love with a whore.

On Friday morning Molly and Gramps received news from Sam that one of the water holes had been poisoned. The carcass of a calf had been dumped in the largest cow pond in the new pasture. Every indication was that this had been done deliberately.

Ten cattle were already dead and another thirty head were sick. Between the vet bills and the loss of cattle, this was one more disaster they didn't need.

"We've got to do something, Gramps!" Molly cried in outrage as she stormed about the kitchen. She wasn't sure how she expected him to respond. She'd thought it over countless times, and her conclusions were always the same. The record books told her they were already in financial trouble. Any more would cripple them. It was clear to her that someone wanted the ranch to fail. "Who would do this to us?" she muttered. "Who?"

"If I knew who'd do such a thing, Molly girl, I wouldn't be sitting here stewing." He'd played solitaire for the past hour, slapping the cards against the table and just as quickly snatching them up again.

"But why?"

Gramps slowly shook his head. "I wish to hell I knew."

"Isn't it obvious someone wants us to bail out?" Surely he hadn't forgotten the offer Russell Letson had brought her a few days after her arrival. That seemed the perfect place to start looking. "Maybe we should ask Letson who his client is."

"Sam already did that."

"He did?" That the two men would exclude her didn't sit well with Molly, but this was an issue she'd take up with Sam, not Gramps.

"Now, don't go gettin' your dander up," her grandfather muttered. "It was a logical decision. You'd just arrived and we couldn't see any need to drag you into something you knew nothing about."

"So do you know who made the offer?" she asked.

"It wasn't someone local, if that's what you're asking. No one from Sweetgrass would want this land so bad he'd be willing to hurt us in order to get it," Gramps told her.

"Who is it, then?"

Gramps scratched the side of his head. "My guess is it's one of those movie-star types outta Hollywood. I hear that's quite common now. These people think they're gonna turn back time and have bison on the land again. Romantic malarkey." The old man rolled his eyes. "Sam talked to Letson for quite a while. Letson couldn't tell him who made the offer, but he didn't say no when Sam mentioned the movie-star idea. So we don't know for sure, but that's who we think it is. Some actor. Most folks around here won't sell to a movie star, so he must've hired Letson." Gramps paused. "Can't see one of those Hollywood pretty boys comin' out here to knock down mailboxes and poison our cattle, though."

Molly agreed. But she was going to ask Sam about it. In the meantime she wanted to clear the air about something else. Something she'd put off since the Fourth of July.

"What exactly do you know about Sam?" she asked in what she hoped was a conversational tone.

"Sam?" Gramps's eyes narrowed suspiciously. "Not that again! Why're you asking *this* time?"

"Sheriff Maynard stopped by for a chat with us before the parade last week."

"Oh?"

"He wasn't particularly…pleasant."

"Oh."

"He seems to know something about Sam that we don't."

"Oh?"

The *oh*'s were beginning to irritate her. "Gramps, I know you like Sam. I do, too, and so do the boys. But something's not right. Why would Sheriff Maynard want to make trouble for Sam? And even more important, why did Sam clam up afterward?"

"You'll have to ask him."

Gramps was hiding something from her. Molly was convinced of that, and it angered her. She was his flesh and blood. His granddaughter. And apparently he didn't trust her enough to tell her the whole truth about a hired hand.

"Fine. I *will* ask him." She was going to have so many questions for Sam she'd have to start a list. "The man responsible for keeping the law in this county looks at Sam as if he isn't to be trusted and you're pushing me to *marry* him. What kind of message does that give me, Gramps?" She didn't allow him an opportunity to answer. "It says you're so desperate to see me married off that you're willing to throw me to anyone. Even a man you hardly—"

"Enough!" Gramps pushed the deck of cards aside. "You ask me what I know about Sam Dakota. I know he's decent and honest. I know he cares for those boys of yours and he'd make you a damn good husband. That's what I know. As for his trouble with the sheriff, you can think what you will, but it was nothing Sam did."

"All Sam's interested in is the land you offered," she said. It still offended her that Gramps had dangled part of *her* inheritance as an inducement.

"Did Sam tell you himself that he'd only marry you if I threw in the land and cattle?" Gramps asked.

"No," she admitted. "But he didn't have to say it," she added sarcastically. His attitude had said it all.

"Do you honestly believe I'd suggest you marry a man I don't trust?" Gramps asked her quietly.

"Why him?" she cried. "Do you think I'm incapable of finding my own husband? What if Sam marries me, sucks the ranch dry and then leaves me?"

Gramps shook his head. "I told you before, Molly, that isn't going to happen."

"How can you be so sure?"

He sighed deeply and looked away. "Without Sam, I would have lost the ranch last winter."

"Any hired hand would have saved the ranch," she argued. "Sam was there when you needed him, but it could have been anyone."

Again Gramps shook his head. "No. For one thing, he got the cattle sold off in time to pay my bank loan. I'll grant you another foreman might've managed that for me. But the other thing he did..." Gramps rubbed at his eyes. "He pawned his silver buckle to pay back taxes. Those things are worth a lot, Molly. Remember I told you he was a world-champion rodeo rider until his accident? It was his prize that he hawked for the ranch. He didn't tell me about it right away, either. I found out when I went in to the assessor's office to ask for some extra time. That was when I discovered Sam had already been in and paid the bill. The only reason he told me was I pressured him into it."

Sam had done that? Molly felt a sudden need to sit down.

"I'd been having a bit of a problem with money," Gramps said, and Molly understood how difficult it was for her grandfather to admit this. "I put off thinking about it as long as I could, but when the dunning letters started coming in, I knew it was time I faced the music."

"You told Sam?"

"No!" This was said with vehemence; she realized it hurt his pride to talk about his financial failures. "Sam was the one who brought in the mail. He saw the final-notice envelope himself."

"How much was it?"

Gramps named a substantial figure. "He hawked the most precious thing he owned to help me. Despite what you think, Sam Dakota is a good man. Give him a chance to prove himself, Molly girl. You might be surprised." Gramps hesitated and his voice grew gentle. "You should have seen him when he first arrived. He was mad as hell and the chip on his shoulder was the size of an oak. But after a while, when he got to working the land, he changed. The land will heal you, too, Molly. If you let it."

Molly *wanted* the land to heal her. She wanted the contentment of a life lived close to the earth. She wanted the sense of accomplishing something real.

"Sam paid the taxes without telling me what he'd done," Gramps whispered. "He's that kind of man. You won't go wrong marrying him. He'll be good to you, Molly, and a decent father to your sons. I won't be with you much longer." He held up his hand to stop her when she started to protest. "Think about marrying him. I promise you, you won't be sorry."

Molly spent the evening doing just that. Thinking. Much later, while the house slept, she was still wide awake. Worrying. Wondering. What would she do without Sam? Who could she trust? Was it *right* to marry him?

Staring out at the moonless night, she felt alone and afraid. Someone was trying to frighten her off her land. Hurt her family. If ever there was a time she needed a strong ally, it was now.

Was that enough for a marriage, being allies?

The house was quiet and dark as she hurried downstairs. The clock on the stove said it was after midnight. She wasn't sure what prompted her to look out the kitchen window, but she did, and the first thing she noticed was that Sam's light was on.

Before she could lose her nerve, she pulled on a sweater and a pair of boots and made her away across the yard.

She knocked twice before he answered.

"Yeah? What is it?" He raked back disheveled hair as he opened the door.

"I...I thought you were up," Molly apologized.

"I must have dozed off in front of the television." He didn't invite her in, which was just as well. She'd say what she had to say quickly and be done with it.

"Two things." She straightened, holding her head high, and forced her voice to remain calm and unemotional. "First, I've decided to approach you about Gramps's suggestion."

He didn't say anything for perhaps a minute. Just stared at her. "You're willing for us to get married?" he finally asked. He didn't sound like he believed her.

"Yes," she said, and nodded once for emphasis. "Are *you* willing?"

"I'm willing." No ands, ifs or buts. No questions or hesitations, but then she'd doubted there would be.

"All right. We can get the license later this week."

He nodded. "You said two things."

"The next one is a question. Please be honest. Would you have agreed to marry me without Gramps's offer of the cattle and land?"

"No," he said, steadily meeting her gaze.

If nothing else, she appreciated his honesty. "That's what I thought."

Ten

Sam was sitting at the kitchen table when Molly came downstairs the following morning. The coffee was made, and she glanced his way before helping herself to a cup. His silence grated on her nerves. The night had been miserable. She'd slept, but only intermittently. Her dreams had been full of strange fearful scenarios. She remembered one in which she was at her wedding—except that the groom turned out to be Daniel and the preacher Sheriff Maynard.

Judging from the dark shadows beneath Sam's eyes, he hadn't slept any better. Neither spoke, although Molly knew he was as aware of her as she was of him. For two people who'd agreed to marry, they didn't appear to have much to say to each other.

She noticed that he waited until she'd had time to drink half her coffee before he spoke. "Have you changed your mind?"

Molly's gaze flew across the room. "Have you?"

"I asked you first."

If he was trying to make her feel like a fool, he was

definitely succeeding. "No. I'm willing to go through with a wedding if you are, but—"

"I am," he interrupted, not giving her a chance to finish. He stood and reached for his hat.

"But," she continued as though he hadn't spoken, "I'd prefer the marriage to be strictly a business arrangement."

Sam's eyes narrowed. "You already know my answer to that. We'll be man and wife in every sense of the word, or the whole thing's off."

"But you said…you admitted you'd never have agreed to the marriage if it wasn't for Gramps's offer."

"Think of that as my guarantee."

"Your guarantee?" she flared. *She* needed a guarantee if anyone did. This was no love match, after all. Even if her husband-to-be thought they were going to share a bed. That issue wasn't resolved yet, as far as she was concerned. "Your guarantee?" she repeated. "Of what?"

"Who's to say that a couple of years down the road, after I've worked my fingers to the bone, you won't file for divorce and kick me off the place?" Sam asked coolly.

"Who's to say you won't sell off the cattle and abscond with the profits?" she threw back.

They glared at each other across the room.

Sam was the one to break the tense silence. "It would help, don't you think, if we could agree to trust each other? The only person who's shown any confidence in our ability to make a go of this marriage is Walt. For his sake—if not our own—let's put aside our doubts and agree to make the best of it. Can we do that?"

This was more difficult than she'd thought it would

be. Faith and trust didn't came easily. "All right," she whispered at last.

He relaxed then. "Good. I'll get Pete and Charlie set for the day and then we can drive into town and apply for the license."

"Already?" she gasped.

"Is there a reason to wait?"

No one knew about this yet, not even Gramps or the boys. Molly needed time to discuss it with her children. It wasn't fair just to spring a stepfather on them. They had the right to express their opinions and concerns first. Not that either boy was likely to object.

"I have to tell my family. Phone my mother in Australia." Molly nervously brushed the hair from her face. "But other than that I don't suppose there's any reason to wait."

"We'll both need a blood test."

She tightened the belt on her dressing gown.

"I thought we could have the test done, get the license and make an appointment with a justice of the peace for tomorrow afternoon."

Molly inhaled sharply. A justice of the peace made the entire proceeding sound so…calculated. This might not be a love match, but she still wanted her wedding to take place in a church.

"What's wrong?"

"What about having a minister marry us?"

"Seeing that we aren't getting married for the normal reasons, saying our vows before a man of God seems somewhat hypocritical, don't you think?"

He was right of course, and Molly was unable to come up with an adequate justification for a church wedding—although she still wanted one. She nodded unhappily.

"Smile, Molly," Sam said with sudden amusement. "It could be worse."

Molly wasn't sure that was true. She was about to pledge her life to a man who didn't love her, who openly admitted he was only marrying her for five hundred acres and fifty head of cattle. Worse, she was going into the marriage for selfish reasons of her own. She needed his help, to run the ranch and to *keep* the ranch.

Truly what you'd describe as a marriage of convenience.

With such odds against them, it seemed doubtful they'd manage to stay married for more than six months, Molly thought with sudden pessimism.

"It's a business agreement—and more," Sam clarified, and waited for her to agree.

"And more," she concurred reluctantly.

Sam left after that, while she lingered over her coffee in the kitchen and prayed she was doing the right thing.

Tom and Clay wandered down for breakfast a few minutes later. Molly gave them time to fill their bowls with cereal and sit down at the table. "What would you say if I told you I was thinking about getting married again?" she asked, avoiding eye contact.

"Who?" Tom asked suspiciously.

"Yeah, who do you want to marry?" Clay echoed.

Molly drew in a deep breath. "Sam."

Tom grinned and punched a fist into the air. "Yes!" He nodded. "I figured it had to be."

"Cool, Mom!"

"Neither one of you objects?" Although it seemed pointless to ask.

"I *like* Sam," Clay said without hesitation.

Molly looked to her oldest. Tom was still grinning widely. "If I'd handpicked a new dad, it would've been Sam."

"I see." Molly could hardly claim to be surprised. And, of course, Sam's closeness to her boys was one of the reasons she'd agreed to this.

"What's all the shouting about in here?" Gramps asked as he slowly made his way into the room.

"Mom's marrying Sam!" Clay burst out.

Gramps went silent as if he wasn't sure he should believe it. "Is that true, Molly girl?"

She nodded.

"Praise be to God." Gramps clasped his hands together. "I haven't heard better news in fifteen years. You won't be sorry, Molly, I promise you," he said again.

What she didn't tell her grandfather was that she already had regrets. An uneasiness in the pit of her stomach refused to go away. Despite the reasons that had led to the decision—sound *convenient* reasons—Molly couldn't shake the feeling she was making a terrible mistake. She still knew next to nothing about Sam, and he barely knew her.

Well, she was committed now. She'd given her word. She'd just have to make sure they learned a little more about each other. And soon.

An hour later, when Sam returned to the house, Molly was dressed and ready for the drive to town.

"I've got to stop off for some supplies," he announced as if that was the main reason for this trip into Sweetgrass. Anything else, he seemed to imply, was just a trifling errand. Or worse, an annoyance.

Once in his truck, she barely had the seat belt snapped before Sam took off down the driveway. He drove as if he couldn't get this whole thing over with fast enough. They bumped over potholes and rocks at a speed well above what Molly considered safe.

"Stop!" she shouted just before they hit the paved highway.

He slammed on the brakes. "What for?" he demanded.

The seat belt was all that kept her from pitching forward into the windshield.

Sam's arms remained on the steering wheel. He waited for her to speak.

"Why are you so angry?" she asked.

"I'm not."

"Is there some logical reason you're driving like a wild man?"

Her question seemed to bring him up short. "I'd like to get this done as quickly as possible so I can get back to work."

Molly had the almost irresistible urge to cover her face and weep. "I realize we're not in love," she said, surprised by how small her voice sounded. "But I'd like us both to treat this wedding as something more than a business agreement. Since you insist you eventually want a real marriage—with a shared bed—then I insist on something, too." Her voice gained confidence as she spoke. "I agree to your stipulation." Molly stared straight ahead of her. She *did* agree; she'd come to a decision about it. She *would* sleep with him. Maybe not right away, but when they felt more comfortable with each other. She'd do anything she could to make the marriage work. "But," she went on, "I have a stipulation of my own."

"All right, what is it?"

"A real wedding."

He went stock-still. "You want a wedding?"

"Yes. One that's more than a five-minute civil ceremony."

"So, what exactly do you want?"

"I want a minister to perform the wedding."

"All right. But I don't know any ministers."

"I'll find one." She could tell he wasn't thrilled with her request; nevertheless he was willing to agree to her terms, just as she'd agreed to his.

"Okay." He glanced at her. "Can I drive again now?"

"No." She had to tell him about Daniel; he deserved to know that much. But she found it excruciatingly difficult.

"No?"

"I have to tell you something." She clenched both hands. "My first marriage wasn't a good one."

"So I gather."

"You know about Daniel? The boys told you?" It made sense when she thought about it. The boys had probably told him. That was fine. She wanted him to understand her fears—that her inability to judge character had scared her to the point of being afraid to marry again.

"Yes," he said. Then, "What were they supposed to tell me?"

They hadn't. Molly stared out the side window. "He's...in prison."

Sam was silent so long she wondered if he'd heard her. "What's he in for?"

"Fraud. He cheated a lot of people out of their retirement income. Especially older people. Pensioners."

"Bastard." Sam grimaced. "What's his sentence?"

"He got twenty years with no possibility of parole," she said. "The trial went on for weeks. People can be so cruel. They asked the boys questions. Kids taunted them."

"I'm sorry, Molly."

"Yeah, well, it's all water under the bridge now. But I thought you should know." It amazed her how much better she felt for having told him. At least it was out in the open and they could discuss it.

"Are you okay now?" he asked.

"Uh-huh." And she was. For the first time since this morning, she felt good about their decision. Not just resigned but genuinely optimistic. Perhaps, with a bit of compromise and a lot of hard work they could make a success of this marriage.

Sam did drive more sensibly after that, but he remained silent. So did she. Twice she caught Sam shifting his attention from the road to her. As they neared town, he slowed the truck down to well below the speed limit. For someone in a hurry, he suddenly seemed to have plenty of time on his hands.

He tapped his index finger against the steering wheel; she could tell he had something on his mind.

"Before we apply for the license," he began, then hesitated.

"Yes?"

"I've lived damn near thirty-six years on my own," he said, as though this was new information.

"I realize that." She didn't mention that other than a four-year marriage, she'd been on her own, too.

"I've lived a...varied life, Molly. For a long time I followed the rodeo circuit."

Although she knew that, it was the first time he'd mentioned it.

"There were plenty of women in those days, and—"

So this was confession time. Frankly Molly didn't want to hear about his groupies and all the women he'd loved. Or slept with. It would be just one more piece of baggage in a marriage that would be burdened with enough.

"Don't tell me," she said, stopping him.

He pulled his gaze off the road long enough to look at her. His brow knit in a puzzled frown. "What do you mean?"

"I don't want to hear it."

"But there're things about me you should know—things that could change your mind about this marriage business. I haven't lived the life of a saint."

"Neither have I."

He ignored that. "I'm not proud of my past, and as my wife you have a right to know what you're getting in the husband department."

"It doesn't matter."

"Some of it does," he said. The stiffness in his back and shoulders made her wonder what that might be.

"Are you healthy? Are there children you're supporting? A common-law wife?" Those were the important issues.

"Yes to the first question—I had enough blood tests in the hospital to be sure of that. And no to the others. To the best of my knowledge I've never fathered a child and I've never had a wife, common-law or otherwise, but my past—"

"Is past," she interrupted. "Confession might be good for the soul, but in this instance...I think not. Let's start with a clean slate, shall we? What's in your past has nothing to do with the future, and the same applies to me."

He was quiet for a moment. "You're sure about this?"

"Very sure." She smiled. "There's lots I want to hear about your life—your family and your childhood, your glory days in the rodeo, where you've worked since. But anything you feel guilty about, you can keep to yourself. Okay?"

He reached for her hand and squeezed it. "I intend to be a good husband, Molly. I realize these circumstances aren't the best, but if we both try, we can make this a good marriage."

Was it possible? Molly didn't have an answer to that, but she was beginning to feel real hope.

Three days later at five o'clock in the afternoon Sam stood with Molly in the office of Reverend Ackerly at Sweetgrass Baptist Church. Tom, Clay and Walt crowded around them. Sam couldn't help smiling at Walt's attempt to appear suitably solemn—as befitted a member of the wedding. He and Mrs. Ackerly had agreed to be their witnesses.

Molly wore a floor-length dress in a pretty shade of pink with big buttons and a wide belt. She wore the cameo that had once belonged to her grandmother and pearl earrings. Her auburn hair was freshly cut and curly. Sam had never seen her look so pretty and had difficulty not staring at her. Although he hadn't said anything, it pleased him that she'd wanted to make something special of this wedding. It boded well for their marriage.

What *didn't* help was that she knew nothing about his prison record. He'd tried to tell her, but had backed down when she'd insisted she didn't want to know about his past scandals. Her insistence had relieved him, because he was afraid that once she heard the truth, she'd change her mind. Not that he'd blame her. She sure wasn't getting any bargain.

Someday, he promised himself, he'd tell her about that part of his past. But not now. When the trust between them was firmly established, then and only then would he feel safe enough to reveal the darkest shadows of his own life.

Before the wedding ceremony they'd stopped at the jeweler's and purchased simple gold bands, but Sam's gaze had wandered over the diamonds. A year or two from now, when he could afford it, he'd buy Molly the diamond she deserved. Maybe by then he'd be the husband she deserved, too.

He quickly reined in his thoughts. Although they both wanted the marriage to work, fooling himself into believing this was a love match would only lead to trouble. He wasn't stupid. He knew why Molly had developed this sudden desire for a husband. She was scared and, frankly, he understood that. Especially when someone—some unknown person—was after the ranch and willing to go to just about any lengths to obtain it.

Sam didn't mean to be so distracted by these problems in the middle of his own wedding, but the worry was there. When it came time to say his vows, he had a few of his own he intended to silently add. He would protect Walt, Molly and the boys or die trying.

On the minister's instructions, he spoke his vows. His voice was strong, firm, clear. The words came directly from his heart. It'd taken him thirty-six years to marry, and he only intended to do it once.

He didn't know if what he felt for Molly was love. He did know he genuinely cared for her and her children. He knew he wanted her in his life and longed to be part of hers.

Molly repeated her vows in a voice just as strong and confident as his. Sam instinctively recognized it as bravado and admired her for it. He respected this woman for a number of reasons. Her love for her grandfather. Her courage in coming to Montana—and in marrying him. The fact that she loved her children and worked hard to be a good mother. His own mother had been a teenager when he was born, little more than a child herself. Her husband, Michael Dakota, had adopted Sam as his own son. Through the years, his stepfather hadn't played favorites among the children, and neither would Sam. If sometime in the future Tom, Clay and Molly were willing, he'd like to look into adopting her boys. He only hoped he could be as good a stepfather as his own had been.

He thought about Michael with renewed sorrow and genuine regret. He wondered about his mother and the rest of his family. He'd call or write them soon....

Then the ceremony was over, and they signed the documents, witnessed by Gramps and Mrs. Ackerly. When they finished, Gramps shook Sam's hand and said he'd have Letson draw up the paperwork on their agreement.

"What about dinner?" Gramps said as they walked out of Pastor Ackerly's study. "My treat." The old man looked pleased with himself, as well he should. Sam suspected that Walt had planned this wedding for quite some time.

"What do you say, Mrs. Dakota?" Gramps asked, smiling at Molly.

Mrs. Dakota. They'd discussed the possibility of her keeping the name Cogan, if for no other reason than it was the name she shared with the boys. Molly had declined. This was Montana, and while it was common practice for women to keep their surnames in other parts of the country, it wasn't here. Besides, she had no loyalty to Daniel or his family.

Mr. and Mrs. Sam Dakota.

Not only did Sam have a wife and two stepsons, but he was a husband now. The unencumbered life was forever behind him. And Sam was glad of it. He felt nothing but gratitude to an old man who'd had the insight to suggest this marriage—and the shrewdness to offer him the right incentive.

Gramps chose the restaurant, claiming he wanted to eat at the new steak house. Sam smiled at the way Clay eyed the dessert platter the minute they entered the place. The hostess greeted them warmly. "Congratulations, you two!" she said. "We'll be bringing you some complimentary champagne and appetizers."

"Thank you," Molly murmured, then cast Sam a puzzled look.

"How'd she know?" Sam asked once they were all seated.

Gramps cleared his throat, looking spry and happy. "I called the radio station and they announced it."

"Gramps!" Molly groaned, and Sam watched the color brighten her cheeks.

"It isn't every day my granddaughter snares herself a husband. I wanted folks to hear the news."

Actually it didn't bother Sam one bit that the town knew he'd married Molly.

"They talk about weddings on the radio?" Tom asked, shaking his head in wonder.

"Between the beef prices and the garage sales," Gramps said with a chuckle. "And after bingo."

That launched a conversation about Clay's most recent bingo success; he'd gotten to the phone fast enough this time and won himself a big five dollars.

"I suspected I'd find you in here," Ginny Dougherty called out as she made her way across the restaurant. She wore clean blue jeans and a red plaid shirt. "So how's the happy couple?"

"Married," Walt answered on their behalf. "I imagine you're looking for an invitation to join us. Damn snoopy neighbors," he grumbled.

It was all for show, Sam realized with a grin. He caught a glimpse of Molly's twinkling eyes. Every time he looked in her direction it was hard to pull his gaze away.

The waitress returned with a bottle of champagne and four glasses.

Walt peered at the label. "Where's it from?" he asked as though he was some kind of connoisseur. Sam hid a smile.

"You never could see worth a damn without your glasses," Ginny said, pulling out a chair and making herself at home. "It's domestic—from California." She took Molly's discarded menu and read through it.

"My eyesight's good enough to know you're an interfering old woman," Walt complained.

"Gramps!"

"Well, she is. No one invited her to dinner."

"I did," Molly said.

"When?"

"Just now. Please join us, Ginny. I apologize for my cantankerous ill-mannered grandfather."

"You'll do no such thing," Walt growled.

"I brought a wedding present. From Fred and me," Ginny said, changing the subject before a full-blown argument broke out, which it often did when Ginny and Walt were together. Sam used to wonder why these two fought so much, but over the months, he'd come to realize they enjoyed sparring with each other. He had to admit Walt showed more life when Ginny was around than any other time.

"A present?" Molly sounded delighted.

Sam wanted to kick himself. He should have bought Molly something. Not that he could afford much, but he should've picked out some little gift just to reassure her that he wasn't a heartless cold-blooded bastard marrying her for a piece of land.

"I figured," Ginny said, "neither Walt nor Sam would've done anything about a honeymoon."

"We couldn't afford one," Molly explained, making it sound as if they'd carefully weighed the decision. In reality, not a word had been uttered by either of them.

Once again Sam felt lacking. He hadn't been a husband more than an hour and already he'd failed Molly. Not once, but twice!

"Well, you're gonna have a honeymoon now," Ginny said, grinning sheepishly. She reached into her jeans pocket and pulled out a key. Holding it up, she let it swing a couple of times before handing it to Sam.

"What's that?" Walt asked, frowning.

"The key to a hotel room, what else? I booked the best room available, so Molly and Sam can celebrate their wedding night in *private*."

Gramps glared at his neighbor. "I wasn't planning on making a video recording of it, if that's what you're implying."

"Gramps!"

"All right, all right," he muttered, looking none too pleased.

"It was a very thoughtful thing to do," Molly said. When she realized Sam was watching her, she lowered her gaze.

Sam wondered if anyone else noticed how the tips of her ears turned as red as her hair. So she was a bit hesitant. That was fair; he had a few qualms of his own. It'd been a long stretch since he'd last made love.

Just then the waitress brought the promised platter of appetizers—tiny ones, no more than one bite each, in Sam's opinion. Things with shrimp and smoked salmon and a white substance that was apparently goat's cheese. Molly and Ginny loved them, Gramps complained about the size and what he considered odd ingredients, and the boys wolfed down a bunch, surprisingly without comment. Sam ate a couple, finding he wasn't all that hungry.

"Can I order the lobster?" Clay asked once the appetizers were gone.

"Not now," Gramps answered. "You can order it when Sam's buying, not me."

Clay closed the menu. "I don't see anything else I'd like."

"I'm sure there's something," Molly said and read

off a number of entrées Clay had apparently enjoyed in the past.

The boy repeatedly shook his head. "Can I have chocolate cake and cherry pie, instead?"

"Sure," Sam answered.

"You most certainly may not," Molly said at the same time.

Clay frowned. "Can I or can't I?"

"You'd better not," Sam answered.

"I suppose it wouldn't hurt you this one time," was Molly's response.

Again they'd spoken simultaneously.

Sam looked at her and she at him, and they both laughed. It felt good. As far as he was concerned, laughter was something this family could use.

The meal was ordered and the champagne was drunk. With great fanfare Gramps asked for a second bottle to accompany their entrées. He proposed a toast that brought tears to Molly's eyes, wishing his granddaughter and her husband a marriage as happy as his own had been.

Ginny wasn't the only one who came to offer congratulations. Twice during the meal, businessmen stopped by their table to shake Sam's hand and to offer their best wishes. The Wheaton name had been part of the Sweetgrass community for a lot of years. In other circumstances Sam might have resented the intrusions, but not now. He was being welcomed. He'd become part of the community, no longer a drifter, a man without roots. This marriage made people feel differently about him; he understood that. It meant he'd made a commitment not only to Molly but to a vision of the future. Sweetgrass was where he belonged and where he intended to stay.

A sense of well-being filled him. In one twenty-four-hour period, he'd gained a wife and family and found a home. A man couldn't ask for much more than that.

By the time they returned to the ranch it was after nine. Sam quickly changed out of his jacket, dress shirt and string tie into a comfortable pair of jeans and Western-style shirt. First thing in the morning, he'd move his things out of the small house and into Molly's bedroom upstairs in the ranch house. Molly might think she'd gotten a reprieve, but he had news for her. She was his wife and he wasn't planning to sleep alone ever again.

For their night in the hotel, Sam packed his shaving kit and little else. When he'd finished, he got the truck and went to pick up Molly. She was ready, a suitcase in her hand. Walt hugged her goodbye and she clung to him.

She lingered over both her children before walking down the porch steps to the truck, where Sam waited patiently. Her eyes shyly met his as he leaned across the seat and opened the passenger door.

In minutes they were on the road again.

Sam toyed with the idea of initiating a conversation, but there was only one subject on his mind and he didn't figure talking about it would help.

As they neared town, he slowed down so that he was driving well within the legal limit. Wouldn't Sheriff Maynard just welcome the opportunity to throw his butt in jail on his wedding night? Sam didn't plan to give him the chance.

The hotel was on the outskirts of town. The neon

sign was old, and the *V* in vacancy had burned out. Molly waited in the truck while he went inside to sign the register.

"Well, hello there," Bob Jenkins greeted him from behind the counter. "I hear congratulations are in order."

"That's right," Sam said. Although he had the key, Ginny had explained he'd need to check in before going up to the room.

"The missus put a bottle of champagne on ice for you and the new wife," Bob said.

"That's great." Although Sam figured they'd probably had enough champagne. "Thank you from us both."

"Don't worry none about neighbors, either. Business has been kinda slow lately and I'll make sure whoever checks in won't be anywhere near your room."

Sam nodded, pleased to know they'd have a lot of privacy. He signed his name with a flourish and hurried back to Molly. She was huddled against the passenger door.

He started the engine. "You aren't nervous, are you?"

"No," she said quickly. Perhaps too quickly.

"Good."

"I…I'm relieved we decided to do the intelligent thing and wait before entering into the, uh, physical aspect of this marriage."

Sam frowned, recalling no such agreement. "Wait? You and me? This is a joke, right?"

"But we agreed…I assumed we had, anyway. When we spoke in the car—the day we applied for the license… You don't actually think we're going to make love tonight, do you? We barely know each other!"

Now Sam was worried. "That's not the way I understood it."

"It isn't?"

"I told you up front that I fully expect this to be more than a business agreement, and you agreed. Not with a lot of enthusiasm, perhaps, but you did agree to become my wife in every sense of the word."

"Yes, I know—but not right away. I thought...I believed you understood that. I wanted us to become... familiar with each other first."

He clenched the steering wheel with a ferocity that whitened his knuckles.

"Molly, I want to make love to you tonight."

"No matter how I feel? You said yourself you don't love me."

"But I like you and respect you. We're attracted to each other—our kisses tell me that much. Isn't that enough?"

She took a long time answering. "No...it's not."

Eleven

Pearl wondered if wives realized how much business she enjoyed because they refused to make love with their husbands. More than one miserable man had sought her out because of his wife's recurring "headaches." As a rule a married man went to his wife first and Pearl second. She was convinced half her clientele would rather have stayed home with their wives, if only the women had been a bit more accommodating.

The man sitting at the bar was a prime example. He looked like he was about to cry in his beer. Pearl read the signs like the pro she was. The gold band on his finger told her he was married. The scenarios ran pretty much alike: husband and wife would argue and he'd leave the house, needing time away to cool down. These couples had forgotten that making up should be fun and it should happen in bed. A few of the men went to Pearl to restore their damaged egos. Some visited her on impulse. Others craved a little tenderness even if they had to pay for it. Then there were the angry men, looking for someone on whom they could take out their rage. Those were the ones Pearl avoided.

It was difficult to tell which category the cowboy at the bar fell into. She walked over to where he sat and slipped onto the stool next to him.

"Hello, there," she said in a husky provocative voice. "You're looking lonely."

He ignored her.

Pearl was accustomed to the cold shoulder, but she knew how to work her way around that. "Is there anything I can help you with?"

No response.

"Al, I'll take a bloody Mary," she called. The bartender acknowledged her order with a nod and she winked. Pearl rarely drank mixed drinks, and Al knew to make hers a virgin.

"Problems at home, cowboy?" she asked gently.

He glanced in her direction—an encouraging sign. She smiled prettily and, without being too obvious about it, made sure he got a good view of her assets. He downed his drink in short order, and Pearl noted the way his hand shook as he lowered the glass. Her guess was the argument he'd had with his wife had to do with sex. This guy was so damned hot, she could feel the heat radiating off him.

"Do you want to talk about it?" she asked, and leaned forward to suck on the colored straw.

"No."

Ever so lightly Pearl placed her long nails on his forearm. "Want to *do* something about it?"

She had his full attention now. In no hurry, she ran the tip of her tongue over her lips, cold now from the iced drink and reddened from the spicy tomato juice. The cowboy didn't seem able to stop looking at her mouth.

"Nobody can take care of you better than Pearl," she promised, and took a long exaggerated suck from the straw.

He shut his eyes.

The battle was half-won. Pearl smiled to herself.

To her surprise he slapped his money on the bar and started to leave. He hadn't taken more than two or three steps before he hesitated.

Pearl sensed that he was weakening and followed him outside. This wouldn't take long. Johns like this cowboy were ready to explode before she had a chance to remove her underwear. She considered them easy money.

"My place is right around the corner," she told him, tucking her hands in her jacket pockets.

"I'm not interested."

"Don't be so hasty. I'm good, cowboy, and I can help you forget whatever's troubling you. Come on, let Pearl make it better."

"Just how good are you, Pearl?" he asked, standing outside his truck, his hand on the door.

It wasn't a question she was often asked. Generally, all men cared about was a willing body. Any sexual finesse was lost on them.

"Good enough to satisfy you, cowboy."

He laughed once, abruptly.

She held her arms open to him. "Pearl will take care of you. Satisfaction guaranteed."

He rubbed his face with a shaking hand. "Are you good enough to satisfy a bridegroom on his wedding night?"

She'd heard some good lines in her time, but this was a new one. "Sure, honey, whatever you need. Let Pearl take the ache away. I promise to do the job a whole lot better than a couple of aspirin." She slipped her arms around his waist and moved suggestively against him, letting him feel the lush fullness of her breasts and inhale the scent of her perfume. She refused to use cheap perfume.

"Sorry. Like I said, I'm not interested." He spoke slowly, thoughtfully, and put his hands on her shoulders, gently pushing her away.

The regret and disappointment she heard in him tugged at her heart. Pearl hadn't really known she possessed a heart until Russell. Although she was grateful for everything he'd done for her, she didn't want to care or have feelings when it came to dealing with her customers. She provided a service, one devoid of emotion or sentiment. She was a businesswoman who appreciated her own value. Repeat business was her staple, and once she'd given a man a satisfactory experience, she encouraged him to set up a regular time with her, even offering a discount program. Monroe didn't know anything about that, not that he would've cared. All that concerned him was the money he collected from her and the other girls.

This cowboy had the potential to become the kind of customer she liked best. She could persuade him; she felt sure of it. She'd persuaded men like him before. Yet she hesitated. He was an emotional wreck. While she offered a temporary solution, sex with her wouldn't help him if his bride found out.

"Do you love her?" Pearl asked softly, barely knowing where the question came from.

The cowboy didn't answer right away. "I guess I

must, otherwise that skirt you're wearing would be over your head by now."

"Then go back."

He shook his head. "She doesn't want me touching her. She's not interested."

Pearl laughed. "Listen, I don't pretend to know a lot about human nature, but if she married you, trust me, she's interested."

The cowboy wanted to believe her. Pearl saw it in the fierce way his eyes held hers. "This isn't a normal marriage," he said, shaking his head.

"What marriage is?" Pearl wrapped her hand around his forearm, letting her long painted nails gently scrape the inside of his elbow. "Listen to me, cowboy, I don't care what led up to your marriage—she wants you."

"That's not what she's saying."

"I'll tell you what. You go back, and if you can't settle this with her, find me and I'll give you one on the house." Pearl had never before made that type of offer. But if his bride wasn't a born idiot, she'd appreciate the good man she'd married and count her blessings.

The cowboy looked like he was in grave danger of smiling. "You honestly think it'd help if I went back?"

"I do."

He gave a deep, shuddering sigh. "Then I will." He opened the truck and bounded inside. As the engine fired to life, he glanced at her. "Thanks."

"Not a problem." But it was. Loving Russell had changed her, and she stood at a crossroads. Either she continued on with the only life she'd ever known or she changed. Russell had repeatedly asked her to marry him. He didn't understand what she was really involved in. Nor did he understand that if they were seen together, he'd be in danger. So would she. He continually told her how smart she was, but it wasn't true. If she was even half as smart as he believed, she'd find a way to marry the only man she'd ever loved.

The ice cooling the champagne had long since melted. Molly sat on the edge of the bed, more miserable than she could remember being since the judge had declared her divorce from Daniel final. A second marriage was quite possibly the only thing that could drag her this low.

For the past few days she'd actually looked forward to marrying Sam, but this evening, as the time for their so-called honeymoon arrived, she'd started to worry. Being alone in a hotel room hadn't been part of the plan. Not *her* plan, anyway. She would have preferred their first night together to be in the comfort and familiarity of the ranch. But then Ginny and Fred had given them this honeymoon night, and Molly didn't have the heart to disappoint them.

The problem was with herself, Molly realized, and her fear of letting anyone get close, even the man she'd married just hours before. Intimacy terrified her, and because she'd been afraid, because the thought of allowing Sam to touch her and hold her had frightened her, she'd sent him away.

Panic had set in when they reached the hotel. Sam had been quick to remind her of her promise to him, and an argument had immediately ensued. Molly couldn't remember everything she'd said, but whatever it was, she regretted it. Sam had dropped her off and driven away, tires squealing. And so Molly had been left to fret and wonder where he was and what he was doing.

With her arms folded around her middle, she paced the floor, feeling wretched and defeated.

For a while she convinced herself she didn't even *want* to know where he'd gone.

Like hell she didn't. This was her wedding night, and she was minus a bridegroom. Minus her pride and dignity. Every doubt she'd harbored after divorcing Daniel returned full force. He'd left her for someone else and claimed she'd driven him away. She'd protested the accusation loud and long, yet she was driving her second husband away in what appeared to be record time. It'd taken all of four years for Daniel to leave her and less than four hours for Sam to walk out.

Although it was useless to try to sleep, she made the effort, slipping between the cool sheets and hugging a pillow to her breast. The shadows from the broken neon light danced against the wall, making her desolate, reminding her what a failure she was.

She must have fallen asleep because her eyes flew open when she heard Sam. He inserted the key into the lock, opened the door and walked silently into the room. A flood of relief and gratitude washed over her. It was all she could do to keep from scrambling out of bed, throwing herself in his arms and begging his forgiveness. Nothing had gone the way she'd planned. Instead of talking about her fears, instead of reasoning everything out, she'd become defensive and unrealistic.

Sam stood uncertainly in the middle of the dark room.

"Sam," she whispered, and sat up in bed.

"Yeah?"

Her chest hurt from holding her breath. "I'm sorry."

She heard his sigh. "Me, too."

"I don't blame you for leaving…" She let the rest fade, fearing her emotion would embarrass them both.

Sam crossed the room and sat on the bed. "I'm afraid you got the short end of the stick in the husband department, Molly. I don't blame you for——"

"It isn't me who's been cheated, it's you."

He turned and stared at her in the darkness. The only light came from the neon sign outside, but it was enough to see the puzzled frown on his face.

Molly owed him the truth. "I'm afraid."

"Of what?"

It hurt to voice her doubts aloud, to confess her flaws, knowing that his rejection now would devastate her. "Of getting hurt again. Of being vulnerable—so many things. I don't think I realized myself how frightened I was until we arrived at the hotel."

"Do you still feel that way?"

"Yes, but not as much."

He lifted his hand as if to touch her face, then hesitated. "Are you willing to try? You can set the pace. If you want to stop, we can."

"Are you willing to give me a second chance?" she asked.

"More than willing," he assured her, leaning forward to gently press his mouth to hers.

Molly's eyes fluttered closed and she slid her hands against his wide shoulders. This wasn't Daniel, she reminded herself, but Sam. He'd married her, wanted her as his wife, needed her.

When they kissed again, it was Molly who initiated the contact. She knelt on the bed and wrapped her arms around his neck. This was good. Better than good. They were both quiet when the kiss ended.

Sam chuckled and got to his feet, then began to un-
snap his shirt with hurried movements. "She was right."

"Who?"

"I met someone tonight at Willie's place."

"The tavern?"

"Yeah. First time I've been there since the fight. I
guess that tells you how bad I was feeling. Anyway,
I talked to this woman for a bit and she urged me to
come back."

Whoever the woman was, Molly owed her a debt
of gratitude.

Sam removed his boots, which landed with a thump
on the floor. "I need you, Molly. I don't claim to be any
prize as a husband, but I'll try." He pulled off his jeans
and got beneath the covers.

"It's…it's been a long time for me, Sam."

"It has been for me, too." He moved closer to her.
"You're wearing far too many clothes for a bride on her
wedding night."

Molly rested her head on his bare shoulder and
placed her hand on his lean hard chest. She could feel
his heart hammering against her palm. "You think so?"

"I know so." He kissed her with a pent-up hunger
that nearly devoured her. Molly's response was immediate and just as heated, surprising even her. The kiss
was wild and wonderful, and their hands moved frantically, touching, arousing, exciting.

Molly let her fingers creep up his chest, enjoying
the smooth feel of his skin, appreciating the man in her
arms. Nothing mattered right now except their fierce
physical craving for each other.

Molly linked her fingers behind his neck and drew
his mouth to hers. The kisses that followed were hot

and urgent. When he positioned himself above her, she shifted her body to accommodate his. Raising her head from the pillow, Molly kissed him, barely allowing their lips to touch. The kiss was more breath than contact.

"Molly." He said her name in a pain-filled groan, then caught her hips, holding her still against the mattress. Sweat glistened on his upper lip and forehead.

Panting beneath him, her arms stretched out at her sides, Molly dragged a harsh breath through her lungs. She lifted her head just enough to touch the tight cords in his neck with her tongue. He tasted of salt and man and smelled faintly of roses.

He made love to her, filled her body with his own, until they reached a wild exhaustive crescendo that left her utterly drained.

There was no sound but their breathing, harsh and rapid. Neither spoke. For her part Molly felt incapable of saying a single word. Sam's breathing steadied first and he smiled at her, then spread soft kisses over her face.

"How do you feel?" he whispered, holding her in the crook of his arm.

"Wonderful."

Sam kissed the crown of her head. "Me, too."

"I want to be a good wife, Sam...I know I started this night off all wrong, and I regret—"

He silenced her with a finger to her lips. "Don't apologize. It isn't necessary. Just promise me that from now on we'll talk everything out. It's the only chance we have. This marriage can be a good one if we're both willing to work at it."

She nodded. "I promise."

Happier than she could remember being in a very long while, Molly hugged him close. If they shared nothing more than incredible sex in this marriage, it would be enough.

She'd been in love once and the love hadn't even lasted the length of her marriage. She was afraid to count on it again. She cared for Sam, respected him, needed him. But loving him would be dangerous. Loving him meant risking more than she could afford to lose. She had too much at stake to let her heart get in the way.

This unbridled feeling of happiness couldn't last. Molly was sure of it. The two weeks following her wedding were the best days of her life. Her boys were content. Each had adjusted in his own way to the change from their lives in California to life here in Montana. Tom spent his days riding with Sam, learning all he could about horses and ranching. He displayed a natural talent that Sam fostered and encouraged. Sam's approval and the attention he paid Tom did wonders for the boy's self-esteem; the changes in him were dramatic. In two months he'd gone from a moody adolescent to a hardworking responsible young man.

Clay stuck close to the ranch house with Molly and Gramps. Her younger son worked countless hours training Bullwinkle. The boy and his puppy were inseparable. Sometimes Clay helped Molly in the garden or with work around the house.

Clay also spent a lot of time with Gramps playing cribbage. Or he'd sit contentedly on the porch with the old man, whittling away at his block of wood, inordinately proud of his masterpiece. He and Gramps had grown very close.

Gramps seemed happy, too—although his health

had declined to the point that he spent most of the day in his chair or listening to the radio. It seemed he had found serenity, a quiet peace.

Molly saw her husband off each morning, then counted the hours until he returned. It wasn't that she didn't keep busy; with the house and the garden she had more than enough to fill her days. Every evening she'd wait for him. He and Tom would ride in, exhausted, and the three of them would walk to the barn. Any outward display of affection between husband and wife was reserved for the privacy of their bedroom.

In two weeks' time their eagerness for each other hadn't dissipated. Always, after they made love, he held her in his arms and they talked. He told her about his years with the rodeo and the accident that had cost him his career. She kissed his scars and her eyes filled with tears at the pain each one must have caused him.

One such night she asked Sam, "Are you happy?"

He went very still at the question and she wondered if she'd unwittingly stepped over the line of what they could openly discuss. Perhaps he thought she was asking him to declare his love for her. She wasn't. If he did love her, he'd tell her in his own good time.

"Yes, I'm happy."

It wasn't the words but his voice. The way he said it. With honesty, looking directly into her eyes. With gratitude, as if she, and only she, had done this. Made him happy.

"I am, too," she whispered.

"No regrets?"

She slid her fingers through the dusting of dark curly hair on his chest. "Not recently," she teased, and was rewarded with a playful swat on the backside.

As she occasionally did, she responded in French, telling him that she'd like to have another child some day. With him.

"Are you going to tell me what you just said?"

"Oh, sometime."

"I understood one word."

"My, my, and what would that be?"

"Baby." His eyes were serious. "Molly, is there a possibility you could be…"

"Don't worry," she assured him. With money tight and the problems around the ranch still unsolved, no one needed to tell her that now wasn't the best time to have a child. Later, though, she'd bring up the subject again.

It was midnight before Molly fell asleep. She wasn't sure what woke her two hours later. The full moon shone like a beacon into the bedroom. Sitting up, she experienced the oddest sensation that something wasn't right.

After a moment, Sam, too, stirred and sat up.

"What is it?" he asked, his voice groggy with sleep.

She shrugged. "I don't know."

"Did you hear something?"

"No. It's just…" She couldn't put it into words.

Sam sat on the edge of the bed and reached for his pants.

Molly threw on her housecoat and followed him downstairs. The first thing she noticed was that the front door was open.

On the hottest days of summer Gramps usually left it open to allow a breeze between his bedroom and the living room. But the evening had been cool with the promise of a rainstorm. The winds had come and then just as quickly shifted north.

As she went to close the door she saw him. Gramps had fallen asleep in his rocking chair. Sam stepped into the kitchen and turned off the light, then hurried through the house to check the other doors.

"Gramps," Molly said softly, sitting in the rocker beside him. "Wake up. It's time to go inside."

He looked so peaceful. Chatting with him, she waited for Sam's return so her husband could help her guide Gramps to his bedroom.

"I love Sam. You knew I would, didn't you?" She rocked contentedly and glanced up at the full moon, now obscured by clouds. "You were so right."

She glanced over at Gramps and could have sworn she saw him smile in his sleep.

"Molly?" Sam called.

"Out here," she said softly. "Gramps fell asleep on the porch."

Sam joined her and gently shook Gramps, trying to wake him. After a moment he turned away and clutched one of the porch railings.

"Sam?"

He turned back and knelt in front of her, taking both her hands in his. "Molly." He kissed her fingertips and held her hands against his lips. "My love. Gramps isn't asleep. I'm afraid he's gone."

Twelve

Molly didn't sleep the rest of the night. She didn't even try. Instead, she sat on the porch holding the cameo Gramps had given her. His Molly's cameo. The one she'd worn at her own wedding. It seemed so unfair that he should die now. Her mind filled with a thousand regrets, begrudging every day she'd wasted before moving to Montana. If only she'd known sooner. The words echoed in her heart. *If only, if only, if only...* But her tears hadn't come yet.

To Molly's gratitude, Sam made the necessary phone calls as soon as the day began to lighten. The coroner was the first to arrive. He'd spoken briefly to Sam and asked her a couple of questions, but afterward she didn't remember either the questions or her responses. Later Mr. Farley from Ross Memorial stopped by to discuss the burial. Gramps had made his preferences clear in a letter he'd mailed to Ross Memorial a few months earlier. Mr. Farley had brought it with him. Gramps had stated that he didn't want money wasted on a funeral, and as for a service, if there was to be one, he wanted it private. Just his immediate family. Then, like an afterthought, he'd granted permission for Ginny to attend if she wanted, but no one else.

Once again Molly was glad to let Sam handle things. When the burial had been arranged, Mr. Farley left with the promise that he'd be in touch shortly.

By far the most difficult task of the day was telling the boys. It astonished Molly that they'd both slept through the commotion that followed her discovery. Rather than wake Tom and Clay, she'd let them sleep. In the morning Clay came downstairs first, took one look at her and knew something was terribly wrong.

"What's going on?" he asked, standing in the middle of the kitchen, socks and sneakers dangling from one hand.

"It's Gramps," Molly said gently. "I'm afraid he's gone. He died last night."

Clay's face showed shock and disbelief. "He *can't* be dead!" her son insisted. "He was all right when I went to bed. We were on the porch together, and he was fine then."

Molly bit her lower lip to keep it from trembling. "I'm sorry, sweetheart, but it's true."

"It can't be!" Clay screamed. "Make her tell me it isn't true," he cried, turning to Sam. "He can't be—he told me about D day and Normandy and the Battle of the Bulge. He lived through the war." Clay's face tightened with desire as he gazed at Sam, begging him to tell a different truth.

"I'm sorry, son." Sam shook his head.

With that Clay burst into tears and buried his face against Molly, sobbing so hard his entire body shook. She wrapped her arms around his thin shoulders, blinking back her own burning tears as the emotion seared through her, as fresh and painful as the moment Sam first told her.

"What's wrong?" Tom asked as he stepped into the kitchen. Sleep blurred his eyes, and his hair was uncombed and wild-looking. He paused, glancing from his brother to Sam and then her, his eyes filled with question.

Molly told him.

Once he realized Gramps was dead, Tom exploded out of the house, leaving the screen door to slam in his wake. He was gone for more than an hour, and when he returned he joined Molly on the porch, silently slipping into the empty rocker at her side. She longed for words to ease his pain, but could find none, so she remained quiet. It didn't matter. She knew he just needed to be close to her.

After about fifteen minutes he stood, his eyes red and puffy. Voice breaking, he said, "I was *proud* to be related to a man like Gramps."

Molly wasn't sure how Tom felt about being embraced just then, but she pretended not to remember that he was too cool to be hugged by his mother. She held out her arms to him and he bent down to hug her, hard. When he left, she watched him rub his forearm across his eyes. Molly cried then, uncontrollably. Cried till she thought she had no tears left.

She sat on the porch all day. Without asking, Sam brought her food and coffee every few hours. She drank the coffee but barely ate. Activity continued around her. Sam kept the boys occupied, granting her the opportunity to seek her own solace. By evening she'd found a certain peace. An acceptance of sorts.

She clung to that and kept it close to her heart, wanting to celebrate Gramps's life, not concentrate on his death. She refused to get swallowed up in the grief of his passing. It was what he would have wanted, and knowing that helped soothe the terrible ache of his loss.

Gramps had never been religious, but he was a man of faith. Many an evening, he'd sat on this very porch with his worn Bible spread open in his lap, reading from the book of Psalms.

One night, shortly after the incident of the downed fence, Molly had found Gramps with his Bible. He'd looked up. "King David was a man who knew trouble," he'd told her. "Real trouble, and he said we aren't to lean unto our own understanding."

Molly wasn't sure what that meant, but it was the only time she could remember him commenting on anything the Bible had to say.

That night at dinnertime—their first at the ranch without Gramps—Molly made an effort to put a meal on the table. Her own appetite was still nonexistent. Picking fresh greens from the garden, she made a huge taco salad and set it in the middle of the table, instructing the boys to help themselves.

"Aren't you going to eat, Mom?" Clay asked.

"I will later when Sam returns," she said, but she wouldn't. Couldn't. Everything hurt just then. Her head. Her heart. Even her stomach.

Sam had run into town, for what she couldn't remember now. In fact, she could remember almost nothing of what had happened that day. Knowing Gramps's death was inevitable, Molly had prepared herself for it. Or so she'd believed. But now that the reality of it was upon her, she realized that it was impossible to ever feel ready for death, the death of someone you loved.

Grief still came unabated. No matter how certain or even welcomed death might be, it was always a shock.

"You okay, Mom?" Tom asked, joining her on the porch after the sun had set. He sat on the top step, turning so he could study her. Clay came with him, silent and sullen, and held the puppy in his lap. Boris and Natasha curled up on the rug outside the door as if they, too, had come to give their farewells to Gramps.

She nodded. "I'd hoped we'd have more time with him."

"Me, too," Tom said.

"I wish you both could have known him better. He was a wonderful man." It hurt to talk and her fingers clenched and unclenched on the wooden chair arms.

"I'm glad for the time we had."

Her fourteen-year-old son's wisdom touched her heart. Tom focused on what he could be grateful for, instead of all he'd lost. He, too, had achieved a hard-won acceptance. He counted his blessings.

"He taught me to whittle and I can play cribbage now," Clay said.

Gramps had taught her the same things when she was about the same age.

"Last night he talked more about the war," Tom told her. "He told us about men dying even before they made it to land, their bodies bloating in the water."

Molly's hand reached for the cameo and gripped it hard. He'd called it his good-luck charm. He'd carried the cameo into battle with him, taking a small tangible piece of the love he shared with his wife. For protection. As a token of faith in the future.

"He talked quite a bit about dying and how it was nothing to fear," Tom added, as if remembering this for the first time. "He said that with some folks death can be a friend."

"A friend?" Molly knew what he meant but had never heard such talk from her grandfather.

"For those who'd made their peace with God," Clay said. "That's what he said. I think Gramps was ready."

"He talked about a lot of things last night," Tom said. "But mainly it was about the war and about your dad and his Molly."

The tears came again, unwanted. Molly hadn't meant to cry, not in front of her sons. She didn't want to upset them further.

"Mom…"

"I know, honey, I'm sorry. I can't seem to stop. I'm going to miss him so much." At least she wasn't alone anymore. At first Gramps's suggestion that she marry Sam had seemed an interference, an insult, but she knew this terrible void inside her would be ten times deeper if it wasn't for her husband. She accepted that Gramps was gone, but she would always miss him.

She held a handkerchief to her eyes. So many tears had been shed that her eyes ached and her nose was red and sore from blowing.

"I liked him," Clay said quietly. "He might have been old, but he knew a lot of stuff and he never treated me like a kid. Even when I made mistakes in cribbage, he never made me think I was dumb."

The burial service was held three days later. Afterward Sam, Molly and the boys stood at one side of the grave and Ginny stood across from them as the casket was lowered into the ground. The minister who'd married her and Sam said a prayer, then briefly hugged

Molly and exchanged handshakes with Sam and the boys. Molly lingered, as did Ginny Dougherty, who repeatedly dabbed a tissue to her eyes.

"I'm gonna miss that crotchety old coot," Ginny said, and blew her nose loudly.

"We'll all miss him," Sam said. His arm rested across Molly's back, and she was grateful for his comfort and support. Molly didn't know what she would have done without him these past few days. He'd given her strength.

"We were neighbors for thirty years," Ginny continued, weeping softly now. "Walt and Molly stood with me when I buried Hank." She rubbed her eyes with one hand and took a couple of moments to compose herself. "Walt and me might not have agreed on a lot of things, but I knew if I ever needed a helping hand, he'd be there."

Ginny's tears came in earnest then, and she raised both hands to her face. "Damn, but I'm gonna miss him."

Molly stepped away from Sam and put her arms around the other woman. "It's going to be mighty lonely without Gramps around," she said, "especially with the boys starting school next week. Do you think you could stop by for tea one day? It'd be good to have a friend."

Ginny nodded and hugged Molly fiercely. "I never had children, you know. If I had, I would've wanted a daughter like you."

Molly savored the compliment. The older woman was a lot like Gramps—just as ornery and just as honest. And just as lonely.

"Would you like to come back to the ranch with us for dinner?" Molly asked.

Ginny shook her head. "No thanks, I've got to get back. Fred's on his own." She kissed Molly's cheek, then hurried to her truck, parked near the cemetery entrance.

As they left the graveyard, Molly realized that Ginny had been sweet on Gramps. She should've guessed it earlier. All the years they'd lived next to each other, watched out for each other, fought, argued and battled. And loved. Silently. Without ever saying a word to each other. Without ever a touch. They'd been the best of friends and the best of enemies.

The shadow-filled alley behind Willie's was deserted now that the tavern had closed for the night. Monroe sat in his car with the lights off and waited for Lance to show. He didn't trust his fellow Loyalist and considered him a loose cannon. In the past couple of months, Lance had grown even more unpredictable, impatient. It grated on Monroe's nerves. He wanted Lance gone, but Burns wouldn't hear of it.

The car door opened and Lance climbed into the front seat.

"You're late," Munroe muttered. He glanced at his watch, letting the man know he begrudged every one of those five minutes.

Not only was Lance out of uniform, he'd grown lazy. Any discipline had vanished from his personal hygiene and his attitude. His face bristled with a two-day beard and his fatigues were rank with body odor. His boots were unpolished, one of the laces broken. Monroe suspected he'd snuck off to attend another rodeo.

"I take it the old man's dead and buried?" Lance said.

"The service was this afternoon," Monroe confirmed.

"Did that lawyer cousin of yours convince his grand-daughter to sell yet?"

Monroe wished to hell it was that easy. "Unfortunately, no, and now that she's married Dakota, we're forced to tighten the screws."

"You got any ideas?"

This was supposed to be Lance's area of expertise. The Loyalists had imported him from Idaho, reasoning that it was better if an outsider handled the dirty work, sparing Monroe any hint of suspicion. Other than to make contact with Monroe, Lance wasn't supposed to venture into town. The less seen of him the better. Only, he'd grown bored living in his wilderness camp and started hanging out with another Loyalist, playing pool and getting drunk.

"I thought you were supposed to be the idea man," Monroe snapped.

"I am. All I need to know is how far you want me to go."

Monroe gritted his teeth, trying to control his irritation. "Do what you have to do and don't bother me with the details, understand? And stay out of town."

"No need to lose your cool," Lance muttered, opening the car door.

The interior light came on, illuminating a section of the alleyway. Suddenly Monroe caught a movement out of the corner of his eye and jerked his head around. It took him a moment to locate the source.

Pearl. She'd crouched down behind the garbage dump in an attempt to hide. He wondered what she'd been doing there, but it went without saying that she was up to no damn good. The bitch needed to be taught a lesson. He'd make sure she kept her nose out of his business from now on. Before the night was over she'd be begging his forgiveness; anticipating that scene excited him. He hadn't seen near enough of Pearl lately, and obviously she'd forgotten some of the lessons he'd given her earlier. This was the type of work he relished best—putting a woman in her place. By the time he was through with her, she wouldn't be sneaking around and listening in on his conversations anymore.

"Who did this to you?" Russell demanded, studying Pearl's battered face. Fierce anger consumed him until he barely recognized the sound of his own voice. By God, whoever beat her would pay for this. She sat before him with both eyes swollen so badly he wondered how she could see out of them. The corner of her mouth had a jagged cut.

"Russell—"

"Tell me, dammit! I want to know." He paced her living room, too furious to sit still.

"It's not so bad," she said in an obvious effort to brush off his concern. It didn't work.

"Who?" he shouted again, his hands in tight fists at his sides. Russell had never been a violent man, but the rage he experienced now led him to believe that he was capable of brutality. Capable of anything.

Pearl lowered her head. "Please, it isn't important."

"It is to me."

He'd known something was wrong when she didn't show up at the cabin Sunday morning. He'd waited an hour and then gone searching for her, assuming her car must have broken down along the way. The cabin was a good fifty miles out of town, and on that isolated road, she could wait hours before someone came by. But he didn't find her, nor did he see her rattletrap of a car.

When he returned to the cabin, the message light was flashing on his answering machine. It was Pearl, telling him she wouldn't be able to come that Sunday and probably not the next one, either. Her voice had sounded odd, and after playing the message a second time, he was sure something was wrong.

Unconcerned about his reputation, he drove directly to Pearl's house. She hadn't wanted to let him in and did so only after he raised a fuss loud enough to call attention to his being there. Reluctantly she unlatched the door and he'd found her beaten and bloody.

"Russell, please, just go," Pearl said now. "I'll be fine, and in a couple of weeks, you won't even know I was hurt. I'll…we can continue just like before. Okay?" She tried to usher him to the door, but he'd have none of it. Again and again he'd asked her to marry him, and each time she'd refused. He couldn't understand it, couldn't fathom that she would choose this kind of life over the love they shared.

"I'm not leaving until we have this out," he insisted.

He could see that talking was painful for her. And her bruised swollen eyes—he could hardly stand looking at them. By all that was right she should be in a doctor's office, perhaps even a hospital.

"Please…"

"I can't pretend this didn't happen," Russell said, and continued his pacing. He rammed his fingers through his hair hard enough to tug painfully at the roots.

"Please…you're making me dizzy. Sit down." She gestured toward the sofa.

He sagged onto the ottoman, but couldn't look at

her. Every time he did his stomach churned and he felt like vomiting.

She held a washcloth to the edge of her mouth, dabbing gingerly at the cut. "There's no reason to carry on like this," she said, dismissing her own pain. "These things happen now and then. It isn't pleasant, it isn't fun, but it's a fact of life. An occupational hazard, so to speak. I'm sorry it upsets you—I wish you hadn't come."

She moved slightly, and her robe opened, exposing ugly bruises high on her shoulders. Dangerously close to her throat. It was almost as if her client had attempted to strangle her.

Russell's blood ran cold at the thought.

He loved her more than he'd realized. For months he'd pushed the reality of her occupation from his mind. It was easier to ignore the way she made her living than to face it, especially since Pearl steadfastly refused to discuss it. Instead, he'd concentrated on the time they shared every Sunday. But he couldn't ignore the truth any longer.

Drawing in a ragged breath, he looked at her, looked hard at the bruises and other injuries. "We're getting married." He wasn't asking this time, he was telling her. He wasn't going to let Pearl put her life on the line again.

Her first reaction was to physically pull away. Her back went against the cushion, and slowly, one movement at a time, she seemed to become smaller and smaller, shrinking into herself. First she tucked her bare feet beneath her and drew her robe together, holding it closed. Then she wrapped her free arm about her waist.

"Did you hear me?" Russell asked.

She turned her head away.

"Well?" He watched her, waiting, wondering. Hoping.

When she did speak, her voice was almost inaudible. "Men like you don't marry women like me."

"*I* do."

Her chin came up slightly and her words gained conviction. "Let me put it another way, then. Women like me don't marry, period."

"What is this? A rule of some kind?"

She refused to answer.

The silence seemed to last forever, but when she spoke again, he sensed a new resolve in her. The woman could be stubborn, he'd say that for her. "We've already been through this," she finally said. "I can't... I'm so sorry, but it just isn't possible."

"Why isn't it? Look at yourself, Pearl! Your face has been beaten to a pulp. You can't ask me to sit by and do nothing. If you won't tell me who hurt you, then at least let me offer you the protection of my name."

She gave him a small crooked smile and grimaced at the pain it caused her. Russell's gut tightened and the bile rose in his throat as he witnessed her discomfort. Feeling the other person's pain—this was what love did.

Slowly she shook her head. "I can't."

His frustration was nearly overwhelming. "Then explain it to me. At least help me understand. I love you and you love me. Marriage is what happens when people feel about each other the way we do."

"In case you haven't noticed, I'm not like other women." She looked him straight in the eye, and it was the hard-edged look of the woman he'd met all those months ago. "I'm a whore."

He could think of only one way to reach her, to get her to listen to reason, to trust him. With the truth. "I love you, Pearl—you know that. I have for months. I live for Sundays when I know I'll be spending time with you. You're all I think about. Okay, you're right, you're not like other women, but I don't *care.* I don't want anyone but you."

She glanced away and he knew from the way her eyes glazed with tears that his words had touched her. She stiffened her shoulders and smiled slightly. "I'm afraid you've confused great sex with love, Russell."

"We met for weeks before we ever slept together," he reminded her. He knelt down in front of her and reached for her hand. She tried to snatch it away, and it was then that he noticed the large welt on her wrist. He grabbed her other hand and saw a similar welt. The son of a bitch had tied her up.

It hurt him to look at her injuries. "Who did this to you?" he begged again. He experienced the highly embarrassing urge to weep. She must have heard it in his voice, because she took hold of his shoulder and squeezed hard.

"Listen to me, please, and hear me this time. *It doesn't matter.*"

"I'm calling the sheriff."

Pearl laughed out loud. "Oh, please! Do you think he gives a damn about a hooker with an overfriendly john?" she asked mockingly.

Russell glared at the ceiling and forcefully expelled his breath. "I care. I can't do this. I can't sit back and see this happen to you. I can't love you like I do and not worry about the fact that you're being abused. I've looked the other way for too long."

"Just forget about this, please. I'm all right. Really." Her eyes pleaded with him to drop his concern, along with his marriage proposal. In the past Russell had given in to her pleadings, but no more. Not when her life was at stake. Not when all she had to do was agree to marry him and let him love and protect her.

"I can't forget." He turned over her hand and kissed the inside of her wrist. The welt was red and ugly, and he felt the heat of it against his lips.

Pearl closed her eyes. "Please," she begged.

"I've never asked another woman to share my life. I'm asking you. I can understand that it might be uncomfortable for us in Sweetgrass. We'll move, and I'll set up a practice in another state. We'll start over, just the two of us."

She shook her head and seemed about to weep. "No. It just isn't possible."

"You can't make me believe this is the kind of life you want. I know better."

She raised her hand to her face, apparently forgetting that her eyes were bruised, and winced at the flash of unexpected pain. "This is something men have never been able to understand about women like me," she said in a half whisper. "I love what I do."

He knew she was lying.

"You might disagree," she went on, "but I provide a valuable service, and if it gets a little rough occasionally—well, that just comes with the territory. I take the beatings, along with the bonuses. You, Russell, were an unexpected bonus, so you see it all evens out in the end."

"I don't want to listen to any more of this." Especially

when he knew she was lying. They were too close, too intimate, for him not to recognize that.

She clamped her hand around his wrist. Her grip was hard and relentless. "Listen, and listen carefully, because what you fail to understand, what most men like you can't accept, is that I do this by choice."

Russell yanked his wrist free of her grasp and bolted upright, angered by her lies and her attitude.

"I have a specialty, you know—then again perhaps you don't." She moistened her lips. "A lot of women are averse to it, but—"

"I've heard all about your specialty," Russell interrupted between clenched teeth.

She laughed as if his anger amused her. "You do? That surprises me because you've never asked for it."

"It's different with us."

"Is it? Are you completely convinced of that, or is there a tiny shred of doubt?"

"Pearl, this tactic isn't going to work. No matter how crude you are, it isn't going to convince me that you don't love me. I know how you feel."

"Because I gave you my body gratis," she said, and laughed. "It isn't often a girl like me gets to laze away a Sunday afternoon in a private getaway. Even a call girl needs time to breathe once in a while, and if all it costs is a freebie, then why not? You're pleasant company, and you were nice enough to teach me to read. You can't blame me if you got a little too…involved, can you? A girl like me is—"

"Stop!" he shouted. "Don't cheapen what we shared."

"Then don't make more of it than it was!" she snapped back.

His skin felt clammy even as a chill raced through

his blood. He had to get away. Escape. Otherwise he was in danger of making an even bigger fool of himself. Not looking at her, he headed for the door.

"Someday you'll thank me for this," she whispered.

He could hear the regret in her words. It was enough to make him pause. Enough to give him hope. Frozen, he stood with his hand grasping her doorknob, his back to her.

"I learned my lesson with you," she called, her voice filled with pain. "I'm not handing out any more freebies."

Russell jerked open the door and walked out.

He managed to stay away from Pearl for all of two weeks, hoping each day that she'd have a change of heart, that she'd call him. She didn't. He reviewed their conversation over and over, and while he was certain she'd lied, her words had left ugly scars.

For the first time he doubted their love, and as the days passed and she didn't call him, those doubts grew into a feeling of bitterness. By the end of the second week he'd convinced himself that Pearl had played him for the fool he was. She couldn't possibly hold any tenderness for him and stay away this long.

Soon his pain turned to anger. Each morning when he gazed at his reflection in the mirror, he called himself a fool. His anger fed on itself and spread, became even larger.

When he could tolerate it no longer, he had his cousin set the appointment for him—the same way he had that first time. He was prompt, ringing her doorbell at precisely the arranged hour.

It did his ego good to see the surprise in her eyes

when she opened the door. "Don't worry, I'm not going to make trouble with your john," he muttered, "because we're one and the same."

Her eyes were only a little puffy now and the bruises had faded. The gash on her lip had healed or, if it hadn't, was cleverly disguised with bright lipstick. She wore black hose and a sexy leather skirt that rode halfway up her thighs. The spike heels added a good four inches to her height. Her breasts spilled out of the halter top, which had to be two sizes too small.

She looked as if she wasn't sure what to do, as if the shock was too much for her.

"I decided to take you up on your offer."

She cast him a puzzled glance. "Offer?"

"I'm here for your specialty," he announced.

Her eyes widened as though he'd slapped her. A stunned silence followed his words.

"I—"

He pulled out his wallet and extracted a one-hundred-dollar bill. "My money's good, isn't it?" He'd practiced what he'd wanted to say for days, but now that the time had come, he realized he couldn't do it, couldn't humiliate and degrade her, because in doing so, he degraded himself.

He stuffed the bill back into his wallet. "Forget it," he whispered.

"Russell..."

Not wanting to hear what she had to say, he pushed past her and escaped, accompanied by the sound of her sobs.

Cleaning out Gramps's bedroom was like reliving the night of his death. Molly knew she had to do it; it was part of coping with grief. And she and Sam had decided to move into Gramps's downstairs bedroom; somehow the prospect was a comforting one.

Each drawer Molly opened revealed more evidence of his love for her and the children. She discovered her letters tucked away inside books and shirt pockets, re-read so many times the edges had frayed.

Pictures of her and of Tom and Clay in various stages of their childhood were all over his room. He'd saved everything she'd ever mailed him. Every photo, every note, every drawing the boys had made. But it was reading his journal that tore her apart.

From the day his Molly had been laid to rest, he'd written his journal as a series of letters to his dead wife. He'd poured out his heart, described his loneliness, his hopes and his doubts. He wrote about how much he loved Molly and her boys, and his fear that his love might suffocate her if she decided to live with him. He spelled out his pain when she decided to stay in California.

Sitting on the edge of the bed, she started to weep and couldn't seem to stop. She wept over the wasted years, when all she'd done was write, instead of making the effort to visit. Not once had he chastised her. Not once had he asked her to come. He'd loved her unselfishly, completely. She broke into renewed sobbing as she realized that his run-down ranch and his one granddaughter were all he had to show for seventy-six years of living. His granddaughter and her sons.

"Mom." Tom walked into the bedroom.

She shook her head, telling him without words that she needed to be alone.

"Are you all right?"

She covered her mouth with her hand and nodded.

Tom hesitated, then took off at a run, hollering, "Sam! Sam, come quick!"

Knowing that her husband would be equally unnerved by this sudden attack of emotion, Molly made a concerted effort to curtail her sobs—and discovered it was impossible.

"She's gonna be sick if she doesn't stop crying," Tom said when Sam came rushing in through the living room.

Sam entered the bedroom slowly. "She'll be all right," he said as he sat down next to Molly. He gathered her in his arms, and she rested her face against his shoulder, letting him absorb her pain and loss.

"It's all right, honey, let it out." Gently he patted her back. "You've been holding it inside for two weeks now. Have a good cry."

Tom looked worried. "Should I get her something?"

"Like what?" Sam asked.

"I don't know. Tissue? Aspirin? If she doesn't stop soon, you're gonna need a dry shirt."

"Will you two kindly shut up?" Molly said through her tears.

"Gramps wouldn't want you to cry like this, Mom."

"Then he shouldn't have left his journal for me to read," she blubbered, scrubbing her cheeks with both hands.

"What's for dinner?" Clay said, walking into the room. He stopped abruptly and looked at his older brother. "Are Mom and Sam kissing again?"

"Of course not," Molly said, straightening. She drew in several deep breaths and squared her shoulders. "I'm all right now."

"Then what's for dinner?" Clay asked again.

"Food," Tom said, and ushered his brother out of the bedroom.

Molly gazed up at her husband, knowing her love shone from her eyes. She no longer felt she had to hide it. In a way, Sam was Gramps's final gift to her, and she knew without question that she loved him.

"When did Clay find us kissing?" he asked.

She blushed. "Probably the other morning." The first day of school, and her youngest son had awakened early. He'd stumbled into the kitchen to find Molly sitting in Sam's lap, the two them deeply involved in each other. Muttering under his breath, Clay had ignored them and popped bread in the toaster.

Sam had headed for the barn almost immediately afterward, but he'd snuck back into the house before he rode out for the day and stolen one last kiss. He was more openly affectionate these days, as they grew more comfortable with each other.

Sam followed her into the kitchen now. "I've got something to ask you, Clay," he said, clearing his throat. "Do you have a problem with me kissing your mother?"

Clay shrugged. "Not really."

"You, Tom?"

"It doesn't bother me. You can kiss her all you like. You're the one who married her."

Her son certainly had an eloquent way of putting things, Molly thought, rolling her eyes.

"When you asked us how we felt about you marrying Mom, you said, you know…" Clay looked from Molly to Sam, then back to Molly.

"You talked to the boys before we got married?"

Molly asked him after dinner. Tom had cleared the table and Sam was helping her put leftovers away.

"Yeah. I figured they should have some say about me being their stepfather."

"Really. And how did they answer you?"

Sam chuckled and reached for the dish towel. "Tom said he was grateful someone was willing to marry you. He'd about given up hope."

Molly didn't believe him for a minute. Lifting her hands out of the soapy water, she flicked suds at him and laughed when they landed square in the middle of his chest.

He was about to retaliate when the phone rang. Sam glanced regretfully at the wall, then grabbed the receiver. "Hello," he said, still laughing as he flung the suds in Molly's direction.

Molly watched as the laughter abruptly left his eyes and he slammed the receiver back on the hook.

"Who was that?" she asked.

Sam was already halfway out the door. He turned toward her, his jaw taut. "Ginny. We've got a grass fire," he said. "We could lose everything. Get the boys and follow me."

Thirteen

Molly wondered what had started the fire—until Sam found a discarded gas can by the side of the road. He was convinced it had been deliberately set. From what he could determine, the blaze had started in some dry grass and spread within minutes. Thankfully, a shift in the wind had saved the house and barn from certain disaster. Using the tractor and shovels and beating out the flames with blankets, Sam, Molly, Ginny, Fred and the boys, plus members of the volunteer fire department, had stopped it before it roared toward the pasture where the herd grazed.

Exhausted from fighting the fire, smelling of smoke, her clothes and skin covered with soot and ashes, Molly trudged back to the house. The boys followed, too tired to squabble, and dragged their shovels behind them. The volunteer firefighters had already left, and so had Ginny and her cousin. The family had stayed in the field, checking to make sure there were no smoldering patches. When they reached the yard, Sam jumped down from the tractor, and placed his arm around her shoulder.

"You okay?" he asked, searching her face.

His concern and love gave her the energy to smile and offer him the reassurance he needed.

"I think it's time you called the sheriff, don't you?" Molly asked as they sat at the kitchen table. The fire had frightened her. She'd thought...hoped...that they'd seen the end of this harassment. The other so-called incidents, while disastrous, hadn't been life-threatening. A fire was serious business, and as far as she was concerned it was time to bring in the authorities.

"Fine," Sam said. His mouth tightened. "Not that I expect Maynard to do anything."

"Why not?" Molly knew that for some reason the two men disliked each other, but she didn't want to believe the sheriff would allow his personal feelings to interfere with law enforcement.

"I just don't," was all Sam would say.

After they'd showered and changed clothes, Sam made the call.

Sheriff Maynard was apparently out of town on business; he didn't show up until the following evening. Molly was standing at the sink, washing the supper dishes, when she heard his car. She hurried over to hold open the screen door for him. "Thank you for coming, Sheriff."

"So you had some trouble out here yesterday?"

"We did. Clay, get Sam for me, would you?"

Her son nodded and hurried toward the barn.

"I took the liberty of contacting Chief Layman of the fire department. He'll want to question you and your... husband himself."

He hesitated over the word *husband* in a manner that suggested disapproval. Molly pretended not to notice. "Could I get you a cup of coffee while we talk?" she offered.

"That'd be real nice." He followed her to the kitchen, sat down at the table and took a small notepad from his shirt pocket.

When Sam came into the house, he chose to lean against the counter, rather than sit at the table with Sheriff Maynard. They eyed each other malevolently.

Molly poured three mugs of coffee and carried the first two to Sam and the sheriff. Both men continued to stare each other down, behaving like junkyard dogs looking for an excuse to fight.

To his credit Sheriff Maynard remained civil. Molly couldn't say the same for Sam.

"You suspect the fire was purposely started?" the sheriff asked, directing the question to Molly.

Sam responded. "I don't think. I know."

"How's that?"

Sam folded his arms. "It doesn't take a genius to figure it out, seeing that it started at the road."

"It could've been an accident," Sheriff Maynard said. "People can be thoughtless and stupid. Someone could have tossed a cigarette out the window. What makes you think this was intentional? I find that hard to believe."

"Believe what you want," Sam returned stiffly, "but the fire wasn't started by any cigarette. Whoever did this left behind a gas can."

The sheriff made a notation on the pad. "No real harm done, though, was there?"

"As a matter of fact there was." Sam's voice grew harder. "I'm getting ready to sell off my herd. If the winds hadn't shifted when they did, we could have lost everything. So I'm telling you right now—"

"Don't raise your voice to me, Dakota, because it wouldn't take much for me to haul your sorry ass to jail." The threat was as shocking as it was real.

"What Sam means, Sheriff," Molly said, intervening quickly, "is that yesterday wasn't the first time something like this has happened. The fire is the latest in a series of such incidents."

"Have you reported everything else that happened?"

Sam looked away, his eyes as dark as a thundercloud.

"I phoned about the cut fence lines," Molly answered.

Sheriff Maynard nodded, studying Sam, regarding him with the same cautious distrust he might give a rattlesnake. When he spoke again, it was directly to Sam. "As I explained to your wife, Dakota, Chief Layman will be out to ask a few questions in the morning. I'll take the evidence back with me for possible prints."

"Whoever did this wouldn't be stupid enough to leave fingerprints. He left the can so we'd know the fire was deliberate."

"As I said, Chief Layman will look things over in the morning. I'm sorry about the fire, but let's just be grateful no one was hurt." The sheriff took a last swallow of coffee and stood, pushing his chair away from the table.

With no thank-you or word of farewell, Sam reached for his hat and headed out the back door. It slammed in his wake.

Molly resisted the urge to apologize for Sam's behavior. She didn't particularly like Sheriff Maynard, either, but he represented the law. Despite personality differences he was a professional, duly elected, and probably a good lawman.

Molly followed him out to his patrol car. "I'm sorry you and my husband don't see eye to eye," she said.

The sheriff opened his door and paused. "Sam and I seem to have gotten off on the wrong foot."

"Do you mind telling me why?" Sam was a lot of things, but unreasonable wasn't usually one of them. And she had to assume that Sheriff Maynard was a rational man, too.

"I think you'd best discuss that with your husband. I can tell you it started the day he arrived in Sweetgrass looking for a fight. With an attitude like that it didn't take him long to find one." He appeared to regret having said this much. "Molly, I wish you'd never married a—" He snapped his mouth closed. "I beg your pardon, it's none of my business."

A *what?*

"Sheriff, please, I need to hear this." Whatever he had to say might help her understand the animosity between the two men. If Sam was going to be part of the Sweetgrass community, he had to learn to put aside differences and make an effort to get along with everyone. The longer she was married, the more Sam reminded her of her grandfather, with his frequently uncompromising beliefs.

"Gramps was fond of Sam, you know," she felt obliged to tell him. "He was delighted when Sam and I got married."

Sheriff Maynard frowned. "That makes me wonder if Walter was aware of all the facts."

"What facts?"

The sheriff studied her long and hard before he spoke again. "Dakota didn't tell you, did he?"

"Tell me what?"

"That son of a bitch," the sheriff snarled.

"Sheriff, whatever it is, tell me!"

He hesitated long enough for her to know this wasn't going to be good news. "It'd be better if your husband had the common decency to tell you this himself before he married you. But seeing that he didn't, I don't trust him to tell you now, so…"

Molly braced herself.

Sheriff Maynard's eyes avoided hers. "Your husband has a prison record, Mrs. Dakota. He served two years in a Washington-state prison for second-degree assault, and left the state as soon as he was released from parole."

A gasp of shock slid involuntarily from the back of her throat. Molly reached blindly for something to support her.

"I'm terribly sorry, Molly. I don't know if Walt ever knew."

Her knees felt as if they were melting. She had to find somewhere to sit before they completely gave out on her.

"Thank you for telling me." Somehow she managed to get the words out.

"Are you going to be all right?" He placed a supportive hand at her elbow.

"Fine. I'm fine." Turning around, she slowly climbed the steps, feeling exhausted by the time she reached the door. She stumbled into the house and sank into a chair at the table, gripping the edge with both hands.

She'd been married twice. The first marriage had nearly destroyed her, and the second was threatening to do the same. Two husbands, years apart, and somehow she'd managed to marry two…criminals.

The anger and resentment toward Sheriff Maynard galvanized Sam. Sweat poured down his forehead as he pitched hay into the stall, working hard, ignoring his aching muscles.

When Molly suggested they phone the sheriff, Sam knew he was making a mistake. With another man, Sam might have put forth some effort to clear the air. But once Maynard made up his mind about someone, his opinion didn't change.

Sam realized his own anger was a form of self-defense. Sheriff Maynard didn't like or trust him, so Sam was unwilling to offer the hand of friendship. Sure as hell, the lawman would slap a handcuff around it.

The interview had gone poorly, and Sam wasn't sure who to blame. The sheriff appeared to be suggesting that the entire episode with the fire was accidental when anyone with a lick of sense could tell it wasn't. Even asking about the earlier incidents, he didn't reveal any real interest. Nor had he bothered to write down pertinent details, other than what Sam had told him about finding the gas can.

The poisoned water hole could have resulted in disaster; so could the damaged windmill. The pasture near Custer Hills was without a running stream, and the windmill pumped drinking water for the herd. Which was no small thing. Luckily Sam had been able to repair it quickly. He didn't want to consider what would have happened if he hadn't discovered it when he did. There'd been too many incidents like this over the summer. Too many not to believe foul play wasn't involved. The fact that there was already a buyer for the land on the off chance Molly wanted to sell made him even more suspicious.

The old man had been smarter than he realized in deeding Sam those five hundred acres. His section sat squarely in the middle of the property. Not until after the funeral did Russell Letson get the final papers to Sam, and only then did he realize what Walt had done. Molly could sell the land, if worse came to worst, but her two sides of the property would be cut off from each other unless his land was included in the sale. Come hell or high water, Sam wouldn't relinquish those acres. In any event, he was prohibited from doing so by the terms of the agreement.

Setting the pitchfork aside, he left the barn and headed back to the house, fully expecting to get an earful from Molly. He wasn't blind to the looks she'd sent him when they'd spoken to Sheriff Maynard. She hadn't been pleased by his attitude. Well, he wasn't going to apologize. The sheriff was equally at fault.

Halfway between the barn and the house, Sam paused. He stood in the middle of the yard and surveyed the grounds, and even in the waning light he saw that the grass was charred and black. He shuddered; he could only be grateful that this latest disaster had passed them by.

He'd purposely delayed going back into the house, giving Molly time to cool down before he showed his face. The burns on his hands still throbbed, his back ached, and he wanted to be with his wife.

When Gramps had first suggested the marriage, Sam had been interested. The promise of land and cattle was one hell of an inducement. Molly could have resembled one of Cinderella's stepsisters and he still would've been tempted. What he hadn't understood at the time was how damn much he'd enjoy married life.

Sometimes when he woke in the middle of the night with Molly lying at his side, he was overcome with a sense of humility. Much of his life had been hard, devoid of tenderness. He'd served time in prison, although he tried to push that memory to the farthest reaches of his mind. In the years since, he'd drifted from one town to the next. One job to the next, until one ranch had looked much like another.

Then he'd met Walter Wheaton, a sick old man about to lose everything. The rancher had offered him a job when no one else wanted him. As it turned out, they'd needed each other. While he'd gratefully accepted Walt's proposal, Sam had suspected this would be the hardest he'd ever work for anyone, and he'd been right.

But he'd gained so much—a home, a wife, a family. His heart seemed to expand in his chest. He'd given up on love, readily admitting that he'd never understood it or experienced it. Until Molly… This was supposed to be a marriage of convenience, not of love. He and Molly had never said the word to each other, had never discussed how their feelings had changed. It didn't matter. He knew they had.

Sam knew he was in love with Molly.

The attraction between them was only part of it. A pretty fantastic part, to tell the truth. Their lovemaking was the most incredible of his life, and it had nothing to do with technique. It was all about *feeling*. He loved Molly, loved her with an intensity that actually hurt.

He'd never been one to indulge in public displays of affection; such exhibitions embarrassed him. Behind closed doors was another matter entirely.

A month was all it had taken. One month as a married man, and Sam found himself looking for reasons to touch Molly. Reasons to linger in the kitchen after the boys left to catch their school bus—just so he could steal a kiss from her. He enjoyed sneaking up behind her when she was washing dishes and slipping his hands beneath her blouse, filling his palms with her breasts. He loved the scent of her, the feel of her, everything about her. Oh, sure, she put up a token protest, but she enjoyed those times as much as he did.

Other than that first night, they'd never really argued, and he was glad. Sam didn't know if he could bear to have her angry with him. He needed her in his life too damn much to risk endangering their relationship.

He glanced at his watch, wondering if she'd already gone to bed. At the thought a smile curved his lips. He couldn't wait to get into bed...with Molly. He suddenly felt a lot less tired.

Taking the steps two at a time, he hurried into the house. Molly stood at the kitchen counter, packing Tom's and Clay's lunches for school.

"Where are the boys?" he asked.

"Upstairs."

He caught a slight coolness in her response, but let it go. She slapped a slice of bread down on top of another with enough force to flatten both pieces. Sam hesitated. "Is something wrong?"

"You tell me."

He sighed and walked slowly toward her. She was still angry about that scene with the sheriff. Okay, so maybe he'd overreacted. It wouldn't have hurt to be a bit friendlier to Maynard. If it would keep the peace, Sam would admit to being at fault.

"Does this have to do with Sheriff Maynard?" he asked, maintaining his composure. He'd made a mistake on their wedding night when he'd allowed her anger to fuel his own. If he didn't let his pride get in the way, maybe they could settle this.

"No."

"No?" Her answer took him by surprise.

She whirled around, and her eyes flashed with indignation and another emotion he couldn't identify.

"You might have told me." Each word was a bitter accusation.

"Told you what?"

"Don't pretend you don't know." She opened the refrigerator and shoved the mayonnaise jar inside. It slammed against the pickle jar and toppled the plastic container of ketchup.

Sam couldn't remember ever seeing her like this. "Molly?"

"How about the truth, Sam? Didn't you think I had a right to know about your prison record? What hurts— what *really* hurts—is that you knew about Daniel and how…how difficult it was for me to tell you my ex-husband was in prison…and you didn't say a word." A sandwich went into the brown paper bag and Sam pitied whichever boy had to eat it.

"I tried to tell you," he argued. "That day we—"

"Don't," she said fiercely. "Don't you dare try to squirm your way out of this."

"It's the truth," he said with enough vehemence to give her pause. "Think back to the day we applied for the wedding license."

She squinted as if deep in thought.

"On the ride into town. I started to tell you, and you stopped me and made this long speech about the past being over and how it'd be best if we both put it behind us and started again."

"I was talking about old lovers!" she flared. "You can't honestly believe I shouldn't know about a felony record. Second-degree assault, Sam. You tried to kill someone and you just conveniently forgot to tell me that before our wedding."

"I didn't forget. I—"

"You deliberately chose to hide it from me! Which leads me to wonder what else you haven't told me."

"You know everything about me—well, not about my time in prison, but everything else." Despite his best intentions, he was fast losing ground and with it his patience. Molly had tried and convicted him without so much as asking the particulars. "As far as I'm concerned you *chose* not to hear it."

Silence throbbed between them. He stood on one side of the kitchen and she on the other, but the distance between them might have been the entire state of Montana.

"I think you should leave," she said finally.

"Leave?" She had to be joking. Apparently she'd failed to remember that they were getting close to roundup. Their entire livelihood was at stake. If ever she'd needed him, it was now. Then there was the matter of the land he owned, deeded to him at the time of their marriage. Land he'd fight to keep.

"Move, then—back to the foreman's house."

"You *are* joking, right?" He prayed she was, but one look said otherwise. "Okay, I'll admit you had a right to know. I should've said something before you married me. I meant to tell you, but hell, I'm not proud of having served time, and I'd prefer to put it behind me. If you're waiting for me to apologize, then I'll do it. I'm sorry, Molly." It wasn't easy, but he managed to choke out the words, hoping that would satisfy her.

"I feel like such a fool," she said miserably. "You didn't tell Gramps, either, did you? He'd never have let me marry another criminal." She turned and leaned heavily against the kitchen counter, bracing her hands on the edge.

Feeling wretched and angry at her unfairness, Sam took one step toward her and stopped. He'd done his damnedest to explain, to apologize, but he wasn't getting down on his knees and begging. If she wanted him gone, then fine, he'd leave—just long enough for her to miss him.

He walked out of the kitchen and slammed the door so she'd know he was going. Half hoping she'd race after him and beg him to stay, Sam climbed into his truck. To be on the safe side, he sat there for a moment or two, just to make sure Molly didn't have a change of heart.

She didn't.

With nowhere else to go, Sam drove to the same tavern he'd gone their wedding night. But he wasn't in the mood to drink. Being stupid enough to think whiskey would solve his problems was exactly what had landed him in jail; that wasn't going to happen again. Sam considered himself a fast learner. Anger and alcohol didn't mix.

Willie's smelled of stale cigarette smoke and beer. He recognized a couple of cowhands who were playing a game of pool in the corner. The music was too loud, the conversation too boisterous. Almost everyone here was looking for a good time.

The only thing Sam wanted was a dark corner to sit in for a while. To think and brood and figure out a way to get Molly to see reason. Dammit all, just when he thought everything was going well, this had to happen. That bastard Maynard couldn't resist telling her, could he?

He claimed the stool at the farthest end of the bar and let it be known that he wasn't seeking company.

He'd been nursing his beer for an hour or so when he saw her. The hooker who'd talked him into returning to the hotel on his wedding night. It might have saved him a whole lot of heartache if he hadn't gone back; at least, that was the way he felt now. Any other night he might have greeted her and thanked her for the best damn advice anyone had ever given him.

Feeling his attention, she swiveled around and held his look. It took her a moment to recognize him. As soon as she did, her face relaxed into an easy smile. It wasn't a hooker's smile, either, but one of—hell, he didn't know—friendship, he guessed.

When her potential customer didn't pan out, she made her way across the room to where he sat.

"How ya doing, cowboy?"

He shrugged.

"Still married?"

He wasn't sure the marriage would last beyond this night, but for the moment he could answer her honestly. "You might say that."

"How's the missus?"

"Madder'n hops on a griddle."

She cocked one expressive eyebrow. "Don't tell me you had another tiff?"

"Looks that way." He glanced down at his near-empty mug. "My fault this time."

"You gonna tell her that?"

"I already did, but she's really pissed off. I don't blame her. Thought I'd give her time to cool off."

She smiled. "Good idea."

"How're you doing?" he asked just to keep the conversation going. He felt lost and more than a little lonely. Being alone had never bothered him until he married Molly, and now it was as if…as if he wasn't complete without her. "It's Pearl, isn't it?"

She nodded. "I'm doing so-so," she said.

"Business good?"

"Fair." She brushed a strand of bleached blond hair away from her face, and he noticed the dark shadows beneath her eyes. They were prominent enough that makeup couldn't completely disguise them.

"Anything I can do to help?" Maybe he wasn't such a fast learner, after all. It was helping a woman that had landed him in jail that first day in Sweetgrass. But dammit, he *owed* Pearl.

Sam wanted to believe he wouldn't have taken her up on her offer the night of his wedding. He didn't think so, but the mood he'd been in…he just didn't know. What she'd done was a generous thing. He'd never heard of a hooker who'd suggest a client go back to his wife.

"I…" She shook her head. "No, but thanks. It's sweet of you to ask."

The door opened and a couple of rough-looking men, dressed in fatigues, walked in. Pearl's attention flashed to them. Potential clients, Sam guessed, but her reaction said otherwise. She whirled around and Sam noted she'd gone pale beneath her makeup.

"I changed my mind, cowboy," she said, her voice trembling. "If you still want to help me, you can."

Sam set his mug down on the bar. "What do you need?"

She bit her lower lip. "A way out of here. I don't want them to see me."

Sam didn't hesitate. "You got it." He wrapped his arm around her as if they were longtime lovers and, using his body as a shield, escorted her toward the door. The bartender glanced over in surprise, but said nothing. The two men climbed onto bar stools, and if they noticed Sam and the woman leaving, they took no heed.

Not knowing what had given Pearl such a fright, Sam thought it prudent to drop her off somewhere safe.

"Where do you want to go?" he asked. "A friend's house?"

"No." Her short laugh was unexpected. "Call girls don't generally have a lot of friends."

"What about other…you know, other girls like you."

"Not in this town, honey. It's every girl for herself."

This was a world Sam didn't know and had no desire to explore. "Where do you want me to drive you?"

He was all the way down Front Street before she answered. "Home, I guess." She gave him the address, which was directly behind Willie's, so he circled back.

"Are you sure it's safe there?"

"I've got protection," she said, "and they know it."

Sam wanted to do more for her, but he'd learned the hard way that he should just hightail it out of the area before whatever was going down got messy. He'd done his good deed for the night.

He pulled up in front of the address she'd given him. She was about to open the door and climb out when she surprised the hell out of him by throwing her arms around his neck and hugging him tight.

"What was that for?" he asked.

"A thank-you. Now go home to your wife and tell her how sorry you are. If she's smart, she'll forgive you. Decent men aren't all that easy to find, and you're one of them."

"Thanks."

She got out of the pickup and he waited until she was safely inside the house and had turned on the lights before he drove off.

She'd given him good advice on his wedding night, and there wasn't any reason to believe her words of wisdom wouldn't work this time. With a renewed sense of hope Sam drove back to the ranch. At least the dogs were glad to see him.

The house was dark and quiet when he entered. Molly must be in bed. Sam was glad; it would be easier to reason with her there. He thought so, anyway. He tiptoed into the bedroom. The moonlight showed Molly's still form, and her slow, even breathing told him she was asleep.

Stripping off his clothes, he lifted the covers and got in beside her.

"I'm home, Molly," he whispered, and slid his arms around her waist. His hand crept up, sought her breast. Probably not the wisest move, but holding her like this had become habit.

Molly sighed and snuggled closer.

"Did you miss me, sweetheart?" he murmured, and gently nibbled at her ear.

Her immediate response gave him a world of hope. Rolling onto her back, Molly wound her arms around his neck. Then she did that thing with her tongue, tickling the hollow of his throat. Goose bumps spread down his arms and legs. "Oh, baby..." he whispered. "I think we should talk, don't you?"

Not answering, she clung to him.

"On second thought we can talk anytime." He eased his leg between hers and was about to kiss her full on the lips when it happened.

The willing pliant woman in his arms went stiff, then bolted up and shoved him away. "Where have you been? Oh, God, you were with another woman! I can smell her all over you!"

Fourteen

Russell Letson's heart stopped cold. He read the head-lines again, certain there'd been some mistake. This couldn't be real! The agony was as fierce as anything physical, perhaps more so.

The paper said that Pearl was dead.

He covered his eyes with one hand in a futile effort to force the fog of pain from his mind. He needed to think, to assimilate what the words said and what he could make himself believe, make himself accept.

Again he read the article, which took up half the front page of the regular Wednesday edition. The *Sweetgrass Weekly* rarely had a murder to write about. Even a murder without a body was big news. The door to Pearl's house had been left open for several days, and when a neighbor had gone to investigate, she discovered the place had been ransacked. It was as though a tornado had been let loose inside, she'd said. Blood splattered the walls, and a deep crimson stain was found on the bed, leaking through to the mattress. So much blood. Dear God, had she suffered?

Bile rose in his throat, and thrusting the newspaper aside, he closed his eyes and drew in several deep breaths. To his amazement he felt tears in his eyes. *Sweet Jesus, please, don't let her have suffered.*

He loved her. He'd known it long before he'd seen her eyes swollen shut and the bruises that marked her upper arms and neck. She'd rejected him, and the pain of that rejection had driven him away, even when he knew she'd lied. Almost everything she'd said to him that Sunday was a lie. What he'd never been able to figure out was why she believed it was necessary.

He'd hoped she'd see reason, but then he'd lost patience and ruined everything. The night he'd gone to her and treated her like a whore had killed any tenderness she might have felt for him.

Ashamed and defeated, Russell hadn't seen Pearl since. But his thoughts had been with her every minute of every day while he tried to sort out what to do next, how to approach her and ask her forgiveness. He'd planned to talk to her, convince her they could make a good life together, if she'd only give them a chance.

But he'd waited too long and now it was too late.

Pearl was dead.

In time someone would find her decomposed body, cast aside like so much garbage on the side of a country road. Perhaps her killer had had the decency to bury her somewhere. He prayed that was the case.

Dear Lord, not Pearl, please not Pearl.

Once he'd composed himself enough to reach for the phone, Russell dialed Sheriff Maynard's office to make a few discreet inquiries.

"Any leads?" he asked in a crisp professional tone, as if a murder case was a routine matter.

Maynard didn't sound pleased to hear from him.

"None yet, but we'll eventually find whoever was responsible."

Russell had never felt anything like this need, this all-consuming drive for justice. He'd gone into law for a number of reasons, none of which had much to do with justice, but in the blink of an eye that had all changed. The minute he'd read the headlines, justice—and punishment—took on the utmost importance.

"Then the killer left evidence behind?" Russell pressed, despite the lawman's obvious reluctance to discuss the case. They knew each other well, and Maynard owed him this.

"There's always evidence."

"Who was her pimp?" Russell demanded. If anyone knew, it was the sheriff. He tried to sound as if the matter were one of casual interest. Asking these questions was bound to lead Russell to potential suspects. If he did nothing else in this life, he'd make sure that whoever murdered Pearl paid for his crime.

"Listen, Russell, I can't talk about this case. Not yet. You'll hear the details as soon as I have them. Now stop pestering me. I've got work to do." He paused, then asked, "Why all the curiosity? How well did you know her, anyway?"

The last thing Russell needed was to become a suspect himself. "Every guy in town knew her, didn't he? You did yourself, right?" he asked, making light of his preoccupation with the crime.

The sheriff laughed. "Knew her intimately, you mean," he joked. "Every cowhand in town slept with her at one time or another. Either that or he was a saint. The lady had a body and knew how to use it. That's what makes cases like this so damned difficult. My guess is that her john got a little too rambunctious and things went further than he intended."

Russell stopped breathing to help prevent the mental picture of a man abusing Pearl from forming in his mind. It didn't work, and he was tormented with what her last minutes must have been like.

"I'll say this, though," the sheriff murmured. "I don't think I've ever seen so much blood."

"Is there any chance she could be alive?" He wanted desperately to believe there was a possibility Pearl had survived the beating and like an injured animal had run off to hide.

"I suppose there's a chance," the sheriff admitted after a moment. "But my guess is she's dead. Hard to see how anyone could lose that much blood and survive."

Russell's throat felt like he'd swallowed the cotton in the top of his vitamin bottle. It hurt to breathe. "Why would the killer take away the body?"

Maynard snickered as if to say the question was unworthy of a response. "Think about it. Physical evidence. Anyone with half a brain isn't going to leave a corpse behind at the scene of a crime. Not these days. Why give investigators an edge?"

Russell nodded, surprised he hadn't realized that himself. "Right."

"I'll let you know more when I can."

At this point Russell didn't care how much his curiosity left him exposed. "I want to know everything. Find the bastard. Do whatever it takes, but find the bastard." His hand trembled as badly as his voice by the time he replaced the telephone receiver.

For two days Russell didn't sleep more than a few minutes at a time or eat anything at all. Whenever he

closed his eyes, he saw Pearl as he had the last time
they'd been together. Her eyes had been bright with un-
shed tears as she called out to him. Unwilling to listen,
he'd turned his back on her and walked away. In those
last moments he'd destroyed any hope of reconciliation.

Now he'd have to live with that for the rest of his life,
and he didn't know if he could.

Although he made a pretense of working, if anyone
had asked him what he'd done, Russell wouldn't have
been able to say. He'd been in the office all week, but
he'd written no letters, prepared no legal briefs, talked
to no clients. He'd had his secretary cancel his appointments. For hours each day he sat and stared into space.
His secretary seemed convinced he had the flu. He let
her believe what she wanted; it saved him from having
to invent excuses.

The buzzer at his desk pulled him out of his reverie.
"Yes," he said, resenting the intrusion.

"Mr. Sam Dakota's here to see you. He says it's urgent."

Russell wearily rubbed his face. Instinct told him to
send the man home; he was in no shape to offer legal
advice. "Tell him I'm already booked solid." A complete lie, but that should let Roberta know how much
he wanted her to turn the rancher away.

"I'm sorry, Mr. Letson, but he insists on speaking
to you personally. He's very persistent and says it's of
the utmost importance."

Russell's head drooped slightly, the weight of the decision almost more than he could bear. "Send him in,"
he said finally. He'd listen to whatever was troubling
Sam, then advise him to hire another attorney.

The door opened and his secretary let Sam into the office.

Russell gestured toward the chair on the other side of his desk, and Sam took a seat. He seemed nervous, sitting on the edge of the cushion and holding his hat with both hands. The first thing Russell noticed was how pale the rancher looked—but then he suspected he wasn't exactly the picture of health himself.

"What can I do for you?" Russell asked when Sam didn't immediately speak. For someone who'd been hellbent to talk to him, he was taking long enough to get down to it.

"I wasn't sure where else to go or who to call," Sam told him with obvious reluctance. "I don't trust the sheriff, and the bartender and four or five others at Willie's are bound to have seen me and what the hell—" He leaped to his feet and walked over to the window. "I have a feeling deep in my gut that I'm going to end up charged with the murder of that poor woman."

Russell felt his blood stir for the first time since he'd read the newspaper headline. "Murder?"

Sam turned around to face him. "I swear by everything I hold dear that I didn't lay a hand on her."

Russell's blood wasn't only stirring, it was surging in his veins. "You were with Pearl the night she died?" His voice rose with each word, although he spoke slowly and clearly.

"I spent time with her," Sam admitted, "but not the way you think."

"Then explain it to me." His voice was cold, hard, as he stared at the other man, seeing him in a new light.

"Molly and I argued," Sam was saying. "She found out about my prison record." He lowered his head.

Russell's gaze narrowed as he studied the man closely. Maynard had told him about it shortly after Walt hired Dakota, but it surprised him that Molly hadn't known.

"Molly—I should've told her, I know that now. I admit I was wrong to go through with the wedding without disclosing my past." His eyes met Russell's. "I love my wife."

The regret on Sam's face told Russell the truth of his words. "Get back to the part having to do with Pearl," he instructed, not wanting Sam to get sidetracked by his marital problems.

"I met Pearl a couple of months earlier," Sam explained, again with a certain reluctance, "but not, uh, on a professional basis."

Had Pearl entertained other men the way she had him? Russell wondered. A rush of jealousy set his nerves on edge. Loving her the way he had made the thought of anyone else sharing that special closeness intolerable. He'd loved her and she'd loved him. What she'd done with her clients had nothing to do with the feelings between them.

"I met her the night Molly and I got married."

"You were with Pearl on your wedding night?" This was beyond real. Dakota honestly couldn't expect Russell to believe that!

"I met her at Willie's," Sam explained, his expression tightly controlled, revealing none of his thoughts. "Molly and I..." He paused, looking uncomfortable. "Let me just say that Molly and I didn't see eye to eye on a certain issue and I left the hotel in a huff."

"And drowned your sorrows in a bottle of beer at Willie's."

"Something like that," Sam admitted. "That's where I met Pearl."

His gaze roved about the room in an agitated way that might have suggested guilt, but Russell could see that Sam was genuinely distressed. His attorney's instinct told him Sam wasn't the one who'd killed Pearl; if it turned out he was wrong, Russell figured he'd save the courts a lot of trouble and expense and see that justice was carried out himself.

Dakota continued with his story, explaining how Pearl had sent him back to his wife. Russell's heart tightened when he realized what a generous thing she'd done for a stranger.

"You'd never seen her before that night?" he asked.

"Never."

Russell believed him. He stared openly at the rancher; Sam's own gaze didn't waver, which he considered a good sign.

"What did you do with her the night she was killed?"

"I gave her a ride home."

"Why?" He couldn't quite keep the suspicion out of his voice. What man played taxi driver for a hooker unless he had an ulterior motive?

Sam braced himself. "I know it sounds incredible, and I can't think of a single reason for you to believe me, but I swear this is the truth. I met her at Willie's again and she seemed a bit down. So because she'd been kind to me, because I liked her, I asked if there was anything I could do for her, and she asked for a ride home."

"Any particular reason?"

"Two unsavory characters came into the tavern and she didn't want them to know she was there."

"Did you get a good look at either of them?"

Sam shook his head sadly. "The lights were dim, and I paid more attention to shielding Pearl than to studying their faces."

"Did anyone see the two of you leave together?"

"Four, possibly five others."

Russell sat back and tried to absorb what he'd learned. "What about outside the tavern?"

"A couple of guys in the parking lot, but that's about it."

Again Russell paused, mentally picturing the setup at Willie's. He hadn't been in there in months. Willie's was where Pearl had sought out customers, and knowing that, he'd avoided the place. Not that he'd ever gone there much.

"Has Sheriff Maynard questioned you yet?"

"No, but he will," Dakota said with an ironic sort of conviction. "Let's just say the sheriff would be delighted with an opportunity to pin this murder on me."

"And you didn't do it?"

"You're damn right! I didn't have anything to do with it."

In his heart he recognized that the rancher was probably guilty of nothing more than poor judgment.

"What about Molly?" Russell asked.

The look in Sam's eyes when he responded was a familiar one to Russell; he saw it every time he saw his own reflection. Pain. Deep desolate pain. "She only speaks to me when necessary," Sam told him. "I don't know what she believes—then again, maybe I do."

"Have you spoken to her about this?"

He shook his head. "I don't know how... I'm not entirely sure she's made the connection. She smelled Pearl's perfume on me, but she has no way of knowing the woman I was with that night was the woman who was murdered. I've tried to come up with a way of explaining what happened and I can't. You're the only one I've talked to about this."

"You made the right decision in coming to me first," Russell said.

"If worse comes to worst, will you represent me?" Sam asked, and his dark brooding gaze refused to release Russell's.

"I'm not a criminal attorney. You'd be better—"

"You're the only one I trust."

Russell hesitated. Pearl had trusted him, too, and he'd single-handedly destroyed that. Sam Dakota would do well to look elsewhere for legal representation. In his present state of mind, he wouldn't do the man a damn bit of good.

"Will you?" Sam pressed.

Russell avoided eye contact. "God's own truth, I don't know. Let's cross that bridge when we come to it."

Sam hesitated and then nodded. "Be warned. That bridge is well within sight."

The alley behind Willie's was dark and deserted as Monroe waited for Lance. His mind was churning with the recent events involving Pearl Mitchell. Her body hadn't been found, and while he hadn't verbalized his suspicions, he fully suspected Lance was the one responsible. Killing a valuable piece of Loyalist property was just the kind of thing he'd come to expect from that troublemaker.

For once Lance was on time. He opened the car door and slid quickly inside.

"You heard about the fire?" he asked. "At Dakota's?"

"I heard," Monroe confirmed. "Do you have any other brilliant ideas?" It was difficult to keep the sarcasm out of his voice.

"A few."

"Perhaps you'd better clear them with me."

Lance's eyes narrowed. "You don't think I can do the job? Then I suggest you try it yourself. Those two are the stubbornest *luckiest* damn pair I've ever seen."

"I just might." This wasn't the first time Monroe had thought to take matters into his own hands, especially since he was dealing with a man he considered completely incompetent.

The silence between them was strained with tension. "I'm going after their weakest link next," Lance said.

"What's that?" Monroe demanded.

"What it is with any family." Lance was smiling now. "The kids."

"You don't look your normal perky self," Ginny commented when Molly brought her a tall cold glass of lemonade, then joined her at the kitchen table. Ginny had dropped by unexpectedly, taking Molly at her word. Her timing was perfect; if ever Molly needed a friend, it was now.

"I've been feeling a bit under the weather," was all Molly would admit. Pride being what it was, she found it difficult to announce that her marriage of less than two months was a failure. She could barely look at Sam. He'd lied to her, misled her and worst of all cheated on her. It was as though she'd searched out and married Daniel's twin brother, she thought bitterly.

Molly's stomach twisted in a knot of pain. She knew how to choose men, all right. From the frying pan into the fire—that was her. When it came to husbands, she seemed to have a knack for choosing the most-likely-to-hurt-her candidates.

What wounded her most was that Sam hadn't bothered to deny he'd been with another woman. She'd ranted and raved and carried on like a fishwife, but all he'd said was that she could believe what she wanted. Which had made Molly all the more furious. He came home smelling like a whorehouse, and *she* was the one who was supposed to feel guilty?

"Sit down, honey," Ginny advised. "What's wrong?" To Molly's utter humiliation her eyes filled with tears. "You want to talk about it?" Ginny asked with a gentleness Molly had rarely heard in the other woman's voice.

She shook her head.

"I suspect you're worried about the price of beef," Ginny murmured, reaching for a cookie. "I'm telling you, it can't get much worse than this."

Molly didn't need any other troubles, but they seemed to come in droves. The cattle were ready for market, and the price per pound was several cents less than it had been the year before. The middlemen were making huge profits and in the process destroying the independent rancher.

As if there weren't enough problems in her life, the current slump in beef prices meant they wouldn't have enough money to meet their accrued expenses. Without a loan or some other way of paying the bills, Molly didn't know what they'd do. It was just one more trouble along with everything else—only the *everything else* seemed more pressing just then.

Ginny leaned over and grabbed her hand. "What's wrong, Molly?" she asked again. "Don't be afraid to tell

me. It doesn't take a four-eyed snake to see that something's troubling you real bad."

That was when Ginny's kindness finally reduced
Molly to sobs. She covered her face with both hands
and wept as if her entire world had shattered hopelessly.

What amazed Molly was that, as she blubbered
out the sorry tale, Ginny seemed to understand every
word. She told her neighbor about the squabble—but
not what they'd fought over—and how Sam had come
home smelling of expensive French perfume. He'd been
with someone else, Molly was convinced of that. He'd
betrayed her.

"You can't really think Sam would cheat on you,
Molly!"

"I…I don't know what to think anymore," Molly
confessed.

"Hogwash. You married him, didn't you?"

"Yes, but—" She'd married Daniel, too.

Ginny didn't allow her to finish. "That man's so
crazy about you he can't see straight. The minute you
come into view his eyes follow you like a hawk watching a prairie rabbit. He'd no more seek out someone else
than he'd court a rattlesnake."

"But…" Molly hesitated. Ginny didn't know all the
details, and Molly couldn't tell her. "He misled me about
his past." She inhaled a quavering breath and continued.
"It's true I told him this was a fresh start for us both,
but I certainly expected him to tell me…certain things."

"Certain things?"

Molly twisted the damp tissue in her hands and
looked away. "Sam's…got a prison record."

"Oh, that. I know all about it. Walt told me," Ginny
surprised her by saying.

"Gramps *knew?*"

"Course he did. Do you think he'd let you marry any man without knowing everything there was to know about him first? You were his only kin."

"But I assumed... I thought..."

Ginny rubbed her forehead as she mulled over this latest bit of information. "It makes sense, doesn't it?"

"Sense?" Molly repeated.

"Sam not telling you. The boy was afraid. Figured if you knew he'd done time, you wouldn't have married him. That doesn't sound like a man who'd step out on his wife first chance he got, now does it?"

"Sure he wanted to marry me! Gramps offered him that land and those cattle, and—"

"Fiddlesticks. That land was incentive, all right, and probably got Sam to thinking about marriage, but that *wasn't* the only reason he married you. He was interested in you right off—I could see it and so could Walt. Not having much time left, Walt did the only thing he could. He hurried the two of you along, is all."

Molly desperately wanted to believe Sam loved her. These past weeks—before the night of the fire—had been the happiest of her adult life. The thought that it had all been a lie hurt more than anything she'd ever faced, including Gramps's death.

Ginny took a long swallow of her drink. "Don't be a fool, Molly Dakota, and make the same mistake as me. I loved your grandfather for longer than I care to admit. We could've enjoyed a few good years together, but we were both too stubborn and set in our ways to let the other know. That was the reason we bickered. We both knew the minute we stopped fighting we'd be making love, and it put the fear of God into us." The older woman sniffed loudly, dabbing at her eyes. "Damn allergies," she muttered and blew her nose.

"Oh, Ginny."

"Trust him, Molly. Walt did, and he was the best judge of character I ever knew. I swear to you that you won't be sorry."

Ginny left soon afterward, and as Molly waved her off, she noted that Sam's truck was back. He hadn't told her where he was headed that afternoon, and she hadn't asked. They weren't exactly on speaking terms. He ignored her except for the most basic conversations about ranch or household matters, and she did the same with him.

Still standing in the back doorway, Molly saw Tom and Clay trudging down the long drive, with Clay's half-grown dog trotting beside them; the school bus dropped them off at the end of the quarter-mile ranch road, where Bullwinkle faithfully waited for Clay. Molly had snacks ready and waiting. Both boys acted as if they were half-starved whenever they walked in the door after school.

"You and Sam still fighting?" Clay asked as he grabbed his lemonade and two chocolate-chip cookies.

"We aren't fighting, exactly," she murmured. She'd done her best to hide the tension between her and Sam from the children and was relieved that he'd done his own part to disguise it.

"Well, hurry up and forgive him, would you?" Tom said. "Sam's about as much fun as fried liver and on-ions these days. How much does he have to suffer be-fore you'll forgive him?"

"Tom!" Molly couldn't believe her son would ask

such a question. "What's between Sam and me is none of your business."

"Is this what happens when people get married?" her youngest son wanted to know. "It's great for a little while, and then you fight and everything changes?"

Difficult as it was to admit, her boys were right. This unpleasantness had gone on long enough. Ginny's observations had hit home, and now her own children were saying essentially the same thing.

Running her fingers through her hair, Molly squared her shoulders, took a deep breath and headed out the back door.

"Where you going?" Clay called after her.

"Where do you think, stupid?" his brother taunted. "Leave them be, all right? And if Mom comes back with straw in her hair, don't ask any questions."

Molly turned to glare at her oldest son, but Tom only smiled and winked. Some of the tension eased from her shoulders and she grinned. At the moment a bit of straw in her hair appealed to her. She'd missed Sam. After a decade without lovemaking, it surprised her how easily she'd adjusted to the routine of married life.

Sam was in the barn cleaning tack and barely glanced up when she entered.

"I have something to ask you and I expect the full truth," she announced.

Her statement was met with silence.

"All right?" she asked, feeling suddenly uncertain. It would've been easier if Sam had approached her, instead.

"Fine. Ask away," he muttered.

"Were you or were you not with a woman the other night?"

"That depends on your definition of *with*."

"I didn't realize this was a technical question." She crossed her arms defensively.

"If you're asking if I slept with—as in had sex with—another woman, then the answer is a flat-out no."

"Oh."

"If you're curious as to what I was doing, I'll tell you. A lady asked for a ride home and I gave her one. She was grateful and hugged me, and I swear to you, Molly, that's all it was. A hug, nothing more."

The intensity of his look burned straight through to her heart. She wanted to believe him so very much.

"I've only loved one woman in my life," he continued, methodically polishing the worn leather of her grandfather's saddle. "And that's you."

Molly felt her chest tighten. She wanted it to be true, and while he'd shown her in a hundred ways that he cared, he'd never said the words. Before she could stop herself, she whispered, "I love you, too."

Slowly Sam stood. "Then why are you all the way over there and I'm all the way over here?"

"Can we meet in the middle?"

He grinned for the first time. "You're a stubborn woman, Molly Dakota."

"I had a good teacher," she said, thinking of Gramps.

They didn't walk toward each other, they ran. Sam caught her about the waist and buried his face in the curve of her neck. She threw her arms around him and clung. And all her doubts fled.

"I've been so miserable," she whispered against his shoulder.

"You?" He chuckled, but his amusement was abruptly cut off when his mouth covered hers.

They'd kissed countless times, but Molly couldn't remember any kiss that had meant this much. It was passion, but it was more—giving, taking, holding, sharing. *Trusting.* They both gasped for breath when the kiss ended.

"Do you realize the torment I've been in the past few nights, sleeping beside you?" he whispered.

"You actually slept?"

"You're joking, right?" He kissed her again—and stopped abruptly. "Listen, Molly, there's something..." He hesitated.

"What?" she asked.

"There's going to be trouble."

"What do you mean?"

"The woman I gave the ride to..."

"Yes?"

"It was Pearl Mitchell."

The name blazed itself across Molly's mind, and she pressed her forehead against his shirt. "Oh, God."

No sooner had she said the words than she heard the sound of an approaching car.

"Are you expecting anyone?" Sam asked.

She shook her head.

Before they could make their way outside, the barn door burst open. Sheriff Maynard stood there, looking like an avenging angel.

"Sam Dakota, I'm taking you into town for questioning in the death of Pearl Mitchell."

Fifteen

Sam had lost track of the hours he'd spent in the back room at the sheriff's office. Four? Six? His eyes burned from lack of sleep, but the questions kept coming, some at shotgun speed, others with a slow nasal contempt and the assumption of guilt. His answer was the same to each and every one.

"I refuse to answer any questions until my attorney is present."

According to Sheriff Maynard, he'd been unable to reach Russell Letson. Sam didn't believe him for a second, but said nothing. And wouldn't. Nor did he question the handcuffs, although he hadn't been charged with any crime. It would do no good to demand his rights.

He'd been this route before and had learned the hard way that a uniform didn't guarantee justice, fairness or truth. When he'd been arrested in the barroom brawl that led to his prison sentence, the investigating officer had to rephrase certain questions three or four times to get the answers he needed in order to arrest Sam. Fool that he was, Sam had trusted the man to be unbiased. As a result he'd ended up in jail. Yes, he'd been involved in the fight. Yes, he'd had a knife. Yes, he'd been drinking. Three yeses was all it took to put him behind bars that first time, and Sam had no intention of making a repeat appearance. Not when his life had finally taken a sharp turn for the better. He wasn't going to mess that up.

The ranch was his future, as were Molly and the boys. They'd worked their way deep into his heart. A man didn't walk away from his family, nor did he walk away from his responsibilities. That was a belief he'd shared with Walt. The old man had treated him like a son; he'd loved Sam enough to encourage him to marry Molly, his only granddaughter. And Sam had no intention of letting his friend down now or becoming a victim of circumstances.

"I *demand* to see my husband."

He could hear Molly's determined voice as the young deputy opened and closed the door. Despite the situation, Sam couldn't keep from smiling. It did his heart good to know someone else was butting heads with Molly. He almost felt sorry for the clerk. His wife was a stubborn headstrong woman, which only made Sam love her more. Knowing she was here and on his side gave him the strength to endure another round of questioning, to listen in silence as the sheriff and his men detailed the "evidence" that pointed directly at Sam. Fortunately he was aware of their game plan. Instinct demanded that he argue his case, protest his innocence. But experience had taught him that his declaration would soon be used as "proof" with which to convict him.

An hour later the door opened a second time, and

Russell Letson stepped inside. He took one look at the handcuffs on Sam's wrists and demanded, "On what grounds are you holding my client?" His voice suggested Maynard had stepped so far over the line he was lucky not to get tossed into a cell himself.

"Dakota was the last known person to be with Pearl Mitchell."

Russell snorted. "If *that's* all you've got, then I suggest you release him now or become the defendant in a lengthy and very expensive lawsuit for unlawful detainment."

Sam was beginning to believe he'd underestimated the attorney. Mild-mannered Letson was hell wearing shoes when it came to defending his clients. Sam wasn't sure what had persuaded the other man to accept his defense, but he suspected Molly had something to do with it.

Sheriff Maynard's face, double chin and all, was as red as a ripe tomato. Openmouthed, he stared at the attorney as if he couldn't believe what he'd heard. The two were obviously familiar with one another, and they waged a silent battle of wills.

"Now just a minute…" Sheriff Maynard scanned the room as if he felt obliged to make a show in front of his deputies.

"You've gone too far this time," Russell said, more calmly now. "Way too far. You know it, I know it, and so does everyone else in this room. You can stop here or we can pursue this issue in a court of law. The decision is yours."

The two men squared off face-to-face before the sheriff growled something incomprehensible and backed away.

Sam stood up and stretched out his arms for the sheriff to unlock the handcuffs. Maynard did so with undisguised reluctance. When his hands were free, Sam rubbed the soreness out of his wrists. Exhilaration filled him. When he'd walked into this office, he'd been terrified that he might never be free again.

He nearly mowed down two men in his eagerness to get to Molly. She got quickly to her feet when he walked into the waiting area in front of the office. Her beautiful blue eyes met his, and the emotion in them was nearly his undoing.

Without speaking a word, they simply walked into each other's arms. Sam's eyes drifted shut as he wrapped his arms around her and felt her love as profoundly as anything he'd ever known. He gave an audible sigh. Molly was sunshine after a fierce storm. Light after dark. Summer after a harsh winter. His joy. His freedom. His love.

"Are you all right?" she asked, her voice trembling. Her fingers investigated his face, brushed back the hair from his brow.

"I'm fine. There's nothing to worry about." He wasn't entirely sure that was true, but he was hopeful. Thanks to Russell Letson.

Russell was at the counter completing some paperwork, and Sam hurried over to thank him. They spoke for a few minutes and exchanged handshakes. Afterward it seemed to him that when Russell saw Molly standing close to his side, a bit of sadness showed in his eyes, as though he envied them the love they shared. Mentally Sam shook his head; he was growing fanciful.

"I only did what was right," Russell said as they prepared to leave. "I'm sorry it took so long for the message to reach me." He looked slightly embarrassed when Molly stepped forward and kissed his cheek. "Go home, you two, and be happy."

"That's what we intend to do," Sam said, grinning at his wife. The problems hadn't disappeared, and as soon as this crisis was over, there'd be another one, but for the moment nothing was more important than breathing in the fresh air of freedom.

"What time is it?" he asked.

"Three, maybe four," Molly said, and yawned. They'd both been up all night. In a couple of hours the ranch would come alive with activity and Sam would be needed to handle the affairs of the day. But for the next two hours, he planned to make love to his wife.

As soon as they arrived at the house, Molly led the way into their bedroom and didn't bother to turn on the lights. In the dark they removed their clothes, and when Sam got into bed, he held his arms wide. She came to him, unresisting, eager, and sighed openly when he touched her.

"It'll be morning soon," he whispered.

"I know." She let him draw her closer, her breasts nestling against his chest. Then she trailed a series of kisses from his ear and down the underside of his jaw and slid her tongue over the ultrasensitive skin there.

He lifted his head to kiss her with the pent-up longing of all the dark lonely nights of wanting her, of hungering for her. Although he was weary to the bone, he needed her now as he never had before. Needed her as an absolution for the life he'd once lived. Needed her to obliterate the pain of being accused of a crime he didn't commit. As proof that he was alive and capable of feeling and loving and caring. He positioned himself above her and thrust deep inside her welcoming body. A sigh that slipped from the back of her throat told him she needed him, too.

The incredible pleasure drove any other thought from his mind. He gave her everything. His heart, his soul, all he ever hoped to become, all he would ever be. In the aftermath of their lovemaking they clung to each other, holding tight the tenderness and unadulterated joy of being in love. Neither spoke, but the communication between them was stronger, more perfect, than any words they might have said.

Soon afterward, their positions reversed, Molly fell asleep with her head on his shoulder. A wiser man might have followed her into that gentle oblivion, but Sam chose, instead, to hold her as long as he could. To love her consciously a while longer.

Finally, exhausted, he closed his eyes. He couldn't remember the last time he'd slept, really slept, without the weight of innumerable problems bearing down on him. As he felt his mind drifting off to the peaceful state of nothingness, he remembered that Molly wasn't on the birth-control pill yet and that—for the first time since their wedding—they hadn't used any protection. He smiled, despite everything. If Molly became pregnant as a result of this night, he knew he wouldn't regret it, hard as an unplanned pregnancy would be.

"Mr. Wilson would like to see you in his office," Tom's English teacher, Mrs. Kirby, informed him before class.

The principal? Why would the principal want to see him? Tom tried to think what he might have done to get in trouble and could think of nothing. He'd played it safe since starting school. It didn't take a genius to figure out which kids were the troublemakers. Most of them were proud of the havoc they caused. Being bad was their claim to individuality—or so they thought.

When he'd entered the school as a new kid, both sides—the bad-ass guys and the serious ones—made overtures of friendship toward him. The decision had been Tom's as to which side he'd join. Last spring he'd learned his lesson about the consequences of being friends with a troublemaker like Eddie Ries.

At the time Tom had tried to play it cool, but he still felt guilty about that incident. He especially felt guilty about the look he'd seen on his mother's face when she'd come to the school to get him. That was all the lesson he needed. For a mother, his was all right. They didn't always agree, but she was pretty easy to get along with, especially now that she was married to Sam. Tom wanted to make both of them proud, so he'd carefully stayed away from anything that hinted of trouble.

Now this.

"Did Mr. Wilson say what it was about?" Tom asked his teacher. She was older, about the same age as his mother. He liked her. While it was true he wasn't ever going to enjoy reading Shakespeare, she made it tolerable.

Mrs. Kirby's look was sympathetic. "I'm afraid not."

There was a sick feeling in his stomach. To the best of his recollection, he didn't have anything to worry about; still, you didn't get called to the principal's office for the fun of it.

"Should I wait until after class?" Tom asked next.

"If I were you, I'd go now."

Tom reached for his books and walked out of the

classroom. It felt like every eye was on him as he walked down the silent hallway toward Mr. Wilson's office.

The secretary, Mrs. Kozar, glanced up when he entered the office. The first thing Tom noticed was that she wasn't smiling. Mrs. Kozar was kind of pretty and she had a funny smile that made anyone who saw it want to smile, too. It started at the edge of her lips with a little quiver and slowly spread across the rest of her mouth. This afternoon there was no quiver and no smile.

Damn, what could he have done?

"Mr. Wilson's waiting for you," Mrs. Kozar said.

Tom wanted to ask her if she knew what this was about, but even if she did, she probably wouldn't tell him. Hell, he hadn't done anything and already he felt guilty!

Tom knocked politely, waited a moment and then walked into Mr. Wilson's office. To his astonishment, he found his mother and Sam sitting there, opposite Mr. Wilson's desk.

His mother cast him a look that spelled *grounded* and worse in one swift eye-meeting glance. It was all Tom could do not to shriek that he'd done nothing wrong, dammit.

"Sit down, Tom," Mr. Wilson invited—no, ordered.

Tom took the chair next to Sam. Although he tried to relax, his body remained stiff. He clutched the chair arms with tense fingers.

"Is something wrong?" he asked, glancing first at Mr. Wilson, then his mother and Sam.

"This morning when I arrived at school," the principal said, "I discovered that someone had spray-painted graffiti on the outside of the gymnasium wall. The north wall."

Everyone focused on Tom. It took him a moment to realize that Mr. Wilson was accusing him of defacing the gym wall.

"Hey, wait a minute!" Tom was on his feet, hardly aware that he'd even moved. "I didn't do it!"

Mr. Wilson sent a sidelong glance at his mother, as if he expected her to leap into the fray.

"Ask anyone," Tom said, gesturing for someone to listen to reason. "I took the school bus this morning, the same as I always do and—"

"What about after school yesterday?" his mother asked.

Tom stared at her because she didn't sound like herself. If he didn't know better, he'd think she was about to cry. Sam and his mother held hands, and that was a good sign because it meant they weren't fighting anymore, but then he noticed that his mother's fingers were white because her grip was so tight.

"I stayed for football practice," Tom said, searching his memory. But that shouldn't be enough to condemn him. He looked at his family and then the principal. "Brian Tucker drove me home, remember?" Brian was the star quarterback and an honor student. Tom made a point of mentioning him, thinking someone would appreciate his wisdom in choosing such a worthwhile friend.

Apparently no one was impressed.

"When you transferred from the San Francisco school district to Sweetgrass," Mr. Wilson said in that prim authoritarian way he had, "we requested and received a copy of your school records."

Good, that ought to show everyone he wasn't a troublemaker. Well, sure there'd been the one incident, but that was it.

"You think because someone spray-painted the gym wall here it was me?" No one had told him *he* was going to be accused every time someone decided to decorate a wall.

"I don't think it could have been anyone else." Mr. Wilson's voice held a frightening certainty.

"I didn't do it." Tom wondered how many times he'd have to say it before someone believed him.

"Your signature's on the graffiti," his mother said, sounding really depressed. It was the same voice he'd heard in the other principal's office. The voice that said he'd failed her and somehow it was her fault. She must be a terrible mother.

"My signature," Tom said, almost relieved now. "That's got to tell you something. I may be a lot of things, but stupid isn't one of them. If I decided to do anything as dumb as spray a wall, I wouldn't sign my name to it." They must think he was some kind of moron!

"Not your name, Tom. Gang symbols."

The blood drained out of his face; Tom could actually feel himself go pale. Even his legs felt weak. He sat back down.

"The identical gang symbols you painted on the wall at your previous school," Mr. Wilson said. "I had your mother look and verify these were the same."

"But I didn't do it!" His words were edged with hysteria.

"Don't lie to me!" his mother cried. "You know how I feel about lies. You've always known. Oh, Tom, how could you do something like this?"

Tom's anger came so fast that it demanded every ounce of self-control not to grab something from Mr. Wilson's desk and hurl it through the window. "Would someone please listen?" he shouted. "I swear to you I didn't do it!"

"You don't expect me to believe that, do you?" Mr. Wilson asked, gazing at him with contempt.

"If you don't mind, I'd like to say something." Sam spoke for the first time, commanding their attention. He was the only one who seemed to be in control. Mr. Wilson was angry and his mother was about to lose it and so was he.

"Please, feel free." Mr. Wilson gestured at Sam.

"I've never known my stepson to lie," he began. "I'm not saying the kid's another George Washington, but in all my dealings with him, he's been honest and fair. If Tom says he isn't responsible for the graffiti, then I feel obliged to believe him."

Tom was so grateful someone trusted him enough to defend him that tears welled in his eyes. It embarrassed him and he looked away and hoped no one noticed when he pressed his sleeve to his face.

"How do you explain the gang symbols then?" Mr. Wilson asked, as if that was all the evidence needed to hang Tom from the nearest tree.

"Tom isn't the only student in the school who knows gang symbols." Again it was Sam who spoke in his defense.

"*California* gang symbols?" the principal said.

"My guess is there are any number of students who have access to that kind of information. Answer me this, Mr. Wilson," Sam said. "Has Tom caused any trouble since the start of school?"

"No, but it's early in the year—"

"In other words, you *expect* me to be a trouble-maker!" Tom shouted, so mad he couldn't sit still.

One sidelong glance from Sam advised him to keep his mouth shut. Seeing that Sam was the only one willing to champion his cause, Tom was willing to follow the unspoken advice.

"What about his friends?"

Mr. Wilson's eyes lowered. "He seems to have made friends with young men who rarely require disciplinary measures."

Like Brian Tucker. Tom nodded profoundly for emphasis, thinking this should be another point in his defense.

"Is there anyone who *saw* Tom do the spray-painting?"

Mr. Wilson cleared his throat. "No."

"Any physical evidence? A can of paint in Tom's locker? Paint on his clothes or shoes the same color as the graffiti?"

Mr. Wilson wasn't making eye contact with them any longer. "None."

Sam paused and glanced over at Tom, giving him a half smile. "Then perhaps it would be best if we decided to forget this unfortunate incident."

"Who's going to repaint the wall?" Mr. Wilson demanded. "I'll have you know that's school property, and it's against policy to deface anything belonging to the school."

"Perhaps you could ask for volunteers?" Sam suggested.

Tom had liked Sam from the first. But even if he'd never gotten along with Sam and resented him for marrying his mother, even if he'd hated the way Sam had become part of their family, everything would have changed this day. Sam was more than his stepfather. He was his friend.

Sam had believed him when no one else did. He'd stuck up for him when his own mother had found him guilty. This was no small thing, and Tom would never forget it.

"Tom," Mr. Wilson said, looking directly into his eyes. "If I misjudged you, then I apologize. What Mr. Dakota said is true. So far you've proved yourself to be a good student and a fine young man. I hope you'll forgive me for leaping to conclusions. Adults do that sometimes." The principal stood and held out his hand.

Tom shook it and met Mr. Wilson's eyes without flinching. He exchanged a firm handshake with the older man. Sam had taught him about handshakes, too—the importance of meeting the other man's eye and firmly shaking his hand. None of that limp-wristed stuff.

"No problem, Mr. Wilson," Tom said, grateful to be back in good standing with the principal. "We all make mistakes. If I find out who did paint the gym wall, I won't worry about being called a snitch. I'll tell you." Whoever it was had tried to frame him, and Tom wasn't going to let that pass.

"You do that. Now get back to Mrs. Kirby's room."

"Thanks." He was halfway out the door when he stopped and turned around. "Thanks, Sam." His mother's look was forlorn and miserable. He wished she'd stuck up for him, too, but Tom kind of understood. It was because his real father was such a jerk and had lied to her so many times. So he had to forgive her.

"I'll see you tonight, Mom."

She nodded and Tom could see she was close to tears. Good, a little guilt now and again wasn't a bad thing. She'd probably cook his favorite dinners all week to make up for this.

Maybe things weren't so bad, after all.

Molly was an emotional wreck. She'd just been through one of the most traumatic weeks of her life. First Sam had been arrested, and when she'd finished dealing with that crisis, the school had phoned. The incident with Tom had taught her some valuable lessons. She'd been willing to believe a stranger over her own son. Her heart ached each time she thought about that afternoon. Sam had been the one to stand up for her son.

She knew why he'd done it, too. Sam understood what it was to be falsely accused. She was convinced of Tom's innocence. But not in the beginning, and that she would always regret. She'd let her son down when he'd needed her most.

If that wasn't enough, Sam sold off part of the herd and was forced, along with the other independent ranchers, to accept the lowest price in a decade. The check wasn't enough to cover expenses. They had no choice but to apply for a loan.

Molly rode into town with Sam when he went to the bank to talk to Mr. Burns. There was some consolation in learning that the Broken Arrow wasn't the only ranch in the area experiencing financial difficulties. Sam and Molly had spent most of every night for the past week reviewing the money situation. It didn't look promising.

Although Molly had applied to the school district for work, there hadn't been an opening for a language teacher. She had mixed feelings about this. They needed the money of course—but she actually enjoyed being a stay-at-home wife and mother. For a while, anyway. It was the first time since Clay's birth that she was able to be with her children. In the beginning she'd expected to be bored within a month, but the house needed a lot of work, a lot of maintenance, and she'd been able to provide it with a minimum of expense.

"Do you mind if I don't go in to see Mr. Burns with you?" she asked Sam. He'd parked in front of the bank and didn't look all that thrilled about the appointment himself.

"No problem," he said, and Molly glanced down the street to the pawnshop. Every week without Sam's knowing, she'd taken a little of her grocery money to pay off what was owed on Sam's rodeo buckle. She'd wanted to give it to him as a wedding present, but the cost had been too high.

"Sure you're okay?" Molly asked, her attention returning to the bank. As she recalled, Mr. Burns seemed a decent enough man, sympathetic to the needs of the community. Surely other ranchers had been forced to ask him for assistance.

"I'm not looking forward to this, if that's what you mean," Sam said, and with an exaggerated groan of dread, opened the door on the driver's side.

Molly placed her hand on his forearm, stopping him. "Need a little fortification?" she asked suggestively, then moistened her lips so there'd be no doubt about exactly what she had in mind.

Sam's eyes sparked as he gazed at her lips, and Molly could see he was tempted. "Later, all right?"

She was mildly disappointed, but smiled and nodded.

"Oh, what the hell," he said in an abrupt change of

mood. He reached for her, his fingers slipping into her hair as he brought her mouth to his.

The kiss was hot enough to cause a nuclear melt-down, and when they broke apart, Molly sincerely wished they were anywhere but Front Street.

"Does the Sweetgrass Motel rent by the hour?" Sam whispered as his lips hovered close to hers.

"Sam!" Molly giggled and prodded her husband's arm. "Go see Mr. Bank President. Smile real nice and let him know how very grateful little ol' us would be if he sees fit to grant us a loan."

Sam chuckled. "You might be a hell of a lot better at this than me."

"Get in there, cowboy, and do your best." They both avoided talking about what would happen if Mr. Burns refused to advance them credit.

Sam frowned suddenly.

"What is it?" Molly asked.

He shook his head, then looked away. "Someone else once called me cowboy."

"A woman, no doubt." Molly pretended to be jealous.

"As a matter of fact it was. Pearl Mitchell."

"Oh." Pearl's body had yet to be found, but there was plenty of speculation. The matter of Pearl's disappearance might have been forgotten if not for the efforts of Russell Letson. Ginny told her that the attorney spent a lot of time riding Sheriff Maynard about the case. It left Molly wondering what connection Russell might have had with Pearl. Had he been one of her clients? Presumably that wasn't something a man like Russell would want broadcasted. According to Ginny, Pearl was said to have been popular with her customers—but no one seemed to care what had happened to her as much as Russell. Were there personal reasons for his obsession, reasons no one knew? Still, Molly couldn't see the attorney with a woman like Pearl.

"I hope they solve that case." An eerie unreal feeling came over her every time she thought about the murder.

"I hope so, too," Sam added.

Molly's own reasons were mostly selfish. Once the real killer was brought in and tried, no one could point a finger at Sam. Molly believed in her husband's innocence with all her heart, but she wasn't sure everyone else in town did.

"I'll meet you back here in a half hour," Sam said as he headed into the bank.

Molly waited until he was out of sight before walking down to the pawnshop. The bell jingled above the door when she entered. Max Anderson hurried out from the back room and nodded in greeting when he saw her. He was a tall skinny man with a lank ponytail and one gold front tooth.

"Making another payment, are you?" Max asked.

"Please." Molly set her purse on the counter and reached inside for the ten-dollar bill. At this rate it would take her years to buy back Sam's award buckle, but she refused to let him lose it.

"That's an interesting cameo you're wearing," Max said.

Molly's fingers closed around the necklace, surprised he hadn't noticed it before. She wore it every day as a reminder of Gramps and of her grandparents' love. The cameo and the plain gold band around her finger were the only pieces of jewelry that had any real meaning for her.

"Gramps gave it to me years ago after my grandmother died."

"Do you mind if I take a look at it?"

Molly hesitated a moment, but at last slipped the chain from around her neck and gave it to Max.

He held it in the palm of his hand, then turned it over and studied the back. "This is a family piece, isn't it?"

"Gramps bought it during the Second World War, someplace in France, I believe."

"It could have been Italy. Quite a few cameos are made there."

Molly hadn't known that.

"It's lovely."

"Thank you." She held out her hand; Max seemed a little reluctant to let the cameo go.

"You take care of it," he said.

"I will," Molly promised with complete confidence. This cameo, like the ranch, was part of her heritage. Someday she'd give it to Tom's wife or perhaps her own granddaughter. When she did, Molly would tell the story of a young man trapped in a war and the woman he loved who waited half a world away for his safe return.

"I didn't think you'd want to sell it." Max accepted her payment and subtracted that amount from what was owed on the silver buckle. "This is a good thing you're doing," he said with a nod of approval.

"Sam's the generous one."

"He's a good man, I agree with you there," the pawnbroker said.

She and Max exchanged friendly goodbyes. Her business finished, she walked back to where Sam had parked the pickup. Assuming he'd still be a while, she decided to look around the J. C. Penney store. She was about to venture inside when she heard Sam call her.

Surprised he was finished so soon, Molly turned around to see him storm across Front Street.

"Let's get out of here," he said, his mouth tight with anger.

"Already?" He hadn't been with Mr. Burns more than ten minutes, if that.

"No need to discuss the matter of a loan any further," Sam muttered. He turned away, as if he'd failed her.

"What happened?" Molly had to know.

"We aren't going to get any loan, Molly. We're going to have to find another way to hold on to the ranch."

Sixteen

The alarm sounded, and Molly groaned as she climbed out of bed, leaving Sam to sleep while she brewed a pot of coffee. These late-October mornings were crisp and cold, and she reached for her robe and tied it securely about her waist, then made her way, blurry-eyed, into the kitchen. Standing in front of the coffeemaker, she waited for the hot water to filter through for the first cup.

"Mornin'," Sam murmured a couple of minutes later as he moved behind her. He wrapped his arms around her waist and buried his face in her neck. Turning into his arms, Molly hugged her husband, savoring the closeness they shared.

Sam yawned. He was exhausted, Molly realized, and wished he'd stayed in bed awhile longer. She didn't know what time he'd gone to sleep, but it was long after she had, and that had been close to midnight. Sam had wanted to review the accounting books one last time before meeting with the other independent ranchers.

"I've got the Cattlemen's Association meeting this morning," he reminded her.

Molly rested her forehead against his shoulder and swallowed a sigh. With money worries crowding in around them, they clung to each other for emotional support. Their lovemaking had taken on an abandonment, a need, as if proving their love often enough would safeguard their world.

Molly tightened her arms around him. She treasured these moments before the boys paraded down the stairs. The serenity of the morning would shatter as soon as Tom and Clay charged into the kitchen.

The coffeepot gurgled. Reluctantly Molly disentangled herself from her husband's arms and brought down two mugs, filling each one. The aroma, which generally revived her, had the opposite effect this morning. Her stomach heaved, and for a couple of seconds she actually thought she might be sick.

"You okay?" Sam asked. "You don't look so good."

"I'm fine," she lied. It was the strain and worry of their financial situation. Molly knew that stress could manifest itself in all kinds of physical ailments. She didn't want to add health concerns to Sam's already heavy load, so she reassured him with a saucy grin. "If you come back to bed, I'll show you exactly how fine I am."

"Don't tempt me." He took a first tentative sip of his coffee and glanced at his watch. "I've got to get moving." He kissed her cheek and, carrying his mug, disappeared into their bedroom.

Still feeling a bit queasy, she leaned against the counter. She remembered the last time the smell of coffee had bothered her—when she was pregnant with Clay. *Pregnant.* Molly frowned and realized she couldn't recall the date of her last period. She thought she'd been on schedule since Gramps's death, but couldn't be sure. It went without saying that the expense of a pregnancy just then would cripple them. The health insurance they did have was limited, and it paid next to nothing for routine medical conditions. Like pregnancies.

The doctor had told her the emotional upheaval of Gramps's death might upset her cycle, so she'd put off starting her birth-control pills for a month or two. But she and Sam had been so careful! She *couldn't* be pregnant.

At the sound of footsteps pounding down the stairs, Molly removed half a dozen eggs from the refrigerator. One of the pleasures of being an at-home mom was that she could indulge her boys with the luxury of a hot meal on these cool autumn mornings.

"What's for breakfast?" Clay asked as he clumped into the kitchen. The half-grown dog trotted behind him, settling beneath the table. Her son pulled out a chair and immediately reached for the radio. Five minutes of world, national and Montana news was followed by the listing of school lunches, beef prices and the reminder of radio bingo and the local sponsors.

"We get hot dogs today," Clay said cheerfully. "Is it all right if I buy my lunch?"

"Sure." Molly cracked the eggs against the side of a ceramic bowl, then added milk and whipped the mixture with a fork.

"I'll take his lunch if you've already got it packed," Tom said. His voice alternated between two octaves; her oldest son was becoming a man, and the evidence showed every time he spoke.

"You need two lunches?" Molly asked him. He'd

grown an inch and a half over the summer, and his appetite had never been better. Must be the country air, Molly concluded.

"I'll eat the second one after school," Tom explained, "before football practice."

Dressed in a pair of freshly laundered jeans, a Western shirt and string tie, Sam joined the others in the kitchen. "Something smells good."

"French toast," Clay informed him.

"You two can set the table," Molly said to the boys.

"Going someplace, Dad?" Tom asked.

Molly smiled every time she heard Tom address Sam as Dad. He'd started shortly after the incident at the school. Sam had never made a big deal of it, but she knew it pleased him. It pleased her, too.

"A meeting with the other cattlemen," Sam answered.

Suddenly the radio announcer had a news flash. Human remains had been discovered along Route 32, about fifteen miles outside town. A couple of hunters had happened upon the decomposed body and reported their find to the sheriff's office.

Molly's hand stilled and her gaze sought Sam's. "Pearl Mitchell?" she asked.

"That would be my guess," he said with a note of sadness.

"Isn't she the lady someone killed?" Clay asked. "I didn't think people got murdered in places like Sweetgrass. That's the kind of stuff that goes on in San Francisco, not Montana."

Molly had believed the same thing. Not once in all the months she'd been in Sweetgrass had she thought to even lock the house. The dogs were protection enough. And as for locking the car—well, according to a crime report she'd heard over the radio, there hadn't been a car stolen in three years.

"How will they know if the remains belong to that missing woman?" Tom wanted to know.

"The sheriff will probably send them to a laboratory in Helena," Sam explained. "With luck, the body could give the authorities enough evidence to locate the murderer."

Molly hoped that was true. Hardly anyone spoke of the killing these days. It had been several weeks now, and with no suspects and few clues, Pearl's murder remained unsolved. Sometimes Molly still worried that the people of Sweetgrass blamed Sam, but that didn't appear to be the case. It was as though the subject of the murdered hooker was forbidden. People felt bad about her death, but she wasn't someone they knew or cared about. The only people who seemed to miss her— besides Russell Letson—were the randy cowhands who came into town looking for a good time. But from what Molly heard, there were plenty of young women willing to take over where Pearl had left off.

The boys grabbed their books and were out the door five minutes before the school bus was due at the end of their drive. Molly carried their syrupy plates to the sink, which she filled with hot sudsy water.

"I'm leaving, too," Sam said, reaching for his Stetson. He paused in the doorway. "Just make dinner for the boys tonight. Something easy."

Molly frowned. "What about us?"

"We're going out to dinner."

They so rarely went out that the idea flustered her. "Where? Why?"

"Dinner and a movie."

Finances didn't allow this sort of thing. "But, Sam—"

"No arguments." He grinned, and any resistance she felt melted away.

"Are we celebrating something special?"

His grin widened. "Yeah, I just don't know what it is yet. How about celebrating the fact that I love you? Is that a good enough reason?"

She nodded, feeling the strangest urge to cry. Sam left then, and in the quiet of the morning, the sun cresting the hill, Molly sat down with a fresh cup of coffee and a piece of toast.

One sip of the coffee and her stomach heaved again. Surprised, she flattened her hand against her abdomen. Her eyes shot to the calendar, pinned to the bulletin board near the phone.

Standing, she took it down. She flipped back to September and studied the notes she'd scribbled—the reminders of meetings and dentist visits, the church women's group, PTA meeting at Clay's school. And there was that terrible night when Sam was arrested. Afterward they'd made love without protection—the one and only time.

Could she possibly be pregnant because they'd been careless just once?

Her stomach was all the answer she needed. She'd enjoyed good health while pregnant with Tom and Clay, but during the first two months she'd suffered frequent bouts of nausea. She'd been forced to give up coffee because the mere smell of it made her retch. Both times.

Molly didn't need a doctor's appointment to confirm what she already knew.

She was pregnant.

* * *

Russell sat in the darkness of his cabin, holding a glass of bourbon. The ice had long since melted and diluted the potency of the drink. He wished he was more of a drinking man. That way he might be able to escape this gut-wrenching pain, at least for a little while. All he needed was a few hours' respite so he could sleep.

Since he'd learned of Pearl's death, he hadn't slept an entire night; he woke up frequently, often hourly. Nightmares, grief and tension hounded him the minute he closed his eyes. Once exhaustion dragged him into a troubled sleep, he'd wake abruptly, Pearl's screams echoing in his ears. More likely they were his own.

The sheriff had phoned late the night before to tell him about the most recent discovery. Although Russell had no official connection with the murder investigation, he'd been allowed to visit the site.

Afterward he'd had no doubt left that the remains were Pearl's. The shallow grave had been unearthed by wild animals, and human bones were scattered in a half-mile radius. An hour after he arrived, he'd driven directly to his cabin. He hadn't been there since the murder. Too many memories. Too much pain. He still hadn't been sure he was ready to handle the place, but he'd been so tired and the cabin so close. Here, he wouldn't need to deal with anyone.

If he had it to do over again, there were so many things he'd change. The regrets stacked up till they reached halfway to the heavens. His fingers were numb with cold, and Russell raised the glass to his lips and gulped down the alcohol.

Soon he felt groggy, but not groggy enough. A so-called friend, offering to help him through this difficult time, had given him a handful of sleeping pills. Russell hadn't wanted them, but now he was tempted. He'd been awake all night following Maynard's call about what the hunters had found. This morning, in the woods, he'd watched deputies scoop up Pearl's remains and shove them into a black plastic garbage bag. That had shattered whatever little peace he'd managed to achieve in the weeks since her murder. He withdrew the brown bottle from his coat pocket and spilled two capsules into his palm.

Sleep. He'd sell his soul for a single night's sleep. Without another thought he tossed the pills into his mouth. It didn't take long for the combination of drugs and alcohol to begin having the desired effect.

Moving into the bedroom, he stripped off his clothes and sank onto the mattress, his back to the wall. When he found the energy, he got up, pulled back the covers and climbed between the cool sheets. Almost immediately his bare feet encountered a silky nightgown.

Pearl's. From her last visit.

With a sense of unbearable grief, he reached for the long peach-colored gown and held it against his heart. He closed his eyes, waiting for oblivion.

When he awoke, the room was cold and dark, so dark it was virtually impossible to see. The gown Russell had pressed against his heart was now wrapped around his upper body. He flung it aside and covered his eyes with the back of his hand.

As he lay there, eyes squeezed shut, the scent of roses, the French perfume Pearl had loved, drifted toward him. His need for her was so great his senses had actually invented it, fulfilling his desperate longing for the woman he'd lost.

The lingering aroma of roses grew stronger. Russell knew that the minute he opened his eyes it'd be gone. He was determined to savor it while he could. Fantasy, whatever, he didn't care. Not if it brought him close to Pearl for even a minute.

Pain tightened his chest and he wondered what he'd say to Pearl if he had the opportunity to speak to her one last time. Even though he knew she was dead, he could pretend she was there with him. He wanted her lying at his side as she so often had in the past.

"I'm so sorry," he whispered, his voice shaking with emotion. "We could have made it work…."

The scent of her perfume seemed even more potent. He kept his eyes closed as he struggled to banish from his mind the horror of her last few minutes on earth. These were the thoughts that had tormented him for weeks. She must have been in horrible pain, experienced terrible fear. He hoped with all his heart that she hadn't been bound, that she'd put up a fight. Dear God, he couldn't bear to think about it any longer. Part of him died with her every time he imagined her final minutes.

He must have drifted off to sleep because when he woke up again it was morning. Sun leaked into the bedroom from between the heavy drapes. Pearl's nightgown was next to his pillow where he'd flung it. Sitting up, he reached for it now and brought it to his chest. He wadded up the soft material as he buried his face in it, longing to immerse himself in her perfumed scent. But the beautiful aroma of the roses, like Pearl, was gone.

Sam was definitely pleased.

Money worries had festered in him for nearly a month. Beef prices were at a record low. Ranchers couldn't afford to raise cattle in this current economic climate. At this price, it actually *cost* them to raise beef.

That was what the cattlemen's meeting had been about. As a group, they'd taken their concerns to the bank and Mr. Burns. It seemed the banker was anxious to help when faced with all the ranchers in the county withdrawing their funds en masse.

That morning when he'd left Molly, Sam had impulsively made a dinner date with her. At the time there'd been nothing to celebrate. Now there was. He had the loan, and although the terms weren't the best, it was the first piece of good news in quite a while.

"Are you going to tell me?" Molly asked, sitting across the table from him. She'd barely glanced at the menu.

"All in good time," he said, grinning at her. She looked especially lovely, and he wondered if he could keep his eyes off her long enough to actually eat.

"Sam, I swear, I'll have a perfectly awful evening until you tell me what happened this morning."

There was no help for it. He would've preferred to hold out a bit longer, but... His grin felt like it spread halfway across his face; that was how good he felt. "We got the loan," he announced.

Molly closed her eyes and brought her fingers to her lips. "Oh, Sam."

"The terms aren't that terrific," he felt obliged to tell her.

"But at least we have the money we'll need for now, right?"

Sam nodded and reached across the table for her hand. "First half's due December first."

Her eyes continued to hold his. "So soon?"

"I'm not worried about it, because I'll sell off the last of the herd then. Even if beef prices stay as low as they have been, we'll be able to meet the payment without a problem."

Molly leaned back in her chair, and the relief he saw in her eyes humbled him. He'd had no idea she'd been this worried. Molly was gutsy and determined, and she'd silently clung to her doubts and fears, rather than place more pressure on him. Sam loved her for it; at the same time he was sorry she hadn't come to him.

Flustered, she brushed her emotion aside. "I'm sorry—I don't know what came over me."

"We're going to be all right." If nothing else, he wanted to reassure her that no matter what happened, they'd find a way. They'd manage.

"I know. It's just that..." Sniffling she picked up her purse and sorted through the contents until she found what she wanted. A tissue. She dabbed at both eyes, then stuffed it back inside the purse.

"Did you get a chance to talk to Tom?" she asked in an obvious effort to change the subject. She blinked furiously to keep back fresh tears.

"He was coming into the house just as I was leaving."

"He had some good news, too," Molly told him.

"About the football team?" Although thin and wiry, Tom had turned out to be an excellent wide receiver. Brian Tucker had made Tom his favorite pass receiver, and Tom had quickly advanced from junior-varsity level to varsity—something of a rarity for a sophomore. Although he had no right to feel proud of Tom's accomplishments, Sam did. Damn proud.

"By the way, they found the person responsible for the graffiti," Molly said.

"Who?" Sam asked with keen interest.

"Tony Hudson."

The name meant nothing to Sam. "Another student?"

"A senior. He was caught doing some more spray-painting by Mr. Wilson himself."

"Why'd he do it?" Sam figured someone—this Tony?—had purposely set Tom up. Either that or it was a coincidence, which wasn't too likely in Sam's opinion.

"So many young people are involved in gangs these days," Molly said. "And just as many want to be. It's frightening."

"Even here in Sweetgrass?" That was incomprehensible to Sam.

"Mr. Wilson seems to think so."

Sam mulled that over for a moment. "Did Tony have anything to say in his defense?"

Molly laughed. "This kid needs a good attorney, because his defense is almost ludicrous. He claims someone hired him to do it."

Sam went still. "Who?"

Molly shook her head at the improbability of such a statement. "I think someone ought to contact Russell, don't you?"

Sam grinned, but he wasn't amused. With everything that had happened at the ranch this summer, he wasn't taking such talk lightly. What better way to undermine and discourage a rancher than to attack his children? It was difficult enough to protect his cattle and land. Now Sam knew he had to shield the boys, as well. The best approach would be to sit down and talk with them, man to man.

"You're so serious all at once," Molly said, her happiness shining through her smile. "This is supposed to be a night to set our worries aside and enjoy each other's company, remember?"

"I couldn't have said it better myself."

"Oh, before I forget, I volunteered you for the school Harvest Moon Festival."

Sam groaned in good-humored resignation. All week, Tom and Clay had been joking about whether or not Sam was going to help out at the school festival. Sam wasn't altogether comfortable with the prospect and had half hoped it wouldn't arise. "Okay. What am I supposed to do?"

"Don't you dare look at me like that!"

Sam couldn't keep from laughing, and at Molly's puzzled smile, he explained, "You sound just like a wife."

"I am a wife, as if I needed to remind you."

Sam was still astonished by how much he loved this sense of belonging, of being a part of her and the boys' lives. A family man. A member of the community. A couple of hours stuck behind some booth at the Harvest Moon Festival was a small price to pay.

"Sam."

Dick Arnold approached the table, and Sam got to his feet to shake hands with him. Then he introduced the other rancher to Molly.

"I wanted to thank you for what you said this morning," Dick said. "Hell, if it hadn't been for you, I don't know what we would've done. You sure helped us keep things on track. So thank you, Sam, and I'm saying this for a whole lot of us."

Sam was too shocked to answer. He wasn't accustomed to dealing with compliments. They embarrassed him. He wished Dick had chosen to speak with him privately, rather than in front of Molly.

At last he said, "I'm glad we were able to come up with a workable solution."

"Yeah, but you're the one who convinced us to present a united front. There was some talk after the meeting about nominating you for president next year. Would you consider running? We need someone with a clear head and a sense of direction." He paused, then chuckled. "Look, I didn't mean to interrupt your evening out. Just wanted to stop off, meet the missus and say thanks." Dick touched the brim of his hat. "Nice meeting you," he said to Molly, then turned and walked away.

Knowing his wife was about to hound him with unnecessary questions, Sam reached for the menu. As if on cue, the waitress appeared and they placed their order. He was a little disappointed when Molly declined a glass of wine. It would have gone nicely with their dinner.

"Tell me what you've volunteered me for," he said, steering the conversation back to the Harvest Moon Festival.

"Frying hamburgers between six and seven."

Sam gave an exaggerated groan.

"I'll be working the cotton-candy machine at the same time," Molly added, as if she needed to prove she was doing her part. "Mrs. Mayfield is an expert at getting people to work together for the common good."

"And who, may I ask, is Mrs. Mayfield?"

"Mrs. Mayfield, the choir director from church. She's coordinating the event this year."

Sam grumbled under his breath, but he didn't really object. In fact, he looked forward to slinging a few burgers. Not bad for a man who'd once feared the future.

A calliope played loudly in the background. The grounds behind the high school had taken on a festive air. Schoolchildren raced in and out of the gymnasium, where they spent their tickets on such wildly popular games as the Balloon Toss and the Jelly Bean Count.

Molly was busy swirling cotton candy around small white tubes. The sticky pink stuff decorated her clothes and tangled in her hair.

Sam dished up hamburgers close by, chatting with their neighbors as if he'd lived in the community all his life. Every now and then she'd look up to see him smiling and exchanging greetings with a fellow rancher. She'd heard from other wives that Sam's speech at the Cattlemen's Association meeting had stirred the ranchers into action. It made her proud to be his wife.

The full yellow moon dominated the evening sky. The air was crisp and cold, but Molly didn't mind. Gaiety and laughter could be heard everywhere, mingled with occasional screams from the Haunted House. Mr. Wilson, the high-school principal, strolled past and introduced her to his wife. Mr. Givens, from the supply store, bought cotton candy for his grandchildren. He'd donated two bales of hay and a thousand pennies for the penny search, scheduled at seven.

Tom and Clay had disappeared the minute they arrived, intent on avoiding the embarrassment of being seen with their parents. Sam had given them each enough money to buy their own dinners, but Molly

guessed the money had gone for fairground junk food—
nothing she would've considered *real* food.

Toward the end of her shift, Russell Letson stopped
by and bought some cotton candy, which he presented
to a toddler who was begging her mother for a goodie.
Molly had guessed there was a kindness about him, a
gentleness. He seemed quiet and more withdrawn than
she remembered, but more at peace with himself, too.

"It's good to see you, Molly."

"You, too."

"Are you happy?"

It wasn't a question she would have expected from
him. "Very."

"I'm really pleased. Walt was right, you know. Sam's
a good man."

"I think so, too."

Russell nodded and with a small wave, walked on
to another booth.

"Mom!" Panting, Tom burst onto the scene a few
minutes later. "I can't find Clay! Not anywhere."

"I'm sure he's around." Molly scanned the crowd,
but to no avail.

"I've looked everywhere! Mom, something's happened to him!"

"Tom—"

"No one's seen him in more than an hour. I've
looked. Everyone's looked."

"I'm sure there's a perfectly logical explanation. He's
probably sitting in a corner petting a dog or something."

"You didn't believe me before!" Tom shouted, gripping her arm. "Believe me now."

A chill raced down Molly's spine.

"An *hour,* Mom. I've been looking for an hour!"

Tom was close to panic. Molly had never seen him like this. She held his look for an instant, then said, "I'll get Sam."

Seventeen

Sam saw the fear in Molly's eyes even before he heard that Clay was nowhere to be found. "I'm sure he's here somewhere," he said, confident the youngster was just off with friends.

"That's what I thought, too," Tom said, clutching Sam's shirtsleeve. "But I looked everywhere and I've talked to all his friends. No one's seen him. No one. I was holding on to some of his money for him, and we were supposed to meet so I could give it to him. He didn't show up. That was an hour ago."

"Do you think he might have gotten involved in something and lost track of the time?" Sam asked.

"I'd think that, except for one thing. He came after me twice for his money, and I told him he had to wait until seven-thirty like we agreed. He'd been bugging me for it earlier, and then he didn't show."

Sam couldn't pretend he wasn't worried. "So that's when you started asking around?"

"Yeah. No one's seen him."

"I'm sure there's a perfectly logical explanation for this," Molly said again, as if that would make it true.

But no one had to remind her that there was a murderer loose in Sweetgrass.

"You're right—I'm sure there's a good reason." Sam slipped his arm around his wife's shoulders. "I suggest we break up and start searching." He glanced at his watch. "We'll go in three different directions and meet back here in fifteen minutes. Okay?"

Both Molly and Tom agreed with a nod. A couple of Clay's friends wanted to help, and Sam asked them to check the gymnasium. Afraid the boy might have been lured into the parking lot, Sam headed in that direction himself. He retrieved a flashlight from the truck and walked slowly down the lanes of parked vehicles.

He called Clay's name repeatedly, and when he'd covered the whole lot with no success, he returned to the rendezvous point. Molly and Tom were waiting for him. He saw by the worry in their eyes that they hadn't found Clay, either. A knot of fear tightened in his stomach. While he didn't want to alarm his family, he was growing more apprehensive by the minute.

This was the worst thing that had happened yet, and it was hard not to believe that everything was connected. He couldn't stand this, couldn't stand the thought of Clay being in danger. If ever he'd needed proof of his feelings for Molly's children, the tension in his gut spelled it out.

"Mom!"

At the sound of Clay's voice, Molly whirled around. The boy ran toward her, legs pumping frantically. He burst into tears and caught her about the waist, clinging as though he never intended to release her.

"Where were you?" Tom demanded, so angry his face was white.

"Someone grabbed me," Clay said, breathless and holding on tightly to his mother. His face was streaked with dirt and tears.

"Who?" Sam asked, squatting down so he was eye level with the boy. He gripped Clay's upper arms and waited for a response.

"I...don't know. I didn't see who it was, 'cept he wore army boots and one of his shoelaces had broken and was tied short. He threw a gunnysack over my head and carried me away. I couldn't see anything! Then he stuffed me in the trunk of a car and closed it."

"Dear Lord!" Molly gasped.

"I pounded and shouted, but no one came—no one heard me." Clay made a gallant effort not to start sobbing again. "At first I thought it was Tom."

"I'd never do that!" his older brother cried in outrage.

"I know you wouldn't," Clay said. "Then I thought they wanted my money, but I'd already spent it, and besides, he didn't even ask."

"Did you hear his voice?"

"No. But he was big and mean, and—"

"I thought you said you didn't see him," Sam reminded the boy.

"I didn't, but he lifted me up as if I didn't weigh hardly anything and I came high off the ground and when I kicked him, he didn't even grunt."

"How'd you get away?" Molly asked in a shaky voice.

"I...I don't know. Someone opened the trunk, pulled me out and untied my hands, then called me a bunch of dirty names. By the time I got the gunnysack off my head he was gone. I was afraid he'd change his mind and come after me again so I took off running."

"I think we'd better report this to the sheriff," Sam said, more angry than he could remember being in a long time. First the incident with Tom and now this. He placed a protective hand on Clay's shoulder.

"No!" Clay shouted. "I don't like Sheriff Maynard."

Lord knew Sam wasn't keen on the man himself, but he wasn't about to let this incident pass. Someone had tried to kidnap his son, and personal feelings aside, Sam wouldn't put Clay at risk. Not for anything.

"We're talking to the sheriff," Molly countered in a tone that said she wouldn't be persuaded otherwise.

They found Maynard sitting at one of the long rows of picnic tables, eating his hamburger off a paper plate. He didn't look like he wanted to be disturbed, but that didn't deter Sam.

He promptly reported the attempted kidnapping. The sheriff listened intently and wrote down the particulars. "I'd like to speak to Clay myself."

"Fine," Sam said.

The sheriff wiped his hands on a paper napkin and stood. He paused, looking back at Sam. "We got started off on the wrong foot, Dakota. I seem to have jumped to conclusions about you. I haven't seen many guys make turnarounds, but you did. You've proved me wrong. If you're willing, I'd like to put the past behind us."

Sam nodded, astonished by the other man's willingness to let bygones be bygones.

Sheriff Maynard stuck out his hand and Sam shook it.

A ruckus broke out on the far side of the football field, close to where the hay had been spread for the penny toss. The lawman headed in that direction and Sam followed. A group of teenage boys had gathered in a wide circle around a fight in progress. Most were too involved in shouting encouragement to notice the sheriff and Sam approach the outer circle. It didn't take Sam long to recognize the smaller of the two boys.

His first instinct was to jump in and break it up, but he knew Tom wouldn't appreciate his interference, nor did Sam want to embarrass the boy. He expected Sheriff Maynard to do it for him, but to his surprise the lawman stood back for a few minutes and did nothing.

"Sometimes it's best to let them get it out of their systems," he said, chewing on a toothpick. "I'll step in if it gets out of hand."

Sam wasn't sure he agreed, seeing that the other boy had a good thirty pounds on Tom. But what Tom lacked in weight, he more than compensated for with agility. He took a solid hit to the face and Sam flinched, knowing the boy would come away with a shiner. Tom slammed a fist into his opponent's gut, and the kid stumbled backward holding on to his belly. After that, the sheriff stepped into the fray.

He spat out his toothpick. "Okay, okay, that's enough. Let's break it up here." The crowd parted and the lawman grabbed each boy by the scruff of the neck. "You two're finished, understand?"

Tom's nose was bleeding and his right eye had already started to swell.

"Now shake hands and be on your way."

Neither boy was willing to extend a hand.

"Let me put it like this," the sheriff said calmly. "Either shake hands or I'll take you both down to the office, charge you with disturbing the peace and give you a hefty fine. The choice is yours."

Tom and his opponent reluctantly shook hands.

"Good. Now get out of here, and if I see you fighting again, you're going to be in more trouble than you want to even know about. You understand me?"

Tom lowered his head and nodded. As the crowd dispersed, Sam hurried over to him. "Do you want to tell me what that was all about?" he asked, giving Tom his handkerchief.

Tom shook his head.

"Okay. That's up to you. We've talked about fights before, and if you chose to take on someone who's bigger and uglier than you, you must've had a good reason. If you want to leave it at that, then I respect your decision."

Tom held the handkerchief to his bloody nose and looked at Sam through his one good eye. "That's Tony Hudson."

The name sounded vaguely familiar. It took Sam a couple of minutes to remember that Tony Hudson was the boy linked to the graffiti incident.

"I think he might have had something to do with what happened to Clay tonight, too," Tom muttered. "I wouldn't put it past him."

Sam gently squeezed the boy's shoulder. He understood that a man had to protect what was his—and that included his reputation. Tony Hudson had tried to destroy that. Although Sam didn't advocate fighting, he wasn't going to lecture Tom. He grimaced; no need to guess what Molly's reaction would be when she saw her son's swollen face.

His wife took one look at Tom, covered her mouth and promptly exploded with questions. "Are you all right, Tom? How's your eye? Who started the fight?" She paused for breath. "What's the matter with you?"

she cried, then turned disgustedly to Sam, as if he was somehow personally responsible for the fight.

"Molly—"

"Stay out of this, Sam. How could you have stood by and let this happen?" she snapped. "I saw you— standing there, encouraging him." Whirling back around, she caught Tom's chin and angled his head upward, none too gently. "Let me see that eye." She gasped when she saw how swollen it was and glared again at Sam.

"I'm ashamed of you, Thomas. Ashamed."

"Ah, Mom. Sam's cool about it. Why can't you be?"

Molly tossed Sam a look that could have turned a man to stone. She steered both boys toward the car and left Sam to follow or remain at the festival and find his own way home.

He had the feeling this evening wouldn't be ending the way he'd planned—making love to his wife. At the rate things were going he'd be lucky if she so much as kissed him good-night.

After the doctor confirmed what Molly already knew, she realized the next step was to tell Sam. She'd planned to do it the night of the Harvest Moon Festival, but then everything had gone so wrong. First Clay's disappearance, followed by Tom's fistfight. Molly had been furious with Sam, claiming it was his influence on her son that had induced Tom to settle a disagreement with his fists. His eye had swollen so badly that by the time they arrived home he could no longer see out of it.

Molly hated violence. Every time she looked at Tom's poor eye, she had to resist the urge to weep. She'd cried that night, and her tears had come as a shock—but this had happened with her first two pregnancies, as well. The minute she was pregnant, her emotions seemed to go askew, and she found herself weeping at the most inappropriate times. Television commercials for greeting cards and dog food. Movies. Even when she won at radio bingo. It was a wonder her husband hadn't already guessed, but experience told her men were obtuse about these things.

Matters being what they were the night of the festival, Molly couldn't very well announce she was pregnant. Nor on the days that followed. Troubles were said to come in threes, and they certainly did with them.

First Sam's truck broke down and he learned he needed a new transmission. While he was able to do the repair work himself, the parts came to more than a thousand dollars. Money they could ill afford, but Sam needed the truck.

Then the roof of the house sprang a huge leak, ruining the ceiling over Clay's bedroom. Sam had to climb onto the steeply pitched roof in the middle of a horrendous downpour. The plastic tarp was a stopgap measure. The whole thing needed to be replaced, and the job couldn't be delayed much longer. The work they'd done earlier in the year had only been a temporary fix.

"I'll go into town and see about the price of shingles," Sam had said when he climbed down from the roof, drenched to the skin.

It went without saying that a new roof wouldn't be cheap. Shivering with cold, he'd showered, then sat at the kitchen table hugging a cup of coffee while he went over their finances. So *that* wasn't the time to tell him she was pregnant.

Finally, with all the rain, it seemed unlikely their

well would go dry—but that was what happened the following week. Sam looked like he'd been punched in the gut when he learned the price of having a new well dug. Again, this wasn't something they could put off.

Molly simply didn't have the heart to add to his troubles by telling him about the pregnancy. She calculated the costs, and with doctor's fees and hospital estimates, having this baby would cost several thousand dollars. Not including baby furniture, clothes and supplies. So Molly kept the news to herself, struggling to hide her morning sickness and lack of appetite. Her emotions were something else entirely. Sam assumed her mood swings were due to financial worries, and she let him believe it.

Ginny was the one who guessed first.

"Sam doesn't know," Molly told her neighbor over hot chocolate the first week of November.

"You've seen Dr. Shaver?"

Molly nodded. "He's got me on vitamins big enough to choke a horse. They don't come cheap, either." Her grocery money would only stretch so far.

"You take them, understand?" Ginny insisted.

"Of course." Molly didn't quibble over doing whatever was necessary for a safe pregnancy. "It's just that Sam doesn't need another financial burden right now," she explained.

"You're looking at this all wrong," Ginny said gruffly, patting Molly's hand. "This is *exactly* the kind of news he needs. That man of yours is carrying the weight of the world on his shoulders. I bet you the first calf of spring he'll be so excited when you tell him I'll hear him all the way over at my place. He's gonna be so proud, Molly. Just you wait and see."

Molly nibbled on her lower lip, wanting to believe Ginny. "You really think so?"

The older woman didn't express the least hesitation. "I know so."

Taking her friend's advice, Molly planned the perfect evening. She arranged for Tom and Clay to spend the following Friday night with friends, thawed out a rib roast and planned the menu right down to a small bottle of champagne. One glass wouldn't hurt the baby, she decided, and it would do the mother a whole lot of good.

The champagne was on ice and dinner in the oven when Sam walked in the back door, looking exhausted. He didn't notice that she'd set the table in the dining room with china normally reserved for holidays and special occasions. Nor did he appear to realize that the boys were away and it was just the two of them.

"What's for dinner?" he asked, appreciatively sniffing the kitchen as he made his way toward the shower.

"Roast," she said, eager to please him with a special meal.

"Smells great."

Molly waited until he'd gone into the shower before she boldly opened the door and stepped in to join him. He sent her a shocked look, almost as though he'd never seen her naked. His astonishment quickly turned to a smiling welcome, and he made room for her under the warming spray.

"I thought I'd wash your back for you," Molly said, reaching for the washcloth and bar of soap.

He hesitated. "What about dinner?"

She sighed; the man knew nothing about romance. "It's in the oven."

"But the boys…"

"Are spending the night with their friends. We're alone, sweetheart. Just the two of us."

A smile lit his face. "Why didn't you say so earlier?"

With the water pelting down on them, Sam backed her into a corner of the stall and his lips grazed hers. Molly wound her arms around his neck, and his hand slipped between their bodies to capture her breast.

This was heaven, Molly thought. This playful time with her husband. They exchanged small nibbling kisses that became more erotic, more intense. She barely noticed that the water had turned lukewarm. The soap and washcloth dropped to the floor, and she could deny him nothing.

Molly had planned a long slow seduction, but Sam wasn't interested in any of that. He soon had her pinned against the tile wall, her legs anchored around his waist, ready to receive him.

But raised as she was, the water hit her directly in the face and she was all but drowning. "Sam," she sputtered, trying to twist away, fighting for each breath.

Once he realized her dilemma, he quickly reversed their positions so that he was the one with his back to the wall.

"I don't think this was such a good idea," she said with some regret. They were both slippery and wet, and she found herself slipping out of his grasp.

"It's a wonderful idea," he insisted, shifting the burden of her weight and holding her thighs more firmly. But it didn't work, and she started slipping again, banging her ankle against the shower door.

"Dammit," she muttered irritably. This did *not* feel sexy.

He grumbled something about her gaining weight,

but she decided to ignore the comment or, more appropriately, forgive him. Sam refused to give up and eventually they managed to arrange their bodies and adjust to each other for the optimum lovemaking position. Sam braced his shoulder against the wall, while holding on to her. Molly's back was to the water, with her knees against the sides of the shower stall for leverage.

Just when everything seemed to be working, the water went abruptly from warm to ice cold.

Molly let out a scream, but because her body blocked his, Sam obviously hadn't noticed the change in temperature yet.

"That's it, honey. That's it." His eyes remained closed, but not for long as she squirmed and bucked in an effort to escape the freezing water. Her movements, however, did wonders for Sam, who closed his eyes, breathing fast. Finally she was able to move in a way that allowed the blast of cold water to hit him full in the face.

He let out a yelp of surprise, lost his balance and promptly dropped her. Molly landed in a heap on the shower floor while Sam reached for the controls and turned off the water.

Her dignity was hurt far more than her derriere; nevertheless, she wasn't pleased.

"Sweetheart, are you all right?" He had the grace to look embarrassed.

"I guess so." Because the soap had melted and the floor was slippery, she had difficulty getting back on her feet.

He opened the shower door, stepped out and handed her a towel. No sooner had she wrapped it around her than he took the smaller hand towel and began to dry her hair.

The towel obstructed her vision, but apparently that didn't worry Sam as he led her out of the bathroom. "Sam," she said, swatting at the towel. "Where in the name of heaven are we going?"

He paused as if the question confused him. "Going? Honey, we're gonna finish what we started."

"But—"

"You don't want to stop, do you?"

"It's just that I'm a little cold," she said, shivering.

"I'll warm you, I promise. You game?" The hopeful need she heard in him was her undoing.

"I'm always game for you," she told him softly, "and you know it."

He rewarded her willingness by lifting her in his arms and carrying her into the bedroom. He groaned as he approached the bed. "You *have* gained weight, haven't you?"

"Sam." She tried to kick herself free, but he wouldn't allow it.

"That was a joke," he whispered, and kissed away any protest she might have voiced. His tongue stroked the curve of her ear as he pressed her against the bed. "Oh, baby," he whispered, "this is the best idea you've had in a long time." He stroked her hip and thigh and peeled open the towel. Taking a moment to smile down at her in the dim light, he gently kissed each nipple before his mouth sought hers. Again and again he kissed her, and in almost no time Molly had completely given herself over to the heat of their lovemaking.

Sam held her for a few minutes afterward, then

brushed his lips across her brow. "Meet you in the kitchen," he said.

Molly got dressed and, after combing the tangles out of her wet hair, she joined him. "This is a very special night," she said, wanting to set the mood for her news.

"You can say that again," he murmured, scooping some frosting off the carrot cake she'd made and licking his finger. "You certainly didn't need to go to all this trouble."

"It's no trouble."

He froze, and she noticed that he stole a glance at the calendar. "I haven't forgotten anything, have I?"

"No, of course not."

"It isn't your birthday?"

"No!"

"Our anniversary's in June, right?"

"Sam, would you kindly stop?" She pulled the roast out of the oven and set it on the stove. "If you like, you can open the champagne."

"Champagne?"

"On the table. And the crystal flutes are in the dining room."

He picked up the bottle and seemed to be looking for the price. "This is real nice, sweetheart, but we can't afford champagne."

"It wasn't any more expensive than a bottle of wine."

He nodded. "Yeah, that's true. And it's not like we do this every night."

He sliced the roast while she carried the dishes out to the table and lit the candles, then he brought out the meat platter and put it carefully in the center. "This is great." He slipped his arm around her waist and kissed her neck.

"Thank you. I wanted tonight to be memorable."

"It's already been memorable." He pulled out his chair and reached for the platter of roast beef before she'd had a chance to sit down herself. Molly cast him a look she normally saved for the boys, and with an apologetic grin, he put the platter back down. When she'd spread the linen napkin on her lap, they smiled at each other. Sam poured the champagne, then helped himself to the meat, the potatoes and squash, the salad.

Throughout the meal, Molly waited for the right moment. She'd planned what she wanted to say, hoping against hope that Ginny was right. She had his reaction all worked out in her mind, too.

In her romantic fantasy Sam would fall quiet and look at her with adoring eyes. Then he'd clasp her hands and say something charming about how her love had forever changed him. That was certainly the way she *wanted* it to happen, but their evening had gotten off to a less than romantic start with their comedy of errors in the shower. True, things had improved later on, and the meal was going well. But this was too important an announcement; the timing had to be perfect.

Sam expressed his appreciation for the dinner over and over. He made every effort to show her how much he enjoyed her cooking, accepting a second piece of carrot cake for dessert.

He helped her clear off the table, and while she put on a pot of decaf coffee, he turned the radio on softly and sat in the living room to wait for her. Starting at nine o'clock in the evenings, the local station played light classics, fifties jazz, instrumental versions of popular songs—music that soothed.

"There's something I need to tell you," Molly said,

growing concerned the night would slip away before she completed her mission. That could happen easily enough, considering how nervous she was about it. She reminded herself that a new life was reason to celebrate, and that she and Sam loved each other. He'd be happy; she knew he would.

She carried in the tray of coffee and set it on the table. "Actually this probably won't come as a surprise." Her back was to him as she poured them each a cup, adding a splash of cream.

"Sam?"

"Hmm?"

"What I wanted to tell you…"

Silence.

She turned around and found him sitting in the recliner with his eyes closed, humming quietly along to the music.

"Sam," she said again.

Seeing this might well be the moment she'd waited for all night, she set the coffee aside and nestled in his lap. His arms automatically came around her and he reached over to turn off the lamp, casting the room into a welcoming dimness. It wasn't hard to imagine her grandparents sharing a special moment in this room, the same way she was with Sam.

Pressing her head to his shoulder, she kissed the underside of his jaw. This was nice. Really nice.

"I love you so much," she whispered.

"Me, too."

"Do you remember how eager we were to make love—"

A smile cracked his mouth. "What do you mean

were? You can tempt me any minute of any day. What happened in the shower should prove that."

She stroked his chest, loving his solid muscular warmth. His head leaned against the back of the chair and his eyes closed.

"These have been a hellish couple of weeks," he murmured.

"But we're doing okay, aren't we?" She continued to kiss his throat, then moved her lips along his jawline.

"It wasn't you on that roof in a pounding rainstorm."

"True." She unbuttoned his shirt and slipped her hand inside. "You know, sometimes things that seem disastrous are really blessings in disguise."

"Next time I'll let *you* crawl under the chassis and discover the transmission's shot."

"I wasn't talking about the truck repairs."

"Obviously."

"There's something else."

He went very still.

"But it's not bad news," she added.

"Good, because I've had more of that than I can handle."

With her head resting against his shoulder, Molly worried her lower lip, uncertain now. She wanted to believe he'd be pleased, but feared he'd look on the pregnancy as just another burden. As it turned out, she waited too long, because the next thing she knew, he was snoring in her ear.

The next morning, Sam knew something was wrong with Molly the minute he awoke. It probably had to do with that dinner scene the night before, but God's honest truth, he'd had one bitch of a day and was dead on his feet. Not wanting to disappoint her, he'd gone along with her romantic charade, and to be fair, he'd been surprised and delighted when she joined him in the shower. Never having made love in an upright position, he'd been required to improvise—admittedly without total success. But all in all it had worked out rather nicely once he got her into bed. He was too much of a traditionalist to be very experimental when it came to making love with his wife. But he was willing to try if she was.

Dinner was wonderful, and it was clear that Molly had gone to a lot of trouble. But now he knew he'd committed some terrible faux pas. Molly was curled up on the far side of the bed, as near the edge as she could possibly get.

"Morning, sweetheart," he whispered, wriggling across the bed to get closer to her.

He knew it probably hadn't been good form to fall asleep in the chair so soon after dinner, but he'd been exhausted. He didn't even remember getting into bed.

Silently Molly tossed aside the covers and climbed out of bed.

"Is something wrong, sweetheart?" he asked.

"Oh, Sam, sometimes you make things so difficult."

He sighed, wondering how often he'd be obliged to apologize for falling asleep in the middle of her romantic evening. He did feel bad about it, but she *could* be a bit more understanding.

"Just tell me what's wrong, okay?"

"Nothing's wrong," she whispered.

He'd swear she was crying. "Molly, for heaven's sake, tell me!"

"You don't know, do you?" She shook her head, her

expression hopeless. "You honestly don't know." Sniffling, she grabbed a tissue from the dresser.

"Uh…"

"Think about it, Sam. Just think. I had a wonderful night planned for us and… I don't know why I should have to tell you anything! You should be able to figure this out yourself. You were the one who noticed I've gained weight."

"Honey, a few pounds. Don't worry about it. You look great. You *are* great. It's just a little more of you to love." He reached out to her, planning to pull her into his arms.

She slapped his hands away and blinked hard. "Sam, there's a reason I've gained a few pounds."

"Sure, it's all the desserts you've been baking lately, but I don't want you to worry about it."

She released a soft groan and left the bedroom.

Sam didn't know what her problem was, but he had work to do. The way he figured, she'd tell him when she was ready. Right now he needed to get over to Lonesome Creek to check on the herd.

Molly had coffee and toast waiting for him when he joined her in the kitchen.

"I gotta go."

"I know." She'd wiped all traces of tears from her cheeks and kissed him. "Think about what I said, all right?" she murmured.

She looked so small and pitiful that Sam held her longer than necessary before he headed for the barn to saddle up Thunder.

As he rode toward Lonesome Creek, it hit him.

Molly was pregnant.

Pregnant!

His heart felt like it would explode with excitement. With happiness. His instinct was to turn around and ride back, kiss her senseless, tell her how thrilled he was. He would have, too, but he heard voices just then, and the sound of a truck. This was *his* land and anyone on it would be up to no good.

Without considering the fact that he was alone and unarmed, he charged for the hill and crested it in time to see four men dressed in fatigues loading up his cattle.

They saw him, too.

What happened next seemed unreal, like something out of a flickering scene in a silent movie. He heard a shout and watched transfixed as one of the men raised a rifle to his shoulder and took aim. It was a moment before Sam realized the man was aiming at *him*.

With a cry of outrage, Sam pulled back on Thunder's reins to reverse the gelding's direction. Bending low over the horse's sleek neck, he made for the ranch, knowing that even the slightest hesitation could cost him his life.

The sound of the rifle blast reached him at the precise moment he experienced the searing pain of the hit. The sheer force of it flung his arms wildly into the air. With his weight off center, he slid from the saddle, just managing to free his feet from the stirrups. The gelding's thundering hoofs echoed like cannon shots as he fell. His last conscious thought before he slammed against the hard ground was a simple prayer. He asked for only one thing. To live long enough to tell Molly how happy he was about the baby.

Eighteen

This wasn't going down the way Monroe had planned. The Loyalists needed the Wheaton land, but the old man had been too damn stubborn. Wouldn't listen to reason. Okay, he'd expected that. Walt Wheaton had been a cantankerous fool most of his life. Monroe had considered it a godsend when his granddaughter arrived, but he'd been wrong. The situation had quickly gone from bad to worse.

Sam Dakota had thrown a monkey wrench into the entire scheme. Without him Molly would've been forced to sell the property, and she'd have been glad to be rid of it. Dakota was as stubborn as the old man, and it was clear he intended to fight for the land with the same unshakable determination.

Monroe leaned forward and planted his elbows on his desk. The situation had taken a sharp turn south starting with Pearl Mitchell's murder. He'd confronted Lance, who claimed he'd had nothing to do with it and offered an alibi. When Monroe checked, he was surprised to learn Lance had been telling the truth. Yeah, he'd come to town that night, but Lance had been at

Willie's playing pool with that hothead Travis. The bartender confirmed it.

It would have been convenient if they'd been able to pin the murder on Dakota, but that hadn't panned out. Monroe could deal with Molly, persuade her it'd be wise to sell—if he could get her husband out of the picture. What shocked him was that his cousin, his own flesh and blood, was the one responsible for seeing the man set free. It angered him every time he thought about it. Damn attorneys weren't to be trusted. Even when they were part of the family.

He wished the hell he knew what Russell's angle was with Pearl. The way his cousin had hounded the sheriff's office for information led him to believe there might have been something between them. That was enough to make him laugh. His cousin falling for a hooker!

Monroe felt bad about Pearl's murder, too, but she was the one who chose to live this life. She knew the risks. If he found out who'd killed her, he'd make the son of a bitch pay, if for no other reason than the lost income she'd provided. The freebies Pearl threw in every other week or so would be sorely missed, but he'd convince one of the other girls to be just as accommodating.

The girls had gotten nervous after Pearl's death, and profits had dropped by thirty percent. He'd been against setting up this prostitution ring in the first place, afraid someone would trace it back to him. But it was the least of his worries now. Lately there'd been any number of problems developing.

Tightening the screws on Dakota had been downright fun, but the bastard had refused to break. Messing around with his stepsons hadn't done it, either. Hiring the Hudson kid to paint the wall had been Lance's idea. He snorted. Lance was a fool and not to be trusted. He was sure Lance's friend was the one who'd set the Cogan boy free. Travis was a good man and a capable soldier, but he couldn't stand seeing anything happen to kids. They were his weakness. Damn fool.

Burns had turned on him, too. Without ready cash Dakota would've been at their mercy, but the bank president had stepped in and rescued him. Monroe understood that Burns had to put business first, but it complicated an already complicated situation. Once Monroe heard the terms of the loan, though, he'd realized what had to be done. Dakota had to be prevented from getting his cattle to market.

The door opened and Lance walked into his office.

Monroe's anger flared like a match to a blowtorch. "I told you never to come here." He was on his feet, prepared to personally drag Lance's sorry ass onto the street. Talk about stupid!

"It went wrong," the other man muttered.

This wasn't what Monroe wanted to hear. "Meet me behind Willie's at midnight."

"Travis shot him."

"Shot who?" he demanded. Forced as he was to deal with incompetence and insubordination, it amazed him the organization had held together this long.

"Dakota," Lance said. "There was nothing we could do."

Monroe gave a slow satisfied smile. So Dakota was a goner. No great loss. And who better to comfort the grieving widow than Monroe himself?

Grumbling to herself about how obtuse men could be, Molly set about her busy day. There never seemed to be any shortage of projects needing attention. She had a list of chores for the boys, as well.

Humming as she sorted laundry on the back porch, she heard the unmistakable sound of a horse galloping into the yard. It didn't seem possible that Sam could be back already—but maybe he'd figured out what she'd been trying to tell him. She felt a bit queasy this morning, and she pressed her palm over her stomach, loving her unborn child with the same fierceness as she loved her boys.

Molly peeked around to see Thunder prancing about in front of the barn door, snorting and jerking his head.

Riderless.

Molly stared at the horse. Where was Sam? Grabbing her sweater from the peg, she raced onto the porch.

"Sam?" she called. She stopped suddenly. She *knew* something was wrong. Terribly wrong.

With her breath coming in short frantic gasps, she stormed back into the house for the truck keys. Her fingers trembled so badly she had trouble inserting the key in the ignition, and she cursed under her breath. Taking a moment to calm herself, she pushed in the clutch, revved the cold engine and headed in the direction she'd seen Sam ride.

The pasture was anything but smooth, and she was hurled, jarred and jolted as she sped across the uneven terrain. All the while she prayed frantically, fear gnawing at her insides. She had no idea what she'd find. If Thunder had thrown Sam, there was a possibility he'd reinjured his back. He'd been forced to give up the rodeo because of a spinal injury; any further damage could leave him paralyzed for life.

Dread roared through her like wildfire. So intent was

she on her worries that she nearly drove right past Sam. When she did see him staggering across the pasture, holding his head, she stomped on the brakes.

Leaping out of the cab, she raced toward him. When he saw her, Sam sank to his knees. Blood oozed between his fingers and flowed onto his face and into his eyes.

Molly gasped.

"It's not as bad as it looks," he assured her, his voice barely audible.

"Sam, oh, Sam."

"We got troubles, sweetheart."

His eyes fluttered and she knew he was going to pass out.

"Rustlers got our herd." With that he toppled over, face first.

Sam awoke and groaned at the hammering in his skull. Pinpoint lasers pierced his brain, blinding him with light. He raised his hand to protect his vision and tried to figure out where he was.

He recognized nothing.

"Sam?"

Molly was with him; that was promising, anyway.

"Where am I?" Each word demanded tremendous effort.

"Home. Dr. Shaver just left. Ginny's here, too. I don't know what I would've done without her and Fred. They helped me carry you into the house. Can you tell us what happened?"

"Rustlers...got the herd."

"I know." He caught the way her voice trembled, but doubted she fully understood the magnitude of what this meant. "The loan, Molly. We have to make a five-thousand-dollar payment in three weeks."

She grasped his hand tightly. "Don't worry about that now. We'll find a way."

"But…" He half lifted himself from the bed, not sure why, but knowing he had to do something. Everything around him had an unreal quality, as though it were all part of a bad dream. The worst nightmare of his life. If so, he wanted to wake up soon.

Dear God, what were they going to do?

"It's all right," she insisted gently. She placed her hands on his shoulders and eased him back against the mattress. He felt her lips on his cheek and for a moment welcomed her comfort and her love. But comfort couldn't last, not when they'd been robbed of every hope for their future.

"Sheriff Maynard." He struggled to speak and clutched her arm, wanting her to know the importance of his request. He needed to talk to the lawman, and the sooner the better.

"I called him already," Molly answered calmly. "He wants to talk to you as soon as you're a bit better."

"Now."

"Soon, I promise. But for now, please rest." Her voice trembled again, and he did as she asked, rather than upset her further.

The pain in his head was vicious. Unable to fight it any longer, he closed his eyes. "Tell Maynard…I can identify one…if I saw him again." The one with the rifle. Sam had gotten a good look at him. Unfortunately it wasn't someone he recognized. A stranger. In another sense, however, the fact that he *was* a stranger brought Sam a measure of relief. It would be difficult to accept that any of his neighbors would involve themselves in something so criminal.

Who? Why? The questions pounded in his brain, as painful as the physical agony.

Although his eyes remained closed, Sam was awake, at least partially so. Bits and pieces of conversation drifted his way.

"Dr. Shaver said another inch to the left and the bullet would have gone directly into his brain," Molly said. "As it is, it gouged a path across the top of his skull."

"Were they trying to kill him?" The voice belonged to Tom, and from his tone Sam knew the boy was fighting mad. "Who would do something like this? Who? If I ever find out—"

"Tom, we don't know," Molly responded. "No one does."

"What are we going to do if we can't make the first payment?" Tom asked. Sam wondered the same thing, and the weight of that burden was heavier than anything he'd ever experienced, including the prison sentence. It crushed him with fear.

Molly hesitated. "I don't know what'll happen, but we don't need to deal with it now."

"Won't the bank give us more time?"

"I already called and explained the situation," Molly said. "And while Mr. Burns is sympathetic, he said he couldn't make allowances."

"We aren't going to lose the ranch, are we?"

Molly hesitated and her voice shook ever so slightly when she answered. "I…don't know."

"Will we move back to San Francisco?"

Sam wanted to protest, reassure Tom and Clay that he'd do everything in his power to see that didn't happen. They belonged in Montana now, as much as he did himself.

"What about Sam? If we have to move, will he go with us?"

Sam living in a big city. Not likely. He nearly snickered out loud. He wouldn't last a day.

"Of course he will," Molly said. "Sam's my husband."

Although his head hurt like a son of a bitch, Sam almost smiled. Molly loved him, and by God he couldn't, wouldn't, let her down now. Walt had brought them together, and the old man knew exactly what he was doing. He and Molly might not have started their marriage in the traditional way, but they were going to make it work.

In his thirty-six years Sam had committed more than his share of sins. In all that time, he'd never asked for much. Mostly he hadn't given a damn about anything or anyone, including himself. Then he'd met Walt Wheaton and fallen in love with Molly.

He cared now. Cared about his family—Molly, the boys, his unborn son or daughter. Cared about his own life. Cared more than he'd ever thought possible. Somehow, some way, he'd get that money.

Russell sat in his office and read over the faxed report a second time. He'd had to pull a number of strings and call in several favors to obtain this information. Now that it was in his hands, right here in black and white, he was even more confused. He knew more about militia groups and domestic terrorists than he'd ever expected to learn. He'd made contact with the FBI and could negotiate the Internet like a pro. And he'd discovered that the paper trail led directly back to the Loyalists in Sweetgrass. To a member of his own family.

Countless hours had gone into his research. It had all started with Pearl's murder. Every time her name passed through his mind he experienced a deep sense of loss. The weeks hadn't eased it. Nothing had, and he suspected nothing ever would.

There'd been little comfort for him, except that one night he'd spent in the cabin. Often he'd close his eyes and bask in the memory, feeling again the cool silk of her nightgown, smelling her rose-scented perfume. Remembering her. It made him more determined than ever to find the man responsible for her death and see that justice was served.

That promise had led him to the papers that lay before him now. The print blurred and he pinched the bridge of his nose, weary in body and mind. It'd been a long day, and if this contract said what he thought it did, Pearl's death hadn't come at the hands of an overzealous john. She'd been a tool used by the Loyalists; he believed she'd been killed because she knew too much. Perhaps she'd threatened to tell what she knew.... For the first time he understood why she'd rejected his marriage proposals. Had she died trying to free herself from the Loyalists in order to marry him? It didn't bear considering. He understood now who was responsible for her death. His cousin. And the irony was that it'd been through his cousin that he first met Pearl.

With this realization came a renewed sense of guilt. Indirectly *he* was responsible for putting her in danger. He'd been the one who taught her to read. Lovely, generous Pearl had been like a child, tasting life for the first time, soaking up everything she learned, each sound, each new word. Her joy had been his own.

Who would have guessed this newly acquired skill would get her killed? Russell was ninety-nine percent sure that was what had happened. She'd read something she shouldn't have and gotten caught. Or perhaps she'd inadvertently let the information slip. Whichever, it had cost Pearl her life.

He'd never be the same without her. He wasn't sure he could continue living the way he had before he loved her. Once this was over he didn't think he could stay in Sweetgrass.

Rubbing his eyes, he studied the paper one last time, then tucked it into a file, which he locked inside the cabinet.

He turned off the light as he left the office and started for the parking lot. The cold was like a physical shock when he stepped outside. Snow was predicted that night.

Climbing into his car, he warmed up the engine and headed home. On impulse he drove past Pearl's house. New renters had moved in a month earlier, apparently unaware or unconcerned that a murder had taken place there.

He stopped off at the minimart and bought himself a sandwich, then drove home and ate it in front of the television while he watched CNN.

"I'm closer," he whispered to Pearl before he got into bed that night. "It won't be long now. I'll know why. You won't have died in vain, my love. Whoever killed you will pay. Whatever you found out—he'll answer for it."

This was his promise, and he fully intended to keep it.

The alarm buzzed in Molly's ear, and blindly stretching out one arm, she fumbled with the knob until the irritating sound ceased. Not wanting to leave the warm comfort of the bed, she cuddled close to Sam and absorbed his body heat for a few extra moments before quietly getting up. Sam had been in such a bad mood since his injury, extra sleep could only do him good.

It was a week ago that he'd spoken to Sheriff Maynard. Because Sam had been unable to name any of the men and because the sheriff had found no concrete evidence, there was little hope the cattle would be recovered. Since then Sam had been listless and cranky. She knew he was physically and emotionally drained. Although Doc Shaver had insisted he remain in bed for at least two days, Sam had simply refused. Molly had done her best, but the man defined stubbornness.

They didn't discuss the loan payment again. Really, what was there to say? Sam couldn't make the money appear out of thin air, and she was no magician, either. And so they didn't speak of it.

Some nights the tension in the house was so oppressive, Molly wanted to shriek. The boys had been restless and ill-tempered, too.

"It snowed!" Clay yelled as he flew down the stairs for breakfast. He said it as though no one else had noticed a thing.

Molly smiled at his enthusiasm, pleased to hear something other than whining or complaints.

"It's beautiful, isn't it?" she said, gazing out the kitchen window. The sun rose over the horizon, casting a pinkish glow on the white perfection.

"It's stupid," Tom said. He'd followed his younger brother down the stairs. Molly set a plate of hotcakes in the middle of the table and Tom helped himself. He poured on enough syrup for the pancakes to float.

"Hey," Clay protested, jerking the plastic container out of his brother's hand. "I want some, too."

A tug of war ensued, and soon the two boys were at each other's throats. Molly quickly broke it up, but the bickering continued until the boys grabbed their school-bags and headed out the door to meet the bus.

Still angry, Clay stood in the open doorway and glared at Molly as though the fight with his brother was all her fault. "I hate Montana."

Molly sighed and shook her head. "Clay, that isn't true and you know it."

"I don't care if we lose this stupid ranch. The only thing I like is Bullwinkle. I want to move back to California." Having said that, he ran out, slamming the door.

Defeated, Molly slumped into the chair and raised her hands to her face. The boys' constant quarreling depleted her energy. It didn't help that Sam had been sullen and pessimistic all week.

"What was that about?" Sam asked. She hadn't heard him come into the kitchen.

Whenever Molly looked at the bandage on his head, she experienced a twinge of pain herself. The head wound was only a small part of what he'd suffered. For reasons as yet unclear to Molly, he blamed himself for the loss of the cattle. He'd never come right out and said so, but she hadn't lived with him and loved him all these months without being able to figure that out.

"The boys got into a fight," she explained. "No one's in a good mood."

"Maybe Clay can have his wish," Sam said with-out emotion.

"What do you mean?"

"Maybe it isn't too late for you and the boys to move back to California."

Her heart seemed to lurch to a sudden stop. He had to be joking, but one look told Molly he was serious.

"Is that what you want?" she asked, barely able to say the words.

He shrugged as if her returning to California or not was of little consequence to him.

"That's a perfectly rotten thing to say, Sam Dakota! It's obvious that you don't understand what marriage really means. I committed myself to you when I said my vows. No ands, ifs or buts. Love isn't just a feeling. It isn't hormones, either. It's commitment, standing beside each other, facing problems together. It's holding on to what's really important." When she finished, her eyes had filled with tears.

"To my way of thinking, you got the short end of the stick in this marriage," he said.

"I could say the same thing about you. I came into this relationship with two children and a complete set of emotional baggage. But we're married now, and no one's keeping score of who got the short end of what stick—or anything else!"

He turned his back and walked out of the kitchen.

Molly heard the radio come on and knew he'd settled down in the living room. He'd gone there in order to avoid her. Well, she wouldn't *force* him to speak to his own wife!

Unable to stay in the house, Molly dressed, fighting back tears and nausea, and drove to Ginny's place. The older woman stepped onto the porch when she heard Molly's car.

"More troubles?" Ginny called out, concern evident on her face.

Molly shook her head. "I came for coffee and a few words of encouragement."

"Encouragement I got, but my coffee tastes like cow piss." She chuckled. "That's what Walt used to tell me, but you know he had more than his share of my coffee and he wasn't too proud to down a slice or two of my apple pie while he was at it."

Molly smiled at the reference to her grandfather. She missed Gramps more than ever. He'd always been there for her; he'd always been willing to look at a problem straight on. She understood now how much courage that took. And he'd had a way of coming up with solutions....

"It's a bit early in the day for pie," Molly said, "but I'll gladly accept a cup of that coffee."

"Great." Ginny led the way into the house.

The warm homey kitchen was where Ginny and Fred spent most of their time. The radio rested on the kitchen counter, and a stack of mail and books and magazines took up at least half the table, along with a deck of cards and an old cribbage board.

"Walt and me used to play cribbage and two-handed pinochle now and again," Ginny explained. "Not often, just enough for me to think of him every time I look at that old board. Can't seem to bring myself to put it away. Sometimes Fred and I play a bit in the evenings, but it's not the same...."

Molly touched the older woman's hand. "I miss him, too."

Ginny sniffled and dabbed at her nose with her hankie. "How's Sam this fine morning?"

Molly looked away, not meeting Ginny's eyes. "He… he suggested I move back to California with the kids."

"You didn't believe him, did you?"

Molly didn't know what to believe any longer.

"What that husband of yours needs is someone to read him the riot act," Ginny said, frowning darkly. "If he feels sorry for himself now, just wait till I get through with him. He should be shot for saying something like that."

"Someone already tried," Molly reminded her.

"From the way Sam's acting, you'd almost think he's disappointed the guy's aim was off."

Molly held on to her mug with both hands and stared into the steaming coffee. "He blames himself for what happened."

"That's ridiculous. It could've been my herd just as easily."

Molly pushed her hair off her forehead. "I don't know what we're going to do, and Sam refuses to talk about it. Now it seems as if he's given up and wants out of the marriage."

"Don't you take him seriously," Ginny chastised. "Not for a moment. Maybe you should tell him about the baby now. It'd give him something else to think about."

"No." Molly was adamant about that. "If he doesn't love me enough to ride out the troubled times, then a baby isn't going to change things." Thinking about the many difficult times her grandparents had faced, Molly gripped the cameo dangling from the gold chain. Somehow it helped her feel closer to them both.

"That cameo's lovely," Ginny said. "Have you ever thought about selling it?"

"No." Molly was horrified Ginny would even suggest such a thing.

"It might be valuable. When was the last time you had it appraised?"

Appraised? Molly had never even given appraisal a thought. She'd always assumed its commercial value wasn't more than a couple of hundred dollars. The sentimental value, however, made it priceless.

"I seem to remember Walt telling me once it was a collector's piece," Ginny murmured. "I know how you feel about it, but it wouldn't hurt to have a jeweler take a look."

Molly held the cameo more tightly as she recalled the pawnbroker's interest. She'd figured it was because he considered the cameo so unusual, not because of its monetary value.

Over the past few days she'd given ample thought to what assets they could sell to raise money. One problem was the fact that they had so little time. As for selling equipment or one of their vehicles, no one in Sweetgrass had money to spare or to spend. Her car, while paid for, wasn't worth five grand, and Sam's pickup was pretty old. Besides, he needed it on the ranch. Walt's old truck was worthless, and everything else they owned was mortgaged to the hilt.

"You're right," Molly said, finding a new resolve. "It wouldn't hurt to have a jeweler look at it."

"You want me to come along? On our way we can stop off at your place and I can beat the crap out of Sam. If he wants to feel sorry for himself, then I'll be sure and give him plenty of reason."

Molly laughed, for probably the first time in a week. "Oh, Ginny," she said, "I'm so glad we're friends." Impulsively she hugged the older woman. "But I can deal with Sam."

Immeasurably cheered, Molly returned home, hoping Sam's mood had improved.

"Sam," she called as she walked into the kitchen.

Silence.

"Sam?" She checked the living room and glanced into the bedroom, thinking he might have gone back to bed for a nap.

He was as familiar with the doctor's orders as she was—in bed for two days, and then quiet and rest for the following week. She knew he was feeling better, but not well enough to leave the house.

Checking outside, she noticed that his truck was missing.

"Sam Dakota, where did you go?" Her instinctive reaction was anger that he'd defied the doctor's orders.

She searched for a note in the kitchen and found none.

Then she noticed that the hall-closet door was ajar, and she understood. That was where they stored the suitcases. She crossed again to the bedroom door, looked in and noticed that each one of the drawers on his side of the dresser had been left open.

Molly's legs felt like they were about to give out on her. She clutched the door frame with both hands as she took it all in.

Sam had left her. Unable to deal with their problems, he'd packed his bags and driven off. Without even saying goodbye.

Nineteen

Paul Harden, the jeweler, gently turned the cameo over in the palm of his hand. "Ginny was right. This piece is a rare collector's item. I couldn't begin to give you an accurate appraisal without making a couple of phone calls first."

"Could you guess?" Molly urged. "Maybe...a thousand?" she asked, hardly daring to believe in the possibility.

Unable to deal with Sam's abandonment, she'd driven into town. With all the problems crashing down around her shoulders, she'd decided to deal with the most pressing one first—the loan payment. She might be able to talk Mr. Burns into accepting a partial payment until they could get back on their feet financially and regroup after the loss of the herd.

"Much more than that. I'd say it was closer to five or six."

"Five or six thousand!" Molly's voice echoed in her ears, and she felt slightly dizzy. "You're not joking, are you?"

"Not about something like this," Paul told her. He

was a jovial man in his early sixties with dark brown eyes that twinkled when he laughed. He'd sold Molly and Sam their wedding bands the day before the ceremony, and as a favor to Gramps had sized them overnight.

"Oh, my…"

"Are you interested in selling?" he asked.

"I…I don't know. I mean, no, I don't want to, but I imagine I'm not going to have any choice."

Paul frowned. "I swear Burns is squeezing every rancher in the area. If you want, I'll make a few calls and ask around, see what I can do to get you the best price."

"I'd appreciate it." Molly couldn't believe her good fortune. Once again, even after his death, Gramps had supplied the solution to her troubles. But giving up the cameo would be so very difficult. She'd worn it all these years and it held such meaning for her.

"Give me a call in the next couple of days," Paul said, "and I'll let you know what I've found out."

Molly nodded, pinching her lips to keep from crying. She'd rather sell her right arm than her grandmother's cameo, but if worse came to worst, there'd be no help for it.

"Don't worry," Paul said, patting her hand. "These things often have a way of working out for the best."

"Thanks," she murmured, and turned away before he saw the tears in her eyes.

This wasn't easy for Molly, but it was either take matters into her own hands or become an emotional casualty. Since Sam had seen fit to abandon her, she had no choice but to do what she could to secure the future for herself and her children. If that meant selling a family heirloom, then so be it.

Molly arrived home thirty minutes before the boys were due back from school. She dreaded telling them Sam was gone. But it wasn't something she'd be able to hide. Tom, especially, would take the news hard.

From past experience she knew her children would look to her for their emotional cues. If she was strong and brave, they would be, too. For their sake, as well as her own, Molly prayed she'd be able to pull it off. While the breakup of her first marriage had devastated her, it didn't compare to the numbed sense of disbelief she felt now.

The phone rang, and Molly stared at it, not sure if she should answer or not. Part of her wanted it to be Sam; at the same time she didn't know if she could talk to him.

She answered on the third ring.

"This is Patrick Sparks from the Butte Rodeo returning Mr. Dakota's phone call."

Molly didn't understand why Sam would be calling Butte. "I'm sorry, he isn't here."

"Would you take a message and let him know I'm sorry I wasn't here to talk to him personally? Naturally I've heard of Sam." He paused and laughed briefly. "Best damn bull rider I've ever had the privilege to watch. I'd heard he was forced into retirement some years ago—but if he wants to ride again, we'd be more than happy to have him in Butte. In fact, we'd consider it an honor."

"Sam called you?" Molly asked, barely able to get the question out.

"Yes. Early this morning. Unfortunately I was out

of the office at the time. I would've enjoyed talking to a rodeo legend like Sam Dakota."

"Are...there any other rodeos going on now?" Molly asked, thinking quickly.

"The season's winding down, but Missoula's putting on a big one this weekend."

"Thank you," Molly said. "Thank you so much."

Racing into the bedroom, she yanked the top drawer on Sam's side of the dresser all the way open. Sure enough, his clothes were there; only the top layer of T-shirts and briefs was missing. Molly berated herself for jumping to conclusions, for assuming the worst. For not trusting Sam. He hadn't left her at all! He'd packed up and gone to compete in a rodeo, hoping to collect the prize money.

Her husband was risking his life for her and the boys in order to make the payment on the ranch.

"Oh, Sam," she whispered, relieved and furious with him at once. "You're an idiot." What he didn't know was that this wasn't necessary, not any longer. She could sell the cameo. *Would* sell it.

The back door opened and the boys wandered in, their faces red from the cold and the long trek down the driveway.

"Each of you, pack an overnight bag," she instructed them, clapping her hands to get them moving.

"Are we going somewhere?" Tom asked, eyes wide with surprise.

"To the rodeo," she said, and because the relief overwhelmed her, she cupped his cold face between her hands and kissed both his cheeks. "First I'm going to phone Ginny—ask if Fred can stop by here to see to the horses and dogs...."

"Rodeo?" Tom ardently scrubbed her kiss from his cheeks. "Mom, have you lost it?"

Laughing and crying at the same time, she nodded. "No. I've *found* it. Found something wonderful."

"What?"

"Love," she whispered, then repeated. "Love."

It amazed Sam that anyone remembered him. He certainly didn't feel entitled to the hero's welcome he'd received when he paid his entry fee. All he cared about was the purse, a hefty five grand, which was exactly the amount needed to make the first payment.

He was the last entrant, the last man to ride. Exactly eight seconds—that was how long he needed to stay on. Eight seconds to win five thousand dollars. He stared down into the chute at the snorting bull, and his blood fired to life. It'd been a long time, and the adrenaline surged through his system. He was ready. He missed the old life—but not enough to trade it for what he had now. Sweetgrass was where he belonged. No, he belonged wherever Molly was, Molly and their family. She'd taught him that with her gentle love.

The bull snorted again, eager to be released from the constraining chute. In a couple of minutes Sam would ease his weight onto the beast's back and the door would open.

He was in top physical condition—strong, fit and agile. Working the ranch had done that for him. He'd recovered from his head injury; if he hadn't, the ride would have been a suicide mission, and he had no intention of dying. Nor did he intend to spend the remainder of his days crippled. He was a man with a lot of reasons to live. The time had come to start counting his blessings, instead of keeping tabs on what he'd lost.

Given the nod, Sam climbed over the top of the chute and settled himself on the bull's massive body. The animal's head reared back, and he slammed from side to side in a futile attempt to unseat his rider. The old boy would have eight seconds to do that once the chute door opened. From what Sam had seen so far, the bull was determined to give him a ride he'd feel all the way to his back molars.

Sam wrapped the bull rope around his hand. His blood roared in his ears, and he focused on the memory of Molly's face. The announcer's voice boomed over the public address system, and Sam heard his name and the cheers that followed. The other riders weren't the only ones who remembered him; apparently the audience did, too.

When the announcer finished, Sam gave the signal and the chute opened. The bull charged out of the pen, and Sam's right arm instinctively went up to maintain his balance.

Colors blurred as he was jerked and yanked and spun about. Yet despite the blurred images, he thought he saw Molly standing on the sidelines with the boys.

Here? How was it possible? He'd gone mad, Sam concluded. He'd tried to reach her at Ginny's and discovered she'd already left. Fred had promised to let her know, but Sam hadn't mentioned *which* rodeo for exactly this reason: he hadn't wanted Molly to come.

It felt as though every bone in his body had been jarred from its socket before the buzzer finally went off. Spectators leaped to their feet and the applause was deafening. He'd done it. He'd stayed on the bull for eight seconds, the longest eight seconds of his life. He had the purse.

Soon Sam was behind the stands, out of the lime-light. He felt weak enough to faint, but exhilaration kept him on his feet. His throat was parched; he accepted a drink of water and gulped it down. As he set the cup aside, he saw her.

Molly stood no more than five feet away. It hadn't been his imagination—she'd been there. She'd watched him ride, had screamed and cheered for him.

"Hello, sweetheart," he whispered, holding out his arms to her. His arms and his heart.

She seemed unsure which to do first: kiss him or give him the lecture of his life. He looked at his oldest son, but Tom shrugged as if to say Sam was on his own.

The lecture won. "Sam Dakota, how could you leave me like that and without so much as a note?" she demanded.

"Fred was supposed to tell you." Unwilling to wait for her to come to him, he covered the distance separating them and gathered her in his arms. The feel of her filled his heart. He'd briefly feared that old life would tempt him once he was back; it hadn't happened. Instead, he'd realized something. The injury that ended his rodeo career had really been a gift, because it had brought him Molly and the boys. Neither fame nor glory could replace the contentment he'd felt since his marriage.

"I didn't talk to Fred—just Ginny." Molly shook her head. "Oh, Sam, how could you have taken such a risk?" she whispered, sounding close to tears.

"That was easy, my love. I did it for us."

"You could've been killed!" she cried, fighting back tears.

"I wasn't."

"Or badly hurt."

"I'm none the worse for wear." He kissed the tip of her nose and she buried her face in his neck. Then he rubbed the side of his face against her hair, loving the fresh scent of it.

"Dad! Dad!" Clay tugged hard at his sleeve, and Sam placed his arm around the boy's shoulders. Clay tugged harder. "That man over there," he said urgently. "He's got a broken shoelace."

"He should be wearing cowboy boots like the rest of us," Sam teased. For a moment he was amused by the things kids noticed. Then he made the connection—just as Clay said, "But he's got those combat boots, exactly like the guy who grabbed me."

"Where?" Sam demanded, releasing Molly.

"Over there." Clay pointed to a tall man dressed in fatigues who stood by the corral, talking to another man.

Sam recognized him immediately as one of the two unsavory characters who'd walked into Willie's the night Pearl was killed. The men she'd wanted to avoid.

Without hesitation Sam started across the yard, anger driving his steps. "Why don't we ask him about it right now?" he said between gritted teeth. He had every intention of finding out why a grown man would want to terrify a boy and his family.

"I'll get the authorities," Molly said, and before Sam could assure her he wouldn't need anything other than his fists to get the answers he wanted, she was gone.

"We need to talk," Sam said, interrupting the two men.

The first man barely glanced at him, but the second one stared back as though he'd seen a ghost. He recovered quickly, however, and asked, "What do we need to talk about?"

"My son."

"I didn't know they let jailbirds like you—" As soon as Sam was within striking distance, the man attacked, hitting him square in the jaw with a powerful right hook.

Sam didn't see it coming and the punch caught him off balance and sent him sprawling to the ground. His jaw hurt, but not nearly as much as his pride. He half rose and hurled himself at the other man, hitting him just above the knees. The force made him topple backward, but Sam wasn't able to pin him down. Dust clogged the air as they rolled around in the dirt.

"Sam, Sam…" Molly's voice drifted toward him. He wanted to tell her to stand clear, but he dared not divert his attention.

"Give it to him, Lance," the man's friend shouted.

Lance outweighed him by some pounds, and Sam was stiff and sore from the recent bull-ride. He guessed from Lance's technique that he'd been trained by the military.

"Sam…Sam!" Molly screamed in warning as he blocked a punch. He turned to tell her to get out of the way and saw that she'd picked up a shovel.

Unfortunately her aim was slightly off and when she slammed it down, it missed Lance entirely and hit Sam on the shoulder instead. Pain shot down his arm and he crumpled to the ground. He must have briefly lost consciousness when his head hit the ground because the next thing he knew two sheriff's deputies were standing beside Molly. Somehow she'd managed to corner Lance with the shovel. His friend was nowhere to be seen.

"What's going on here?" one of the lawmen asked, moving between the two men.

Molly and Sam both started talking at once. Molly stopped and signaled Sam to continue. He explained what had happened with Clay.

"Someone stole our winter herd last week and shot my husband," Molly threw out. "Ask him about *that* while you're at it." She pointed at Lance, her face a study in contempt.

"Hey, you're not pinning that on me." Lance wiped away blood at the corner of his mouth. He glared at Sam. "If you want to ask anyone questions, you can ask Mr. Hero over there about a certain woman who disappeared. He knows a lot more than he's saying."

Sam tensed at the mention of Pearl's murder. "You're the one she was hiding from," he accused, vividly remembering the fear on Pearl's face when she saw Lance.

"My husband had nothing to do with the poor woman's death," Molly said righteously. "Now arrest that man." She pointed in Lance's direction. "On kidnapping charges."

"Is there a problem here?" Sheriff Maynard stepped through the crowd of curious onlookers and presented his badge to the deputies.

"Sheriff Maynard." Molly sounded relieved, and truth be known, Sam was pleased to see the other man, too. Surely now he could count on the sheriff of Sweetgrass to clear his name.

"I have a warrant for that man's arrest. He's charged with the murder of Pearl Mitchell," Maynard announced.

As everyone watched openmouthed, he slapped handcuffs on Lance's wrists and led him away.

"You're an idiot," Sheriff Gene Maynard—alias Monroe—shouted at Lance.

The younger man sat in the back of the patrol car. "Come on, Monroe," he whined. "This is a joke, right?"

Monroe could sense Lance's resentment—and frankly it felt good to put handcuffs on that bastard. It was what he deserved for all the screwups. The incompetence Monroe was left to deal with was like an aching tooth. The pain never seemed to lessen nor was it likely to go away. You'd have a bad tooth pulled, he thought. You'd get rid of it. Lance was a disgrace to the Loyalists. A hothead. Insubordinate.

"You're the one who killed her, aren't you?" he muttered as he drove toward Sweetgrass. Despite the so-called alibi provided by the bartender, Monroe believed that Lance was responsible for Pearl's death. It was the only scenario that made sense.

"How many times do I have to tell you I didn't do it?" Lance growled from the back seat.

Monroe felt such a blinding flash of anger he had trouble keeping the car on the road.

"Where you takin' me?" Lance demanded.

Monroe wasn't sure until precisely that moment. "I'm hauling your sorry ass to jail where it belongs."

"Oh, no, you don't," Lance squawked. "You can't! You wouldn't!"

Monroe experienced a deep sense of satisfaction on informing him otherwise. "Just watch me."

Lance fell into a sulk. As they neared Sweetgrass,

Monroe asked him, "How'd the kid know it was you?" His gaze met the other man's in the rearview mirror.

Lance shrugged. "No idea."

"You should've stayed away from the rodeo."

"Couldn't help myself. I like rodeos. How was I supposed to know Dakota was riding? His name wasn't on the program."

"Good thing for you that you didn't know."

"Whaddaya mean?"

Monroe sighed. The question was another example of the man's incompetence. "Well, if you'd known, you might've been able to keep him from picking up the prize money, right?"

"Oh, yeah. Right."

"So at least you have an excuse for screwing up— again." Monroe's hands tightened around the steering wheel. Burns and the others weren't going to be pleased when they learned Sam and Molly had managed to come up with the first payment. Damn stubborn fools, Dakota and his wife. They would have saved themselves a lot of grief if they'd given up the ranch sooner. Now Monroe had no choice. The Loyalists needed that land and they intended to get it, but the matter was in Monroe's hands now. He couldn't trust Lance; the man was useless. Besides, freeing him would raise too many questions. Monroe grinned. He couldn't deny he relished this assignment. Sam Dakota needed to be taught a lesson, set down a peg or two. And he was just the man to do it.

Sam was tired but happy. He had his family around him and, at least for the moment, all was right with the world. They were home, and the ranch house had never looked more inviting. Especially now that they'd be able to make the loan payment. Sam suppressed the sudden urge to laugh. It was a ticklish sort of feeling, one that bubbled up from the soles of his feet and touched every part of him. The crushing burden of this financial worry had been lifted from his shoulders. And that was only part of the good news.

Lance Elkins had been arrested, and judging by the anger brewing in Sheriff Maynard, Sam guessed that Lance would be making a few more confessions. Perhaps they'd finally be able to get to the bottom of the freak "accidents." If anyone could persuade Lance to talk, it was the sheriff. Sam almost felt sorry for Lance.

"Sam?"

Then there was Molly. His love, his wife. His pregnant wife. They hadn't spoken about it yet and it had taken him long enough to figure out, but he was sure. So sure. "In here." He sat in the living room, his feet propped on the ottoman, more tired than he'd ever been in his life. His head ached, his back throbbed, and there didn't seem to be a single muscle in his body unwilling to raise a protest over his return to bull-riding. The fistfight with Elkins hadn't helped.

"Oh." Molly walked into the room and stopped abruptly.

He opened his eyes. "Oh, what?"

"You…you look tired."

"That depends," he said, grinning up at her. "I'm certainly not too tired to make love to my wife."

"Sam!" She chastised him in a whisper and glanced over her shoulder to make sure the boys weren't listening in.

"They're upstairs," Sam assured her.

"We need to talk," she said, and then, as if the subject distressed her, she looked away. "I realize now isn't the best time for me to get pregnant but—"

"Why isn't it?" he asked. He'd given this more than a little thought in the past week, and try as he might, he couldn't make himself regret the fact that they'd been careless. His heart felt as though it might burst with joy, and all because Molly was carrying his child. Burst with joy. He'd heard that expression before; he'd never understood it till now.

"Our insurance only covers a small portion of the cost."

"Then we'll make payments to the doctor," he said with complete confidence.

"You never said how you felt about us having a baby..." She clamped her teeth on her lower lip.

Holding back a smile would have been impossible just then. "I don't think I've ever been happier in my life."

He held out his arms to her and she'd just started toward him when there was a loud crack of sound against the wall. Sam knew a rifle when he heard one. Grabbing Molly's arm, he leaped out of the chair and jerked her forward, pulling her down.

Together they hit the floor. Sam took the brunt of the impact and yelped at the flash of pain.

"What is it?" Molly asked, her eyes wide with terror.

"Someone's shooting at us."

"No—that's impossible!"

The dogs started barking frantically and Clay raced into the living room. Sam yelled, "Get down!"

The boy dropped to the carpet just as a bullet whizzed by where his head had been a second earlier.

"That does it." Sam crawled on his hands and knees

into the kitchen. "Nobody move." Just then a blaze of bullets ripped a line in the wall directly across from him.

Molly's cry of alarm intensified his anger and his fear. She covered her head with both hands and buried her face in the carpet.

Clay screamed as a window exploded, spraying glass about the room.

"Sam! Sam!" Tom shouted from upstairs. "What should I do? Tell me what to do."

"Stay where you are," he instructed. "Don't move."

Molly raised her head enough to reach for Clay and drag him to her side where she could protect him.

Sam didn't know what the hell was happening, but he wasn't going to sit still and let his family be used for target practice. All that he held dear was in this house, and whoever was shooting had best make peace with his maker, because Sam wasn't going to wait around for answers.

Slipping into the master bedroom, he opened the bottom dresser drawer and removed a handgun. Exiting the house undetected was no easy matter, but the safest room from which to leave was the bathroom. He climbed over the window ledge and fell into the darkness, landing hard.

Once outside, he crouched low and headed in the direction he'd seen the first round of bullets. His advantage was his knowledge of the land. The horses moved restlessly in their stalls; their tension strong and pungent.

Carefully he made his way along the wall to the corner of the barn.

"That's far enough, Dakota. Drop your weapon."

Sam stopped abruptly. A chill ran down his spine when he recognized the voice.

"Do it *now,* or you're a dead man."

Sam's fingers relaxed as he bent forward and cautiously dropped the pistol on the ground. "Maynard?" Slowly he turned around to face the other man.

"I can see you're surprised."

Sam didn't bother to deny it. "Why?"

Sheriff Maynard continued as if he hadn't heard. "It's a real shame, seeing how you managed to make good and all. Just when it looked like you'd done a turnaround, an unknown assailant attacked the family. In your effort to see to their safety, you were shot and killed. Then a few weeks after you're buried, the town will learn how you swindled old man Wheaton and duped Molly into marrying you. She won't be able to hold her head up in public, and she'll sell out at a lower price than originally offered."

"What's so important about this land?" Sam demanded, his hands doubled into fists.

"Me and my friends, we need it."

"Friends?"

A slow grin twisted the lawman's face. "The Loyalists."

Sam had heard of the militia group and knew they were active in the area, but he didn't know much about them. None of this made sense.

"This country's losing everything it stands for," Gene Maynard explained. "That's what we believe. The only way to hold on to our freedom is to overthrow the government. It just so happens this land is perfect for training purposes. We knew Wheaton was on his way out, so we had the plans drawn up and we aren't going to change things now." His mouth thinned. "You threw a wrench into our plans when you arrived."

Sam realized that his appearance on the scene was one thing, but his marriage to Molly another. No wonder the lawman had had it in for him.

"It's a shame to kill you, Dakota. You've kind of grown on me. But I could see a long time ago that you don't share our views, and that's unfortunate because you could've done us good. You've got guts."

"Why'd you kill Pearl?"

Maynard ignored the question. "Not long after you're dead, the town will discover you were the one responsible for her death."

"But he isn't the one who killed her, is he, Gene?" Russell Letson's voice rang out from behind the sheriff.

Maynard froze.

"Drop the gun."

"Russell, get out of here," Maynard said, glancing over his shoulder. "Go before I forget we're related."

"I know who killed Pearl."

"Great. You can tell me all about it later. Now, for your own sake, leave, and forget you ever saw me here with Dakota."

"That's one difference between you and me, cousin," Russell murmured sarcastically. "I have a very long memory. I'm not going to forget anything I heard or saw tonight."

"This has nothing to do with you."

"That's where you're wrong. Did she suffer, Gene? Did she beg you to let her live? Did she plead for mercy?"

"For the love of God, man, it wasn't me! Now drop the gun."

"You beat her." The words were full of anger and accusation.

"All right, all right, I beat her," Maynard confessed, "but I wasn't the one who killed her, I swear it." As he spoke, he swung around toward Russell.

Instinctively Sam knew what Maynard intended and with a wild cry leaped toward him, wanting to knock him off balance before he could fire. But a gun exploded before Sam was two inches off the ground.

Gene Maynard slumped down. Rearing back, he aimed at his cousin, but Sam used the momentum of his leap to kick the gun out of his hand.

Slowly Russell walked toward the moaning sheriff. His eyes burned with hatred as he leveled his weapon at the man's chest.

Whimpering for mercy, the sheriff twitched and tried to crawl away.

"Don't do it, Russell," Sam said. "He isn't worth spending the rest of your life in prison. Let *him* rot there, not you. The inmates will have a field day with him. Let them dole out the punishment."

Russell blinked and Sam knew his words had found their way through his hatred and into his mind. "I want him to suffer."

"He will," Sam promised.

"No!" Maynard shouted. "I didn't kill Pearl. I swear it." Blood flowed from his wound as he stared up at them with glazed eyes. Russell hesitated for the first time. "Why'd you want the Broken Arrow Ranch?"

"It was for the militia—the Loyalists. We were going to use it ourselves, build our training grounds here. This place and the one next to it. Two old people about to die…"

"Burns is involved, as well, isn't he?" Russell asked, and it was clear from Maynard's reaction that he was surprised the attorney knew it.

"Yes," he moaned.

"He's losing a lot of blood," Sam warned.

"Let him. I want him to rot in hell."

"She was a hooker, man! Why do you care?" Maynard asked, clutching his wounded shoulder.

"I cared," Russell said slowly. "I cared."

"Sam...Sam!" The lights went on and Molly raced across the yard. He caught her in his arms and hugged her fiercely.

"Tom," Sam said to the older boy, who'd followed his mother out, "call for an ambulance. After that I'll contact the authorities in Missoula."

Molly continued to hug him, as if she was afraid to let him go. "It's all right, sweetheart, not to worry," he murmured. "I'm fine."

"Sheriff Maynard?"

"I'm afraid so."

"But why?"

"It's a long story." He kissed her, then removed the pistol from Russell's fingers. "How'd you know it was Maynard?"

Russell's smile was infinitely sad. "You might say Pearl told me." His face darkened with pain and he looked from Molly to Sam. "I hope the two of you will be very happy."

"We already are," Molly said gently, and smiled up at her husband. "And that's not going to change."

Epilogue

Molly gave birth to a healthy baby girl the afternoon Gene Maynard, alias Monroe, Lance Elkins and David Burns were sentenced. They were convicted on a number of federal charges and would spend the rest of their natural lives in prison.

Sam had gone into the delivery room with Molly and coached her through the final stage of labor. When the baby was born, the physician had placed her in his arms for the first time. As Sam held his daughter and stared awestruck at her beautiful face, his eyes filled with tears.

The emotion he felt today far surpassed what he'd felt when he won the silver buckle—his rodeo triumph. *This* triumph, the birth of his child, made his rodeo accomplishments seem hollow. The buckle had attained a new meaning for him, though—because Molly had given it back to him. When he looked at it now, what he thought of was her love.

"She's perfect," he whispered, his voice hoarse with emotion. "Just like her mother."

Exhausted by the long hours of labor, Molly smiled contentedly.

"Welcome to the world, Cassie Marie Dakota." Sam gently kissed her brow. "You have two older brothers who're gonna spoil you something terrible."

"And a daddy, too."

"Oh, Molly," Sam said, gazing at his wife. "How did a saddle bum like me ever get so lucky? I have you, Tom, Clay and now Cassie. My heart's so full it feels like it's about to jump out of my chest." He stroked the baby's face. "Hey, Cassie. Your Grandma Dakota's gonna love you. And your aunts and uncles…" Sam had called his family Christmas Day; they'd come to visit a week later, just in time for New Year's. Another new beginning. They'd be back, all of them, once Molly and the baby had settled into a routine.

Molly's eyes drifted shut.

"I love you so damn much," Sam added.

"I love you, too, sweetheart…but right now I have to sleep…."

While she was wheeled into the recovery room, Sam took Cassie into the nursery and handed her to a nurse.

When Molly woke up, she was in her hospital bed, and Sam was asleep in the chair beside her. Clay and Tom tiptoed silently into the room. "How d'you feel, Mom?"

"Wonderful," she assured them.

"We just went to see Cassie. For a girl she's not bad-looking," Clay said, then gave a small sigh just so she'd know he was only a *little* disappointed she hadn't given him the brother he'd requested.

Tom claimed he'd wanted a sister all along and beamed her a proud smile as if she'd purposely ordered a girl on his behalf. "The way I figure it, she'll need an older brother to look out for her."

"Hey, she's going to need two older brothers," Clay said. "You're not her only brother, you know."

"What about changing her diapers? Will her older brothers be willing to do that?" Molly asked.

"Sure," Tom said, sending Clay a sidelong glance. "*He'll* be more than happy to help change poopy diapers."

Molly laughed, and Sam opened his eyes. Stretching his arms high above his head, he looked around the room. "I'm certainly glad you boys gave me a little practice in this fathering business," he said with a grin.

"Hey, glad to do it," Tom teased. "Cassie will thank us later."

"You willing to do this again?" Clay asked. "Next time, get me a little brother, all right?"

"Anything you say, son." Sam reached for Molly's hand. He brought it to his lips and gently kissed her palm. His eyes were bright with love. "I wish your grandfather were here."

"He's here, Sam," she assured him. "I'm as sure of that as I am of your love for me. Both my grandparents." She closed her eyes and could almost hear her grandmother whisper to her beloved husband.

"Walter, you chose well for our Molly. You chose well."

As Russell sat in his office reading, the door opened and two men dressed in dark suits stepped inside.

"I'm sorry," he said, "we're already closed for the day."

"Come with us," the first man said without explanation.

Russell stood. "I beg your pardon?"

"You're to come with us."

The second man pulled out a badge and flashed it, but Russell wasn't able to read the identification card. All he knew was that these two men worked for the federal government.

"Where are we going?" he asked as he followed them out the door. Neither one answered. "Should I call someone?"

"That wouldn't be advisable."

Not that there was anyone to call. His mother had died that past Thanksgiving, and the only close friend he had these days was Sam Dakota. Molly had come home from the hospital the day before, and he'd been out to visit her and hold Cassie. The infant had immediately charmed him; he'd found it difficult to leave.

One man drove and the other sat in the back seat with him. They'd been on the road twenty minutes, still refusing to answer his questions, when Russell realized where they were headed. His cabin. This puzzled him even more.

A little later they pulled into the driveway and parked in his usual spot. A second car was already there.

"We'll wait for you here," one of the men told him.

"I'm to go inside?"

"That's right." This was said as if it should have been obvious.

Not knowing what to expect, Russell walked into the house. A woman stood at the far side of the living room, at the window that overlooked the valley. The first thing he noticed was how familiar she seemed.

"Hello, Russell."

Not until she spoke did he recognize her. His voice nearly failed him. *"Pearl?"*

"It's a shock, isn't it?" she asked softly.

Her hair was different and she'd gained a few pounds; the hollowed places in her face were filled out. She'd been pretty before, but there was a gentle beauty about her now, a serenity.

His knees were too weak to hold him and he sank into the first available seat.

"I'm sorry to do this to you," she said. "I didn't think I'd ever see you again, but now that the trial's over, they said I was free to contact you." Her voice wavered a bit and she stopped.

"The trial?" His head buzzed with questions.

"I was the one who got in touch with the FBI," she explained. "They staged my death.... I couldn't tell you, Russell. I couldn't get you involved."

"But all that blood?"

"It wasn't mine."

"The body? They found the body."

"That was...fortuitous. Some poor murdered woman—I feel terrible about that. She still hasn't been identified...." Her voice trailed off.

Anger propelled him to his feet. "You let me believe you were dead!"

"I didn't have any choice."

He whirled around, away from her, while he thought this through.

"Monroe...Gene didn't know I could read," she whispered. "He...he left information around without any fear that I'd read it and understand. But then you taught me and I was able to tell the authorities the Loyalists' plans.

I remember almost everything I've read—I have a good memory. Please, oh, please, don't be angry with me."

What was the matter with him? Russell mused. He had Pearl back. It was far more than he'd dared hope, more than he'd dared dream.

"I love you," she whispered, tears shining from her eyes. "Now you know why I did what I did." After an awkward silence she bowed her head. "You can go now if you want—the agents will take you back to town."

"I'm not going anywhere without you," Russell said, walking toward her. He wrapped his arms around her and she clung to him, weeping softly. "Not ever again."

"You'll have to give up your life as you know it. Take on a new identity. Become part of the Witness Protection program."

"Done."

"And love me for the rest of your life."

"Done," he whispered brokenly. "For the rest of my life."

"And mine," Pearl said, smiling up at him, her eyes bright with tears.

* * * * *

RANSOM CANYON

Jodi Thomas

I dedicate this book to my dear friend DeWanna Pace. We met in a writing class and spent the next twenty-five years helping each other follow our dreams.

I miss her, but know she's Heaven's blessing now.

One

Staten Kirkland lowered the brim of his felt Resistol as he turned into the wind. The hat was about to live up to its name. Hell was blowing down from the north, and he would have to ride hard to make it back to headquarters before the full fury of the storm broke. His new mount, a roan he'd bought last week, was green and spooked by the winter lightning. Staten had no time to put on the gloves in his back pocket. He had to ride.

When the mare bucked in protest, he twisted the reins around his hand and felt the cut of leather across his palm as he fought for control of both his horse and the memories threatening as low as the dark clouds above his head.

Icy rain had poured that night five years ago, only he hadn't been on his ranch; he'd been trapped in the hallway of the county hospital fifty miles away. His son had lain at one end, fighting for his life, and reporters had huddled just beyond the entrance at the other end, hollering for news.

All they'd cared about was that the kid's grandfather was a United States senator. No one had cared that Staten, the boy's father and only parent, held them back. All they'd wanted was a headline. All Staten had wanted was for his son to live.

But, he didn't get what he wanted.

Randall, only child of Staten Kirkland, only grandchild of Senator Samuel Kirkland, had died that night. The reporters had gotten their headline, complete with pictures of Staten storming through the double doors, swinging at every man who tried to stop him. He'd left two reporters and a clueless intern on the floor, but he hadn't slowed.

He'd run into the storm that night not caring about the rain. Not caring about his own life. Two years before he'd buried his wife, and now he would put his son in the ground beside her because of a car crash. He'd had to run from the ache so deep in his heart it would never heal.

Now, five years later, another storm was blowing through, but the ache inside him hadn't lessened. He rode toward headquarters on the half-wild horse. Rain mixed with tears he never let anyone see. He'd wanted to die that night. He had no one. His wife's illness had left both father and son bitter, lost. If she'd lived, maybe Randall would have been different. Calmer. Maybe if he'd had her love, the boy wouldn't have been so wild. He wouldn't have thought himself so invincible.

Only, taking a winding road at over a hundred miles per hour *had* killed him. The car his grandfather had given him for his sixteenth birthday a month earlier had missed the curve heading into Ransom Canyon and rolled over and over. The newspapers had quoted one first responder as saying, *"Thank God he'd been alone. No one in that sports car would have survived."*

Staten wished he'd been with his boy. He'd felt dead inside the day he buried Randall next to his wife, and he felt dead now as memories pounded.

He rode close to the canyon rim as the storm raged, almost wishing the jagged earth would claim him, too. But, he was fifth generation born to this land. There would be no more Kirklands after him, and he wouldn't go without a fight.

As he raced, he remembered the horror of seeing his son pulled out of the wreck, too beat up and bloody for even a father to recognize. Kirkland blood had poured over the red dirt of the canyon that night.

He rode feeling the pounding of his horse's hooves match the beat of his heart.

When Staten crossed under the Double K gate and let the horse gallop to the barn, he took a deep breath, knowing what he had to do.

Looking up, he saw Jake there at the barn door waiting for him. The rodeo had crippled the old man, but Jake Longbow was still the best hand on the ranch.

"Dry him off!" Staten yelled above the storm as he handed over the mare to Jake's care. "I have to go."

The old cowboy, his face like twisted rawhide, nodded once as if he knew what Staten would say. A thousand times over the years, Jake had moved into action before Staten issued the order. "I got this, Mr. Kirkland. You do what you got to do."

Darting across the back corral, Staten climbed into the huge Dodge 3500 with its Cummins diesel engine and four-wheel drive. The truck might guzzle gas and ride rough, but if he slid off the road tonight, it wouldn't roll.

Half an hour later he finally slowed as he turned into a farm twenty miles north of Crossroads, Texas. A sign, in need of painting and with a few bullet holes in it, read simply "Lavender Lane." Even in the rain the air here smelled of lavender. He'd made it to Quinn's place. One house, one farm, sat alone with nothing near enough to call a neighbor.

Quinn O'Grady's home always reminded him of a little girl's fancy dollhouse: brightly painted shutters and gingerbread trim everywhere. Folks sometimes commented on how the house was as fancy as the woman who owned it was plain, but Staten had never thought of her that way. She was shy, had kept to herself even in grade school, but she was her own woman. She'd built a living out of the worthless land her parents had left her.

He might have gone his whole life saying no more than hello to her, but Quinn O'Grady had been his wife's best friend. Even after he'd married Amalah, she'd still have her "girls' days" with Quinn.

They'd can peaches in the fall and take courses at the church on quilting and pottery. They'd take off to Dallas for an art show or to Canton for the world's biggest garage sale. He couldn't count the times his wife had climbed into Quinn's old green pickup and simply called out that they were going shopping as if that were all he needed to know. Half the time they didn't come back with anything but ice-cream-sundae smiles.

Quinn hadn't talked to him much in those early years, but she'd been a good friend to his wife, and that mattered. Near the end, she'd sat with Amalah in the hospital so he could go home to shower and change clothes. That last month, it seemed she was always near.

The two women had been best friends all their lives, and they would be to the end.

Staten didn't smile as he cut the engine in front of Quinn O'Grady's house. He never smiled. Not anymore. For years he'd worked hard thinking he'd be passing on the Double K to his son. Now, if Staten died, the ranch would probably be sold at auction to help support his father's run for the senate or, who knows, the old guy might run for governor next time. Even though Samuel Kirkland was in his sixties, his fourth wife was keeping him young, he claimed. He'd never had much interest in the ranch and hadn't spent a night on Kirkland soil since Staten had taken over the place.

Quinn caught Staten's attention as she opened her door and stared out at him. She had a big towel in one hand as she leaned against the door frame and waited for him to climb out of the truck and come inside. She was tall, almost six feet, and ordinary in her simple clothes. He couldn't imagine Quinn in heels or her hair fixed any way except the long braid she always wore down the center of her back. She'd worn jeans since she started school; only, there had been two braids trailing down her back then.

Funny, Staten thought as he climbed out and tried to outrun the rain, *a woman who wants nothing to do with frills or lace lives in a dollhouse.*

After he reached the porch and shook like a big dog, she handed him the towel. "When I saw the storm moving in, I figured you'd be coming. Tug off those muddy boots while I dip up some soup for supper. I made taco soup when I saw the clouds rolling in from the north."

No one ordered any Kirkland around. No one. Only here, in her house, he did what she asked. He might never have another drop of love in him, but he'd still respect Quinn.

His spurs jingled as his boots hit the porch. In his stocking feet he stood only a few inches taller than her, but with his broad shoulders he guessed he probably doubled her in weight. "Any chance the clouds made you think of coconut pie?"

She laughed softly. "It's in the oven. Be out in a minute."

They watched the stormy afternoon turn into evening, with lightning putting on a show outside her kitchen window. He liked how he felt comfortable being silent around her. They sometimes talked about Amalah and the funny things that had happened when they were growing up. He felt as if he and Quinn were the leftovers, for the best of them had both died with Amalah.

Only, tonight his thoughts were on his son, and Staten didn't really want to talk at all. As the sun set, the temperature dropped, and the icy rain turned to a dusting of soft mushy snow while they ate in silence.

When he reached for his dishes and started to stand, she stopped him with a touch on his damp sleeve. "I'll do that," she said. "Finish your coffee."

He sat quiet and still for a few minutes, thinking how this place of hers seemed to slow his heart and make it easier to breathe. He finally left the table and silently moved to stand behind her as she worked at the sink. With rough hands scabbed over in places where the reins had cut, he began to untie her braid.

"I did this once when we were in third grade. I remember you didn't say a word, but Amalah called me an idiot after school."

Quinn nodded but didn't speak. Shared memories settled comfortably between them.

He liked the way Quinn's sunshine hair felt, even now. It was thick and hung down straight except for the slight waves left by the braid.

She turned and frowned up at him as she took his hand. Without asking questions she pulled his injured palm under running water and then patted it dry. When she rubbed lotion over his hand, it felt more like a caress than doctoring.

He was so close behind her their bodies brushed as she worked. Leaning down, he tickled her neck with a light kiss. "Play for me tonight," he whispered.

Turning toward the old piano across the open living area, she shook her head. "I can't."

He didn't question or try to change her mind. He never did. Sometimes, she'd play for him, other times something deep inside her wouldn't let her.

Without a word, she tugged him to the only bedroom, turning off lights as they moved through the house.

For a while he stood at the doorway, watching her remove her plain work clothes: worn jeans, a faded plaid shirt that probably belonged to her father years ago and a T-shirt that hugged her slender frame. As piece by piece fell, pale white skin glowed in the low light of her nightstand.

When he didn't move, she turned toward him. Her breasts were small, her body lean, her tummy flat from never bearing a child. All she wore was a pair of red panties.

"Finish undressing me," she whispered, then waited.

He walked toward her, knowing that he wouldn't have moved if she hadn't invited him. Maybe it was just a game they played, or maybe they'd silently agreed on unwritten rules when they'd begun. He couldn't remember.

Pulling her against him, he just held her for a long time. Somehow on that worst night of his life five years ago, he'd knocked at her door. He'd been muddy, grieving and lost to himself.

She hadn't said a word. She'd just taken his hand. He'd let her pull off his muddy clothes and clean him up while he tried to think of a way to stop breathing and die. She'd tucked him into her bed and then climbed in with him, holding him until he finally fell asleep. He hadn't said a word, either, guessing that she'd heard the news reports of the crash. Knowing by the sorrow in her light blue eyes that she shared his grief.

A thousand feelings had careened through his mind that night, all dark, but she'd held on to him. He remembered thinking that if she had tried to comfort him with words, even a few, he would have shattered into a million pieces.

Just before dawn, he remembered waking and turning to her. She'd welcomed him, not as a lover, but as a friend silently letting him know it was all right to touch her. All right to hold on.

In the five years since, they'd had long talks, sometimes when he sought her out. They'd had stormy nights when they didn't talk at all. He always made love to her with a gentle touch, never hurried, always with more caring and less passion than he would have liked. Somehow, it felt right that way.

She wasn't interested in going out on a date or meeting him anywhere. She never called or emailed. If she passed him in the little town that sat between them called Crossroads, she'd wave, but they never spoke more than a few words in public. She had no interest in changing her last name for his, even if he'd asked.

Yet, he knew her body. He knew what she liked him to do and how she wanted to be held. He knew how she slept, rolled up beside him as if she were cold.

Only, he didn't know her favorite color or why she'd never married or even why sometimes she couldn't go near her piano. In many ways they didn't know each other at all.

She was his rainy-day woman. When the memories got to him, she was his refuge. When loneliness ached through his body, she was his cure. She saved him simply by being there, by waiting, by loving a man who had no love to give back.

As the storm raged and calmed, she pulled him into her bed. They made love in the silence of the evening, and then he held her against him and slept.

Two

When her old hall clock chimed eleven times, Staten Kirkland left Quinn O'Grady's bed. While she slept, he dressed in the shadows, watching her with only the light of the full moon. She'd given him what he needed tonight, and, as always, he felt as if he'd given her nothing.

Walking out to her porch, he studied the newly washed earth, thinking of how empty his life was except for these few hours he shared with Quinn. He'd never love her or anyone, but he wished he could do something for her. Thanks to hard work and inherited land, he was a rich man. She was making a go of her farm, but barely. He could help her if she'd let him. But he knew she'd never let him.

As he pulled on his boots, he thought of a dozen things he could do around the place. Like fixing that old tractor out in the mud or modernizing her irrigation system. The tractor had been sitting out by the road for months. If she'd accept his help, it wouldn't take him an hour to pull the old John Deere out and get the engine running again.

Only, she wouldn't accept anything from him. He knew better than to ask.

He wasn't even sure they were friends some days. Maybe they were more. Maybe less. He looked down at his palm, remembering how she'd rubbed cream on it and worried that all they had in common was loss and the need, now and then, to touch another human being.

The screen door creaked. He turned as Quinn, wrapped in an old quilt, moved out into the night.

"I didn't mean to wake you," he said as she tiptoed across the snow-dusted porch. "I need to get back. Got eighty new yearlings coming in early." He never apologized for leaving, and he wasn't now. He was simply stating facts. With the cattle rustling going on and his plan to enlarge his herd, he might have to hire more men. As always, he felt as though he needed to be on his land and on alert.

She nodded and moved to stand in front of him.

Staten waited. They never touched after they made love. He usually left without a word, but tonight she obviously had something she wanted to say.

Another thing he probably did wrong, he thought. He never complimented her, never kissed her on the mouth, never said any words after he touched her. If she didn't make little sounds of pleasure now and then, he wouldn't have been sure he satisfied her.

Now, standing so close to her, he felt more a stranger than a lover. He knew the smell of her skin, but he had no idea what she was thinking most of the time. She knew quilting and how to make soap from her lavender. She played the piano like an angel and didn't even own a TV. He knew ranching and watched from his recliner every game the Dallas Cowboys played.

If they ever spent over an hour talking they'd probably figure out they had nothing in common. He'd played every sport in high school, and she'd played in both the orchestra and the band. He'd collected most of his college hours online, and she'd gone all the way to New York to school. But, they'd loved the same person. Amalah had been Quinn's best friend and his one love. Only, they rarely talked about how they felt. Not anymore. Not ever really. It was too painful, he guessed, for both of them.

Tonight the air was so still, moisture hung like invisible lace. She looked to be closer to her twenties than her forties. Quinn had her own quiet kind of beauty. She always had, and he guessed she still would even when she was old.

To his surprise, she leaned in and kissed his mouth.

He watched her. "You want more?" he finally asked, figuring it was probably the dumbest thing to say to a naked woman standing two inches away from him. He had no idea what *more* would be. They always had sex once, if they had it at all, when he knocked on her door. Sometimes neither made the first move, and they just cuddled on the couch and held each other. Quinn wasn't a passionate woman. What they did was just satisfying a need that they both had now and then.

She kissed him again without saying a word. When her cheek brushed against his stubbled chin, it was wet and tasted newborn like the rain.

Slowly, Staten moved his hands under her blanket and circled her warm body, then he pulled her closer and kissed her fully like he hadn't kissed a woman since his wife died.

Her lips were soft and inviting. When he opened her

mouth and invaded, it felt far more intimate than anything they had ever done, but he didn't stop. She wanted
this from him, and he had no intention of denying her.
No one would ever know that she was the thread that
kept him together some days.

When he finally broke the kiss, Quinn was out of
breath. She pressed her forehead against his jaw and
he waited.

"From now on," she whispered so low he felt her
words more than heard them, "when you come to see
me, I need you to kiss me goodbye before you go. If
I'm asleep, wake me. You don't have to say a word, but
you have to kiss me."

She'd never asked him for anything. He had no intention of saying no. His hand spread across the small
of her back and pulled her hard against him. "I won't
forget if that's what you want." He could feel her heart
pounding and knew her asking had not come easy.

She nodded. "It's what I want."

He brushed his lips over hers, loving the way she
sighed as if wanting more before she pulled away.

"Good night," she said as though rationing pleasure.
Stepping inside, she closed the screen door between
them.

Raking his hair back, he put on his hat as he watched
her fade into the shadows. The need to return was already building in him. "I'll be back Friday night if it's
all right. It'll be late, I've got to visit with my grandmother and do her list of chores before I'll be free. If
you like, I could bring barbecue for supper?" He felt as

if he was rambling, but something needed to be said, and he had no idea what.

"And vegetables," she suggested.

He nodded. She wanted a meal, not just the meat. "I'll have them toss in sweet potato fries and okra."

She held the blanket tight as if he might see her body. She didn't meet his eyes when he added, "I enjoyed kissing you, Quinn. I look forward to doing so again."

With her head down, she nodded as she vanished into the darkness without a word.

He walked off the porch, deciding if he lived to be a hundred he'd never understand Quinn. As far as he knew, she'd never had a boyfriend when they were in school. And his wife had never told him about Quinn dating anyone special when she went to New York to that fancy music school. Now, in her forties, she'd never had a date, much less a lover that he knew of. But she hadn't been a virgin when they'd made love the first time.

Asking her about her love life seemed far too personal a question.

Climbing in his truck he forced his thoughts toward problems at the ranch. He needed to hire men; they'd lost three cattle to rustlers this month. As he planned the coming day, Staten did what he always did: he pushed Quinn to a corner of his mind, where she'd wait until he saw her again.

As he passed through the little town of Crossroads, all the businesses were closed up tight except for a gas station that stayed open twenty-four hours to handle the few travelers needing to refuel or brave enough to sample their food.

Half a block away from the station was his grand-mother's bungalow, dark amid the cluster of senior citizens' homes. One huge light in the middle of all the little homes shone a low glow onto the porch of each house. The tiny white cottages reminded him of a circle of wagons camped just off the main road. She'd lived fifty years on Kirkland land, but when Staten's grand-dad, her husband, had died, she'd wanted to move to town. She'd been a teacher in her early years and said she needed to be with her friends in the retirement community, not alone in the big house on the ranch.

He swore without anger, remembering all her instructions the day she moved to town. She wanted her only grandson to drop by every week to switch out batteries, screw in lightbulbs, and reprogram the TV that she'd spent the week messing up. He didn't mind dropping by. Besides his father, who considered his home—when he wasn't in Washington—to be Dallas, Granny was the only family Staten had.

A quarter mile past the one main street of Crossroads, his truck lights flashed across four teenagers walking along the road between the Catholic church and the gas station.

Three boys and a girl. Fifteen or sixteen, Staten guessed.

For a moment the memory of Randall came to mind. He'd been about their age when he'd crashed, and he'd worn the same type of blue-and-white letter jacket that two of the boys wore tonight.

Staten slowed as he passed them. "You kids need a ride?" The lights were still on at the church, and a few cars were in the parking lot. Saturday night, Staten remembered. Members of 4-H would probably be working in the basement on projects.

One kid waved. A tall, Hispanic boy named Lucas whom he thought was the oldest son of the head wrangler on the Collins ranch. Reyes was his last name, and Staten remembered the boy being one of a dozen young kids who were often hired part-time at the ranch.

Staten had heard the kid was almost as good a wrangler as his father. The magic of working with horses must have been passed down from father to son, along with the height. Young Reyes might be lean but, thanks to working, he would be in better shape than either of the football boys. When Lucas Reyes finished high school, he'd have no trouble hiring on at any of the big ranches, including the Double K.

"No, we're fine, Mr. Kirkland," the Reyes boy said politely. "We're just walking down to the station for a Coke. Reid Collins's brother is picking us up soon."

"No crime in that, mister," a redheaded kid in a letter jacket answered. His words came fast and clipped, reminding Staten of how his son had sounded.

Volume from a boy trying to prove he was a man, Staten thought.

He couldn't see the faces of the two boys with letter jackets, but the girl kept her head up. "We've been working on a project for the fair," she answered politely. "I'm Lauren Brigman, Mr. Kirkland."

Staten nodded. *Sheriff Brigman's daughter, I remember you.* She knew enough to be polite, but it was none of his business. "Good evening, Lauren," he said. "Nice to see you again. Good luck with the project."

When he pulled away, he shook his head. Normally,

he wouldn't have bothered to stop. This might be small-town Texas, but they were not his problem. If he saw the Reyes boy again, he would apologize.

Staten swore. At this rate he'd turn into a nosy old man by forty-five. It didn't seem that long ago that he and Amalah used to walk up to the gas station after meetings at the church.

Hell, maybe Quinn asking to kiss him had rattled him more than he thought. He needed to get his head straight. She was just a friend. A woman he turned to when the storms came. Nothing more. That was the way they both wanted it.

Until he made it back to her porch next Friday night, he had a truckload of trouble at the ranch to worry about.

Twenty miles away Quinn O'Grady curled into her blanket on her front porch and watched the night sky, knowing that Staten was still driving home. He always came to her like a raging storm and left as calm as dawn.

Only tonight, she'd surprised him with her request. Tonight when he'd walked away at midnight, it felt different. Somehow after five years, their relationship felt newborn.

She grinned, loving that she had made the first move. She had demanded a kiss, and he hadn't hesitated. She knew he came to her house out of need and loneliness, but for her it had always been more. In her quiet way, she could not remember a time she hadn't loved him.

Yet from grade school on, Staten Kirkland had belonged to her best friend, and Quinn had promised herself she'd never try to step between them. Even now, seven years after Amalah's death, a part of Staten still belonged to his wife. Maybe not his heart, Quinn decided, but more his willingness to be open to caring. He was a man determined never to allow anyone close again. He didn't want love in his life; he only wanted to survive having loved and lost Amalah.

Amalah had wanted to be Mrs. Kirkland since the day she and Quinn had gone riding on the Double K ranch. She'd loved the big house, the luncheons and the committees. She knew how to smile for the press, how to dress, and how to manage the Kirkland men to get just what she wanted. Amalah had been a perfect wife for a rich rancher.

Quinn only wanted Staten, but never, not for one moment, would she have wished Amalah dead. Staten was a love Quinn kept locked away in her heart, knowing from the beginning that it would never see light.

When her best friend died, Quinn never went to Staten. She couldn't. It wouldn't have been fair. She never called or tried to *accidentally* run into him in town. Amalah might be gone, but Staten still didn't belong to her. She was not the kind of woman who could live in his world.

Two years passed after Amalah died. Staten would stop by now and then just to check on Quinn, but her shyness kept their conversations short.

Then, Randall died.

She'd heard about the car crash on the local radio station and cried for the boy she'd known all his life.

Tears for a boy's life cut short and for a father who she knew must be hurting, but who she couldn't go to. She wouldn't have known what to say. He'd be surrounded by people, and Quinn was afraid of most people.

When she'd heard a pounding on her door that night, she almost didn't answer. Then she'd seen Staten, broken and needing someone, and she couldn't turn him away.

That night she'd held him, thinking that just this one time, he needed her. Tomorrow he'd be strong and they'd go back to simply being polite to one another, but for one night she could help.

That next morning he'd left without a word. She had never expected him to return, but he did. This strong, hard man never asked anything of her, but he took what she offered. Reason told her it wouldn't last. He'd called the two of them the leftovers, as if they were the ones abandoned on a shelf. But, Staten wasn't a leftover. One day he would no longer suffer the storms. One day he would go back to living again, and when he did, he'd forget the way to her door.

As the five years passed, Quinn began to store up memories to keep her warm when he stopped coming. As simple as it seemed, she wanted to be kissed. Not out of passion or need, but gently.

Every time he walked away might be the last time. She wanted to remember that she'd been kissed goodbye that last time, even if neither of them knew it at the moment.

Three

Lauren

A midnight moon blinked its way between storm clouds as Lauren Brigman cleaned the mud off her shoes. The guys had gone inside the gas station for Cokes. She didn't really want anything to drink, but it was either walk over with the others after working on their fair projects or stay back at the church and talk to Mrs. Patterson.

Somewhere Mrs. Patterson had gotten the idea that since Lauren didn't have a mother around, she should take every opportunity to have a "girl talk" with the sheriff's daughter.

Lauren wanted to tell the old woman that she had known all the facts of life by the age of seven, and she really did not need a buddy to share her teenage years with. Besides, her mother lived in Dallas. It wasn't like she died. She'd just left. Just because she couldn't stand the sight of Lauren's dad didn't mean she didn't call and talk to Lauren almost every week. Maybe Mom had just gotten tired of the sheriff's nightly lectures. Lauren had heard every one of Pop's talks so many times that she had them memorized in alphabetical order.

Her grades put her at the top of the sophomore class, and she saw herself bound for college in less than three years. Lauren had no intention of getting pregnant, or doing drugs, or any of the other fearful situations Mrs. Patterson and her father had hinted might befall her. Her pop didn't even want her dating until she was sixteen, and, judging from the boys she knew in high school, she'd just as soon go dateless until eighteen. Maybe college would have better pickings. Some of these guys were so dumb she was surprised they got their cowboy hats on straight every morning.

Reid Collins walked out from the gas station first with a can of Coke in each hand. "I bought you one even though you said you didn't want anything to drink," he announced as he neared. "Want to lean on me while you clean your shoes?"

Lauren rolled her eyes. Since he'd grown a few inches and started working out, Reid thought he was God's gift to girls.

"Why?" she asked as she tossed the stick. "I have a brick wall to lean on. And don't get any ideas we're on a date, Reid, just because I walked over here with you."

"I don't date sophomores," he snapped. "I'm on first string, you know. I could probably date any senior I want to. Besides, you're like a little sister, Lauren. We've known each other since you were in the first grade."

She thought of mentioning that playing first string on a football team that only had forty players total, including the coaches and water boy, wasn't any great accomplishment, but arguing with Reid would rot her brain. He'd been born rich, and he'd thought he knew everything since he cleared the birth canal. She feared his disease was terminal.

"If you're cold, I'll let you wear my football jacket." When she didn't comment, he bragged, "I had to reorder a bigger size after a month of working out."

She hated to, but if she didn't compliment him soon, he'd never stop begging. "You look great in the jacket, Reid. Half the seniors on the team aren't as big as you." There was nothing wrong with Reid from the neck down. In a few years he'd be a knockout with the Collins good looks and trademark rusty hair, not quite brown, not quite red. But he still wouldn't interest her.

"So, when I get my driver's license next month, do you want to take a ride?"

Lauren laughed. "You've been asking that since I was in the third grade and you got your first bike. The answer is still no. We're friends, Reid. We'll always be friends, I'm guessing."

He smiled a smile that looked like he'd been practicing. "I know, Lauren, but I keep wanting to give you a chance now and then. You know, some guys don't want to date the sheriff's daughter, and I hate to point it out, babe, but if you don't fill out some, it's going to be bad news in college." He had the nerve to point at her chest.

"I know." She managed to pull off a sad look. "Having my father is a cross I have to bear. Half the guys in town are afraid of him. Like he might arrest them for talking to me. Which he might." She had no intention of discussing her lack of curves with Reid.

"No, it's not fear of him, exactly," Reid corrected. "I think it's more the bullet holes they're afraid of. Every time a guy looks at you, your old man starts patting his service weapon. Nerve-racking habit, if you ask me. From the looks of it, I seem to be the only one he'll let stand beside you, and that's just because our dads are friends."

She grinned. Reid was spoiled and conceited and self-centered, but he was right. They'd probably always be friends. Her dad was the sheriff, and his was the mayor of Crossroads, even though he lived five miles from town on one of the first ranches established near Ransom Canyon.

With her luck, Reid would be the only guy in the state that her father would let her date. Grumpy old Pop had what she called Terminal Cop Disease. Her father thought everyone, except his few friends, was most likely a criminal, anyone under thirty should be stopped and searched, and anyone who'd ever smoked pot could not be trusted.

Tim O'Grady, Reid's eternal shadow, walked out of the station with a huge frozen drink. The clear cup showed off its red-and-yellow layers of cherry-and-pineapple-flavored sugar.

Where Reid was balanced in his build, Tim was lanky, disjointed. He seemed to be made of mismatched parts. His arms were too long. His feet seemed too big, and his wired smile barely fit in his mouth. When he took a deep draw on his drink, he staggered and held his forehead from the brain freeze.

Lauren laughed as he danced around like a puppet with his strings crossed. Timothy, as the teachers called him, was always good for a laugh. He had the depth of cheap paint but the imagination of a natural-born storyteller.

"Maybe I shouldn't have gotten an icy drink on such

a cold night," he mumbled between gulps. "If I freeze from the inside out, put me up on Main Street as a statue."

Lauren giggled.

Lucas Reyes was the last of their small group to come outside. Lucas hadn't bought anything, but he evidently was avoiding standing outside with her. She'd known Lucas Reyes for a few years, maybe longer, but he never talked to her. Like Reid and Tim, he was a year ahead of her, but since he rarely talked, she usually only noticed him as a background person in her world.

Unlike them, Lucas didn't have a family name following him around opening doors for a hundred miles.

They all four lived east of Crossroads along the rambling canyon called Ransom Canyon. Lauren and her father lived in one of a cluster of houses near the lake, as did Tim's parents. Reid's family ranch was five miles farther out. She had no idea where Lucas's family lived. Maybe on the Collins ranch. His father worked on the Bar W, which had been in the Collins family for over a hundred years. The area around the headquarters looked like a small village.

Reid repeated the plan. "My brother said he'd drop Sharon off and be back for us. But if they get busy doing their thing it could be an hour. We might as well walk back and sit on the church steps."

"Great fun," Tim complained. "Everything's closed. It's freezing out here, and I swear this town is so dead somebody should bury it."

"We could start walking toward home," Lauren suggested as she pulled a tiny flashlight from her key chain. The canyon lake wasn't more than a mile. If they walked they wouldn't be so cold. She could probably be home before Reid's dumb brother could get his lips off Sharon. If rumors were true, Sharon had very kissable lips, among other body parts.

"Better than standing around here," Reid said as Tim kicked mud toward the building. "I'd rather be walking than sitting. Plus, if we go back to the church, Mrs. Patterson will probably come out to keep us company."

Without a vote, they started walking. Lauren didn't like the idea of stumbling into mud holes now covered up by a dusting of snow along the side of the road, but it sounded better than standing out front of the gas station. Besides, the moon offered enough light, making the tiny flashlight her father insisted she carry worthless.

Within a few yards, Reid and Tim had fallen behind and were lighting up a smoke. To her surprise, Lucas stayed beside her.

"You don't smoke?" she asked, not really expecting him to answer.

"No, can't afford the habit," he said, surprising her. "I've got plans, and they don't include lung cancer."

Maybe the dark night made it easier to talk, or maybe Lauren didn't want to feel so alone in the shadows. "I was starting to think you were a mute. We've had a few classes together, and you've never said a word. Even tonight you were the only one who didn't talk about your project."

Lucas shrugged. "Didn't see the point. I'm just entering for the prize money, not trying to save the world or build a better tomorrow."

She giggled.

He laughed, too, realizing he'd just made fun of the whole point of the projects. "Plus," he added, "there's just not much opportunity to get a word in around those two." He nodded his head at the two letter jackets falling farther behind as a cloud of smoke haloed above them.

She saw his point. The pair trailed them by maybe twenty feet or more, and both were talking about football. Neither seemed to require a listener.

"Why do you hang out with them?" she asked. Lucas didn't seem to fit. Studious and quiet, he hadn't gone out for sports or joined many clubs that she knew about. "Jocks usually hang out together."

"I wanted to work on my project tonight, and Reid offered me a ride. Listening to football talk beats walking in this weather."

Lauren tripped into a pothole. Lucas's hand shot out and caught her in the darkness. He steadied her, then let go.

"Thanks. You saved my life," she joked.

"Hardly, but if I had, you'd owe me a blood debt."

"Would I have to pay?"

"Of course. It would be a point of honor. You'd have to save me or be doomed to a coward's hell."

"Lucky you just kept me from tripping, or I'd be following you around for years waiting to repay the debt." She rubbed her arm where he'd touched her. He was stronger than she'd thought he would be. "You lift weights?"

The soft laughter came again. "Yeah, it's called work. Until I was sixteen, I spent the summers and every weekend working on Reid's father's ranch. Once I was old enough, I signed up at the Kirkland place to cowboy when they need extras. Every dime I make is going to college tuition in a year. That's why I don't have a car yet. When I get to college, I won't need it, and the money will go toward books."

"But you're just a junior. You've still got a year and a half of high school."

"I've got it worked out so I can graduate early. High school's a waste of time. I've got plans. I can make a hundred-fifty a day working, and my dad says he thinks I'll be able to cowboy every day I'm not in school this spring and all summer."

She tripped again, and his hand steadied her once more. Maybe it was her imagination, but she swore he held on a little longer than necessary.

"You're an interesting guy, Lucas Reyes."

"I will be," he said. "Once I'm in college, I can still come home and work breaks and weekends. I'm thinking I can take a few online classes during the summer, live at home, and save enough to pay for the next year. I'm going to Tech no matter what it takes."

"You planning on getting through college in three years, too?"

He shook his head. "Don't know if I can. But I'll have the degree, whatever it is, before I'm twenty-two."

No one her age had ever talked of the future like that. Like they were just passing through this time in their life, and something yet to come mattered far more. "When you are somebody, I think I'd like to be your friend."

"I hope we will be more than that, Lauren." His words were so low, she wasn't sure she heard them.

"Hey, you two deadbeats up there!" Reid yelled. "I got an idea."

Lauren didn't want the conversation with Lucas to end, but if she ignored Reid he'd just get louder. "What?"

Reid ran up between them and put an arm over both

her and Lucas's shoulders. "How about we break into the Gypsy House? I hear it's haunted by Gypsies who died a hundred years ago."

Tim caught up to them. As always, he agreed with Reid. "Look over there in the trees. The place is just waiting for us. Heard if you rattle a Gypsy's bones, the dead will speak to you." Tim's eyes glowed in the moonlight. "I had a cousin once who said he heard voices in that old place, and no one was there but him."

"This is not a good idea." Lauren tried to back away, but Reid held her shoulder tight.

"Come on, Lauren, for once in your life, do something that's not safe. No one's lived in the old place for years. How much trouble can we get into?"

Tim's imagination had gone wild. According to him all kinds of things could happen. They might find a body. Ghosts could run them out, or the spirit of a Gypsy might take over their minds. Who knew, zombies might sleep in the rubble of old houses.

Lauren rolled her eyes. She didn't want to think of the zombies getting Tim. A walking dead with braces was too much.

"It's just a rotting old house," Lucas said so low no one heard but Lauren. "There's probably rats or rotten floors. It's an accident waiting to happen. How about you come back in the daylight, Reid, if you really want to explore the place?"

"We're all going now," Reid announced, as he shoved Lauren off the road and into the trees that blocked the view of the old homestead from passing cars. "Think of the story we'll have to tell everyone Monday. We will have explored a haunted house and lived to tell the tale."

Reason told her to protest more strongly, but at fifteen, reason wasn't as intense as the possibility of an adventure. Just once, she'd have a story to tell. Just this once…her father wouldn't find out.

They rattled across the rotting porch steps fighting tumbleweeds that stood like flimsy guards around the place. The door was locked and boarded up. The smell of decay hung in the foggy air, and a tree branch scraped against one side of the house as if whispering for them to stay back.

The old place didn't look like much. It might have been the remains of an early settlement, built solid to face the winters with no style or charm. Odds were, Gypsies never even lived in it. It appeared to be a half dugout with a second floor built on years later. The first floor was planted down into the earth a few feet, so the second floor windows were just above their heads giving the place the look of a house that had been stepped on by a giant.

Everyone called it the Gypsy House because a group of hippies had squatted there in the '70s. They'd painted a peace sign on one wall, but it had faded and been rained on until it almost looked like a witching sign. No one remembered when the hippies had moved on, or who owned the house now, but somewhere in its past a family named Stanley must have lived there because old-timers called it the Stanley house.

"I heard devil worshippers lived here years ago." Tim began making scary movie soundtrack noises. "Body parts are probably scattered in the basement. They say once Satan moves in, only the blood of a virgin will wash the place clean."

Reid's laughter sounded nervous. "That leaves me out."

Tim jabbed his friend. "You wish. I say you'll be the first to scream when a dead hand, not connected to a body, touches you."

"Shut up, Tim," Reid's uneasy voice echoed in the night. "You're freaking me out. Besides, there is no basement. It's just a half dugout built into the ground, so we'll find no buried bodies."

Lauren screamed as Reid kicked a low window in, and all the guys laughed.

"You go first, Lucas," Reid ordered. "I'll stand guard."

To Lauren's surprise, Lucas slipped into the space. His feet hit the ground with a thud somewhere in the blackness.

"You next, Tim," Reid announced as if he were the commander.

"Nope. I'll go after you." All Tim's laughter had disappeared. Apparently he'd frightened himself.

"I'll go." Lauren suddenly wanted this entire adventure to be over with. With her luck, animals were wintering in the old place.

"I'll help you down." Reid lowered her into the window space.

As she moved through total darkness, her feet wouldn't quite touch the bottom. For a moment she just hung, afraid to tell Reid to drop her.

Then, she felt Lucas's hands at her waist. Slowly he took her weight.

"I'm in," she called back to Reid. He let her hands go, and she dropped against Lucas.

"You all right?" Lucas whispered near her hair.

"This was a dumb idea."

She felt him laugh more than she heard it. "That you

talking or the Gypsy's advice? Of all the brains dropping in here tonight, yours would probably be the most interesting to take over, so watch out. A ghost might just climb in your head and let free all the secret thoughts you keep inside, Lauren."

He pulled her a foot into the blackness as a letter jacket dropped through the window. His hands circled her waist. She could feel him breathing as Reid finally landed, cussing the darkness. For a moment it seemed all right for Lucas to stay close; then in a blink, he was gone from her side.

Now the tiny flashlight offered Lauren some much-needed light. The house was empty except for an old wire bed frame and a few broken stools. With Reid in the lead, they moved up rickety stairs to the second floor, where shadowy light came from big dirty windows.

Tim hesitated when the floor's boards began to rock as if the entire second story were on some kind of seesaw. He backed down the steps a few feet, letting the others go first. "I don't know if this second story will hold us all." Fear rattled in his voice.

Reid laughed and teased Tim as he stomped across the second floor, making the entire room buck and pitch. "Come on up, Tim. This place is better than a fun house."

Stepping hesitantly on the upstairs floor, Lauren felt Lucas just behind her and knew he was watching over her.

Tim dropped down a few more steps, not wanting to even try.

Lucas backed against the wall between the windows, his hand still brushing Lauren's waist to keep her steady as Reid jumped to make the floor shake. The whole house seemed to moan in pain, like a hundred-year-old man standing up one arthritic joint at a time.

When Reid yelled for Tim to join them, Tim started back up the broken stairs, just before the second floor buckled and crumbled. Tim dropped out of sight as rotten lumber pinned him halfway between floors.

His scream of pain ended Reid's laughter.

In a blink, dust and boards flew as pieces of the roof rained down on them and the second floor vanished below them, board by rotting board.

Lucas reached for Lauren as she felt the floor beneath her feet crack and split. Her legs slid down, scraping against the sharp teeth of decaying wood.

The moment before she disappeared amid the tumbling lumber, Lucas's hand grabbed her arm just above her wrist and jerked hard. She rocked like some kind of human bell as boards continued to fall, hitting her in the face and knocking the air from her lungs.

But Lucas held on. He didn't let her disappear into the rubble. He'd braced his feet wide on the few inches of floor remaining near the wall and leaned back.

When the dust settled, she looked up. He'd wrapped his free arm around a beam that braced a window. His face was bloody. The sleeve had pulled from his shirt, and she saw a shard of wood like a stake sticking out of his arm, but he hadn't let her go. His grip was solid.

Tim was crying now, but in the darkness no one could see where he was. He was somewhere below. He had to be hurting, but he was alive. The others had been above when the second floor crumbled, but Tim had still been below.

Reid jumped into the window frame that now leaned

out over the remains of the porch. The entire structure looked as if it were about to crash like a hundred deformed pickup sticks dumped from a can.

Reid didn't look hurt, but with the moon on his face, Lauren had no trouble seeing the terror. He was frozen, afraid to move for fear something else might tumble.

"Call for help." Lucas's voice sounded calm amid the echoes of destruction. "Reid! Reach in your pocket. Get your phone. Just hit Redial and tell whoever answers that we need help."

Reid nodded, but his hand was shaking so badly Lauren feared he'd drop the phone. He finally gripped it in one hand and jumped carefully from the window to the ground below. He yelped a moment after he hit the dirt and complained that he'd twisted his ankle. Then he was yelling into his cell for help. They were still close enough to town to see a few lights in the distance. It wouldn't be long before someone arrived.

Lucas looked down at Lauren. "Hang on," he whispered.

She crossed her free hand over where his grip still held her arm. "Don't worry. I'm not letting go."

Slowly, he pulled her up until she was close enough to transfer her free hand to around his neck. Her body swung against his and remained there. Nothing had ever felt so good as the solid wall of Lucas to hang on to.

"Can you walk?"

"I think so. Don't turn loose of me, Lucas. Please, don't turn loose."

She felt laughter in his chest. "Don't worry, I won't. I got you, *mi cielo*."

They inched along the edge of the wall where pieces of what had once been the floor were holding. "Tim?"

she called. She tried to shine her light down to see Tim, but there was too much debris below. His crying began to echo through the night, as did Reid talking to Mrs. Patterson on the phone.

"She must have been the last person he called," Lucas whispered near Lauren's ear. "So when he hit Redial, he got her."

Lauren brushed her cheek against his. "She's the last person I'd turn to for help."

"I agree," Lucas answered.

Their private conversation amid the chaos helped her relax a bit.

"Send everybody!" Reid kept yelling. "We need help, Mrs. Patterson." When he hung up he must have dialed his brother because all at once Reid was cussing, blaming the mess they were in on whoever answered.

"Hang on, Lauren," Lucas whispered against her hair. "I'll try to reach the window."

"I'm scared. Don't let me fall."

He bumped the top of her head with his chin. "So am I, but I promise I'm not letting you go."

Finally Lucas reached the window that Reid had dropped from, and he lowered Lauren slowly to the ground outside.

"I got her," Reid shouted just as car lights began to shine through the trees. Emergency vehicles turned off the main road and headed toward the Gypsy House—one volunteer ambulance, a small fire truck, along with one sheriff's cruiser and Mrs. Patterson's old gray Buick tailing the parade.

Lauren watched Reid move toward the men storming through brush.

"We're all right," he shouted. "I got Lauren out, but

Lucas and Tim are still in the house. I was going in after them next." When he spotted the sheriff in the half dozen flashlights surrounding him, he added, "I tried to tell them this was a bad idea, sir, but thank God I went in to help Lauren, just in case she got into trouble."

The first men hurried past Reid, ignoring him, but finally Sheriff Brigman and an EMT stopped.

Men with bright flashlights moved into the house with ropes and a portable stretcher. She could hear Lucas yelling for them to be careful and guiding their steps. Tim was somewhere below, still crying.

Her father shone his light along her body. She could feel warm blood trickling down her face, and more blood dripped down from a gash on her thigh. "I'll take her from here, son," he said to Reid as if she were a puppy found in the road. "You all right to walk, Reid?"

"I can make it, sir." Reid limped, making a show of soldiering through great pain.

"We've got the boy," someone yelled from inside the house. "He's breathing, but we'll need the stretcher to get him out. Looks like his leg is broken in more than one place."

Her father never let go his hold of her as they watched Tim being lifted out of the house. One of the EMTs said that, besides the broken leg, the boy probably had broken ribs. The sound of Tim's crying was shrill now, like that of a wounded animal.

She listened as her father instructed the ambulance driver to take Reid and Tim. They needed care on the way to the hospital. He picked up Lauren and carried her to his car as if she were still his little girl. "I'll transport her to the emergency room. She's got wounds, but she's not losing much blood."

"Lucas is hurt, too," she said as the boy who'd saved her life was helped down from the second floor window. Lucas was the last to leave the haunted house. He'd made sure everyone got out first.

The sheriff nodded. "Make sure he's stable and put him in my car, too. I can get them both there faster than the ambulance can."

Two firemen followed his orders.

Lauren looked over her father's shoulder as Lucas moved clear of the shadow of the house. She'd had far more than the little adventure she'd wanted tonight. When her father set her in the back of his cruiser, she wondered at what point she'd gone wrong and swore for the rest of her life she'd never do something so dumb again.

One of the men from the volunteer fire department bandaged up Lucas's arm and wrapped something around her leg. The sheriff oversaw the loading of the other two injured, then returned. She could almost feel anger coming off him like steam, but he wouldn't step out of his role here. Here he was the sheriff. Later he'd be one outraged father.

Wrapped in blankets, she sat in the backseat of her father's cruiser with Lucas and watched everyone load up like a small army. Mrs. Patterson had tripped in the darkness, and two firemen were taking her home for treatment.

She looked over at Lucas sitting a foot away. He was leaning his head back, not seeming to notice that his forehead dripped blood. He'd saved her and helped bring out Tim. She realized he'd passed her to Reid so he could go back for Tim. No one was patting him on the back and saying things like "great job" as they were to Reid.

Lauren seemed to have been labeled "poor victim" and Lucas was invisible.

"You saved me tonight," she whispered. "Why didn't you tell my dad? He thinks this whole thing was your fault, thanks to Reid."

"The truth isn't worth crossing Reid. Let him play the hero. All I care about is that you're all right. If I spoke up, I might not have a job tomorrow. One word from Reid and the foreman will take me off the list of extras hires, or worse, tell my father to find another job."

"We're alive, thanks to you." She was touched that he worried about her. "The cut on my leg isn't deep. But I owe you a blood debt for real now."

"I know." His white teeth flashed. "I'll be waiting to collect it. You've got to save my life now."

Her father climbed into the car without saying a word to them. He spoke into his radio and raced toward the county hospital, half an hour away.

Lauren didn't feel like talking. She knew the sheriff was probably already mentally composing the lecture he planned to give her for the next ten years. Worry over her would be replaced by anger as soon as he knew she was all right. She'd be lucky if he let her out of the house again before she was twenty-one.

In the darkness, she found Lucas's hand. She didn't look at him, but for the rest of the ride, her fingers laced with his. They might never talk of this night again, but they both knew that a blood debt bound them together, and sometime in the future she'd pay him back.

Four

Yancy

The Greyhound bus pulled up beside the tiny building with Crossroads, Texas, United States Post Office painted on it in red, white and blue, and Yancy Grey almost laughed. The box of a structure looked like it had been rolled in on wheels and set atop a concrete square. He had seen food trucks at county fairs that were bigger.

This wasn't even a town, just a wide spot in the road where a few buildings clustered together. He saw the steeples of two churches, a dozen little stores that looked as though they were on their last legs framed in the main street, and maybe fifty homes scattered around, not counting trailers parked behind one of the gas stations.

A half mile north there stood what looked like a school, complete with a grass football field with stands on either side. To the east was a grain elevator with a few buildings near the base. Each one was painted a different shade of green. Yancy couldn't see behind the post office, but he couldn't imagine that direction being any more interesting than the rest of the town.

"This is the Crossroads stop, mister," a huge bus driver called back to Yancy from the driver's seat. "We're early, but I guess that don't matter. Post office is closed Sundays anyway."

Yancy stood and moved down the empty aisle as the bus door swished open. He'd watched one after another of the mostly sorry-looking passengers step off this bus at every small town through Oklahoma and half of Texas. He didn't bother to thank the driver for doing his job. Yancy had been riding for ten hours and simply wanted to plant his feet on solid ground.

"You got any luggage?" the driver asked. "It's been so long since Oklahoma City, I forgot."

"No," Yancy answered as he took his first breath of the dawn's damp air. "Just my pack."

"Good." The driver pulled out his cigarettes. "Normally I stop here for breakfast. That café across the street serves an endless stack of pancakes, but since there are no cars out front, I think I'll move on. I'll be in Lubbock next stop, and that's home."

Yancy didn't care what the driver did. In fact, he hoped the fat guy would forget where he left off his last passenger. All Yancy Grey wanted was silence, and this town just might be the place to find it.

For the past five years in prison he'd made a habit of not talking any more than necessary. It served no purpose. Friends, he didn't need, and enemies didn't bother chatting. He kept to himself. The inmates he'd met and got along with weren't friends. In fact, he'd just as soon never see any of them again. One of them, a dead-eyed murderer named Freddie, had promised to kill him every time he'd passed within hearing distance, and another who went by "Cowboy" would skin a dead man for the hide.

And the guards and teachers for the most part were little more than ghosts passing through the empty house of his life. He had learned one fact from every group-counseling session he'd attended, and that was if he was going to stay out of prison, he needed to plan his life. So he'd taken every course offered and planned how not to get caught when he next stepped out into the free world.

He dropped his almost empty backpack on the post office steps and watched the bus leave. Then, alone with nothing but the sounds of freedom around him, he closed his eyes and simply breathed for a while. He'd known he was low-down worthless since he was five, but now and then Yancy wanted to forget and just think of himself as a regular person like everyone else who walked the planet.

At twenty-five, he wasn't the green kid who'd gone to jail. He was a hardened man. He had no job or family. No future. Nowhere to go. But, thanks to positive-thinking classes, he had goals.

The first one was simple: get rich. After he got past that one all the others would fall in line: Big house. Pool. Fast car.

On the positive side, he had a lot going for him. Without a plan, he didn't have to worry about holes in his strategy. He wasn't running away from anything or anyone, and that was a first. He'd also learned a little about every trade the prison tried to teach.

Yancy had bought a bus ticket to a town he'd once heard his mother say was the most nothing place on earth. Crossroads, Texas. He figured that was where he'd start over, like he was newborn. He'd rebuild himself one brick at a time until no one who ever knew him would recognize Yancy Grey. Hell, he might even give himself a middle name. That'd be something he hadn't had in twenty-five years of being alive.

Sitting down on the steps, he leaned against the tin door of the twelve-foot square post office and looked around at a tiny nothing of a town that sparkled in the early light. He might not have much, but he had his goals, and with some thinking, he'd have a plan.

He wasn't sure, but he thought his mother met his dad here. She never talked about the man who'd fathered him except to say he'd been a hand on one of the big ranches around. She'd fallen in love with the hat and boots before she knew the man in between. Yancy liked to think that, once, she might have been happy in Crossroads, but knowing his mother, she wouldn't be happy anywhere unless she was raising hell.

Yancy warmed in the sun. The café would probably be open in an hour or two. His first plan was to eat his fill of pancakes, and then he'd think about what to do next. Maybe he'd ask around for a job. He used to be a fair mechanic, and he'd spent most of his free time in the prison shop. There were two gas stations in town. One might have an opening. Or maybe the café needed a dishwasher? He'd worked in the prison kitchen for a year. If he was lucky, there would be a community posting somewhere around for jobs, and he'd bluff his way into whatever was open.

If nothing came up, he'd hitch a ride to the next town. Maybe he'd steal enough lying around here to hock for pocket money. Six years ago he'd caught a ride with a family in Arkansas. By the time they let him out a hundred miles down the road, he'd collected fifty dollars from the granny who rode in the back with him. The old bat had been senile and probably wouldn't ever remember having the money in the first place. That fifty sure had felt good in his pocket.

Another time, when he was about sixteen, he'd hitched a ride with some college kids. They'd been a fun bunch, smoking pot as they sang songs. When he'd said goodbye, they'd driven away without a camera that was worth a couple hundred. Served them right for just wandering around the country spending their parents' money. No one ever gave him a dime, and he'd made it just fine. Except for one dumb partner and one smart cop in Norman, Oklahoma.

Yancy pushed the memories aside. He had to keep his wits about him. Maybe try to go straight this time. He was halfway through his twenties, and hard time would start to take a toll on him soon. He'd seen guys in prison who were forty and looked sixty.

Taking a deep breath, he let the air sit in his lungs for a minute. It felt pure and light. Like rain and dust and nothing else.

A few cars passed as the sun warmed, but none stopped at the café. Yancy guessed the place might not open until eight or even nine on Sunday. He'd wait. With twenty dollars in his pocket, he planned to celebrate. Maybe if they had pie out early, he'd have it for breakfast.

One man in a pickup stopped and stuffed a few letters in the outside drop. He tipped his hat in greeting, and Yancy did the same with his baseball cap. It had been so long since he'd been in the free world he wasn't sure how to act. He needed to be careful so no one would recognize him as an ex-con. Most folks probably wouldn't anyway, but cops seemed to have a knack for spotting someone who'd served time.

Yancy went over a few rules he'd made up when he was thinking about getting out of jail. Look people in the eyes but not too closely. Greet them however they greeted him. Stand up straight. At six-one he wasn't tall enough to be frightening or short enough to be bothered. He continued with his rules. Answer questions directly. Don't volunteer much information, but never appear to be hiding anything.

About eight o'clock he heard one of the church bells. The day was cold but sunny and already promising to be warm. The dusting of snow from last night was blowing in the street like a ghost snake wiggling in the frosty air. In an hour it would be gone.

He decided to set his first freedom goal. He'd buy a coat. After all, winter was already here. The first year in prison he'd been either hot or freezing. If he had a good wool coat, he could be warm all winter, and then if he ever got hot, he'd just take off his good coat. He sighed, almost feeling it already covering his shoulders. The old sweatshirt he'd found in the lost-and-found bin at one of the bus stops last night was too worn to last the winter.

Yancy smiled, knowing that if anyone passed by, they'd think he was an idiot, but he didn't care. He had to start somewhere. Daydreaming might not get him anywhere, but a goal—now, that was something he could sink his teeth into. He'd listened to all the tapes. He had to think positive and do it right this time, because he was never going back to prison.

Two old men came out of a couple of the small houses across the street. One had a saw and the other carried a folding chair. They must live in the cluster of little bungalows surrounded by a chain-link fence. The sign out front, looking as old as the two men, said Evening Shadows Retirement Community.

As he watched the men, he almost felt sorry for them. In Yancy's mind the place looked little better than prison. The homes were in bad shape. One roof sank in at a corner. One porch was missing a railing. The yard had been left on its own for so long it looked like nothing but prairie grass and weeds. A few of the homes had flowers in pots with leftover Christmas greenery, and all had tiny flags tacked up by the door as if they'd been put up as Fourth of July decorations, and no one had bothered to take them down.

Yancy stopped studying the place and decided to pass his time watching the old men. One at a time they each tried to stand on the folding chair to cut dead branches off the elms between the little houses. One kept dropping the saw. The other fell through the opening in the back of the chair and would have tumbled to the ground if his partner hadn't braced him.

Yancy laughed. The two were an accident about to happen, and he had a front row seat.

The second time he laughed, one of the old men turned toward Yancy and pointed his cane like a rifle. "You think you can do any better, mister, you get over here and try."

"All right, I will." He headed toward them. "If one of you break a leg I'll probably get blamed." With nothing to do until the café opened, he might as well lend a hand. That's what normal people did, right? And Yancy wanted to be nothing but normal.

Sawing a branch that had been scraping against the

house was no problem, even with both the old guys telling him how. Yancy had planned to stop there, but they pointed to another branch that needed cutting and then another. As he moved from house to house, more old people came out. Everyone had elms bothering their roof or windows or walls. Before long he felt as if he was leading a walker parade around the place. Every time he cut a branch down, one of the residents would grab it and haul it outside the chain-link fence to the lot beyond.

Listening to them chatter and compliment him was like music to his ears. None of the senior citizens ordered him around or threatened him. They all acted as if he was some kind of hero fighting off the dragon elms that had been torturing them when the wind blew or robbing them of sleep.

"We should pile them up and have us a bonfire," yelled the one old man with *Cap* written on his baseball hat.

"Great idea," his friend said, joining in. "I'll buy the hot dogs and we can have us a weenie roast."

"Won't that be a fire hazard?" Yancy asked as he used a stool to climb high enough to cut the last of the dead branches off a tree.

Cap-hat puffed up, making him about half an inch taller. "I was the captain of the volunteer fire department here for twenty years. I think if I say it's all right, nobody will argue."

To Yancy's shock they all agreed, and now the rush was on to collect firewood.

In general, Yancy hated people. He thought of some of them as evil, like Freddie and Cowboy who'd threatened to murder him for no reason, and others he feared were simply fools. The rest were stupid, destined to be played by the evil walking the earth. That pretty much summed up the population he'd been living with for five years, and those he'd grown up with were no better.

Only, these folks were different. They treated him as if he were a kid who needed praise and direction. Each had stories to tell, and each, in their way, appeared to have lived rich, full lives. None suspected the crimes he'd committed or regrets he had in life. To them he was a hero, not an ex-con.

Yancy swore he felt like Snow White stumbling into the elderly dwarves' camp. All of them were at least a head shorter than him, and most offered him a cup of coffee or something to eat. One little round woman dressed in pink from her shoes to her hair even brought him out a slice of pie. Mrs. Butterfield was her name, and she claimed her husband always ate pie for breakfast.

She also giggled and told Yancy that he reminded her of her first husband when he was young. "Black hair and strange eyes," she whispered. "Just like you, young man."

"Yancy," he said. "My name's Yancy Grey." He didn't want her thinking he was the ghost of husband number one returning.

All agreed that was a strong, good name, except Mrs. Butterfield who'd gone inside to look for a picture of her first husband.

An hour passed, and the café still wasn't open, but Yancy felt stuffed. By now the trees were trimmed and the eight geezers pulled their chairs around a crumbling swimming pool full of tumbleweeds and dead leaves.

The pool deck was one of the few places that was out of the wind and offered sunshine.

Yancy used the tree-trimming chair to join them and was welcomed with smiles. Thank goodness Mrs. Butterfield had forgotten what she'd gone to look for and returned with another slice of pie for him.

The short senior citizen who'd fallen through the chair earlier introduced himself as he offered Yancy a wrinkled hand. "Leo is my name and farming was my game until I settled here. I used to grow pumpkins so big we could have hollowed them out and used them for carriages."

A few rusty red hairs waved at the top of Leo's head as he laughed. "Let me fill you in on the protocol here. Every Sunday we get up early and sit out here, if the weather permits, until ten-thirty when two vans drive up. Until then we eat Mrs. Ollie's deliciously sinful banana bread and Mrs. Butterfield's pie if she remembers it's Sunday. Of course, we do this so the Catholics will have something to confess and the Baptists will have something to sing about. Those feeling the calling load the vans for church and the rest of us finish off the bread before our kin drop by to take us to their low-fat, no sugar, high-fiber Sunday dinners."

"Which van you climbing into, Mr. Leo?" Yancy smiled as he took another piece of the best banana bread he'd ever eaten.

"Neither," Leo snapped. "I was married twice. Once to a Baptist. Once to a Catholic. After spending twenty years in each church I gave up religion for superstition." Mr. Leo leaned forward. "Like, I've been noticing something about you, Yancy. You may be a good-looking fellow, but you got one gray-colored eye and one blue. Like Mrs. Butterfield said, that's strange. Some folks might think you to be the son of a witch, or maybe a witch yourself. I've heard tell a man with two colored eyes can see death coming for any one he stares at. Gypsy blood in you, I'm guessing, with that black hair. They say every Gypsy is born with a gift, and yours just might be death's sight. Am I right, Yancy?"

"That's me," Yancy lied. He had no idea where his people came from, but seeing death hanging around these folks wouldn't be too hard. He was surprised the Grim Reaper didn't make regular minivan stops by this place.

Mrs. Ollie passed by to offer him the last slice of bread. "Don't believe a word Leo says," she whispered. "He ain't never farmed in his life. He taught drama at the high school for forty years, and if he had two wives he must have kept them in a box, because no one in town ever saw them." She laughed. "We don't know if his brain is addled, or if he's just trying to make life more interesting. Either way, he's always fun to listen to."

It took Yancy a moment to wrap his mind around what he heard. He'd known many liars but not one who did so for fun, and nobody in the group seemed to care.

"Don't rat me out, Ollie," Leo grumbled, "or I'll tell him about when you came to town as a lazy streetwalker and settled here just so you'd only have to walk a few blocks to cover the whole town."

The very proper baker hit him with her empty banana-bread pan. Crumbs showered over him, but Leo didn't seem to notice. He just grinned and winked at her because he knew he'd flustered her. "She's Baptist," he whispered. "Never confesses to a thing she's done all her life. Taught home economics down the hall from me, and I can tell you there were some wild parties in that food lab."

She raised the pan as if planning to hit him again, but decided to laugh.

Yancy studied the circle of people. "How many of you taught school?"

To his surprise all but one raised his hand. A tall, frail man in a black suit, wearing hearing aids in both ears, finally lifted his hand to join the others. "I think I qualify, even though I was the principal. I'm Mr. Halls. Many a student made a joke about my name." His announcement was a bit loud. "A man's name sets his course at birth."

They all nodded as if he were the bravest among the brave. Battle-scarred veterans of decades of fighting their grand war against ignorance might have honed them, but age now left them crippled and alone. One to a house. No husbands or wives surviving, apparently. But they had each other. Somehow in the middle of nowhere, they'd found their place, like a flock of birds huddled together on a tiny lake.

When the two church vans arrived, most of the group climbed on. Only Leo, Cap and the principal remained in the circle with Yancy. When the principal went inside to get his cap, Yancy had to ask, "Isn't he going to church? He's all dressed up."

Cap shook his head. "He dresses like that every day. Old habits are hard to break. He's almost deaf, so whoever sits on his right tends to yell."

When Mr. Halls returned wearing his very proper hat, he didn't seem to notice they were still talking about him.

Yancy leaned back in his metal chair and relaxed. *This is it,* he thought, *my river of peace that prison preacher used to talk about.* They might not know it, but these old folks were offering him the bridge to cross from one life to another. He listened as they told him of Crossroads and their lives growing up, of growing old in the Panhandle of Texas, where canyons cut across the flat land and sunsets spread out over miles rich in history wild and deep.

Finally when one of the old men got around to asking what he was doing here in Crossroads, Yancy pointed to the post office and explained that he was looking for a job.

"I'm traveling light. Just a pack." As he said the words, he stared at the steps and noticed his pack wasn't where he'd left it.

"My pack!" he yelled as he stood and ran toward the post office.

By the time the three old men caught up to him, Yancy had been around the little building twice. The pack was nowhere to be found. No one was around. He'd been in sight of the post office all morning, and he hadn't seen a soul walk past. The only person he'd observed stop had been the guy in the pickup, and he'd been long gone before Yancy walked across the street.

"I've been robbed," he said, more surprised that a crime had been committed against him before he'd had time to commit one himself than he was worried about his few possessions.

"Everything I had was in that pack." He didn't mention that most of it was stuff the prison had given him. A toothbrush. All his socks and underwear. The bloody shirt he'd worn when he was arrested and a deck of cards he'd spent hours marking.

"This is serious," Cap said, passing like an elderly, short General Patton before his troops. "This is a crime right in the middle of town. This is outrageous."

Leo didn't seem near as upset. "What'd you have, sonny?"

Yancy didn't move. He couldn't tell them how little he had. They'd probably figure out he'd come from prison. All he'd walked out with were his goals. "I had a good winter coat made of wool," he lied. "And a great pair of boots. A shaving kit in a leather carrier and three hundred dollars."

All three old men patted him on the shoulder. They all agreed that that was a great deal to lose.

Cap spoke first. "Come on home with me, son. We'll call the sheriff, then you can join the few of us who are lucky enough not to have family dragging us to Sunday dinner. Mrs. Ollie always cooks for us."

Yancy was getting into his lie now. "I don't have the money to make it to Arizona. A friend of mine said if I could make it to Flagstaff I might have a job waiting."

They patted him again. "Don't you worry," Mr. Halls said. "We'll take up a collection if we don't find who did this. And do you know, my daughter gave me a winter coat that's too big for me. You can have it. I got half a dozen in the closet. She sends either that or two sweaters every Christmas."

"Is your coat wool?" Yancy asked. After all, it had to match his dream.

"It is," Mr. Halls said, "and if I remember right, it's got one of them heavy zip-out linings."

Yancy tried not to sound too excited. "I think it'll do, thanks."

"Don't thank me. It's the least I can do for a man who was robbed right under our noses."

"I can cover the shaving kit," Leo added. "I have four I've never used. If you need gloves, I got half a dozen you can try on. Can't seem to convince my daughter-in-law that I don't like gloves. Why waste time on gloves when you got pockets, I always say, but I swear that woman never listens. Since my birthday is in November, she mails gloves every year. Lucky I wasn't born in July or I'd be getting a swimsuit."

Yancy choked down a laugh. This was better than stealing. These folks were giving him more than he could carry off. "One thing, Mr. Leo, I'd rather not call the sheriff. You see, it's my religion to forgive any wrong done me."

Leo swore. "Hell, I knew you was one of them van riders all along. Well, if you won't consider converting to my religion of superstition, I'll have to be tolerant of yours. But I got to tell you, son, that forgive-and-forget kind of thinking will lead you down a penniless path."

Yancy did his best to look thoughtful. "I'm set on my faith, Mr. Leo. For all I know, whoever stole my pack thought he needed it more than I did." Yancy didn't add that was usually his philosophy when he robbed someone.

Leo saw the light. "You're a good man, Yancy Grey, and we'd all be lucky to call you a friend. It'll be our pleasure to help you out with anything you need. We might even offer you some handyman work around this place to help you get back on your feet."

"Thanks," Yancy managed as he started a list of

things that he'd forgotten were in his pack. A watch. A new wallet. "I'd be thankful for any work. I've been laid off for a while."

Everyone jumped as Mr. Halls shouted, "A man on a mission is a man who can't be bested."

Leo and Cap nodded, but Yancy had a feeling the old principal was walking the halls in his mind reading quotes he'd seen along the walls of the high school.

Five

The county hospital had its own kind of sounds. Like echoes in Ransom Canyon and the lone clank of a windmill turning on the prairie or the rustle of paper in empty school hallways, hospital noise was unique.

The place rumbled like a train station. Phones rang, pagers beeped, and machines hummed and ticked like the final clock measuring someone's life away.

There was a rush about the people in white one moment and a stillness the next. Lauren had no idea what time it was. She'd seen a clock not long after she'd been wheeled in that said 2:00 a.m., but that had been hours ago.

In a hospital, only the smell of antiseptic seemed to remain the same. In her windowless space, she could have been waiting a few hours or a day.

Lauren sat alone in the third curtained-off emergency room cubicle, drifting off now and then, only to wake to the same nightmare.

She knew Tim was in the first bed. Everyone had

rushed toward him when the emergency room doors opened, which told her he was in danger. Funny Tim O'Grady, whom she'd known all her life, might die! No one she'd ever been close to had ever died. Thinking about it wasn't funny at all, she realized.

A nurse had helped her onto the examination table when she'd first arrived and checked her leg. At least she thought she was a nurse. Without her glasses she couldn't read any of the name tags. For all she knew, she was the janitor. For a while she worried that Pop would be mad that she'd lost another pair of glasses, but decided that was so far down the lecture list it didn't matter.

The nurse was back.

"You're going to need a few stitches and a few shots," no-name in white said. "You're lucky. That first boy looks like he took a Humpty Dumpty fall."

"Can they put him back together again?" Lauren smiled at their nursery-rhyme code.

The nurse frowned as if she'd crossed some line in protocol. "I'm sure he'll be fine. He's getting the best care here."

Lauren nodded, but she didn't feel very lucky, and she wasn't at all sure Tim would be fine. If she were lucky, she wouldn't have gone into that haunted house. Following Reid Collins was the dumbest thing she'd ever done. He might have twice her muscles, but he only had about half her brain cells. If his dad wasn't rich, Reid would be lost. As it was, he'd probably run for Crossroads mayor in another twenty years. First he thought he was a football star because he had the jacket, and now he considered himself a hero.

No-name carefully pulled the curtain closed as she

vanished. Lauren waited, fighting the need to slip under one of the fabric walls and escape. In her mind she kept backtracking all the way to the church, thinking of every wrong turn she must have taken to end up here. If she could get do-overs, she'd have stayed with Mrs. Patterson to talk about all the things the old lady thought were on Lauren's mind.

As time dragged by, her father dropped in twice to glare at her. She was in major trouble. During his first one-minute visit, he said he had to call Tim's and Reid's parents and get them out of bed. The second visit, an hour later, was to inform her that Tim was going into surgery. After that, Lauren just acted as if she was asleep when he made his hourly rounds.

He said the word surgery as if it was something terrible she'd done to Tim, but Lauren couldn't bear to think about it. Somewhere in this very building someone was cutting into Tim.

She wanted to ask about Lucas Reyes. Her father seemed to have forgotten about him. Or maybe he was still angry, thinking that somehow this was all Lucas's fault.

When the nurse finally came back, she was with a doctor who looked as though he wasn't old enough to be out of college. The nurse did all the talking, and the young doc just nodded and signed the chart. As Lauren had suspected, her injury wasn't worth much attention. A few stitches, just like the no-name nurse had said. Within minutes both the nurse and the doctor were finished. They had that why-are-you-wasting-our-time look about them. The emergency room had been busy for hours, and she'd been shoved to the back of the line several times.

About the time Lauren wondered whatever happened to bedside manner, the nurse poked her with an injection and announced, "Tetanus shot going in."

"Do I get a sucker?" Lauren asked, and to her surprise the nurse smiled.

Encouraged, Lauren continued, "How are the others?"

The nurse patted her hand. "They'll all be fine. Two will be released this morning, but the boy they took upstairs to surgery will have to stay a few days."

"You mean Tim's not going to die?"

The nurse shook her head. "Not from a broken leg. They're doing X-rays to make sure he didn't break a rib."

Lauren was so relieved that Tim wasn't headed for the afterlife she didn't feel the second needle. He might be dumb as a rock, but if his brain ever caught up to his imagination, who knows, he could make something of himself, other than being Reid's sidekick.

"What about Lucas?"

"Lucas Reyes?"

Lauren nodded.

"He's fine. Lost some blood, but we stitched him up. I think he's already been released. I saw him sitting in the lobby about half an hour ago."

"And Reid Collins?" Lauren was so mad at him she really didn't care. First, he'd gotten them into this mess, and then, when help showed up, he took all the credit for saving everyone.

"The Collins boy sprained his ankle. He was really complaining about the pain until the doc told him he'd have to use crutches for a few weeks. He seemed to cheer up after that." The nurse grinned. "He might have been cured if they'd offered him a wheelchair."

Lauren smiled, knowing that Reid would make the most of his injury. She thanked the nurse then closed her eyes, deciding that now that she knew all the guys were all right, she might as well sleep awhile. Her dad wouldn't be by to take her home until Reid and Lucas were released and Tim was settled into a real hospital room.

She almost drifted into a dream when she felt someone take her hand. The touch was gentle, comforting, and for a moment she smiled, thinking that her Pop was finally showing her how much he cared.

But when she opened her eyes, Lucas was standing beside the examining table.

"How you feeling?" he said quietly, so low no one on the other side of the curtain could have heard.

She rose to her elbows. "I'll survive."

"I gotta go. Half my family came to pick me up, and I think the hospital is worried about the mob scene. I just wanted to say goodbye. Despite all that happened, I liked being with you tonight."

"Me, too," she said, wishing that she could think of something clever to add. But fighting down nervous giggling seemed to be the limit of her communication skills. Lucas was at least a year older than her, good-looking, and *he* was holding her hand.

"You ever been kissed?" He flashed a smile.

"No," she answered. He could have probably already figured that out. Glasses, sheriff's daughter, homely, brainy type. How many more strikes against her did she need? Oh, yeah, and flat chested.

Without a word, he leaned in and touched his lips

to hers. As he pulled away he winked. "How about we keep this to ourselves?"

She nodded, deciding one kiss and her brain cells must be dying. Now she couldn't even talk.

"See you around." He backed away.

As he vanished through the curtain door, she whispered, "See you around."

Six

Staten

Staten dropped by his grandmother's house, but she didn't have any chores for him. It seemed the cluster of retirees at Evening Shadows had hired a handyman to run the place. In truth, he'd never seen the community looking so good. The swimming pool had been cleaned out, the fence fixed and the porches painted, every house a different color.

"Yancy says," Granny shouted over the news blaring from her TV, "if each door is a different color, some of the folks won't get confused and keep going in the wrong house." She shook her head. "I've never been so embarrassed in my life than when I saw Leo naked."

Staten stood, his fists clenched. He didn't care how old the little man was, he wasn't putting up...

Granny continued, "It was my fault. I must have miscounted. I thought I turned into my house, but it was his. But I blame him, of course, for not locking his door."

Staten calmed. "Granny, you live in number three, he lives in four. How hard could it be to count to three?"

She shook her finger at him. "Now, don't get smart with me. After about eighty years, things like numbers started falling out of the back of my head. I can't even remember my phone number, much less anyone else's."

"Don't worry about it. Everyone you know is programmed into your phone. All you have to do is flip it open, punch a button and say their name."

She raised an eyebrow as if she suspected a trick. "So, what is going to happen if one day I'm somewhere lost and lose my phone? Even if I can borrow someone else's phone, I won't know a number to call, and the stranger I asked to help probably doesn't have Aunt Doodles's number in his phone anyway." She crossed her arms over her chest. "With my luck, the stranger will be one of them serial killers, just looking for his next victim, and there I'll be, up a creek without a phone."

Staten patted her shoulder. Every week she had a new worry. He should keep a list. Eventually she was bound to get around to repeating one. "First of all, you can't drive. So if you're lost, you're still in the county. Anyone you stop will probably know you and be happy to bring you back here. Second, if you do see a serial killer, he probably does know Aunt Doodles. She went to jail several times, remember."

Granny's finger started wagging again. "She did not. Not many anyway. And every single time was that dumb husband of hers' fault, not hers."

Staten leaned down and whispered, "How do you know? You can't count to three."

She slapped his cheek too hard to be a pat. "Stop it, Staten. You remind me of numbers I couldn't remem-

ber, and that reminds me of Mr. Leo and his wrinkled...
body. Now, that's a sight I'd like to unsee."

All at once laughter erupted from her. Staten enjoyed
the sound from the dear old woman who'd loved him
every day of his life.

As always, her sweet chuckle was music to Staten's
ears. When he was growing up, his parents were either traveling or fighting. By the time he was in middle
school, his father had divorced his mother and found
wife number two. Neither of them had seemed to want
custody of him in the split. His mother had remarried
and moved to England within six months, without leaving a forwarding address.

Staten had spent most of his time with his grandparents on the ranch. He'd loved working the land with
his granddad and living in their little place where his
granny's laughter always seemed to fill every nook
and cranny. The visits from his father and wife number whatever had grown further apart. Senator Samuel
Kirkland showed no interest in the ranch. No one was
surprised when Granddad died and left it to Staten, his
only grandson.

"Sorry you had to see Old Leo, Granny." He smiled
at his grandmother. "Maybe the new handyman was
right about the doors. It must have been a shock for you
and Leo when you walked into his house."

Granny was busy cleaning up the coffee cups. "Not
so much. I've seen him naked before." She turned and
headed to the tiny kitchen.

Staten had no intention of asking more. He didn't
want to know.

Since it was too early to go to Quinn's for supper,

he dropped by the volunteer fire department's weekly meeting.

This time of year grass fires were rare, and guys were drinking coffee and talking about how the chamber of commerce was planning something big. The men got their information from their wives, who'd passed it around some. So, no telling how accurate it might be. The leaders in Crossroads were looking for ideas to help the town grow and that meant raising money.

"A fund-raiser to beat all fund-raisers," Hollis shouted. "We plan to raise enough money to improve both the fire station and the clinic. Ellie could use the space at the clinic, and when she graduates, most folks would like to see her stay in town and run it full-time."

"That waiting room is too small," one of the other farmers said. "She'll be stacking folks in chairs before long. With all the pregnancies lately, she'll want to add a birthing room. We can handle a doc coming in once a week, but we need a nurse there full-time."

G.W. Polk, who farmed next to Hollis, shook his head. "There's a good hospital in Lubbock. I was born in a car headed that way. To my way of thinking, kids should be born the same place they're conceived."

Hollis nodded. "My point exactly. You were born in a car and you haven't been the same since."

Staten was distracted by thoughts of Quinn and the way she kissed him, but he tried his best to listen. He rarely participated in the town's problems, but he always sent a check to help out with any fund-raiser. Every year the chamber of commerce thought up a grand plan to improve the town, but nothing ever really changed. Correction, he thought, the dozen reindeer they'd put up at Christmas on all the light posts along Main looked great.

After an hour, he excused himself and told the men that whatever they decided, he was behind the chamber one hundred percent. He took his time leaving. Reason told him he was being a fool worrying about what time he got to Quinn's house. She was the same shy woman he'd known all his life. Nothing unusual would happen tonight, and he'd be wasting worry to think otherwise.

For the past five years he had never given their unusual relationship much thought. Maybe because it seemed to have grown naturally with neither of them planning it. He never considered finding another woman, though he knew a few who'd welcome him in their bed if he showed up.

Only, they would come with strings. They'd want eventually to become Mrs. Kirkland, and Staten wasn't sure he ever wanted that again. Being numb most days was far better than hurting.

Maybe he should just be satisfied with what he had with Quinn. It was good. It was enough. She probably felt the same, even if she had asked to be kissed.

He told himself when he got to her house he'd act exactly the same as he always did. Nothing different. Nothing changed. One little kiss didn't mean anything.

As he pulled up to her place, he noticed her working in the barn, elbow deep in the engine of her old tractor. Even after all his stops, he'd arrived early. He'd said supper. It wasn't even five o'clock.

Halfway to her barn he remembered the bag of barbecue in the truck. If she hadn't already waved, he would have turned around. But it was too late. Maybe she'd rather drive over to Bailee and eat hamburgers or maybe even try something at the café in town. They didn't have to always do everything the same. He could be flexible. The kiss was proof, wasn't it?

No, going into a café would seem too strange. They never ate out. They both thought it would seem too much like a couple thing.

"Need some help?" he asked when he reached her.

"No. I've about got it." She stepped down to face him. "Where's the barbecue?"

"In the truck. I brought beer, too. That all right with you?"

He rubbed away a smudge on her cheek with his finger. The touch was casual, but her eyes watched his every movement.

Stepping out of his reach, Quinn moved toward the house. "I'll clean up while you get the food." She was almost to the porch when she looked back and added, "I already set the table."

He watched her until she disappeared. She'd never seemed quite so nervous around him. Suddenly, he wished he could take back the kiss from last week. He wanted everything to stay the same. They had it good and good was enough.

The shower pipes rattled from down the hallway as he set out the food. The paper containers looked out of place amid her china. He hadn't given it much thought before, but she always set the table with her few pieces of hundred-year-old china and nice flatware. He tossed the plastic cutlery he'd picked up into the trash.

When she finally joined him in the kitchen, he was halfway through his first beer. He offered one to her, but she poured herself a glass of cold tea instead.

She was wearing a blue silk blouse that floated

around her. He liked the look. Something different. Brushing his hand over the soft material, he breathed in her fresh smell. "It seems like I've been fighting all week to get back to you."

"I know how you feel." She leaned against him. "I missed you, too."

They sat down where they always ate and filled their plates. He wasn't sure what she'd like, so he'd bought a pound of every kind of grilled meat the café had. Then he'd tossed in fries and okra for the vegetable.

She asked about the meeting, and he told her the gossip that she probably cared nothing about. Neither ate much. Neither wanted to talk.

Finally, Staten stood. She hadn't offered to take him to her bedroom, and if he stayed longer, he'd say more than he should.

"I should call it a night." He reached for his hat. "We saddle up before dawn tomorrow."

"All right," she said in a flat tone that revealed nothing as she stood.

He took two steps to the door and remembered how he'd promised he would kiss her goodbye before he left.

With his hat in one hand and Quinn holding their plates between them, he leaned over and kissed her cheek.

When he straightened, he saw a tear roll down her face.

He doubted he'd get an answer if he asked her why she was crying, but it was obvious that he was doing something wrong.

Tossing his hat on the bar, he took the plates from her and set them aside. "I didn't do that right," he muttered, more like a swear than an apology.

She waited.

He brushed her shoulders lightly as he leaned in again and touched his lips to hers.

Quinn's mouth was so soft. Her bottom lip trembled slightly.

His fingers tightened over her shoulders, and he pulled her closer, kissing her lightly until her mouth opened. Then, without hesitation, he kissed her completely.

She didn't pull away. She simply accepted his advance. He lifted her arms and set them on his shoulders as he continued. If she wanted to be kissed, by hell he'd kiss her.

Slowly, her body melted against him.

He finally broke the kiss, but he didn't turn loose of her. "Any objections if I undress you?" His hand moved over her back and came to rest on her hip. "I've never said so, but I like doing that."

She leaned her head back as his fingers moved over her blouse. He watched her face as he slowly unbuttoned first her blouse, then her jeans. He liked the way she always left something on for him to finish, and tonight he was doing it all.

Standing before him she closed her eyes as he kissed his way down her body. Then, she took his hand and led him to her bedroom.

They made love slowly, tenderly, as they always did. Only after both were satisfied Staten held her tighter than ever before as though just discovering what a treasure he had in his arms.

When she drifted to sleep, he found himself kissing her. He couldn't get enough of the feel of her. He'd been starving all week and finally she was beside him, warm and soft. For a while she moved in her sleep, welcoming his touch, but when he deepened the kiss she woke with a jerk.

For a few minutes he held her tight, gently caressing her, whispering her name in the darkness.

When she calmed, he pulled her close. "I want you again if you've no objections, Quinn. I don't want to leave and wait a week to be with you again."

Her big eyes widened with uncertainty, but she nodded slightly, and he made love to her for the second time. But this time they both knew he wasn't just loving a woman out of need. He was loving Quinn.

Seven

Lucas

Lucas Reyes stood in the corner of the cafeteria and watched the mayhem. School was like the gathering of the clans in Scotland at Culloden. He'd read all about the great battle on the moors when the MacDonalds, the Jacobites and the French all met to fight the English in 1746. The English brought rifles and the men of the mighty clans of Scotland were wiped out that day. Highlander blood turned the earth red, and some said the thunder of the muskets still echoed off the hills.

Maybe the cafeteria wasn't quite that bad, but the cliques were clear. In his grandfather's day they would have been separated by race, but that no longer played a role. Neither did money. Now the division was more by interest. Each clan at Ransom Canyon High wore the markings of their tribe, though. The geeks, who always seemed to carry more books than anyone else. The jocks in their letter jackets. The cheerleaders with their designer purses and perfect spray-on tans even in January.

Several tiny towns and dozens of ranches fed into

Ransom High, so there were more groups than he could name. Lately the goths were making an appearance, along with a dozen or so freshmen who looked like they were straight out of the Harry Potter movies. Big round black glasses and all that.

For a country school, this place was the best, Lucas thought. Folks around poured money into computer labs and libraries for their kids. Where city schools were cutting extra programs, Ransom Canyon High had the best in music and arts. Lucas knew when he headed to college he'd be prepared.

The idea of learning, without the cliques around, excited him.

"Hi, Lucas," Sarah Rodriguez said as she circled him.

"*Hola*, Sarah," he answered. He'd known Sarah most of his life and she'd always been sweet. He almost hated to see her grow up and join one of the groups. Maybe she'd be one of the few, like Lauren, who kept her own identity.

"My folks are having a belated New Year's party this weekend. You coming with your folks?"

"If I get off work in time. I'm riding for the Kirkland ranch all weekend. He'll have us working cattle until dark, but I'm not complaining. He pays great."

The bell rang, and she started off. "See you, if you make it in."

He waved back, thinking that with her three older brothers, she was comfortable talking to guys. Sarah was pretty, like her mother, with long midnight-black hair that hung down to her waist, but Lucas couldn't help but think he was starting to prefer sunny blond hair that fell down straight without a hint of a curl and bangs long enough to shade eyes framed in glasses.

Lucas glanced across the cafeteria as Lauren left a table where she'd been studying alone. Despite the noise, she read her history book while she ate her sack lunch. Her blond hair had curtained her off from the world. He thought of catching up with her but decided not to.

Somehow in all the talk about what had happened at the Gypsy House last Saturday night, Lucas had fallen out of the picture. Reid Collins had told everyone about how he saved Tim and Lauren, about how they were trapped at one point, about how Tim almost died. But Lucas's part in the whole thing must have gotten left on the cutting room floor.

He didn't care. If kids knew he'd been there, they'd only ask him questions, and at some point, his account of the night and Reid's would cross.

Better to let Reid tell the story. Tim wouldn't be back at school for another week or more, and by then the topic would be past tense. Lauren was so shy, he was sure she wouldn't talk about it. If Tim had any brains left, he would say he couldn't remember how it all happened, so with luck the whole thing would be yesterday's news very soon.

Lucas walked toward class, smiling. He'd remember the blood debt Lauren owed him. Maybe someday he'd tease her about it. And, he remembered kissing her. She was the first girl he'd really liked that he had kissed. He might be leaving after summer for college, but he'd remember Lauren long after he forgot everyone else at this school.

He rushed alone down the emptying hallway, feeling

proud that he'd managed to stay out of any cliques. He saw no point to them. High school was only a passageway to what he wanted in life, nothing more.

To his surprise, Lauren caught up to him and fell into step beside him. For several seconds they just walked, but he slowed his pace a bit to match hers.

"I want to talk to you," she finally said without looking at him. "The story of what happened Saturday night has changed so much I don't even think I was there. Now Reid Collins claims Tim was hanging on by a thread, and we could all hear the ghosts whispering. I would have probably broken both legs in the fall from the window if he hadn't caught me. And—"

"I know," Lucas interrupted her. "According to Reid, I wasn't even there. Which is fine with me."

She stopped and turned to him. "But you were there. You saved my life. Reid can lie all he wants to, but I'll never forget. I owe you a blood debt."

"Let Reid's legend live, *querida*. You and I will remember and that is enough."

"Like the kiss at the hospital. Between you and me, right?"

"Right." He smiled, remembering.

"It was the best kiss I ever had." She laughed.

"It was the only one you've ever had," he teased. "When I find you in a few years, I'll ask you again how I compare and see where I stand then."

She blushed and ran ahead of him into her class.

Lucas stood watching her disappear, knowing they were both late but not caring. She'd forget about him, but he'd remember Lauren. She'd be the only girl he'd ever call darling in any language. Funny thing was,

Lauren would probably never know just how special she was.

"Reyes?" Mr. Paris, his math teacher, snapped. "Are you planning on joining us this afternoon?"

"Of course," Lucas answered. "I'm sorry I'm late."

He wasn't sorry at all, but Mr. Paris didn't need to know that. Being late because he was talking to a girl didn't compute in the old guy's world.

Eight

Yancy Grey had worked ten days straight at the Evening Shadows Retirement Community and loved every minute. The first few evenings he'd cleaned out an old office that stood apart from the rest of the bungalows. The front of the building was lined with dirty windows with a long counter separating the lobby area from the back storage and living quarters. A tiny, windowless bedroom and bath ran across part of the back. The living quarters were barely wide enough to fit a full bed, but it was bigger than his cell had been.

Originally, in the '50s, this place had been a motel, boasting that every cabin had a kitchen, bath and sun porch. Eventually, the sun porches had been enclosed to make living rooms, and the bungalows had been rented by the month. Oil field workers and seasonal farmhands had taken over the place, but the owner had never bothered repairing any of the buildings. Finally, he'd let them sell to pay his back taxes.

Cap had told him the school board bought them in the

'90s, planning to offer discount housing to new teachers for the first two years in the county school system. That had only lasted a short time before retiring teachers asked to buy them.

Yancy hadn't figured out why only teachers wanted to live in the place, but he didn't really care. All he knew was he had a great find. All eight of the residents, except maybe Miss Bees who lived in the first unit, seemed to like him. Old lady Bees didn't like anyone. She sometimes came out to sit with the group, but, if she talked, she only complained. She went to church on Sunday and played bingo over in Westland on Wednesday nights, but she didn't talk to Yancy.

Mr. Halls told him that she thought every stranger was probably a criminal. Yancy figured she might have a few more marbles than the others. He'd be smart to stay out of her way. He had Cap ask her what color she wanted her door and wasn't surprised she chose white. Only interesting thing about Miss Bees seemed to be her nickname, Bunny.

Yancy, with the advice of everyone except Miss Bees, had painted his one-room-and-bath behind the office. He'd used leftover paint from the porches, so every wall was a different color, but he didn't care. He'd spent too many years without color. He'd bought a used mattress and frame from the secondhand store a block away and a desk he could also use as his one table. The owner agreed to let him pay the furniture out at twenty-five dollars a week.

He'd turned what had been the front office into a sunny sitting room. That way, on cold days the old folks could sit in the long row of sunshine and watch their former students go by. The men would drink coffee while the women knitted or worked puzzles. Then, just for fun they'd argue politics. Cap, Leo and Mrs. Kirkland kept up with what was going on, but Mr. Halls only heard half of any news, and Mrs. Butterfield kept forgetting who was president.

About three in the afternoon they'd all wander back to their little cottages for naps.

Yancy started lists on the office wall. The first was things that needed fixing fast, like Miss Bee's roof and Mr. Halls's porch. The second list was for repairs that he could get to when he had time, like Mrs. Ollie's sink that had been dripping for six months and Mrs. Kirkland's broken window in the back. She'd covered it up with colored paper so her grandson wouldn't notice.

"If he sees it, Staten will only ask questions, and I'm not in the mood to tell him the truth," she'd said one morning.

As soon as she'd left, all the men stayed behind, trying to guess what she'd been doing to break a window higher than her head. Leo had explained that during World War II, he'd seen a female member of the French underground who could kick higher than six feet and knock a man out cold. Mr. Halls had pointed out that, since Leo was seventy-four, he would have been fourteen when the war ended.

Yancy went back to his lists, angry that he'd bought into Leo's story completely before Mr. Halls did the math.

The last list he kept on the wall was a wish list. Everyone had something to add to that list.

Miss Abernathy wanted bookshelves in the living room. Mrs. Ollie needed a railing for her hand-painted plates running high around her dining area. She explained to him that they were very valuable, but Yancy figured they'd be the last thing he'd steal if he robbed her place.

Leo wanted his TV hooked up high almost to the ceiling so he could watch sports in bed all night. He grinned and said that if he lost the remote control he could always get Mrs. Kirkland to come in and kick it off and on.

Yancy had worried at first that he wouldn't know how to do any of the repairs well enough to please them, but, to his surprise, Cap Fuller was a wealth of information. His hand wasn't steady, but his mind was sharp. By the end of the first week, Yancy had learned enough about plumbing, woodworking, painting and bricklaying to feel like he could hire himself out as a repairman.

Lying in his little room behind what everyone called the office, Yancy thought about all he had accomplished so far: Working in the sun without anyone yelling at him. Learning. Laughing. Talking to folks he'd never thought he would ever talk to about everything. For the first time in his life he was living a regular life.

Of course, the main topic of conversation was always their health, but he didn't mind. All he had to say was "how you feeling today" and they'd be off talking for half an hour. But, they knew so much more than him, things he'd never even heard about. The minute he acted interested, they showed up with a book or an article he should read. They worried if he was warm at night or if he ate proper meals.

No one had ever worried about him, and now he was into overload.

As each day passed he thought less and less about

robbing them and more about how for the first time in his life he felt as if he had something to contribute.

The whole group had even gotten together and decided to up the dues of their home owner's association a hundred dollars each and pay him eight hundred a month, plus a free place to stay.

Cap had slapped Yancy on the back and said that should beat any offer he'd get in Flagstaff, so he might as well stay here. "A for-sure job here has got to be better than a maybe job there."

Yancy hadn't argued.

In truth, Yancy felt rich. If he could winter here, he could save enough money to buy a car and drive wherever he wanted. Even if he ate at the café three times a week and bought something new to wear once a month, he'd still have plenty of money to save.

On the nights one of them didn't bring him food, he'd heat up a can of soup over a hot plate in his room and swear, right out of the can, it was better than anything he'd had to eat in prison. The kitchen workers used to say they served miracle meals because it was a miracle if you kept it down.

On the eleventh day of work, Yancy was curled up in one of the office chairs reading a book Cap had given him on bricklaying when the glass door banged open.

He felt the cold air rush ahead of a young woman as if to get out of her way as she stormed into the room wearing a navy cape and a frown.

Yancy stood up, wondering if she was lost, or maybe she thought this place was a motel. With the roof fixed and a few of the bungalows painted, it *was* starting to look better.

But when he finally faced her nose to nose, he knew she wasn't lost. He saw anger firing in her gaze, and it all seemed to be aimed directly at him.

"You are not," she started as she slammed a case on the counter and raised her hand like a pointed weapon, "going to take advantage of these dear people."

"All right," he answered carefully, thinking it might not be too healthy to object. She still held a huge purse in one hand and was close enough to reach the case. Either was big enough to pack a gun. Plus, at almost his height and thirty pounds heavier, she'd have the advantage in a fight. The leather bag could prove a weapon if she knew how to use it, and this no-makeup, flat-shoed warrior looked as though she probably could.

Her tight mouth relaxed, but she didn't smile. "I care about these people, and I want you to know that I come by twice a month to check on them. So don't even think about trying anything."

Out of curiosity more than any need to continue the conversation, he asked, "Exactly what is it you think I'm going to do?"

"I don't know. I'm not a criminal."

"Neither am I," he lied, shoving all his thoughts of robbing the old folks blind under the carpet in his mind. "They just offered me a job, lady, so I took it."

"Why is that?"

She set her purse down next to the case and crossed her arms over what he noticed was an ample chest beneath her navy blue cape.

He studied her short hair and unpainted fingernails. "You any kin to Miss Bees?"

"No. Answer the question. Why did they offer you a job?"

"I guess because I needed one, and they needed work done around the place. Seems all their kids say they'll drop by and help with fixing stuff, but Mrs. Kirkland's grandson is the only one who even makes an effort."

She cocked her head. "Jerry at the hardware store said you've charged several hundred dollars to this place."

"I have." He didn't like her tone. "Who are you, lady?"

He swore he saw fire flash in her green eyes for a second. "I'm Miss Ellie, the nurse who checks on them. I make sure they have their medicines and get to their doctors' appointments."

"You don't look old enough to be a nurse." Most of the women he had seen over the past five years were either on TV or models in magazines. This woman didn't look like any of them. She was athletic, solidly built and pretty, even without the makeup.

He saw the lie on her face before she spoke to correct it. "Well, I will have my degree, in a year. I work for the doctor over in Bailee, and she travels here two days a week, then sends me the other three days to keep the office open. If there's an emergency or someone needs something more than a refill, I call her in by phone."

Yancy straightened. "Well, I care about these folks, too, and I'm telling you right now you're not going to drop in every other week and take advantage of them."

Finally, she smiled. "Fair enough. I'll watch you and you watch me. Now I have to get back to work. I make the rounds to every house to check their blood sugar and blood pressure."

She picked up her bags and marched back out of the office with her cape whirling in the wind.

And Yancy started doing just what she'd told him to do...watching her.

Nine

Lauren

Lauren sat in the Ransom Canyon High School auditorium while the volunteer fire department chief gave Reid Collins the Hero-of-the-Month award. It looked like an Olympic medal. Everyone yelled while the cheerleaders bounced around shouting, "Reid, Reid, he's our man. Reid, Reid, ain't he grand."

The fact that no one had ever won a Hero-of-the-Month award didn't seem to matter. Neither did the truth about what happened that night at the Gypsy House. When Tim finally got off the painkillers, he told a different story about how he'd been hurt, but no one paid any attention. After all, he'd been on drugs, and Tim tended to tell stories anyway.

Lauren and Lucas, as they'd agreed, said nothing. They let the story Reid told run. And, as Lucas had predicted, his part that night was completely cut from the script.

Reid hobbled up to the podium on his crutches to give a speech that sounded like he'd copied it from

Teddy Roosevelt. Everyone cheered, and his parents hugged him.

Lauren had the feeling that when he could drive, if he ever recovered from his sprained ankle, he'd have all the dates he wanted. Only, he'd never have her, even as a friend, again. The sad thing about it was that he would never know how she felt, and if he did suspect or remember that they'd been friends, he probably wouldn't even care what had happened to make things change.

Winter would age into spring in a few months, but Lauren had grown up a little already. Maybe one of the ghosts *had* whispered to her in the blackness of that old house, because now she knew that people were not always what they seemed. No matter how many awards they gave Reid Collins, the truth hadn't changed. He was no hero.

She watched him pose for the camera and wondered if he was starting to believe his own press.

She walked out as everyone was shaking hands on the stage like they'd bred a wonder in their midst.

Her father's cruiser was in the parking lot. Without much thought, she walked over to it and climbed on the fender to wait for him.

Her pop, the always bossy sheriff, had also changed in the past week, or maybe she finally saw something she'd been too young to notice before. He watched over her like a hawk, but not out of anger or for punishment. That Saturday night had frightened him, she realized it sometime during the fourth or fifth lecture. He was afraid. If he lost her, he'd be alone. Big and strong as he was, she wasn't sure Sheriff Dan Brigman wanted to be alone. That might present a problem when she went away to college.

Lauren considered getting her father to start dating. There weren't many single women around his age that he hadn't given a ticket to or booked into jail. Plus, they might come with children, and she wouldn't wish her father on any child. There was the possibility that her mother might come back; after all, she'd only been gone ten years for her six-month internship.

Margaret Brigman said she still loved him, but she couldn't live with the man. Maybe if Lauren could scrub him up a bit. Have him wear something besides his uniform. Let his hair grow out. Maybe add a mustache. Maybe change his diet. He only ate from the "B" group of foods: bread, butter, beef and banana nut ice cream. She'd started cooking for herself after she'd spent two weeks one summer with her mother and tried vegetables.

Lauren laughed. She'd begun worrying about her parents—she must be growing up. Funny how wisdom came in big hunks and not little bites. She could almost see the argument she'd have with her pop one day about how it was time for him to move into the home.

"Shouldn't you be in class?"

Her father's voice always made her jump.

"Shouldn't you be at work, Pop?"

"It's hero day," he answered.

"Exactly. Looks like we're both free." As free as I ever am, she thought. "How about we go grocery shopping in Lubbock?"

"We have a good food store here in town. Small, but it has all we need. Why would you want to drive all the way to Lubbock? Traffic. Crowds."

Lauren decided it was worth arguing. "The chicken and the vegetables are both the same color brown here."

While everything else was up for debate, he usually gave in on food matters. "Oh, all right." He tossed his hat in the back of the cruiser. "But we go home and switch cars. I want you driving the back roads every chance we get. Before you apply for your license next summer, we will have logged a thousand miles with me by your side."

Lecturing all the way, she thought, but decided it would be safer to just nod.

Reid and his parents walked by. Mr. Collins called out for the sheriff and Lauren to come over for steaks tonight. "We're having a party for our boy," he added. "Not every day we realize we gave birth to a hero."

Her father looked at her, and Lauren shook her head slightly. He turned back to Davis Collins. "I'll be glad to come, but I have to take Lauren home first. She has to study tonight."

She nodded, backing up her father. They both knew that the men would talk, and she'd spend the evening sitting in a corner with a book. "Maybe next time, Mr. Collins," she answered.

They climbed into the cruiser. "Thanks, Dad," she whispered.

"You're welcome, honey. The whole town may think Reid is a hero for saving you and Tim, but if he had any sense he would have suggested you stay out of that old death trap in the first place."

"I agree." She patted his arm.

Her father covered his big hand over both hers. "He's also a year older than you. He should have known better. I expect you to show more sense after your birthday. Being fifteen and trying something like that is one thing, but at sixteen you'll be almost a woman."

Lauren closed her eyes, praying he didn't start that *growing into a woman in body and mind* talk again. It echoed too many of Mrs. Patterson's words for her father to have thought it up himself.

They were almost home when he spoke again. "Your mother called me this morning. She's coming in next week. She's worried about you, and she's mad at me. That's a hard problem to solve long distance."

"Can she stay with us, Dad? I'll clean the extra bedroom."

He was turning into the long drive down toward the lake when he finally answered, "I guess so, if she will agree to it. She can yell at both of us in the house as easy as she can in public."

"And," Lauren said, grinning, "she won't have far to drag the body if she murders you."

"True. I seem to bring out the worst in Margaret. She wasn't like that when we first married."

"You mean before me?"

"No," he said. "It wasn't you, honey. I think, if anything, it was me. I didn't have enough ambition for her." He was silent for a minute, then added, "Or maybe she had too much for me. Anyway, once the arguments started, neither of us seemed to find a way to stop."

He glanced at her and added, "Margaret would never murder me. Who would she have left to pick on?"

Lauren laughed. "You're right, Pop, you got to outlive her because I'd be the next one she turned on if you disappeared."

Pop smiled. "So if she stays, we hide the guns and knives, just in case."

"Deal." They pulled into the lake house driveway

with its wraparound porch and long dock that went all the way to the water.

This was the only home she remembered, and Pop, flaws and all, was the only parent she truly had.

Ten

The wind blew icy across Staten Kirkland's land. It might be only noon, but he decided to call it a day. Fog was moving in over the canyon rim along his back pasture. With the canyon so close, it wasn't safe to keep working cattle. His men had been out in the below-freezing wind since dawn, and the trucks were all loaded.

With a wave to the cowhands turning their horses toward the bunkhouse, Staten headed over to his home to do paperwork.

If he was being honest with himself, he knew there was another reason he'd stopped work early. Staten wanted to be alone. He wanted to think about Quinn. It had been almost a week since he'd last seen her, but she never quite left his mind.

Most of the time when he needed to think, he'd ride out to the pastures and move among his horses or cattle. The low sounds they made, the click of their hooves over rocky ground, the crackle of the wind in ice-packed trees, all relaxed him. He found his sanity there on his land where the work was never done and he could watch the clouds of heaven pass over and make shadows on the winter grass.

Today he needed to close himself off, to empty his mind so his thoughts could roam.

Once he reached the rambling two-story house that stepmother number two had built but left before she decorated, he made himself a bowl of chili and ate at his desk. His dad had finished the place with furniture bought in room groupings, but the things Staten loved were the few pieces his grandmother had sent over from her house a quarter mile away. The old place his grandparents had was still more a home to him than this house. It was still nestled in the breaks with trees on three sides. When his grandfather died, his grandmother had moved to town, claiming she was living with a memory there. Staten never could bring himself to go back inside. The old house had been locked up and empty for twenty years, but it still shone bright in the morning sun.

He shoved aside his half-eaten bowl of chili. He couldn't concentrate on reading stock reports, so he moved to the huge leather chair that had been his grandfather's. There, with the smell of the old man's pipe still lingering, Staten leaned back and remembered last Friday night.

Even in dreams he'd never made love like that. Over the past five years, he and Quinn had learned each other. Or so he thought. Last Friday night he'd learned a few things about her he hadn't known. For the first time he'd felt her hunger for his touch, needing it, almost demanding it.

He'd loved his wife, but somehow in the whirlwind of taking over the ranch and having Randall, they'd grown apart. The love had been there, always, from the beginning to the day she died, but the passion had vanished. He'd filled his days with work, and Amalah had poured her life into projects and spoiling Randall. They both had worked hard and shared dreams that all wrapped around Randall.

He remembered always looking forward to coming home and sharing with her, sleeping with her, making love to her, but somewhere passion had slipped away. By thirty they were married, settled, content. Three years later she was ill, and they'd both fought for her life.

Unlike his father, Staten had had only one wife, and she'd died. He knew he could never have that partnership again, and he had no intention of trying.

Quinn wasn't what he wanted in a wife, even if he thought he could marry again. She was too shy. She would hate going to dinners in Austin or Dallas when Samuel Kirkland needed family present. Quinn wasn't a joiner and never attended charity functions, even over in Crossroads. Staten wasn't much good at that kind of thing, either, but he felt a duty to do his part.

What he and Quinn had was special. He told himself it couldn't last. She was just someone to turn to when the pain of being alone got to be too much. She was a friend.

Only, lately what they shared seemed deeper, and he wanted more than an occasional day or two out of each month.

Pulling his cell out of his pocket, he pressed her number and wasn't surprised it took forever for her to answer.

"Hello," she finally said, sounding out of breath.

"Quinn, it's Staten."

She laughed. "I know."

It dawned on him he hadn't planned what he was going to say. In the past five years, they'd rarely phoned each other. "I was wondering what you'd like for supper. I thought I'd come over tonight, if you've no objection, and I could pick something up."

She took a while to answer, then her voice was soft. "I put on a roast about an hour ago, just in case you dropped by. With the weather so cold, I thought you might quit early and head on over."

She knew him well, but he didn't want to impose. "I'll be there. I just called in case you wanted to go out. We could—"

"No," she said. "I don't want to go anywhere."

He wasn't surprised. She never wanted to go out. Once, he'd taken her to a farm-and-ranch show in Abilene and lost track of her. He'd found her an hour later sitting in his truck reading. She'd made no apology, and he hadn't commented on the waste of time. They'd just driven back to her place in silence. That night he'd remembered there seemed to be miles between them. She hadn't taken his hand, and he hadn't suggested staying over. After that night he'd waited six weeks before going back, but when he did, she'd welcomed him without a single question.

"I'll be there before dark," he said and hung up, wondering if she'd even miss him if he never saw her again. She was his rainy-day woman, and he shouldn't try to make her more. Amalah had loved parties and eating out and travel. She'd spend weeks talking about what she'd wear to one of his father's big balls in Austin.

She'd loved having fancy lunches with the ladies in the half-dozen clubs she belonged to. Quinn didn't, and, after the drive back and forth to Abilene in one day, Staten never got them confused again.

Quinn would never like things like that. She didn't want to go to the café in Crossroads. What they had was private, between them alone. No one knew he drove the road between his place and hers. He wouldn't have cared, but Quinn wanted it that way.

Drifting off in the leather chair, he was already with her in his mind. At sunset he woke with a start, realizing he was almost late for dinner.

The wind blew him inside when he opened her door without knocking, and Quinn laughed as she caught his hat tumbling in ahead of him.

When she closed the door, he kissed her awkwardly.

She smiled but backed away out of reach. "I'll put the food on the table."

Staten nodded, feeling a bit out of place. Since she'd told him she wanted him to kiss her goodbye every time before he left, something had shifted. He wasn't sure what the rules were anymore. Hell, with Quinn he was never sure what the rules ever were. She never turned him away, but he had no illusion that he was in control. She was his friend. They shared a history since grade school. They had sex now and then, but in many ways he didn't feel as if they were lovers. Not until last week anyway. The way they'd made love that second time was different.

He sat down at her table and didn't miss the fact that she'd taken extra effort tonight. Cloth napkins, a little pot of mums as a centerpiece. "It looks great," he said as she set a platter of roast and vegetables between their plates.

He'd sent her a quarter of beef, freezer wrapped, last spring, and she'd sent him lavender soap. They'd both gotten the joke. She rarely ate beef, and he wasn't about to shower with lavender soap. But she sometimes cooked the meat when he was coming over, and his housekeeper had put the soap in the three guest bathrooms he never used.

"I've been practicing today and thought I'd play for you after supper." She brushed her hip against his shoulder as she filled his coffee cup.

"I'd love that."

When she returned to the table, he stood and pulled out her chair for her. It seemed awkward, new.

"You don't have to," she said, not looking at him.

"I just need to touch you, Quinn." His hand brushed over her shoulder. "I don't know why, but I missed you this week."

"Me, too." She smiled up at him. "Especially when the tractor broke down again."

He took his seat and grumbled. "I know you don't like help, but I'm coming over one day and getting that thing in working order."

To his surprise, she didn't argue. They settled in. He cut her a slice, then filled half his plate with meat. She served the vegetables, giving him one of each, then filled her plate with the potatoes, carrots and celery. As wind rattled the windows, they ate in silence, neither feeling the need to keep conversation going.

His leg bumped her beneath the table, then settled against hers. When she handed him a bowl of cobbler for dessert, he rested his hand on her thigh. She looked up at him, and he saw a fire in her eyes. They'd make love tonight. She must have been thinking about last week, too. They might be in their early forties, but the way they'd made love last time seemed newly born to each.

She stood and put away the leftovers. He simply watched, his hands almost feeling what he saw. The soft flannel of her old shirt. The cotton of her white T-shirt.

Staten stopped his line of thinking. He and Quinn had never been about sex. They were friends first. She'd been there for him when he needed her. They were simply two people who needed someone. They trusted each other. They liked each other.

She took his hand, and they walked to her tiny living room. The piano seemed to take up half the space. He could almost see her as a little girl with pigtails swaying as she practiced. Music would have drifted out the open windows and across her parents' farm.

He leaned back on a couch too small for him and listened as she began to play. They both knew she was giving him a rare gift, and he enjoyed every minute of it. He might not know composers or understand much about music, but he knew that when she played he could hear angels singing.

When she stopped, she turned and smiled. "How did you like that?"

"I loved it, Quinn. You know I did. I wish the world could hear you play."

"It's enough that I play for you. I enjoy that."

He leaned forward, his elbows on his knees. "Oh, I forgot to tell you that the chamber of commerce—"

She laughed. "You mean you, the store owners and a few old women who think they run this town?"

He didn't argue. "Don't pick on me, Quinn. My grandmother made me take her place on the chamber of commerce last year. Claimed at eighty-four she needed a rest from all the decisions they have to make."

"And you never say no to her."

"Nope. She raised me while my dad and his line of wives went to Washington. I figure when she does die, she'll probably leave instructions for how I should live the rest of my life."

"I find it endearing that everyone thinks you're this big powerful rancher, and you still follow orders from her." She moved to kneel in front of him, her hands on his knees. "Your love for her is touching. She's a lucky woman to have you and a smart one for moving to town and not living with you. I'm afraid you'd drive each other crazy."

"Definitely." He cupped her face. "Don't distract me, Quinn, I've got some news. Real news, and that's rare in Crossroads."

Only, she did distract him. She pouted, and he couldn't resist her bottom lip. He leaned forward and kissed her lightly.

"The big news?" she asked.

He brushed his fingers along her jaw. "You know the chamber has been trying to think of a fund-raiser for a year. Well, Miss Abernathy—" he stopped and winked at her "—she was your first piano teacher, I believe. I should thank her for that someday."

Quinn didn't look impressed. "She was everyone in town's first piano teacher. She's also the reason I went to New York to study. She talked my parents into it."

Staten nodded. "Someone mentioned that to everyone at the meeting. Said you might know the pianist she wants to bring in for a one-night concert. Evidently, he is performing in Dallas in March, and she's talked him into stopping here for one performance. We signed the contracts last meeting."

Quinn shook her head. "New York was twenty years ago. I doubt I'd know anyone who's still there."

"Miss Abernathy said he wasn't a student, but a teacher then. When he agreed to come, he asked about you. He had a funny name, Lloyd deBellome I believe."

Quinn pulled away so fast Staten didn't have time to stop her. For a flash he saw the fear in her eyes. She ran to the bedroom and slammed the door behind her.

For a moment he just sat there, having no idea what to do. Then fury rose in him. Whoever this guy was, whatever had happened, didn't matter. All that mattered was that he'd hurt Quinn. She'd done a good job of hiding it from him and probably everyone in town, but that one look hadn't lied.

Staten stood and stormed after her.

He didn't hesitate when he saw the closed door to her bedroom. If it had been locked, he would have knocked it down. His announcement had hurt Quinn, and he'd be damned if he'd leave without knowing why.

Quinn couldn't stop shaking. She curled in a ball and pulled the bedcovers all around her. Staten stormed down the hallway after her and shoved the door open. He was halfway to her bed before he froze. "What is it? What's happened?" His words sounded angry, worried, frightened.

"It's nothing. Go away." She couldn't talk now. He was the last person she'd ever tell what had happened.

He knelt beside the bed. "Like hell, Quinn. I'm not

going anywhere." He climbed in beside her and held her as she cried. He might have no idea what had happened with Lloyd deBellome and her in New York, but while she cried he swore he'd make it right.

"How could anyone in the world hurt you, Quinn?" he finally whispered.

Finally she stopped crying and hugged him back. She was no longer a young girl. She needed to hang on to the one person she knew was safe—him.

He moved his hands over her in comfort. "Tell me what happened, Quinn."

She dried her eyes on his shirt. The clean air smell of him made her smile. She'd always loved the way Staten smelled of the earth and sky and rain and work. Slowly, one long breath at a time, she calmed.

"I'm not going anywhere. Tell me what still hurts you after twenty years." He kissed her cheek. "I wish I could take your sorrow away. I've seen you cry before but never like this. If I could, I would put all your troubles on my shoulders right now. Just tell me, Quinn."

She shook her head. She couldn't. How could she mix such ugliness into what they had? What if it changed the way he looked at her? What if her memories destroyed them? Staten's pain that first night had opened her heart to him. She'd let him into her world like she'd never let another man. She loved the way he always hesitated, always waited for her to make the first move.

He waited now. She knew he was wondering how the mention of a name could be so painful.

She rested her head against his heart and listened to the beat.

Finally, gulping back a cry, she began. "In my last year at the academy I was assigned to a master for private lessons. He would get me ready for my first professional recital. Lloyd deBellome was hard on me from the beginning, telling me I didn't have the talent, pointing out everything that I did wrong and never encouraging me.

"I took the lessons, thinking somehow he was making me stronger, but I hated every minute I had to spend in that little practice room. He was about ten years older than me, and, when he wasn't yelling at me, he was asking me out. Correction, ordering me to go out with him. I was half afraid of him and always said no.

"Finally he insisted, and I went out with him once just to prove that we could never be a couple. I drank too much because of nerves. We ended up in his apartment. We must have had sex, but I don't remember much, only that the next morning I was bruised all over. I collected my clothes and left before he woke."

She took another calming breath before continuing. What was Staten thinking?

"Later, he said I got drunk and fell on the stairs, but I knew he lied.

"At rehearsal he was cold and took every opportunity to touch me. With each hard pat on the shoulder I remembered a little more of what the night before had been like. Sex had been there in the fog, but it was the pain, the times I cried out, that brought him pleasure.

"The next day he told me we would be staying at his place that night, and I said no. He argued through most of my lesson and then seemed to let the subject drop. As I was leaving he said something about how he would give me his special wine again, and I wouldn't care what he did to me. He even laughed and said that in time I wouldn't mind being slapped around or tied down. I might even like it.

"When I shook my head, he laughed and called me a fool for not knowing that pain is only the other side of passion, and I obviously needed both to break out of my shell. He said I would beg to come back to him. I'd beg to be taught how to enjoy the pain."

Quinn felt the muscles in Staten's body tighten, but his hand remained gentle along her back as she continued.

"But I did mind being hurt. I hated him even after the bruises on my body faded. My memory of the night was more like a vague nightmare that still wakes me sometimes.

"One afternoon a month later, he made a pass while he was supposed to be teaching me. He demanded I respond. When I wouldn't, he started shaking me. I'm not sure what would have happened if someone hadn't accidentally opened the wrong door. He was like an insane man, claiming no one but an idiot would turn him down.

"Once the student who'd interrupted us apologized and left, Lloyd demanded I play an impossible piece even for my level of training. I tried, but I was too angry, too frightened. All I wanted to do was get out of that room. While I tried to play, he threatened me not to ever tell anyone what I'd made him do. He said he'd just deny it, and I'd be laughed at. He said, homely girls always are. Again and again he kept yelling for me to play faster. Nothing I did was right."

She shook as if freezing, and Staten held her more closely, but he didn't speak. He seemed to understand that she had to tell her story all at once or she'd never finish.

"I was crying and playing and shaking from fear. Suddenly, he slammed the piano cover on my hands and swore I'd never learn to play correctly. I wasn't worth his time.

"I stood and ran from the room. He'd broken three of my fingers." She shook as if her sobs were too deep inside to come out.

Staten waited.

She could feel the rage building in him, but his touch was still soft and loving. In a forced whisper, he asked, "Then what happened?"

"I went to the emergency room and waited hours before I saw a doctor. Then, they kept me overnight before letting me return to the dorm. When I got back, my roommate had packed my things, and my parents were on their way to get me. Lloyd had made up some story about me being too mentally fragile to take criticism and I'd been suspended. I never finished college, and I never played again in public."

"I'll kill him," Staten whispered as he pulled her against his chest.

To her surprise, Quinn laughed. "You can't. That happened twenty years ago. He was right about me never wanting or being able to play in public. Maybe he did me a favor by breaking those fingers. I came home and got to spend ten years with my parents before they died. I got to be with my best friend until the day she passed. I've built a good life here. He was wrong about my not playing. I play for you. That's enough."

Staten kissed her hands. He kissed the thin scars on her middle fingers. "But you missed having a career."

She shook her head. "My parents always wanted that for me, and I wanted to please them. If I'd had my choice

I would have stayed home, but they'd saved since the day I was born to be able to send me to some grand school. I couldn't disappoint them, but it was never my dream."

"Why were they so set on sending you?" He gently encouraged her to keep talking.

"My great-grandmother had been the best pianist in London in her day. My grandmother always wanted my mother to play, but she didn't have the talent. In me, she thought the family gift would come out. Every teacher, including Miss Abernathy from the chamber of commerce, thought I could make it. Only, no one ever asked me if it's what I wanted."

He began unbraiding her hair. "No one in my family ever had talent for anything but yelling and ranching. While your great-grandmother was entertaining royalty, my great-grandfather was trading a watch for his wife a few miles away in Ransom Canyon. Legend is she didn't speak to him until their third child was born. Family history claims he was from English blue bloods who had disowned him, and she was a captive, part Indian, part crazy."

Quinn laughed. "You Kirklands are a wild bunch. Lucky your father doesn't have to buy his wives or he'd run out of money, or watches."

Staten tickled her, then kissed her. When he pulled away she fought begging him not to leave. She wanted him to hold her until she fell asleep. But he slipped from her bed, then pulled off his clothes and floated a quilt over them both as he climbed back in beside her.

"Mind if I stay awhile, Quinn?"

"Only if you'll hold me." She cuddled against him. She'd told him her worst secret, and he had stayed by her side. For the first time in twenty years the pain of what she'd suffered seemed to be cut in half.

Much later, in the darkness just before dawn, she turned to him, hungry with need. He undressed her and made love to her slowly, with more gentleness than she thought he possessed.

When they finished she cried softly and whispered a thank you.

"You're welcome," he answered. "Thanks for playing for me last night. You're so beautiful when you're lost in the music."

"No."

"Yes, Quinn. You are."

A wind raged outside, but it didn't matter.

"Can we make love again?" she whispered.

"We can," he whispered back. "You make me wish I knew how to be gentle."

"You are, Staten. You always are with me."

He rose above her and stared down at her as if really seeing her for the first time in his life. Then slowly, he smiled and kissed her.

Eleven

Yancy

Sundays were always strange days for Yancy. Most of the old folks went to church or off to visit their kids. The few who stayed around seemed to think Sunday was a day for napping. It was also Yancy's only day off.

When he'd first started, the eight old dwarves told him to take the weekend off, but he didn't have anywhere to go, or a car to go anywhere in. After the first weekend in Crossroads, he talked them into letting him work half a day on both Friday and Saturday instead. That way the weekend didn't seem so long.

The first few Sundays he'd been busy working on his boxcar-size apartment behind the office. He'd painted the walls, put new linoleum down on the four-feet square of a bathroom, and built a shelf for his hot plate and cans of soup.

Yancy bought every kind of soup the store had. It was nice to know that anytime he got hungry he could eat, and there was always a selection. The shelf also had room for a box of crackers and two boxes of cereal.

Whenever he ate alone, he made dinner in his room, not the front office. If the old folks saw him eating alone, they'd come over to keep him company, and he'd had all the noisy meals he wanted for a lifetime.

But, on Sundays, he couldn't just stay in his room all day, so he usually went for long walks in the morning, then over to the café midafternoon. The lunch crowd was long gone by then, and the families having dinner there wouldn't be in until later.

Sunday was the only day the café wasn't open for breakfast. Which had turned out to be a good thing, since if it had been, Yancy would have never met the residents of the Evening Shadows Retirement Community that first day.

He made a point to dress in his cleanest clothes. He now had three pairs of jeans and four shirts. The morning had been cold, but by three o'clock it was warm enough to walk across the street without a coat, which he didn't want to get dirty, or a jacket, which he didn't have. The heavy shirt he'd found at the secondhand shop was warm enough.

Taking his usual seat at the end of the counter, he smiled at the petite waitress who worked Sundays. He never asked her name, and Dorothy, the owner of the place, would never waste money on name tags in a town where everyone pretty much knew everyone else. The little waitress was probably about twenty, cute, with a rounded belly that looked like she was stealing a basketball.

If he sat at the end, Yancy could talk to her when she wasn't busy. In a way he felt like a foreigner practicing English. She might not know it, but he was learning to speak.

"Afternoon." She smiled. "I saved you a slice of cherry pie. Figured we'd be out by one if I didn't set one back."

He nodded his thank you. "How'd you know it was my favorite?"

"'Cause when we have it, you always eat two slices."

He glanced at the menu. "I'll have the turkey and dressing plate and one slice of the pie to start, ma'am."

She made out the ticket. "You don't have to 'ma'am' me. You're in here enough to be a regular by now. My name's Sissy. Call me that."

"Sissy," he said with a nod. "I'm Yancy."

"I know. Mr. Halls told me when he came in last week with his granddaughter. Told me you do a great job."

Sissy went to welcome two truckers coming in.

Yancy acted as if he was reading the menu. He noticed she didn't have a wedding ring on, but she wasn't flirting with him, just being polite. He had five years of catching up to do. If he was going straight, he had to learn how to talk to people. Not too bold. Not too shy.

The café was perfect. On the slow afternoons he could hear every conversation going on in the place. He'd met the owner, Dorothy, when she'd delivered a cake for Miss Bees to take to her Sunday School potluck. Dorothy had told him she did all the cooking at the café, so if he didn't like something he needed to come straight to her.

When he'd said he liked everything, she smiled with pride. She was a woman built to withstand a storm, he thought. She reminded him of a tugboat he saw once. Solid, wide-bottomed and steady moving, with hair that stood straight up, reminding him of a porcupine. Her smile was broad and warm.

As if his thoughts materialized, Dorothy yelled across the pass-through for Sissy to come quick.

The waitress dropped the menus on the counter and bolted into the kitchen. Yancy could hear water rushing. He thought about it a few seconds before standing and catching the swinging door between swings. His thin body slipped into the kitchen.

A pipe was shooting out hot water in an arc as high as his head.

"Need some help?" he said as he moved to the big sink that looked almost exactly like the prison one. Most of the water was tumbling over dirty dishes stacked in soapy water. Before Sissy or Dorothy said a word, he slid under the wash station and turned off the water.

Dorothy looked down at him, her face red from fighting off hot water. "Oh, thank you!" She turned to Sissy. "We might as well close down. We'll never get a plumber from Bailee on a Sunday, and getting one from Lubbock would cost a fortune."

"I can fix it," Yancy said as he stood, very aware that he was dripping wet.

Dorothy glared at him as if about to call him a liar. "If you can, mister, you'll have a month of Sunday dinners coming."

"With pie?"

The cook grinned. "Sure, with pie."

Yancy ran across the street and got the box of tools Cap had put together for him. When he got back he was shivering in his wet shirt, but he didn't want to take time to change. The kitchen was warm. He'd dry.

An hour later the pipe was fixed, and Yancy was

starving. He washed his hands and turned to Dorothy. "You think I could have that first meal today since you're still open?" It was almost the end of the month, and he'd had to count his ones to make sure he had enough money to eat today.

"Sure. You've got four coming. To tell the truth it would have cost me a lot more to call the plumber in Bailee. He charges me seventy-five for just driving over."

Yancy went back out to the dining room, took his seat at the end of the counter and ate his meal. Pie first and last. Sissy told everyone who came in that the café almost had to close, but Yancy had saved the day. Several stopped by to shake his hand. For the first time in his life, Yancy felt like a hero.

When he was leaving, he opened the door for a sturdy woman in a long blue cape. He'd seen her before.

She looked up at him and frowned without bothering to say thank you for opening the door. Her eyes flashed across him as if she were taking mental notes in case she had to identify him later.

"I ain't taking advantage of these people, either, Miss Ellie." He winked. "I did, however, eat all the cherry pie if you're looking for something to yell at me about, and I didn't pay for my meal."

Almost-a-nurse Ellie glared at him. "Folks pay for what they eat around this town. Don't think you can just walk out."

Sissy wiggled her round pregnant belly between them. "He don't have to pay, Ellie. He's got a month of Sunday dinners free for fixing the plumbing."

The nurse settled, but as usual, she didn't apologize. She straightened her back, and Yancy forced himself not to look at her chest. He'd like to see what was under that navy blue cape, but asking her to strip didn't sound like a good idea.

"You here for supper?" Sissy asked the other woman.

"No. I dropped by to bring your vitamins. You left them in the clinic."

"Thanks. I was going to send Harry over to get them."

Ellie glanced at Yancy, as if making sure he wasn't sneaking closer, and then gave her attention to Sissy. "Don't send your brother into the clinic unless he's burning or bleeding. He frightens the patients."

Sissy laughed. "He frightens me half the time. Since he was twelve I make him yell before he enters the house because if he don't, one of the family is likely to mistake him for a bear. I think he's the only sixth grader in town who could grow a full beard."

Yancy wasn't a part of their conversation, but they were standing in the exit. He was afraid to bump into Sissy. She looked like she was about to pop. Though he wouldn't mind brushing by Nurse Ellie, he wasn't sure she'd take to the idea. She'd already made up her mind that he was some kind of outlaw. He didn't want to fall into the category of pervert, too.

Finally Ellie turned her fiery green eyes on him and announced, "I'll be watching you. Don't you forget it."

"I'm not likely to forget your threat. It seems to be echoing." He moved closer to her. "Now if you'll excuse me, I've got to be leaving."

Ellie backed against the door to allow him to leave, but he still couldn't keep from brushing her cape. He was as close to a woman as he'd been in five years.

"You smell good," he said without thinking.

"You don't." She wrinkled her nose. "You smell like dirty dishwater."

Yancy hurried out and didn't look back. It occurred to him that maybe she'd been in prison and didn't know what was proper to say, either. Or maybe she'd just taken an instant dislike to him. Or, who knows, maybe she was simply the meanest woman in town. Someone had to be, and, to his knowledge, she was definitely in the running.

Either way, he would be wise to avoid her. At the rate he was going, he wouldn't have to worry about getting involved with any woman in Crossroads, Texas. All the ones he'd met were either old, pregnant or mean as snakes.

Twelve

Lauren

Lauren Brigman had always been glad February was the shortest month of the year. She hated it. First, the weather was usually crummy. Second, nothing was ever going on in school. And who cared about Valentine's Day. In March she'd be sixteen, so she'd just as soon February got out of the way.

Her father usually got her one of those small hearts with five chocolates inside and a frog or cartoon character on the outside saying something like, *Have a hopping good Valentine's Day.*

Her mother, whom she'd called Margaret since she was five, mailed an expensive card with the usual twenty dollars for every holiday. She always signed *x*'s and *o*'s, but she had no idea what her one child would want on any occasion.

But now Margaret was coming for the weekend, and Saturday was Valentine's Day. At least, Lauren thought she would come by then; she'd already canceled twice, once at the end of January because a storm in Dallas promised a dusting of snow and again in February when she said something came up at work.

Lauren's father had simply shrugged, but Lauren had no trouble reading his mind. Silently he was cussing, knowing Margaret the Great could have driven in if she wanted to, and she was the boss at work, so she could probably have moved her *something came up* to Monday. Crossroads was only five hours from Dallas, but for Margaret Brigman, it always took a Mount Everest effort to get to Lauren.

Work had always been more important than anything else to Margaret. It was important to Pop also. Dan Brigman considered himself the guardian of every person from county line to county line, but Lauren knew his first and last thought every day was saved for his daughter. Even when he wasn't at home he texted her, listing rules and checking in. During the first few years after her mother left, if he had to work late, he'd have Mrs. O'Grady walk over and stay with Lauren or take her back to their place for dinner. The O'Gradys lived a few hundred yards along the lakeshore, so having someone to watch over her was never a problem.

Her mom and dad had separated soon after Pop had taken the job of county sheriff. Evidently, Margaret thought they should move up, which meant a bigger city than Crossroads, Texas. For her, the move to a lake house in the middle of nowhere was definitely down. She couldn't see the beauty in the sunsets on the plains or the colors in the canyon walls as shadows stretched. For Margaret, Crossroads was no more that its name: a wide spot in the road where two highways crossed. A place where travelers stopped for gas or a meal and drove on.

She went off to Dallas to intern with an advertising agency. After all, she'd said, her master's degree *was* in marketing, and how could she practice her skills in a small town? She'd left Lauren's father to manage with a kindergartener and the promise to be back in six months. The internship stretched into a job offer she couldn't turn down, and that slipped into a partnership. The trips home once a month quickly changed to weekly phone calls and apologies.

Pop had done his best when Margaret left, but even at five Lauren had known he was broken. For the first two years she'd expected her mother to come back and fix him. There had been weeks sometimes when they ate nothing but cereal or hamburgers. The house had become a mountain range of piles: work piles, school piles, dirty clothes piles, clean clothes piles. Plus, there'd been ever-growing foothills of shoes, toys and trash that might be needed at some point, like empty boxes and old Popsicle sticks.

Then one day a letter had come. She'd watched her father read it slowly, before folding it back into the envelope and putting it in his work satchel. "Well, honey," he'd started in a voice that sounded forced with calmness. "Looks like it's going to be just you and me. How about we clean up this place and make it right for the two of us?"

They'd redecorated the dining room and called it Lauren's library, and every month they'd driven to Lubbock and added half a dozen new books. He'd let her paint her room, which she did every summer. He'd moved his favorite chair to the porch and sat out there until sundown almost every night. They ate at the kitchen bar or in front of the TV.

They set rules and patterns to their lives. Two trips a year to shop for clothes and once a month for groceries. Lauren became the only kindergartener to pack her own lunch. If she needed anything new, she picked it from a catalog, and he ordered whatever she circled. By age eight she was ordering all her clothes, shoes and supplies that way.

Her mother sent fancy dresses that Lauren never wore and little purses she never carried.

Pop tried to do holidays. He bought the meal-in-a-bag for Thanksgiving that became leftovers all weekend. He stocked up on pizza and frozen dinners for the Christmas break and hung one string of lights on the porch. They always picked out three presents each from all the catalogs that came in December. He'd bring home a tree the day she got out of school and let her decorate it with ornaments she bought at the Dollar Store.

When she was little, he'd take her fishing on the lake. She begged to be left at home as soon as she got old enough to stay by herself. Every Friday night they fought over what movie to watch. He'd burn popcorn and she'd make the sandwiches.

Once a month he found a babysitter and left for the night. It was usually a school night, so she barely missed him. When she was little she used to think he went to see Margaret. Now she doubted that was true. Lauren had never asked him where he went, but he'd only been thirty when Margaret left, so once in a while maybe he wanted to get away to be young again. Maybe one night a month he just needed the load of being a single father and a county sheriff off his shoulders.

Lauren had grown comfortable with her life. She visited her mother for a few weeks during summer break.

Margaret would work, and Lauren would spend the days reading or hanging out at the pool at her mom's condo complex while she counted the days until she could go back home. Pop wasn't much fun, but at least he was there.

As far as she could remember, this was the first time her mother had come back to the Ransom Canyon lake house in ten years. On the rare occasions she *came to visit* she usually stayed at a hotel in one of the small nearby towns. Pop always dropped Lauren off wherever she booked the room. The three of them tried dinners out during those times, but it was usually a disaster. Sometimes Lauren wondered how her parents had ever gotten along well enough to make her.

"You got everything you need?" Her father poked his head into what they called the spare bedroom.

She smiled. The sheriff looked nervous, something she rarely saw in Pop. "I got it all. In an hour you won't recognize this place."

"Good. I have to wash down the porch, and I think we're ready for her. She's had a month to build her case against me for not taking proper care of you, so I figure she'll be yelling at me for hours. Try to hide that scar on your leg as long as possible." He smiled. "Oh, and be prepared to take her out to the old house. She'll want to see where you got hurt."

Lauren giggled, knowing if Margaret saw the tiny scar left by her stitches she'd be angry, very angry. "I made snacks, so we won't starve, no matter how long the yelling lasts." Lauren was very familiar with the fights. Most were over her. He wasn't raising her right. She needed to see more of the world. He should watch her closer, make sure she did her homework. Give her piano and dance lessons. Expose her to more than county fairs and rodeos. The Gypsy House disaster was a forest worth of fuel.

Margaret criticized, but she never offered to take over the job, either. Her role seemed to be simply to yell at him.

"If it gets bad, Pop, I'll walk down to Tim's place. Since he's permanently grounded, he could probably use the company."

"Good idea. Have a plan of escape." He smiled, suddenly in a good mood. "In fact, I might let you date Timothy O'Grady. With a broken leg, he's not likely to step out of line, and I could remind him that it really wouldn't be hard to break his other leg."

"I'm not dating injured boys just to make you happy, Pop. In fact, I'm not dating anyone."

"Good," he said. "Let's keep it that way until you're in your twenties, then we'll talk about group dating, or maybe online dating. That seems germ free, and, of course, I'll be the one meeting them with you those first few times. Maybe I'll even go on the first dozen or so dates. After all, it could be fun."

She tossed a new accent pillow at him. "No way."

He caught it, examined the pillow, frowned and tossed it back. It was the rustic red of the canyon, with lace trim framing it. He'd let her order a whole bedding set: comforter, pillow and sheets, even curtains for the room. The place looked almost like the picture in the catalog.

As he turned to leave, she said, "I love you, Pop, I really do."

"I know. I love you, too. We'll get through Margaret's visit. This time, whatever your mother says, she's right. I should have watched over you, told you not to go in old houses. I shouldn't have been working late, so I could have picked you up."

"It wasn't your fault. You let me learn a lesson, that's all." Since that night, things had changed between them. The lectures were still there, the questioning about every detail of her life, the hovering to make sure she was fine, but she saw something else. The love.

The doorbell made them both jump, but Lauren reacted first. "It's only Quinn O'Grady. I asked her if she'd bring some lavender to put in Margaret's room."

He followed her down the hallway. "We ordered flowers delivered?"

Lauren took time to turn around and glare at him. "Of course."

He shrugged. "Of course. That's probably why Margaret left. The house didn't smell like lavender."

When Lauren opened the door, she saw Quinn O'Grady standing outside with an armful of flowers. "I picked a few wildflowers to mix in, Lauren. It's too early for most, but I found a few near the well house."

As Lauren welcomed her, Quinn passed Pop and smiled shyly. "If you'd like, Lauren, I'll help arrange them?"

"I'd be thankful for the help, Miss O'Grady. You're very kind to have brought them by." Pop stiffened. He was back to being sheriff again.

"No problem," Quinn answered with her head down.

Quinn was almost as tall as Pop. They were about the same age, but since he called her Miss O'Grady, she supposed he didn't know her very well.

Lauren thought of adding her to an ever-growing list of possible women her father could date, but Quinn seemed very, very shy and they had nothing in common. Her father tended to yell when he was mad, drink when he was off duty, and smell like fish when he'd been out on the lake more than an hour. Quinn always smelled of lavender, never raised her voice, and barely talked to anyone. If Lauren hadn't done a report on different types of farming in the area, she would have never met the kind woman.

Today, Lauren appreciated the help. Quinn spread her flowers on the table and began to do her magic. In what seemed like minutes, the house smelled like spring. She even helped Lauren finish off the bedroom and suggested rearranging the furniture so Margaret could see the lake from her bed.

"It'll be a beautiful view for her to wake up to," she claimed.

Lauren doubted Margaret would even open the curtains. For her, the only great view was of the skyline of downtown Dallas.

When Quinn left, Lauren found herself wishing she had a woman like her for a mother. She didn't seem to know anything about fashion or makeup or hairstyles, but there was a gentleness about her.

Her father must have noticed it, too, because he insisted on walking Quinn to her car.

Lauren heard him ask what he owed for the flowers, and Quinn replied nothing. "They are a gift to your lovely daughter. She's a great kid."

"You'll get no argument from me," he answered. "Sometimes I wonder if I'm raising her, or she's raising me. I've heard you used to play piano. You wouldn't be interested in teaching her?"

"If I ever teach, she'd be the first in line," Quinn said and smiled at him.

Lauren doubted they were flirting, but at least Pop was talking to a woman. That was progress.

Pop leaned down to her window and said that if she ever needed a favor that didn't involve where to bury a body, all she had to do was call. He owed her one.

"I'll remember that," she answered as she started her old pickup and turned toward Tim O'Grady's place. "I thought I'd stop in on my cousin and see how her boy is doing. I heard he was hurt."

Pop stepped back and waved, then went around the side of the house to clean the deck.

Lauren walked around the place, checking every detail. They'd cleaned the first weekend Margaret was supposed to come and the second. Now, after the third cleaning, she feared she would scrub off the finish if she dusted anymore. Even after ten years, there were still touches of Margaret in every room.

Apparently when Margaret left them, she'd only taken her clothes. The chest that had been her grandmother's was still in the hallway. Half the books in her father's study must have been her mother's because he never touched them. The nightstands in the guest bedroom, the dishes, the pots and pans had all been abandoned, just like Lauren.

Suddenly, Lauren wished she hadn't fussed so much over Margaret's coming.

But it was too late to take the flowers out or put the old quilt back on the bed. She could hear the hum of a car coming down the drive.

Margaret had arrived.

Thirteen

Lucas

Lucas Reyes rode his horse slowly along the sandy breaks that snaked between Kirkland's Double K Ranch and the Collins's Bar W border. He liked taking this way home. No matter the season, there was a beauty about this quarter mile of in-between land where all he saw was nature in every direction, and the sounds were the same as those that must have floated over this land a hundred years ago.

The slender thread of dried-up creek bed wasn't claimed by Kirkland or Collins. A no-man's-land, where outlaws could have roamed in the early days of Texas. The stillness here was like music to Lucas. All he heard were the low sounds of the wild and his own breathing. He wondered if in the big cities people might live their whole lives without ever knowing this kind of beautiful silence.

His grandfather had told him that this path had once been a hidden entrance to Ransom Canyon where in the 1800s tribes and Comancheros traded hostages and

slaves from one tribe to the other. Texas Rangers had
traveled to the bottom of Ransom Canyon now and then,
without their badges showing, so they could pay the
ransom on children and wives stolen from early settle-
ments.

Lucas felt like it could almost be years ago tonight,
and he might accidentally ride into a campsite that followed no law.

Slowly, as he crossed onto Collins land, he turned
his thoughts back to the present.

Mr. Kirkland had hired him to string wire most of
the day. Every muscle in his body hurt, but the money
was good. He had already saved enough for one semester of college, and, with luck, he would have the next
semester's money in the bank before summer. Then
he'd start working on a cushion. If he worked part-
time during the year, he could cover food and housing
on campus, but he'd have to make tuition by working
every summer and break.

Every cowboy around knew the Double K was the
best place to work. Staten Kirkland paid well, and his
ranch bordered the Collins place, so Lucas could ride
his horse the few miles home when he finished.

Lucas's father was the head wrangler at the Bar W,
Davis Collins's ranch. Lucas and his family lived at the
headquarters in a house only slightly smaller than the
foreman's place. The Collins family lived half a mile
away on a rise that offered a full view of the land they'd
owned for generations, but Reid Collins's dad wasn't
like Staten Kirkland.

Davis Collins was several years older than Kirkland and ran his ranch from his office. The cattle they
raised and horses they trained and sold were no more

than numbers to him. On the rare occasion Collins was seen on his land, it was in a four-wheeler. His two sons were far more interested in riding dirt bikes across unbroken pastures than learning the business their family had been in for over a hundred years.

To put it simply, Kirkland was a rancher and Collins was a businessman. If a drought came, Collins would sell off his herd. Kirkland would haul in feed and keep his best stock to rebuild for when times were better. Kirkland would weather any storm. But Lucas feared that if Reid or his brother didn't show some interest in ranching, the Collins place might be up for sale in ten years.

When he reached the barn, Lucas took care of his horse like his father had taught him, before heading in to supper. It was Saturday night, and he had nothing planned. Maybe he'd ask his papa if he could borrow the old pickup and drive over to see Tim O'Grady. Lucas had noticed that since the accident, Tim and Reid weren't hanging out at school, and to his knowledge, Reid hadn't dropped by to visit Tim. Their friendship apparently hadn't survived the Gypsy House.

The great thing about stringing wire all day was that it gave him time to think. Maybe Tim had seen the light as far as Reid Collins was concerned. Maybe Reid didn't want a constant reminder that he wasn't a real hero hobbling behind him. They'd been friends for as long as Lucas could remember, but football season was over, and Tim was grounded. He would only slow Reid down this last half of their junior year.

After grabbing a bite, Lucas lifted the keys off the nail by the door, held them up and jingled them. His father nodded. With five other kids at home to worry

about, his father never asked questions. Lucas often
wondered if his dad trusted his oldest so completely, or
if he just didn't have the time or energy to ask.

It was almost eight o'clock when Lucas pulled up to
Tim's house on the lake. He liked to park down the road
a little and walk along the shoreline. Tim's house wasn't
big like Reid's, but the O'Gradys were both artists, so it
always seemed to be bursting with life and color. Tim's
dad taught art, and his mother was a painter. Lucas had
no idea if she ever sold any paintings to anyone other
than family, but there were so many O'Gradys around
this part of the state, they could probably keep her busy.

Tim's mom answered the door. "Evening, Lucas, I
wondered if you'd make it tonight."

"I worked until almost dark. Mr. Kirkland ran me
off in time for me to ride home before sunset. He said
I wander around his place enough after dark. I didn't
think he noticed. I've done roundup work several times
for his foreman, but the other night when he offered us
a ride was the first time I think he really saw me, you
know, as a person."

"Do you think he minds you walking his land?" she
asked politely.

Lucas shook his head. "I told him I was just watching
the night sky, and he reminded me to always close the
gates and don't spook the damn cattle." Lucas grinned.
"You know, I've figured out that Kirkland thinks *damn*
and *hell* are adverbs or adjectives to toss into any sentence."

Tim's mom laughed and turned down the hallway
leading to Tim's room.

She didn't need to show him the way. Lucas had
dropped Tim's homework off for two weeks after the

accident, but he guessed, like Tim, she enjoyed the company.

It didn't take much to know few kids came by to visit Tim. Lucas wasn't really sure why he did.

Mrs. O'Grady grinned. "You boys will have a third person for the visit tonight. I want you both to be on your best behavior. No 'adverbs,' if you know what I mean."

If Mrs. Patterson was the company, Lucas had better think of an exit plan fast. The Baptist preacher's wife could have been the next plague to hit the Egyptians if Moses had needed another one.

"Lauren Brigman walked down from her house just to bring Tim cookies." Mrs. O'Grady relieved Lucas's panic. "She's such a sweet girl."

Lucas heard the laughter behind Tim's closed bedroom door.

When he shoved it open, he saw Lauren sitting in the desk chair rocking back and forth like she was on a mechanical bull. Tim had his cast propped on a pillow on his half-bed. They were both staring at the floor.

Tim spotted Lucas and grinned. "Hey, Lucas, look what Lauren brought me."

Lucas glanced down at a box turtle slowly climbing across a shaggy rug. "I was hoping she brought cookies."

When Lauren raised her head her eyes were full of laughter, and he couldn't look away.

"I brought chocolate chip cookies, too. They're in the bag. But, I found this turtle on the way over. Since Tim can't walk around the lake, I brought a lake friend to visit him."

"Tim," his mother's voice came from the hallway.

"You are not keeping that turtle." When no one commented, she added, "I'll bring milk to go with the cookies."

All three waited until they heard her footsteps retreating before Tim whispered, "Mom's driving me nuts. If I could get this cast off I'd beat myself to death with it. She's been babying me since I got home from the hospital. If you two didn't come over now and then, I'd go mad, and, believe me, you don't want to see an insane man on crutches."

Lucas winked at Lauren. They'd seen each other at school in passing, different times, different days, but tonight they'd managed to accidentally bump into one another. Neither was paying any attention to Tim as he rambled on about how his mother tried to spoon-feed him.

"What can we do to help?" Lucas finally broke the rant. He took a seat on the other side of the bed, where he could talk to Tim and look at Lauren. "You're in a cast. I guess waterskiing is out, and it's too cold to swim. You'd sink anyway." When no one laughed, he added, "We could watch a movie."

"No, my parents got the bill for all the movies I've rented on cable." Tim frowned. "I can't buy another one. My mom says we've got eighty channels, surely I can find something free to watch."

Lucas shook his head. "It would almost be worth the trouble of sawing that cast off to watch you try to beat yourself to death. At least it's something the reality shows haven't thought of yet."

All three laughed and began to just talk. About everything: school, sports, graduation, movies they hated. The one topic no one of the three brought up was Reid

Collins or the night at the Gypsy House. Lucas figured each had their reasons for letting the legend live about what had happened that night at the old abandoned house. Lauren was too shy to go up against Reid. Tim might be foggy about what really happened, and Lucas simply wanted to stay out of trouble. If he said anything, Mr. Collins might let his father go.

It mattered little who'd done what that night, but Lucas would never get to go to college if his dad got fired and he had to help out his family.

After an hour, when the cookies were gone and Tim looked tired, Lucas offered to walk Lauren home. "It's on my way. I'm parked about halfway between your place and here."

She nodded like it wasn't necessary, or maybe she didn't care.

As they left Tim's house, Lucas said, "I don't have to walk you if you'd rather be alone."

"No. It's not that. I just don't want to go back. My mother spent the night last night. She was all nice for a while, even drove me to Bailee so we could get our nails done today, then we spent time going through old photo albums at the house. But at dinner she started arguing over how bad pizza was for her diet as well as mine, and my father jumped right into the fight. From my dietary habits they spun off on why I'm second in the class and not first and how the high school isn't good enough for someone with my mind."

"What did you say?" Lucas took her hand as they stepped onto the damp grass near the shore.

"I said goodbye. Pop and I already agreed I could use visiting Tim as my escape plan." She laughed suddenly. "I didn't really make the cookies. I got them at the bakery, but since my mom freaked out over the pizza, I decided I'd better make sure the cookies disappeared."

They walked for a while in silence. The night held the smell of a storm in the thick air, but he barely felt it. He knew this moment would only last for a short time, and he wanted to remember everything. The wind whipping up off the water. The new moon so thin it looked like a tear in the night's canvas. The feel of Lauren's hand in his as if it were the most natural thing in the world.

He thought of asking her out on a date, but she was fifteen and he was seventeen. Her father, or mother, probably wouldn't let her go. Plus, he didn't have the time or the money to date. "How long do you have before you have to be home?"

"Why?"

"I'd like to show you something, but it will take half an hour."

Her fingers laced with his. "Let's go."

Then, they were running as if every second counted. A few minutes later they were laughing as they climbed into his truck. He shoved ropes, spurs and all kinds of cowboy gear out of the way to clear enough room for her to sit beside him.

"I could always ride in back," she offered.

"Nope. It's a mess back there. Saddles and bloody chaps from working yearlings. I leave it back there so it can air out before I put it in the tack room."

They both laughed again as he piled books in her lap. He slipped in beside her and shifted the pickup into gear.

She ducked low as he slowly drove past her house as if they were running away on an adventure.

Lucas never felt lighthearted, he had too many plans, too much to do, too much responsibility on his shoulders as the oldest child. But at this moment, with Lauren at his side, he was Peter Pan and she was his Wendy. They were flying.

Five miles out, he turned at a back entrance of the Double K Ranch. No one but cattle trucks used the road, and it was too far from the headquarters of the ranch or town for anyone to see his lights.

She giggled as they bounced their way across open land to an old windmill painted in black across a shadowy sky. The stars were out now, the Milky Way sparkling like a cluster of tiny diamonds scattered above them.

He cut the engine, stepped out and offered his hand. "I found this place one night when I was late going home."

They moved over the uneven ground to where a water trough stretched below the windmill. "If you step in something soft, you'll know cattle have been here lately getting a drink, but I don't think this pasture is used much in the winter."

Neither looked down as he whispered, "Listen. It's like a symphony out here." The clank of the windmill as the rusty fan blades turned in the wind did seem like music. Closing his eyes, Lucas heard it all. The slough of the water, the dripping from the pipe. The rustle of the dried leaves. The swish of buffalo grass. The lonely sound of a meadowlark's call.

Somewhere in the stand of trees a quarter mile away, an owl hooted and a hawk's cry sounded on the breeze. This was his idea of heaven.

"I love standing here listening and knowing that it must have sounded just the same for years."

"It's beautiful." She moved against his shoulder.

"I hoped you'd hear it. I come out here once in a while. It makes me feel at peace. Around my house it's never quiet. When the noise gets too much for me, I come here and listen to the quiet. Sometimes when the crowd at school is nothing but nervous yelling and giggling or I'm somewhere I don't want to be, I think of here."

They were silent for a while. He put his arm around her shoulders, and she cuddled against his side.

"You know, Lauren, it's Valentine's Day."

"I know. My pop gave me his usual candy heart."

Lucas pulled her against him and kissed her forehead. "Happy Valentine's Day. If you were older and my girl, I'd get you flowers, not candy."

She laughed softly. "Eventually, I will be older. I'd love to get flowers. Yellow roses, of course."

"I'll remember that."

Then without a word they walked back to the truck.

Neither said a word as he drove back, but her hand rested in his. He wasn't sure how she felt, but for him Lauren was like the windmill place. She felt so right by his side.

When they were close to the lake, she asked, "Why'd you take me out there, Lucas?"

"I wanted you to know about it, so when life gets too much, you'll always have a place to go. Mr. Kirkland probably won't know you're there, and my guess is even if he did know, he wouldn't care. I'll be leaving for college soon. You can have my secret place if you like. Sounds like, with your folks, you'll be needing it."

"You're right, and I'll go out there, too. My mom told

me she's giving me her old car for my sixteenth birthday. She said after three years she really needs a new one anyway. I don't imagine Pop will take that well."

"Do they ever agree?"

"No. It's like fighting is the only way they know how to talk."

He turned down the long decline to the lake and her house. "My folks never fight. They don't have time with all us kids. Sometimes I hear them whispering after we've all gone to bed. I imagine they're reintroducing themselves to one another."

Lauren smiled. "I'd love to be part of a big family."

He stopped just before the last bend in the road and turned off his car lights. "Who knows, maybe someday you will be. You'd better get out here, so it'll look like you walked in from Tim's place."

She leaned closer and kissed him on the cheek. "Thanks for taking me to a symphony tonight."

"You're welcome, *mi cielo*."

As she climbed out, she asked, "What does that mean?"

"I'll tell you one day," he said.

She shrugged and closed the door to his old pickup.

He watched her until she disappeared around the bend, then he drove home.

When he left here and times got stressful, he'd think of his special place and picture every detail in his mind. Maybe the memory would calm him.

When he visualized, Lucas knew he'd see Lauren there, too.

Lauren slipped through the back door and tugged off her tennis shoes, now covered in mud and sand. The air in the house was warm on her skin, but she could almost feel the frost between her parents. Pop was glaring at the TV. Mom was in the kitchen, checking messages on her phone.

"How was Tim?" Pop asked.

"Better. Says his mother is babying him so badly he's thinking of beating himself to death with his cast."

The sheriff didn't blink. "That would be one horrible crime scene. Tell him to drag his ass over the county line first. I don't want to be the one to have to deal with his body."

She smiled at her pop's sense of humor.

Her mother stood and walked to the doorway. "That's a sick thing to say, Dan. I wonder that you haven't warped the child."

Pop ignored Margaret. "I saw Reyes's old pickup rattle past about half an hour ago. Was Lucas visiting Tim, too?"

Lauren nodded. "Yeah, we figured since he wanted to die, we would throw him in the lake. With that cast he sank like a rock, and bubbles rose for five minutes. Lucas headed back home after the assisted suicide. After all, with Tim gone, there was no one to do all the talking. I had to stay behind and clean up the milk and cookies mess. Wouldn't want Tim's mom to deal with a funeral and crumbs everywhere."

Pop glanced at her, holding up one finger as if to say *wait for it*.

Then he smiled as Margaret fired. "You have warped her with your perverted cop humor. She'll probably be scarred for life. I can just imagine what the breakfast conversation is like around here."

Her parents were so busy bickering, neither noticed

Lauren leaving. She walked to her room as an amazing realization hit her. Her father had baited her mother. She'd guessed a long time ago that Margaret loved fighting, and now, apparently, her pop had caught the bug.

As she curled up on her bed, she tried to push the sounds of their voices aside and remember the way the night sounded out by the windmill.

This time in her life, this night, what had happened between her and Lucas all felt so good except for one thing.

She knew she could never mention how she was feeling now to her pop. For the first time in her life she had a secret she'd never share with anyone but Lucas. Just between us, he had said. The way he'd saved her life, the kiss at the hospital and now tonight.

Lauren closed her eyes, knowing she'd never mention Lucas, or the way she felt about him, to anyone. But she'd never forget the way she felt when his hand covered hers.

Fourteen

Staten

The last thing Staten had told Quinn when he'd left her place Saturday morning was for her to call him. He wanted her to know he would be there when she needed him, or if she just wanted to talk and have dinner. He wasn't going anywhere just because he learned her dark secret, and he wasn't planning to push to know details.

She had become more to him than just a friend. He now felt protective of her. Hell, it was more than that, but Staten didn't need to think about it now.

When she didn't call, he waited. He would give her space.

After a month, he figured he'd given her enough time. He wanted to see his gentle Quinn again. He wanted her to know that if the past still haunted her, he'd stand near. He needed to make sure *they* were all right. Quinn wasn't an emotional woman. Hell, she'd carried around the horror of what Lloyd had done to her for years. The news that the piano master was coming to her world had upset her deeply. As her friend, he saw it as his job to walk beside her through this. If conflict came, he was more than willing to stand in front of her and fight her fight.

The idea of catching the next flight to New York and flattening the guy had crossed his mind a few hundred times, but he had a feeling that wasn't what Quinn would want him to do.

Staten had tried calling Quinn several times but wasn't surprised she hadn't answered. She didn't carry her phone when she worked outside. The first two weeks of February had been cold, but most of the days were sunny. So the Monday after Valentine's Day, he drove into town to make a few stops, and one of them would be at Quinn's place.

After he had breakfast with his grandmother and ate a few of her leftover Valentine's cookies, his mind turned to Quinn, even while his granny rattled on.

He liked the idea of showing up to Quinn's place in the morning. She'd know he came to check on her, and that was all. They could have coffee and talk.

"Thanks for delivering the magazines, dear." Granny patted him on the shoulder, pulling Staten from his thoughts of Quinn.

Granny ordered a half dozen tabloids every month and refused to have them mailed to her address at the Evening Shadows Retirement Community.

"You're welcome. I needed to be in town this morning for a few errands anyway." He walked around, noticing a new shelf in her kitchen. "You know, you could have the magazines delivered here."

She laughed. "I know, but I like seeing you. The mailman never eats my French toast."

"See you next week." Staten kissed her goodbye and headed over to Lavender Lane.

The need to see Quinn was an ache deep inside him. He told himself he was worried about her, but Staten knew it was more than that. Things were changing between them, and he had no way of stopping what was happening. He liked being in control of his world. He believed when something changed it was usually for the worse. He had spent a month working hard trying to keep his mind off her and their new relationship. He'd kept saying she would call, but she hadn't.

When he pulled on to her place the air was as silent as ever. It couldn't be much past eight in the morning. Maybe Quinn was sleeping in.

Staten grinned. He'd like waking her up. They'd be starting just where he planned to end up tonight…in bed. He never made love to her in daylight. He wasn't sure she'd even be open to the idea.

As he pulled his truck around back so it wouldn't be seen from the road, he glanced toward the house and slammed on the brakes.

The sheriff's cruiser was pulled up close to the porch, where Staten always parked.

Staten switched off the engine and was out of his truck before the motor settled. He ran, heart pounding, toward the door. She worked out here all alone. A million accidents could have happened. She could have been hurt in the fields—snake bites happened all the time—or she might have been shot by some idiot popping off rounds at her Lavender Lane sign.

Hell, she could have fallen in her house. Could have lain there for days, dying an inch at a time.

His boots stormed across the porch, and he hit her

door so hard it rattled off the hinges. "Quinn!" he yelled. "Quinn."

Nothing. No Quinn. No sheriff.

Staten stomped through the house, noticing her phone was still on the stand charging. For a second he hesitated at the door to her bedroom. If she was in bed with the sheriff, what would he do? No, impossible, he thought as he shoved the door open and saw a neatly made bed.

Just the fact that he thought of her with another man bothered him. It frustrated the hell out of Staten. They'd made no promises to each other. Hell, they didn't even buy each other Valentine's gifts.

Slowing his pace, he walked back through the house and stepped out on the porch, realizing he'd acted like a fool. The door leaning against its frame was proof. There was part of him that wanted to be considerate and understanding like he guessed women wanted, but some days he knew he hadn't quite evolved that far.

Staten stared at the cruiser, trying to guess what could have happened. She could have been hurt, and the sheriff rode with her in the ambulance. He could have had car trouble and asked her to give him a lift.

That made sense.

A tapping came from the barn, and Staten took a deep breath. Maybe she was simply working on one of the machines. Maybe the sheriff had stopped by to warn her about crime in the area. A woman living alone on a farm needed to know if something was going on. Staten didn't know if she had a gun, but if he had anything to do with it, she would by sundown.

He lowered his hat against the sun and walked slowly toward the noise. Staten was through guessing. It was wearing a bald spot in his brain. If he wanted to worry, he should go back home and worry about how someone had hit one of his bulls last night out on the county road and didn't total their car. That made no sense. The road ran through open range, but the black bull, even at night, still had the right-of-way. Anyone crossing should have been going slow with their high beams on.

The tapping grew louder as Staten stepped into the barn's shadows. Quinn was all right, he told himself. She was simply working on that old tractor. If he ever went crazy and did buy her a gift, it'd be a new John Deere.

"Morning," he yelled, trying not to allow the roller-coaster ride of emotions he'd just stepped off of to show in his tone.

"Morning," a low voice answered. "How are you today, Mr. Kirkland?"

The sheriff straightened from his perch on the tractor. The two men had known one another for years, worked together when need arose, but neither called the other friend. Staten rarely socialized, and Brigman had a daughter to raise.

"I'm fine, Sheriff." Staten removed his hat. "I just dropped by to order some more soap from Quinn. My grandmother loves giving it as gifts." Granny had told him to pick up some if he went by the farm, so Staten didn't consider it a complete lie. "You happen to know where she is?"

The sheriff jumped down. He wasn't as tall as Staten, but he looked like a man who could hold his own in a fight. "I came out to help when she told me this old bucket of bolts wouldn't start."

When Staten didn't comment, the sheriff continued,

"She was leaving when I pulled up. Said something about having to go to the doctor this morning. I'm sure she'll be back soon. The clinic never gets busy until school is out in the afternoon." He grinned. "Moms around here probably do what my mother used to. No matter how I complained, she always made me go to school, claiming that if I was really sick the school nurse would send me home."

Staten didn't want to talk to Dan Brigman. He was fighting not to think about what terminal illness Quinn might have. She could be finding out the bad news right now while he was visiting with the sheriff about nothing.

But he couldn't just turn around and run.

He glanced at the tractor. "Did you get it running?"

Sheriff Brigman shook his head. "Got a minute? I could use your help. If you could start it up a few times, I might be able to see why it's missing down here."

"Sure thing," Staten said, wondering why Quinn had asked the sheriff and not him to work on the piece of junk. Hell, he'd offered a dozen times.

Staten might as well help out. The day had started with him in a good mood, he'd made his grandmother laugh, but from that point things seemed to be going steadily downhill. He had a full day's work waiting back at the Double K. He was wasting time here.

As soon as the engine started sounding right, he planned to drive back through town and see if he could spot Quinn's old green pickup. If she was still at the clinic, he might just stop by and get that flu shot. Ellie, the girl working on becoming a nurse practitioner, ran the place. She'd told him back in September to get the shot. By getting it now, it should be good to the last month of winter and maybe next fall, too.

If he walked in to get the shot, he could casually check on Quinn.

"That does it," Brigman yelled. "She's running smooth as new."

Staten cut the engine and climbed down as the sheriff strapped back on his heavy belt. They walked toward the house side by side.

"Someone hit one of my prize bulls last night," Staten mentioned.

"What was he worth?"

"About twenty thousand before he was hit. About five hundred now."

Dan pulled out his notepad. "Someone ran his car into the back of a couple of thousand pounds on a moonless night. He shouldn't be too hard to find. Even a truck would take major damage." The sheriff jotted down a few notes as he walked. "I'll keep my eye out. Can't help but wonder what a car or truck would be doing on a back county road late at night."

"That makes two of us. It's my land. I'd like to know who'd be barreling across my property." Staten had a fair idea. Rustlers. They'd been growing bolder since beef prices went up.

"You know of anyone who comes on your land after dark?" Brigman asked.

Staten shrugged. "The oldest Reyes boy, maybe. He likes to look at the stars out where no lights from town interfere, he says. But he's never caused any trouble, and the few times I've seen him, he was walking or riding a horse."

"He drives now." Brigman's voice was low, almost

as if he were talking to himself. "I saw him pass my house last weekend in an old pickup."

They reached the cruiser.

The sheriff offered his hand. "Thanks for taking the time to help me out. I owed Quinn a favor."

"Anytime." Staten touched his hat with two fingers and headed to his truck.

Twenty minutes later, he was driving slowly down the one main street of Crossroads. If speed-limit signs didn't slow highway traffic through town, the shops on the main street would be nothing more than a blur. As it was, strangers heading south from Amarillo or north from Abilene or west from Oklahoma only saw mostly what *once was* when they drove through. They didn't see the two fine churches that had stood solidly for a hundred years, or the first-rate school, or the little museum that sat back in a wide park of mature trees just east of town. Grade schools for a hundred miles around brought buses to tour the pioneer museum and see the beauty of the canyon that opened up all at once across the plain, flat land.

Staten was proud of what his family had done to put the town on the map. Maybe by some standards it wasn't much, but, like most of the farmers and ranchers around, it was all that was needed. Someday, after he was gone, there'd be a wing built onto the museum to hold all the Kirkland files and papers. His family had kept records further back than any settler. His great-grandfather had even kept a journal of the weather, what he did each day and even his thoughts. They might all be gone, but their story would be there on display.

He pulled himself back to his search. Quinn's old green pickup was nowhere in sight.

He turned around at the rest stop just out of town and circled back. Half the parking spots in front of the clinic were empty, so she would have had no trouble getting a parking place.

He crossed the Country Grocery lot and both gas stations. Maybe he'd simply missed her? It was doubtful she went anywhere else to shop. As far as he knew, she only did major shopping trips for supplies a couple of times a year.

When he left the farm- and ranch-supply parking lot, he decided to go in for his flu shot anyway. Even if Quinn wasn't there, he was six months past due, and with his luck he'd be the last human in Texas to have the flu.

Ten minutes later the nurse's aide pushed a needle into his arm, talking, chewing gum and twirling her shoe with her big toe. "You're late getting this, Mr. Kirkland. Folks your age should have a flu shot."

He had no idea how old she thought he was, and he wasn't about to ask. If he thought he could get away with it, he'd simply ignore her, but she'd probably think he'd gone into shock and yell for Ellie. Ellie Emerson was the nearest thing they had to a doctor in Crossroads most days.

So, to save himself trouble, Staten decided to talk to the gum-chewing rattle-box. "I know I'm late, but I was running errands this morning and thought I'd take the time." He tried to remember what her name tag said. Britney or Binky, he couldn't remember. He refused to look at the tag pinned almost at the point of her breast. "I see the clinic is not busy, nurse."

She giggled. "I'm not a nurse, just an aide. I can give shots and take blood. What kind of errands does a big-time rancher like you do? I love your boots, by the way. What brand are they? Don't you have an assistant on the ranch to run errands?"

He had no idea which question to answer first, so he ignored all three.

When she stared at him, he figured he'd better pick one to answer or he'd be in the cramped room all day until Binky had to go for more caffeine.

Staten answered simply, "I drove out to Lavender Lane to get my grandmother some soap." He almost added that it wasn't the kind of thing he could ask one of the cowhands to do, but he didn't want to talk more than necessary to this woman. Her brain reminded him of a flea, small and jumpy.

"Did you buy any?" she asked as she pulled the needle out of his arm and told him to hold a ball of cotton over the site.

"No. Quinn O'Grady wasn't home."

The bloodsucker giggled as her wiggly shoe flew off her big toe. "I could have told you that. She was in here bright and early. The nurse saw her and sent her straight to Lubbock for testing."

Staten forced calm into his words. "For what?" He kept his tone even by staring at the girl's multicolored toenails.

The nurse's aide slapped a strip of tape over the cotton. "I don't know, and even if I did, it would be confidential. All I did was call the ob-gyn and tell him she was on her way."

Staten walked back to his truck and just sat staring at the dust whirling down the middle of Main Street.

Something was wrong with Quinn. She might be dying. He knew the drill. He'd gone through it with

Amalah. First in for a checkup. A simple Pap smear. Then another test. Then another. One day you're fine, just a little tired, and the next day you're fighting for your life.

If he thought he could find her, he'd drive down every street in Lubbock. He couldn't call her. She hadn't taken her phone. All he could do was wait.

Staten turned his truck toward her farm. If he was going to wait, it would be in her house. He wanted to at least be there when she got home, whether the news was good or bad.

On the way back to her place, he swore he almost felt the cold paddles over his chest as the electricity shocked his heart back alive.

The first beats hurt so much he didn't think he would survive. Like it or not. Healthy or dying. Quinn mattered to him.

Fifteen

Staten

Staten Kirkland sat in Quinn O'Grady's kitchen for an hour, making several calls to his men. Just because he wasn't there didn't mean that work would stop on the ranch, but his mind didn't seem to be fully in the game.

All he could think about was Quinn. Maybe while he waited at her place, she was getting the news she had cancer. She might be dying, and she'd find out all alone. He knew she'd take the news hard, but in her shy, quiet way she wouldn't let anyone know. They'd think she was handling it well. They wouldn't see that she was falling apart.

Finally, when he could think of no one else to pester, he walked to the barn and collected enough tools to put Quinn's door back on. Now that he had other things to worry about, he realized what a fool he'd been to storm her house. She'd lived out here for years by herself and never had an accident that he knew about. Plus, everyone in town knew Sheriff Brigman was still in love with his invisible wife. People would say things about how the sheriff was trapped. He loved his job, and he still loved a woman who didn't love him.

If Sheriff Brigman had looked out from the barn when Staten had kicked the door in, no telling what he would have thought. Yet, when they'd walked back together to their vehicles, he either hadn't noticed, or simply hadn't commented on the back door sitting beside its frame.

While Staten was worrying about the sheriff's eyesight, he might as well take some time and worry about why the sheriff thought he owed Quinn a favor.

Just as he finished repairing the door, Staten heard Quinn's pickup. If the thing rattled any louder, parts were bound to start falling off.

Sliding the tools behind one of the porch rockers, he waited as she pulled next to his truck.

"Well, hello, stranger," she said as she climbed out. "I wasn't expecting you this morning."

"I gave up waiting for you to call," he admitted.

"I'm sorry. I've had a lot on my mind these past few weeks, and I haven't been feeling very well." She reached the porch but stopped a few feet away as if unsure what to do. "Are you angry with me about not calling, Staten?"

He realized he was frowning, and his fists were knotted at his side. "No." He forced himself to breathe. "I was worried, though. Are you all right?"

She touched his shoulder. "I'm fine, Staten. Don't worry about me. After you left last month, I had some thinking to do. If Lloyd deBellome comes to Crossroads, I'll simply leave town for the night, or maybe I'll go to the fund-raiser and act like I don't remember him. That would crush his ego, and, with you as my date, he's not likely to say anything."

"You'd go with me?"

"I would." She laughed as if she thought he was kidding. "There is no one on this planet who worries about me as much as you do, but we've got to consider that maybe Lloyd stopping by here is for the best. It's time I stopped hiding from a memory. I'm turning over a new leaf. Might even give up some of the farm work and take up a new calling. Maybe remodel this old house. Once I enlarge the living room, I could probably teach piano lessons. I've always thought that would be fun, and Dan said his daughter would want to take lessons if I was interested."

He started frowning again. Something was definitely wrong. Quinn was rattling, and she'd never said so many words all at one time. Plus, she'd tossed the sheriff into the conversation as if they were friends.

It wasn't like her to stay inside, and she'd never once mentioned teaching anything before. Something was wrong, maybe not with Lloyd deBellome coming to town, but with Quinn. She was getting Staten off track talking about piano lessons and not farming. The real problem was obviously whatever had her going to the doctor. Maybe she'd learned she only had a few years to live. That might explain all these changes.

Staten had never run from a fight in his life, and he wouldn't run now. If she had cancer or some other disease, he'd help her through it. "Quinn, tell me what's wrong with you. How ill are you?"

To his surprise she laughed. "I'm not ill, I promise. In fact I'm very healthy. I just had a checkup this morning. I had all kinds of tests run, and there is not a thing wrong."

Her hand spread over his chest. "Can we talk later? I'm starving for food and for you. For the past few nights I've been having these dreams of you making love to me, and I wake up desperately wanting you. I've even thought of driving over to your place and pounding on the door. I'd politely ask if I could borrow your body for a while."

He covered her hand as it rested over his heart. "The door's not locked. Just come on in. You are always welcome."

"I might just do that one night."

He finally relaxed. This was a different Quinn than he had ever seen, but maybe that wasn't all bad. Staten had no idea when that happened to women. Maybe her hormones were out of whack. But he didn't really care. She was happy and saying she was healthy. He could stop worrying.

Leaning over, he kissed her cheek and whispered, "Let's eat in bed."

She tugged him inside and went straight to the refrigerator. While she made sandwiches, she munched on everything she pulled out of the crisper. He watched her, feeling a peace wash over him. Quinn wasn't ill, she wasn't dying. Their life would go on just as before. They were simply getting to know one another better. Feeling more comfortable around each other.

"We've never made love before dark, Quinn," he said as he played with her braid. "Are you sure about this?"

"I know we never have, but for some reason you look irresistible, and I don't want to wait until dark. Would you mind wasting a bit of daylight?"

"Not at all." He undid the first few buttons of her blouse while she took a bite of one of the sandwiches. In the daylight, he swore her breasts looked bigger.

She handed him two glasses of tea and picked up their plate. "Come on, you can undress me while I eat, and when you're finished I'll watch you strip."

"I'm not really very hungry for food."

"Neither am I," she said around a bite. "I want you, Staten."

She carried his sandwich and the few remaining crumbs of hers toward the bedroom. He'd expected her to move under the covers, his shy Quinn, but she didn't.

They made love with a wildness he'd never felt with her. This was a side of Quinn that he had never seen, but he'd gladly get used to. He loved watching her body as his hand moved over her. He'd never seen her in sunlight. Now, when he woke late at night and thought of her, his memories would no longer be in shadows. He took his time memorizing the look of her in daylight as he had learned the feel of her body in moonlight.

When the afternoon sun sparkled across them, she laughed, saying that they'd both be suntanned all over if they did this often.

"I wouldn't mind," he whispered as he kissed his way down her body.

When they both lay sweaty and nude atop her bed, she whispered, "Are you going to eat that other sandwich?"

He studied her, thinking she looked so beautiful with her hair all around her shoulders and her face flushed from passion. "I figured out why you went to the doctor. You've got a tapeworm."

"No, but close. I was planning to call you tonight

after I saw the doctor. I've suspected for most of the month, but I found out for sure today. Staten, I'm pregnant. Almost three months."

He took her words like a blow. All the air left his lungs, and he fought to keep from passing out. "What did you say?"

"I'm pregnant." She sat up and reached for his sandwich.

"How is that possible?" It wasn't registering. "Didn't you use protection?"

"Didn't you?" she answered.

He sat up, put his feet on the floor and tried reason. "I thought you couldn't have children. That first night I came over, I asked. You said not to worry."

"Apparently I was wrong. It took five years, but you proved me wrong. I am going to have a baby."

Change, he almost screamed. *I hate change.* "But I don't want…" He couldn't say the words. He didn't want complication in his life. He didn't want to start a family, not now, not at forty-three. He'd sworn he'd never marry again. He'd sworn he'd never love anyone again. She was messing it all up. From this moment on, everything would change. Her two words would finally be the blow that split his mind in half.

But he wouldn't say he didn't want a baby. He couldn't tell that big a lie.

A baby. Quinn's baby. His baby.

She stood and pulled on her jeans and top, watching him as if she'd found a stranger in her bed.

He just stared at her, feeling betrayed. She'd never had a child. She couldn't know how much it would hurt to lose one.

"Look, Staten, this is my baby. You don't have to

deal with it if you don't want to. I understand. You didn't ask for this. I can handle it alone. No one has to know it's yours."

Her words sounded rehearsed, as if she'd expected him to react this way when she told him.

"Are you sure it's mine?" he asked, remembering the sheriff who'd been on her property this morning.

Quinn slapped him so hard, his eyes watered, but he didn't move. He took the blow fully, barely feeling the pain.

"I think you'd better leave." Tears ran down her face, but she didn't cry out. "I'm going to the barn. When I get back, you'd better not be in my house, or I swear I'll shoot you in that hole you have for a heart."

Then, before he could take back what he'd said, she was gone.

Staten dressed and tried to piece things together in his mind. Quinn was pregnant, and, of course, it was his. If he'd had any doubt, the slap had knocked it out of him. Also, she obviously didn't want to talk to him anymore. Maybe he'd be wise to follow her orders and leave.

After all, she'd answered another question he'd worried about.

She was armed, and right now her primary target was him.

Sixteen

Yancy

Around four in the afternoon Yancy found Cap sunning in the office lobby like an old gray cat. Yancy touched the old guy's shoulder and asked if Cap would drive him the four blocks to the hardware store.

Several of the aging dwarves had cars, most of them rarely used, but Cap liked to drive, so his car looked as if it would start. Yancy had asked him to go with him a few times to pick up supplies and thought, for his age, Cap was a great driver.

"You can just borrow my car, Yancy," Cap said as he tried to snuggle back into his dreams. "With the promise of rain, I wasn't planning on going anywhere."

Yancy tried to think of an answer. He wasn't about to tell Cap that he didn't have a license, and if he didn't go today, Miss Bees and Mrs. Ollie would just be in again tomorrow with their list of repairs in hand. "Cap, I think I can get everything I need, but I might want a little help picking out a new smoke detector for Miss Bees. You know how particular she is."

Cap sat up, mumbling something while he scratched his goatee. "There ain't nothing wrong with the one she has. I put it in three years ago. A couple of young guys from the fire department came around to check all the batteries before Christmas."

He got up out of his favorite chair in the sunny room and shuffled to the door. He put on his jacket without stopping talking. "You ask me, she hides in her little hallway, where there's no windows, just in case someone's spying on her. Then, she holes up like a criminal and smokes half a pack at a time." He grabbed his blue hat that had *Cap* stitched across the top. "I'll go with you, son. She shouldn't have any complaints when the retired captain of the volunteer fire department picks it out." He always straightened a bit when he reminded anyone of his title.

Yancy grinned. Cap liked nothing more than being on a mission. A few minutes later they backed his boat of a car out of the line of carports built beyond the north fence of the property. It was little more than a lean-to, offering no protection from the wind or cold, but it kept snow off the vehicles in winter.

Cap shook his head. "Miss Abernathy is gone for her weekly trip to the cemetery. She'll get my spot when she comes back, and I'll be on the end again. Last time that happened tumbleweeds about scratched the paint off my whole left side."

Yancy leaned back in the plush seat of what had once been a fine car. As far as he could tell the thirty-year-old Chevy looked pretty much the same all over, so he changed the subject. "Who does Miss Abernathy visit at the cemetery?"

"I have no idea. Near as I know, she came here alone

in the early '60s. I asked her once why she never married. She was a fine-looking woman in her day. Always wore four-inch heels and her hair on top of her head, real proper. When she played concerts at PTA, she'd push out that ample chest and keep her nose in the air like she was playing for the gods and not just us mortals." He snorted. "Always reminded me of a turkey."

Yancy knew if he didn't remind Cap of the question, the old man would go on down first one path, then another. "What'd she say about never getting married?"

"She said she was wed to her music. She was a good teacher, but so was I, and I never thought for a minute that I was married to math." Cap smiled as if seeing something that wasn't there. "I was married to my wife for thirty-two years. When she passed, I filled my time volunteering and teaching. Since the day of her funeral I've never gone back to the cemetery." He looked up with tears in his eyes. "She ain't there. She's gone on to wait for me. I've enjoyed my life, but it'll be a grand day when I walk up to her."

He laughed. "I'm betting she'll act all mad at first 'cause I kept her waiting, then she'll say 'Where have you been, darlin'?'"

Yancy didn't say anything, but he felt it again. The strange sensation that all the people of the Evening Shadows Retirement Community had lived rich, full lives, while Yancy had simply been existing. They had their stories, their children, their secrets. The only stories he had weren't worth the breath it would take to tell them. He couldn't think of a relative he'd claim, and his secrets would stay buried as long as he kept practicing being normal just like everyone else. It was getting easier every day.

A few minutes later they picked out the smoke alarm from the two choices at the hardware store.

Cap stopped to visit with someone he knew on aisle three, and Yancy went in search of nails. He was always running out of screws, nails and duct tape, maybe because he figured that half the things needing fixing around the place only really needed one of the three.

At aisle seven, he began searching for just the right size of nails. Since he planned to put everything on the account, he thought he'd pick up hooks also. With his head down, he heard two men talking as they neared. A drifting conversation not meant for him. At first, he didn't listen. The voices were no more than background noise. But, as they grew closer, he stilled, and that constant tension he had lived with for five years in prison moved over him.

Fear, alarm, a longing to vanish. He recognized the voices, and panic warmed his blood.

"Look, Cowboy, I see your point, but this isn't the place to set up camp. One, it's too small a town. Someone's bound to notice us, and two, I'm not sure I can get all we need."

The second voice was hoarse, as if from a man who'd spent years yelling or smoking. "It's perfect. Less people around, less chance of anyone knowing us. Arlo's got a job at the Collins ranch, and we've got a great spot to stash our load. A month, maybe two, and we'll have taken enough for a real start."

Two men walked past Yancy. He never looked up. Chances were good they wouldn't recognize him, but if they did, he'd be the one in trouble.

He grabbed a few packages of nails and followed, watching them from a distance. The one called Cowboy had been the leader of a gang in prison when Yancy had first arrived. His name was Zane, but no one but a fool with a death wish would call him that. Cons had called him Insane Zane behind his back. He'd taken care of the stock for the prison's annual rodeo. Twice, before Cowboy got transferred, cons had been involved in accidents in the barn. One man had died, supposedly trampled, and another had been paralyzed after falling from his horse. Both had been listed as accidents, but word got around that they weren't.

The other man, shorter and bald, had tried to take Cowboy's place after Cowboy was released, but he hadn't been strong enough to manage the rough cowhands who worked with the prison stock. Yancy couldn't remember the details, but he heard something about Freddie, the bald guy, being in a fight and spending time in solitary. Freddie had the nervous habit of hitting people who got close.

Yancy had hated and feared them both. He didn't want to be in the same state with either, and now they were both in Crossroads.

"You find the nails?"

Yancy staggered, preparing to run, before he recognized Cap's dry tone. When he turned, the old guy was concentrating on a display, giving Yancy a second to force calm into a body intent on flight.

"Yeah, I found what I needed." Yancy rattled the box of nails. "Thanks for picking out the fire alarm. Now Miss Bees can yell at you when it goes off."

Cap shrugged. "That don't bother me. I'm hard of hearing."

They moved toward the checkout as the two men Yancy had been watching headed through the main door. Cowboy hadn't aged well in the past five years, but he was still good-looking in a rough kind of way, but Freddie was more like the perfect poster child for the death penalty. He had scars across his nose, a permanent sneer on fat lips and one eye that never cooperated with the other.

"You know those two, Cap?" Yancy still hadn't seen their faces close up, but the build and the walk were the same. He had heard both their voices in his nightmares that first year in jail. He wasn't likely to forget what they sounded like.

Cap shook his head. "Nope. The tall one, with the worn Stetson, looks like he works on one of the ranches. I heard somewhere that a couple of the outfits are already hiring for spring. Are they friends of yours?"

Yancy shook his head, almost saying that he had no friends. No one from prison. No one from back home. If he died today, Miss Bees, who didn't even like him, would probably be the only one visiting his grave.

As Cap always did, he wanted to stop at the café on the way home as if their journey had been a long one and not simply four blocks.

Even though Dorothy's place was just across the street from where he lived, Cap turned into the café lot and parked out front. The old sign had once said Dorothy's Fine Dining, then it had been painted over to read Dorothy's Café. Only as the second paint job faded, the old sign came back like a shadow that didn't match.

Yancy waved at Sissy as they stepped inside the warm café. She smiled at him while Cap slid into one side of the nearest booth and he took the other.

The place always smelled of cinnamon, and Yancy loved taking the time to breathe in the aroma. Though the drizzle had mostly stopped, the day was spotty with fog, and the sweet-smelling air was heaven.

"Afternoon." Sissy waddled over. "You guys looking for breakfast, lunch or dinner?"

Yancy calculated the cost of each in his head. By getting Sunday lunches free, he had extra money for a few meals on weekdays, so lunch sounded good, but the breakfasts were a few dollars cheaper.

"I'll have pancakes," he said.

Sissy didn't ask more. She knew he always wanted buttermilk pancakes with raisins and pecans on top, and he knew if there was any bacon left, she'd toss it on the plate at no extra charge.

Cap ordered coffee and soup. "Whatever kind you got warming on the back burner." He winked.

"We got potato soup today." She turned her head and grinned as a woman in a blue cape blew in. "Come to see me, Ellie?"

The almost-nurse shook her head. "I've come to see Cap. I was passing and I saw his car." She leaned over the table and kissed the old man's cheek. "How's my favorite uncle today?"

Cap shooed her hug away. "Yancy, this is my pesky niece. I'm sure you've seen her across the street. Comes by to poke on us all every other week. She makes the wellness rounds for the clinic."

Ellie didn't look at Yancy. Which was good because he had nothing to say to her. He thought of asking if he could have the hug she'd tried to give her uncle. Something told him she'd probably karate chop his windpipe closed or give him brain damage from that bag she carried slamming against his head. Ellie was no small girl; a blow from her would probably hurt.

"Sit down and have a visit." Cap pointed to the side of the booth where Yancy sat.

She hesitated, then perched on the edge of his booth. "Uncle, did you drive that car of yours? You know you're not supposed to drive until you've had your eyes checked."

"My eyes are fine," Cap said. "Stop worrying. Yancy drove us around today."

Finally, the young woman turned and stared at Yancy with her cold green eyes. She had to be younger than him and she was definitely several inches shorter, but he swore the woman looked down at him. "Is my uncle telling the truth?"

Yancy was trapped. No matter what he said, someone at the table would be mad at him.

"No," he finally answered.

She bounced up. "I knew it." One finger pointed at her uncle. "I'm going to go wash my hands, and, when I get back, we'll have a serious talk about you taking care of yourself, Uncle Cap."

She was gone in a whirl of blue wool. The swinging door that led to the restrooms flapped so hard it hit both walls.

"Why didn't you lie for me, son?" Cap sounded more curious than angry.

Yancy grinned. "I'm more afraid of her than you."

Cap laughed. "Me, too. I'll go tell Sissy to turn in Ellie's lunch order. She'll know what week it is."

"What week?"

Cap slowly pushed himself out of the booth. "One week she's on a diet, and the next week she's recovering from it. She's a sweet girl, my Ellie, but she's bossy like her mother. Wants everyone to follow the rules." Cap's head kept shaking as he shuffled off toward the counter.

Yancy looked out the window wondering if he should "follow the rules" and tell the sheriff about the two ex-cons he'd seen, but if he did, he'd have to admit to how he knew them. Yancy had seen the sheriff's car drive by but hadn't spoken to the lawman. He'd like to keep it that way for as long as possible. Something told him that once it got out that his last address was prison, not many people would want him around.

"Scoot over," a voice said from beside Yancy as Ellie slid into his side of the booth.

"I was here first." He meant to say it with conviction, but her leg was pushing against his from hip to knee, and his tongue lost traction.

"Do you mind if I join you and my uncle?" she asked as if she couldn't care less whether he did or not.

"No, Ellie, I don't mind. I'm glad you're watching over your uncle. He's a good old guy."

She seemed to relax a little, but the booth was small and her leg remained next to his. "Thanks for not lying for him. You're right, Uncle Cap is a great man, but he doesn't take care of himself. The whole family worries about him."

Yancy felt light-headed. He hadn't been next to any female near his age in years, and here she was touching him. Even if it was through layers of clothing, he swore she felt soft. "I'll watch out for him," he managed to say.

"Thanks." She didn't look his way.

He wanted to keep the conversation going. "You smell good."

Now she looked at him and frowned. Obviously he'd stepped over some invisible line. Then she held up her hands. "It's that soap in the bathroom. Lemon coco-nut, I think."

He blushed and was glad to see she did, too.

He wanted to say that she smelled good all over and then ask, would she mind much if he lowered his hand to her leg and felt the length of just the one resting against his. After all, they were already touching. What did it matter if it was his leg touching or his hand? But he doubted he'd get a sentence out before she drop-kicked him through the open pass-through between the café and the kitchen.

So, he just sat next to her, touching from hip to knee, as he ate his pancakes and listened to her lecture Cap about taking better care of himself.

Yancy lowered his head when the two men from the hardware store came in. Cowboy and Freddie. There was no doubt.

He saw their profiles clearly this time. They were the cons he'd crossed a few times the first year he was in prison. They were both meaner than wild hogs, but Cowboy could fool people because he had an easy smile and a laid-back way of moving that hid his ruthless ways. Cowboy's hair might be longer, but Yancy knew exactly who he was.

"Morning, little lady," Cowboy said to Sissy. "All right if we have a seat at your counter?"

"Of course. I'll take your order in a minute."

Sissy wasn't rude, but she wasn't as friendly as she'd been to Yancy. That made him feel proud. Maybe he no longer looked like a con. Maybe he just looked like a regular guy.

Yancy watched them fold onto the counter stools. They had their backs to him, but he could tell by the way Freddie looked around that he was casing the café. Before he left, the con would know where the money was kept. The real money, not just what they kept in the cash drawer for change. Yancy knew the tricks. All Freddie would have to do was pay with a hundred, then watch across the pass-through as Sissy rushed into the kitchen and pulled a bank bag from somewhere.

Yancy had no proof, but he knew this place was on their list of places to rob in Crossroads. He didn't miss the fact that both their heads turned when Sissy rang up a bill. They would come in fast and hard when they robbed the café. They'd be armed and probably use more force than was necessary. The fact that Sissy was small and pregnant wouldn't slow them down.

He also knew neither of the men had spotted him. Too many years maybe. He'd been nobody, just one more kid in prison for robbery. They'd both always been surrounded by their gangs. He was nothing to them, but for a time they'd been his greatest fear.

When he and Cap left the café, Yancy walked back while Cap drove across to the parking lot. Ellie had left with them, but she hadn't bothered to say goodbye to Yancy even though they'd touched legs for half an hour.

The air was cooler, but Yancy didn't feel it. He'd taken to wearing his flannel shirt over his thermal underwear. It was almost as good as a jacket. Only today he had far more to worry about than the weather.

Somehow he had to keep an eye on Cowboy and Freddie while staying out of their way. A few months ago he wouldn't have cared what they did, but now the old folks were his friends and the idea that someone might hurt Sissy made him sick to his stomach.

He decided if he saw them do one thing wrong, he

was going to the sheriff, even if it meant his secret got out. One fact he remembered about every encounter Cowboy had with anyone on the yard; he was meaner than he had to be. Hitting, hurting, maybe even killing. If a bystander got in the way, that wasn't Cowboy's problem. Freddie tended to move in fast and leave anyone bleeding who got too close to him.

The rest of the afternoon Yancy worked on the gutters, keeping watch like a lone sentinel at the palace gate.

Ellie kept circling in his mind, even though he did his best to keep focused. He liked the way she smelled and how she'd felt against him. Something was obviously wrong with him. He was probably some kind of pervert. He could still feel her warm, soft thigh resting against his. A man could lose sleep on just that one thought.

As he worked, he watched the traffic moving through town. Most were people simply passing by, but he was learning the locals one story at a time. When he went in for a cup of coffee, the folks in the sunroom were talking about the ranches around and pointing as their trucks passed by.

The Collins ranch had silver trucks and pickups. "Think they're uppity," Mrs. Ollie said without missing a stitch. "Old Adam Collins, Davis's father and Reid's grandfather, was like that, too. Always wore an expensive Western hat but never had any manure on his boots. I swear Davis buried the old man in thirty-year-old boots that had never touched dirt."

Mrs. Kirkland pressed her lips together so hard they disappeared, but didn't comment. If she had stories about the men who had been her next door neighbors, as ranches go, she wasn't saying.

"Looks like the plumber got a new truck," Leo added as if anyone cared.

They moved on to a conversation about students who'd grown up, and Yancy went back to watching the traffic as he worked.

The Kirkland ranch trucks weren't as fancy as the Collins ranch vehicles, but every one Kirkland owned had two K's on the driver's door. They were back-to-back mirror images. Double K's. Yancy thought they kind of looked like stars or maybe a real stiff spider. Maybe, if he ever met Kirkland, he'd ask him what the K's looked like to the man who owned the ranch.

Twice, Yancy thought he saw a suspicious one-ton truck go down the street. No markings and whatever logo had been on the driver's side looked to have been spray-painted over. The guy driving wore a cowboy hat low on his forehead. Yancy couldn't see his face for the shadows, but it could have been Cowboy. Whatever they were doing in town was keeping them busy.

He shook off the nervous feeling. Maybe he was wrong. After all, he hadn't gotten a real good look at the two men except for a moment, and it had been almost five years since he'd seen them. What were the odds that three men from an Oklahoma prison could end up in a small town in Texas? And if they were here, it was no business of his.

Yet that night Yancy couldn't sleep. About midnight he put on the long, black wool coat Mr. Halls had given him and went outside.

The town was asleep, and the air so still he heard his own breath going in and out. Crossing over the road, where the night's shadows were deeper, he walked with no particular destination in mind. He moved past the high school and tried to remember one good thing that had happened when he spent time in classes at any one of the dozen schools he had attended.

His mom had moved around, living first with one relative, then another. She'd start a new job and he'd think they'd be fine, then she'd begin drinking, and before he knew it, they'd be moving again. When she finally ran out of relatives, they'd lived in hotel rooms and dumps with men she always wanted him to call uncle.

By the time he was fourteen he was staying out all night. She never noticed. Never asked about school. Never offered him lunch money.

One night he just didn't come home. After that he never went back to school. He didn't care what happened to her any more than she probably cared where he was. He ran the streets with other kids no one wanted. For a few years, he felt wild and free. Then he was caught stealing. Once trouble found him, it never let go for long. Serving time became the norm between vacations of freedom.

As he walked past what Cap had pointed out as the Gypsy House, Yancy heard the eerie sound of branches scratching against the roof. He stood perfectly still and stared. The air was calm, but he swore he heard the branches clawing over the top of the house.

The house seemed out of place along the two-lane road. It was still within sight of town, but no longer a part of it. Years of weathering had turned the outside to the color of dirt, but the way the windows sagged left dark holes just like blind eyes watching him from the crumbling home.

Crossing the road, he walked through the twisted

trees to the remains of the homestead everyone called the Gypsy House. Nothing moved. He heard no sound to indicate that anyone, or anything, had caused the sound, yet he swore he'd heard branches scraping. As he stood close he heard the whirl of the night air circling through the rooms from one broken window to holes in the roof. For a moment he swore the house was breathing.

It crossed his mind that the house was luring him closer, and he couldn't help but wonder if it had done the same to the kids who got hurt there. Maybe the house hadn't wanted them.

Maybe it wouldn't want him if he stepped any closer. Maybe it would. Folks called it the Gypsy House, and one of the old-timers had asked if he had Gypsy blood. Maybe he did. Maybe the place was calling him home.

His mother used to tell him, when he was growing up, about a town called Crossroads where she had to live with a crazy old grandmother one summer.

He'd always thought she made the story up, but now, staring at the house, he wondered if this could have been the very house his mother feared.

Turning, he hurried away. The wind was whipping up, and he needed to head back. He had a full day of work to do tomorrow. He needed sleep.

As he crossed the road, he swore he heard the sound of branches move over ancient tiles on a roof, rotten and caving. The pull to go back and look closer was strong, but Yancy forced his steps to put distance between him and the old house. Ghosts and hauntings were for children. He was a man of twenty-five. He would not give in to fear.

"I'll come back," he whispered. "It's nothing but an

old house. There are a lot worse things to fear that are real. I'll come back and prove it one day," he swore, and he knew he would.

Seventeen

Staten

Staten Kirkland didn't remember much about driving back from Quinn's farm. He must have gone a hundred through town. There didn't seem enough air in Texas to breathe until the cliffs of Ransom Canyon rose before him, and he knew he was almost home. His always-pessimistic thoughts were piling up in his brain.

She wasn't a young girl barely out of her teens as Amalah had been. What if Quinn died during delivery or lost the baby? Hell, even with a healthy baby they'd be living on Social Security before the kid could graduate from college.

But no matter how the worries stacked up, a tiny part of him knew that he wanted to be involved in his child's life. He wanted this baby. He felt as if he'd just awakened on Christmas morning and been given a gift he didn't know to even ask for. A wonderful gift that came with a bucket-load of worry and a ton of excitement.

Quinn would be a good mother, no doubt about that, only Staten had no idea what kind of father he might be. He was no longer in his twenties. He had hardened so much, he might not have enough love to spread out over all the growing-up years.

Might not be an option anyway. He may have slammed the door on any chance he had by asking if she was sure it was his kid. Staten swore for a few miles. He should write a manual of the dumbest thing to say when a woman tells you she's pregnant. Apparently, he was a natural-born expert.

Think. You've got to straighten this out. All he had to do was talk Quinn into speaking to him again. Right about now the mother of his future child was probably plotting to murder him.

What had she said? *This is my baby. I'll take care of it. People don't even have to know it's yours.*

Damn, he didn't care if the whole country knew it was his. It *was* his. In six months he'd be a father again, and damn it, he planned to do it right.

Hell, he thought, *I have six months to stop saying damn and hell.* Women didn't think much of a man who cussed around newborns. Which made no sense. They didn't understand a word you were saying anyway.

Eighteen

Quinn

Quinn walked the rows of plowed earth surrounding her house. The lingering smells of lavender and the warm rich dirt blended. She was home. This land. This place. She'd grown up here. Her child would grow up here.

She hadn't had time to think about how Staten would react to her news. Part of her didn't believe it was possible until a few hours ago. Her periods had never been regular. The few other times she'd been late, she'd simply waited, but this time was different. When she'd missed her cycle, Quinn had hoped that she could dream it might be true if only for a short while.

For once she'd wanted to be selfish and keep it to herself. Over the years she'd watched her friends who were pregnant. She wanted the private kind of joy of knowing every moment of every day that you carried life inside you.

Staten had never mentioned love or a future between them. If he'd wanted more than what they had, surely he'd have voiced one thought about it. But the way he'd acted, all angry and sharp, hurt her. It was like she was trying to force him into something.

Quinn smiled through her tears. She wanted this baby, her baby. If Staten didn't want to be part of that, it didn't change anything.

Staten

Staten felt as if his brain might explode. Too much joy, too much sorrow in this life. He handled it the only way he knew how. He moved all feelings aside and tried to concentrate on work. That was the way his grandfather had taught him, and he'd practiced it religiously. Tonight he'd think of the right thing to say to Quinn, but right now he had problems he had to deal with.

When he crossed the cattle guard onto the Double K, he decided to take the county road. The land would relax him, help him get all the details of his life in order.

The bull that someone had run into last night would be gone, but, who knew, the guy who had hit his prize stock might have returned to the scene of the crime. Maybe it wasn't rustlers. It could have been a drunk on the wrong road. Maybe the drunk hadn't realized what he hit. If he just drove off, he might try to retrace his path.

Staten's men would have hauled off the bull, but maybe somewhere there would be a clue. Besides, Staten decided, he was in no shape to carry on a conversation with anyone, so going into headquarters didn't sound like a good idea.

For the second time in his life he was about to be a fa-

ther, and right now, if he told anyone, Quinn would probably be even more angry than she already was at him.

This wasn't something that she could keep secret
long. He didn't care who knew, but there were a few
people he needed to talk to before word got out. His
granny, for one.

Two miles up the county road, he spied the sheriff's
cruiser parked up on the hill half a mile away.

Staten pulled his truck alongside Sheriff Brigman
and leaned out the window. "Can I help you, Sheriff,
or are you just out for a stroll?"

"I thought I'd see if I could spot anything strange.
Right now a dead bull is the only clue we've got to your
destruction of property claim."

Pulling his truck off the road, Staten joined the sheriff. He almost argued that a dead bull was a hell of a lot
more than just destruction of property. Every man on his
ranch carried a rifle or handgun in his truck. If they'd
seen whoever hit the bull racing away from the crime
scene, shots would have been fired. To the man, they
all rode for the brand and would protect his property.

"What are we looking for exactly?" Staten asked.
He wasn't in the mood to act normal, but maybe trying would calm him down. Part of him wanted to turn
around and race back to Quinn, but reason told him he
needed to get over wanting to murder the driver first.

"Tire marks," the sheriff said, breaking into Stat-
en's worries. "Maybe something that blew out of the
bed of the truck. Broken glass. There had to be damage
done to whatever, or whoever, hit him. To hit a bull hard
enough to kill him, the front of any car or pickup would
be smashed to pieces. I've seen what a deer can do. A

bull must have done a great deal more." Brigman glanced over at Staten. "Did you ever lose a cow like this before?"

"First, I didn't lose a cow, it was a prize bull. And second, of course I've lost both cows and bulls, even calves. The boys and I are guessing we've taken a hit on half a dozen since fall, all to rustlers. That's over twice what we lost by this time last year."

"Would they show up at the sale barns? The brand inspector is surely watching for them."

Staten shook his head. "Most end up in the freezer by morning. Once they're slaughtered, they're gone. Now and then a small-time farmer will steal a few head and mix them in with his own. They breed with his herd, and as long as he doesn't sell them, chances of someone spotting a brand is slight."

An old pickup rattled down the road toward them. Staten knew from the sound that it belonged to Reyes, the head wrangler on the next ranch. He'd seen Lucas drive it around town and into headquarters last month to pick up his pay. Funny how the boy had been nearby and on the ranch for a while, but kind of off Staten's radar until the night the kids got hurt at that old house near town. Ever since, he'd made a point to talk to the tall, lean Reyes boy every time he saw him.

Sheriff Brigman moved closer to Staten. "I asked one of your men to have Lucas Reyes drive his truck over here. You said once that he comes on your land, so he's my most likely cattle-killer. Correction, bull-killer."

Staten frowned. "Lucas didn't do it." He'd watched the kid work stock. He knew too much to barrel across open range at night. His father had worked for the Collins operation for years. Lucas was raised on a ranch, and, legal or not, like most farm and ranch kids, he'd probably been driving since his feet could reach the gas pedal.

Quinn crossed Staten's mind. In about six months she'd have a son or daughter. Whichever didn't matter, but Staten wanted the baby to feel born to the land the way he always felt. He wanted his offspring to grow up on Kirkland ground.

He almost laughed aloud. Not much chance of that happening with Quinn not speaking to him.

Lucas pulled up, jumped from his truck and headed right to Staten. "You need me out here, sir? I was planning on finishing that fence in the west pasture before dark."

Staten didn't like the idea of Lucas thinking he had any part of this interrogation Brigman was about to launch into. He liked Lucas. There was a real intelligence in his eyes, and he didn't back away from hard work. "The sheriff is asking me questions, and I thought you might lend a hand. I told him you like to come out in this back pasture after dark. We were hoping you might have seen something if you were here last night."

"I haven't been out here for a few nights, Mr. Kirkland. If I ever did see something, you'd be the first to know."

The boy was still looking directly at his boss, not the sheriff.

Brigman moved closer. "Exactly what night were you last here, Lucas? Two, three, four."

"It was Saturday night, Sheriff Brigman."

"Before or after you visited Tim O'Grady?"

Staten didn't miss Lucas's surprise, but he didn't hesitate. "After."

"Did you see anything out of the ordinary?" The

sheriff moved between Staten and the kid. "Like someone who shouldn't have been on this land."

"No, sir."

"Were you alone?" Brigman snapped.

For a blink the kid glanced his direction, and Staten saw the boy panic, then Lucas straightened his shoulders as if preparing to take a blow straight on.

"Yes, sir," he said. "I always come out here alone. With five brothers and sisters, I like the silence of this back pasture, and Mr. Kirkland doesn't mind that I walk across this corner of his land."

Staten had never considered himself a mind reader, but he understood his men. He knew the cloth they were made from. Lucas was a hard worker. The other men liked him. Staten had seen them kid him about still being wet behind the ears one minute, then turn around to help him the next. He'd also seen Lucas help others, even working overtime to make sure they got their job done.

Staten would bet his ranch on two facts. First, Lucas Reyes hadn't killed the bull. Surely, even the sheriff could see that there wasn't a dent in Reyes's truck. And the second fact he knew beyond any doubt was that Lucas Reyes had just lied to a county sheriff.

Since the sheriff looked as though he had more questions and Staten figured the discussion was over, he slapped his hand on Lucas's shoulder and said, "Walk with us. We're looking for any clue that would tell us who could have plowed into my bull."

"Yes, sir." Lucas joined Staten on the other side of the road from where the sheriff walked. "What exactly are we looking for?"

"Glass, a fender, anything. Rain's coming in tonight. If we don't look now, a clue might be washed away."

Lucas smiled. "Whoever it was must have been going fast or was a complete idiot. Probably drunk or on drugs if he missed a bull."

"I agree," Staten said. "You wouldn't happen to know anyone who fits the description?"

"No, sir." Lucas hesitated then added, "It could be someone wanting to test how fast a car would go. Everyone knows these back roads aren't likely to have radar on them."

"Good point." The sheriff kicked at dirt as if he thought he might dig up something. "Could have been kids. They steal a car, go for a joyride."

Lucas glanced at Brigman. "You have any stolen cars turned in?"

"No. If it was just joyriders, we would have found the wrecked car. They always leave it somewhere along the side of the road once it runs out of gas."

"That leaves someone testing out a new car," Staten said to himself, thinking he knew of one person who'd gotten a car early last week for his birthday. Reid Collins. Only, Staten wasn't going to suggest anything to the sheriff. Brigman would have to figure that out on his own, and he would. After all, he and half the county had been at the kid's birthday party.

Staten saw something shiny and knelt. Broken glass. Could be a headlight, but it was small, only a sliver.

Brigman joined him. "Looks like they missed this piece. See the markings in the dirt. Someone swept the ground here. Probably cleaning up the wreck. A drunk wouldn't do that."

"Blood," Lucas yelled from ten feet in front of them. "Leading off that way."

Staten walked the blood trail. What happened was obvious. The vehicle had hit the bull where they found the glass. The bull had managed to wander off, bleeding for another hundred yards, before it died.

Brigman got a call and rushed toward his cruiser. "I got to take this," he yelled.

Staring straight at the kid, Staten said, "I don't think you had anything to do with this, Lucas, but I need to ask. Were you here last night?"

"No, sir." Lucas met his stare.

"Then tell me why you lied to the sheriff about being alone out here a few nights ago." Before Lucas could think about his answer, Staten added, "I don't plan on telling anyone, but this is my land, and I need the truth from my men. The whole truth."

Lucas took a slow breath and met Staten's gaze once more. "I couldn't tell the sheriff I wasn't alone the last time I was in this pasture. I was with his daughter." He didn't look away when he added, "We weren't doing anything, sir. I just wanted to show her my favorite place to watch the stars."

Staten nodded. "You were wrong to lie, but I guess I might have done the same if I was facing my girlfriend's father and he was armed."

Lucas grinned. "She's not my girlfriend. At least not yet. We're just friends."

Staten turned back to the road. The sheriff shouted that he had to get to town.

As they watched the cruiser pull away, Staten issued a low order, "Take care of the west fence before dark."

"I will, sir, and thanks."

"For what? I'm a man of my word, Lucas. You be that, too."

"I plan to be."

Staten could almost see the future. This kid was going to make something of himself. "I've got more than twenty years on you, son, but let's shake on something. We'll never lie to each other. Between you and me, it'll always be nothing but truth."

"Deal." Lucas offered his hand.

"Deal." Staten shook on it. "Now get to work."

As the kid ran off toward his old pickup, Staten remembered how he used to say that Quinn and he were just friends. They'd gone far beyond that now, and he'd better find a way to mend a few fences, too, or this stubborn bull of a man would be walking his own blood trail alone until death took him.

Nineteen

Quinn

Quinn stared in the mirror, looking for any signs that she was pregnant. Her breasts were a bit bigger and her tummy slightly rounded. With her height and slim build she could probably carry a child unseen into the fifth or even sixth month.

She could handle three months of listening to folks ask questions. The answers were simple. Of course, the baby was hers. Yes, she knew who the father was, but that wasn't anyone's business. She planned to raise the child alone right here on her farm.

In the days waiting for Staten to call, she'd figured out a few things during the silence. She might be shy and like keeping to herself, but she was strong. She could do this. She could have the baby and raise it herself.

She'd thought of making up a story about how she'd had an old boyfriend show up for a few days, and she'd thought they might rekindle their love. But, she'd realized that they weren't meant to be together. He'd already gone his own way, she'd say. He wouldn't be interested in a baby, but she was.

Quinn laughed. No one would believe such a ridiculous story.

She never had an old love, and, with her luck, the kid would look exactly like Staten.

Maybe she should leave for six months or so and come back with a ring and a kid. But there would be people who would do the math and realize she'd been pregnant when she left. Also, it was time to plant. She couldn't leave the farm now.

This was the twenty-first century, not a hundred years ago. No one cared where the father was, and everyone who loved her would love the baby. She wasn't rich, but they'd never go hungry.

Just as she finished dressing, someone pounded on her door. Quinn didn't hurry. She knew who it was. The only surprise was that he'd taken two weeks to come back.

Walking through the house she saw Staten standing just beyond the screen door. Quinn found herself slowing so she could take him in for a moment longer. He was big, well-built, powerful-looking. His face was as cloudy as the storm rolling across the sky behind him, but even now she thought him the handsomest man she'd ever met.

When she reached the door, she didn't open the screen or invite him in. "If you've come to tell me to abort, you're wasting your time. No matter what the argument, I wouldn't."

He braced the sides of the door frame as if it were strong enough to keep him out. "You know I wouldn't do that, Quinn."

She did know. She knew him better than anyone alive. "Then why are you here, Staten?" Quinn needed to hear the words.

"I want to be in your life." He paused as if he thought one sentence might work. When it didn't, he continued, "I miss you. I need to help you with this baby or at least be around if you need me."

She still didn't move.

"I can't handle the thought of losing you." He pushed away from the door, walked a few feet, swore, and came back. "I don't know the words to say. I can't sleep. I can't eat. I'll be dead in a week if you don't let me come in."

He looked so sad, she unlatched the screen.

He stepped one foot inside and waited, his hat in his big hands.

Quinn remained close. She wasn't afraid of him, she never had been. "I know what you're saying, Staten, but you hurt me too badly."

"It was the shock of it all." He took a deep breath. "I hate not talking to you. You're the only friend I have, Quinn."

She smiled. "I've no doubt. Folks say you're hard as rock. Leaves me wondering if you'll be any good for a baby."

"I'll try. Truth is, I don't know much about babies. Amalah's mom moved in when Randall was born, and Granny drove over to help out almost every morning. Between working hard to get the place going and trying to stay out of my mother-in-law's way, I don't remember much from birth to the day he could talk."

He met her gaze. "I'd try harder if I had another chance. I swear I would."

Quinn shook her head. "I don't want to hurt you, Staten, but I need time to think. We're not two kids. I didn't plan this, but now it's here I want to experience every minute. I don't want to make a decision that I'll end up regretting."

He gave one jerk of a nod. "I understand. Do you want to know what I want?"

"No," she said softly. "Not yet, maybe not ever." She guessed he'd suggest marriage and her moving over to the ranch. She wouldn't fit in his world, and he'd never fit in this place. Or, he might not suggest they marry, and somehow that would be sad. He'd never said he loved her, but she knew she mattered to him. Maybe that's how it would be with the baby, too. He'd come see their child. The kid would matter to him, but there would be no love involved, just a duty to take care of his responsibility.

Kirkland men tended to marry outgoing women. For a hundred years, Kirkland women had taken leading roles in running the town and socials. The library was named after his great-grandmother. Kirkland money kept the museum going. His grandmother had run the chamber of commerce for years. Even Amalah had chaired several charities before she became ill.

Quinn wasn't the wife for Staten, and she never wanted his sense of duty to force them both into something they couldn't live with.

"Can we talk?" Staten carefully set his hat on the back of the nearest kitchen chair as if testing the waters. "Not about the baby, but just talk. I've missed you."

"Me, too." She hadn't really realized how much until she'd seen him standing at the door.

"We could go into town for breakfast. I could buy

you a cup of coffee if you've already eaten. It looks like rain, so we won't get much done today anyway." His low voice rumbled, echoing the distant thunder.

She thought of all the times he'd offered to take her out and she'd said no, but somehow, this time it seemed right. "If I go, will you promise we won't talk about the baby?"

"If that's what you want. You have my word."

She lifted her jacket from the hook by the door and walked out of her house without bothering to lock up.

He followed her to his truck and opened the passenger side for her. "Need any help?"

She swung up. "No, thanks."

They drove toward town talking of the weather. Both lived by the seasons. It was the last thing they checked at night and the first thing they checked in the morning.

When he passed the high school, he recalled a few things that had happened when they were in school. Amalah and Staten had been seriously dating by the time they were all three juniors. Quinn swore she'd heard every detail of every date her best friend had with Staten.

"Remember the time Amalah fell when all the cheerleaders were building a pyramid? I think it was the last football game of the season."

Quinn grinned. "I was in the band. It was halftime, and we were playing the school song when I saw her tumble. I stopped playing and ran out of line, but I couldn't get to her."

"I was huddled up listening to the coach when I heard someone scream and turned to see her falling. I thought my heart would stop when she didn't get up. I wanted to pick her up and make sure she was all right, but she had a crowd around her."

"After the game she laughed at us both for overreacting." Quinn smiled. That was one of the few times she'd felt sorry for Staten because she knew exactly the fear he'd felt. In an odd way they shared Amalah. Over the years her loss was something they also shared.

He covered Quinn's hand with his. "She loved us both, you know."

"I know. She had shone so bright during those years. I always felt like a shadow next to her. I was never jealous, you know. I wouldn't have wanted her life, and I'm guessing she wouldn't have wanted mine."

To her surprise he shook his head. "No, Quinn, you're wrong. You had talent. Real talent. Amalah once told me she wished she could play like you, and she was green when you got to go to New York to study. Miss Abernathy used to brag on you all the time. She'd say you were the brightest, shining star to ever grow up around here. Amalah was proud to be your friend, but I think she would have traded if she could have."

"Sure. Some star." Quinn shrugged.

"You're just as bright, whether you play in New York or just for me. If you decide to teach, I think you'll be great at that, too."

They pulled up to the café. He rushed around and helped her out of the truck. Neither bothered with opening an umbrella or even pulling up their hoods. The gentle rain made both smile.

"Staten," she whispered as they hurried inside, "don't let me eat any bacon."

He raised an eyebrow and then seemed to figure it out. "Right."

The café was long past the breakfast crowd, and the waitress was new, so they could eat in peace. He told her about the mystery of his murdered bull, and she talked about how she planned to change up her fields some this spring. She even planned to lease out the back forty acres of her land to the farmer behind her. "The lease will probably pay me more than any profit I could make growing lavender off the land."

If anyone had been there to listen in, they'd simply think that two old friends were having breakfast together. A farmer and a rancher talking about their problems with the land.

When the waitress brought the breakfast plates, she commented that Dorothy piled on extra bacon. "She said when she saw you, Miss Quinn, she remembered you always ate double the bacon when you came in with your parents several years back."

Quinn thanked the waitress. Without a word Staten ate the bacon on both plates, making her smile. This hard businessman was doing his best to be charming.

He drove her home and walked her to the porch.

She said goodbye twice and thanked him for the breakfast, but he just stood there blocking her way into the house.

When she could think of nothing else to say, she just stared.

"I'm not leaving." He set his hat down on the railing. "I have a promise to keep. I'll kiss you goodbye first, then I'll leave."

Since she was the one who'd made him promise, she couldn't complain. She just waited.

He took his time moving closer, placing his arms at

her waist and tugging her against him. Then, tenderly, he kissed her.

Quinn felt herself melting as the kiss deepened. There was something about how he held her just right, making her feel needed and cherished.

When he finally ended the kiss, she didn't step away. His hands moved over her back, and she wished this one moment might last forever. His words came to her low and loving. "I want to undress you, Quinn. I don't want to talk or even think. I just want to hold you."

She understood all he wasn't saying. Change was coming and like it or not, for better or worse, what they had would never be the same. She'd been his shelter for five years, and he'd been her rock.

Without a word she took his hand and led him into the house and down the hallway. She stood in the shadows of the cloudy day and watched him slowly undress her. Silently he moved Quinn onto the bed and turned her on her side while he untied her braid. Then he lay beside her, letting his hand move over her hair and down her body.

The air was damp and cool, so they cuddled under the covers when they began to make love as if for the first time…as if for the last time. A pure kind of loving without words. No agenda, only showing each other how much they cared.

As she drifted to sleep in his arms, she felt his hand spread wide over her abdomen.

Hours later, when she woke, he was gone. She tried to recall the last moment before she'd fallen asleep. Had he leaned down and kissed her tummy, or had she dreamed it?

Quinn spent most of the week drifting from project

to project while she waited for Staten to return. She had no doubt he would.

Her mind kept going back to the few words he'd said and the way he'd touched her. She knew there were a hundred things to do, a hundred decisions to make, but the memory of the way they'd made love wouldn't seem to leave her mind.

He'd kept to his word. They hadn't talked about the baby. The time would come when they would have to, but for right now, there were enough days left before the world changed to just enjoy being together.

A little before dark on Saturday night Quinn got a text from Staten.

Got invitation to Lauren Brigman's birthday party at the lake next week. I'm not going unless you are.

Quinn laughed. She liked Lauren; they'd become friends, but Quinn had no idea why Staten would be invited.

I'm going.

Good, he texted back. I'll drop by later tonight and we can talk about what I'm supposed to get a sixteen-year-old.

Sounds good, she answered. Supper? Or Dessert?

His answer came back in a blink.

YOU!

She held her breath during the long pause, then he

added, I loved holding you while you slept. Any chance we can do that again?

A river of unsaid words ran between them, but for now the place where they were was enough. He wasn't pushing her or trying to talk her into anything. He was giving her time and letting her know how he felt about her.

Thirty minutes later when she called his cell, thinking he'd be on his way, a stranger answered.

"Kirkland's phone, this is Jake Longbow," a voice rusty with age said.

"Jake," she laughed, remembering the ranch hand from years ago when she and Amalah used to ride horses out on the Double K ranch. "This is Quinn O'Grady. I'm trying to reach Staten."

There was a long pause, then Jake said, "He ran out and jumped in his pickup when we heard gunfire a few minutes ago. Tossed me his phone and told me to call the sheriff. I called the county office, and the sheriff didn't even bother saying goodbye to me. Sounded like he dropped the phone and started running."

Quinn took a quick breath. Probably only hunters. They tended to ignore posted signs. "Jake—" she tried to sound calm "—could you have him call me when he gets back?"

"Will do, but if he's wanting the sheriff, he's planning to press charges this time."

Quinn hung up the phone and picked up a blanket. She'd watch the sunset from the porch and pray Staten called.

Twenty

Staten

The last light of day played along the jagged edge of Ransom Canyon as Staten raced toward the far pasture that bordered the Collins ranch. For him the colors of sunsets across the wide horizon reminded him of Quinn's music. Whenever she played, he thought of his land, ever changing, through the seasons, through the years. Some would describe the terrain as desolate and barren, but if he lived to be a hundred he'd love the views every day.

As much as he loved the land, he hated the sound of gunfire rattling across the calm air. One shot after another seemed to clatter off the clouds and echo through the canyon, warning that trouble was coming to call.

Over the years, Davis Collins had opened his place to friends wanting to hunt, and he also offered leasing rights to companies he didn't know, but Staten never considered doing such a thing even if the money was good. Most of the hunters were respectful, following all the rules, keeping to the property boundaries. But some were drunks and careless, dangerous men who only handled a rifle a few times a year. They'd cross at the sandy ravines and step over low fences without really being aware, or caring, that they were on some-one else's property. Some hunted at sunset and shot at eyes in the darkness, not aware that the eyes looking back were those of a cow and not a deer. Most of the drunks even left their kill in the field. With the Bar W over-hunted, they moved onto neighboring land. Staten planned to at least act as though he was pressing charges this time.

Once, he'd questioned Davis about the hunters, and Collins had sworn no hunters crossed property lines. Staten had only two choices, call the man a liar or walk away. He'd walked away, knowing that getting along with his neighbor was more important, at least until he had proof.

As Staten bounced toward the back pasture, he saw the Reyes pickup turning onto his land and heading straight toward him.

He smiled. Lucas, he'd bet. The kid might live on the Collins spread, but he'd made a hand for the Double K. Staten was more impressed with his skill and brains every time they worked together. Reyes had raised a good boy. Though the boots of a cowhand fit him now, Lucas would go on to greater things, and Staten planned to be there watching.

"Mr. Kirkland," Lucas yelled out his pickup window as he pulled alongside. "I heard shots. They had to be from near here."

Staten slowed to a stop. "Hop in my truck, Lucas. We're liable to run into one another out here once it gets dark."

Lucas pulled off the road and cut his engine. In a blink he was climbing into the big cab of Staten's truck.

"Wow, Mr. Kirkland, this place is big enough to be a mobile home. You got a microwave in this thing?"

"Nope, but I'll order that next time."

Lucas settled in, knowing that if they crossed pasture lines he'd be the one hopping out to open the gates. "How can I help? I know this is your land, but I think of it as my special place and I hate the thought of someone out here bothering it."

Staten nodded. "I know how you feel. I like knowing you're out here watching the stars, but I'll be madder than hell if I find out that someone cut fence to come in. So just listen, kid. If trespassers are still on this section, we'll hear them." Staten turned the truck off the road so they'd travel more quietly on grass.

Lucas's voice was high with excitement. "You think it's rustlers? My dad says they've hit the Collins place twice lately. Maybe a dozen head in the past month.

"Jake said you've been having trouble with them, too. They wouldn't come out this early, would they? It's barely dark. My guess is they'd feel safest cutting fence and rounding up cattle long after midnight."

"Breathe, kid," Staten ordered. "It's not rustlers, it's idiots. Drunk hunters or, worse, high ones. I was thinking they might have come from the Collins place and crossed over at the ravine."

Lucas shook his head. "Dad said at supper that the whole family has gone down to check out colleges for Reid's older brother, Charley. If they're not home, the guest quarters should be empty."

"Charley bright enough to go to college?"

Lucas looked over at him, and Staten had his answer without Lucas having to say a word.

"No surprise. I've watched him grow up. IQ and shoe size seem about the same. Collins is putting his bet on Reid to take over the ranch, but I don't know. Any boy dumb enough to talk you three kids into going into that death-trap Gypsy House might want to run for office. He's got persuasion skills and no brains, just like my old man."

Lucas laughed. "What makes you think Reid didn't try to talk us *out* of going in that night?"

Staten lowered his speed along with his voice. "I thought about it. You and Lauren both have too much brains to do something like that after dark, even though you'd been carrying flashlights. Only she's fifteen, so she might have just wanted an adventure. Tim always seems to be following Reid, never leading. That leaves you, Lucas. Why'd you go in?"

Lucas was silent.

Staten turned to look at him in the low light of the dashboard. "I'm guessing you went in to watch over your friend Lauren."

The kid didn't say a word. He didn't have to. Staten read the surprise in Lucas's face.

"Don't worry about it, Lucas, we all do foolish things, take chances when we should have hesitated, and sometimes the end result turns out to be great." Quinn walked through Staten's mind. They'd been foolish not to use protection at their age, but who knew, it might turn out all right. The idea of sharing a child with Quinn was settling in his mind. After all, they weren't that old. Lots of people started families in their forties these days.

Lucas pointed toward a stand of elms scattered along the creek. "Something moved over there by the water." Half the trees had died during the drought, leaving barkless white bony skeletons strewn among the live trees.

Staten slowly turned the truck so the lights flashed across the rocky ground near the water. "Pull my Colt from the glove compartment and follow me," he said as he lifted a rifle from the rack behind his head.

Side by side they moved down the rocky slope. A young deer, not yet full grown, lay jerking in the mud. Staten smelled the blood even before he saw it. "Keep your eyes open for anyone. If they're hunting for food, they'll be tracking the animal. I want to know they're near before they see us."

As Lucas stood guard, Staten lowered to his knee beside the doe. She didn't try to pull away when he placed his hand on her side and felt her heart racing.

Slowly his eyes adjusted to the shadows, and he made out her wound. She'd been shot in the head, but the bullet hadn't killed her. Another wound, halfway down her back, left a gaping hole so deep it looked like someone had hacked a chunk out of her.

"How is the deer?" Lucas whispered through the silence.

"Dying and in pain." Staten moved his hand along her neck as if making one last attempt to calm her. "Easy now, girl."

Lucas had been raised on a ranch. He knew what had to be done without Staten having to say the words. He passed the rancher the Colt.

One lone shot rang through the night. The deer stopped moving. The men didn't make a sound. Staten's hand moved once more along the deer's neck and whispered, "Jake Longbow always says the same thing when a wild animal dies. *Go. Run with the wind in a place of no pain.*"

Lucas took the Colt back as Staten shouldered the deer. "Sounds almost like a prayer."

Slowly, Staten stood and passed his rifle to Lucas. "Let's put her in the truck bed. I don't want the coyotes getting her."

Lucas carried both the Colt and the rifle back to Staten's pickup. After the rancher covered the animal with a tarp, both men stood watching the night. Someone was out there who didn't belong.

"They're waiting for us to move on," Staten finally whispered as he shoved his rifle back in its place. "I can feel them."

"What are we going to do?" Lucas walked a few feet away from the truck and into the grass without making a sound.

Staten followed. He knew the sounds of his ranch. He'd recognized the rush of quail, the gobbles of wild turkey, the tapping of mule deer when a small herd crossed the road. He also had no doubt that whatever happened, Lucas Reyes would stand by his side now, but he had no idea what they were about to face.

"The sheriff's on his way. First thing he'll do is order a block on the county road. If they think they can't go out that way, they'll have to cross open land. Unless they know this section of pasture far better than I think they do, they'll pick the easiest route and that will be straight past us. If we wait, they'll be heading our way soon."

"We're going to confront men with guns out here in the dark?"

Staten barked a laugh. "I didn't live to be forty-three

by being that dumb. Chances are slim they'll even see us. They probably left their trucks in the shadows of the elms. Once they pass us, we'll follow them. I know this area well enough to drive it without headlights."

"Oh, I understand. Good plan, Mr. Kirkland. I wasn't much on the 'Gun-fight at the O.K. Corral' idea."

Staten chuckled and picked up the Colt, and they moved forward to the shadow of a cluster of mesquite trees. There, they'd wait. The night wind rustled over the tops of tall buffalo grass. Staten forced out slow breaths, thinking that he could feel trouble coming and wondering if that was how men had felt on this land for hundreds of years. Bones and weapons had been found at Yellow Creek and at the south bend of the Red River miles northeast. A dozen cavalry men had died at Antelope Peak little more than a hundred years ago. Maybe their cries still circled high in the air like smoke from a long spent fire.

He widened his stance and waited. An uneasiness galloped over his thoughts. He couldn't hear it or see it, but he could feel it in his blood.

After fifteen minutes of silence, Lucas whispered, "You think we missed them?"

"Nope."

"Maybe you should call the sheriff and make sure the road block got set up?"

Staten swore. "I would if I hadn't left my phone back at the barn. Any chance you've got one I could borrow?"

Lucas shrugged. "I'd let you if I had one."

"A teenager without a phone? Impossible."

The sound of an engine silenced them both. They stood still, their shadows blending with those of the trees.

Staten held his breath as the grind of a motor grew louder, but underneath the roar of what had to be a truck was something else—a smaller motor. A car, or maybe a small pickup. For a few minutes they seemed to be traveling together, then the smaller engine veered off and grew fainter. Maybe going another way? Maybe slowing down to see if the truck made it?

The starless night revealed little but finally, as foggy as a day-old dream, came a lone truck moving across the night no more than shadow on shadow.

"There he goes!" Lucas jumped from the trees and started running for Staten's truck.

Staten reacted like a parent reaching for a child who darts into the street. If he'd been three feet closer he could have stopped the boy. Now all he could do was join him.

If they were lucky, they'd make it to the truck before the smaller engine came into view. Once inside, he'd wait for the second car to pass before following.

Lucas ran full out, fast and light.

"If we're lucky," Staten whispered just as his luck ran out.

Pain, like lightning volting from his shoulder, hit him out of nowhere. Time slowed and didn't pick up until he heard the sound of a round being fired. He waited a second, expecting to hear the bullet fly by. Only it didn't. It had already hit him.

Staten's strong body crumbled. His face hit the cold ground as fire raged through his shoulder. The Colt tumbled from his hand as all feeling seemed to leave his arm.

As he jerked, Staten swore he heard Jake Longbow whisper, *"Go. Run with the wind in a place of no pain."*

Helpless to move, Staten watched Lucas make it to the truck before the shot registered. He glanced back, and to the kid's credit, he didn't hesitate as he reversed his route.

"Get down!" Staten yelled, knowing it didn't matter if he was hurt. Whoever was out there knew exactly where he and the boy were.

Lucas dropped and spider-crawled toward Staten.

"Are you hit?"

"Stay down, kid. They'll come closer. Fire off two rounds toward the moon. That should slow them down and bring any of my men within hearing distance running toward us."

Staten fought to keep from passing out. "If you hear movement coming toward you, fire again, high. If it's my men coming in to help, they'll be yelling." Staten felt like an elephant just sat down on his head, but he had to stay conscious long enough to make sure Lucas would be all right. "If someone shoots back," he said weakly, "lay down and wait until you've got a clear shot, then aim for their legs. Even if you miss, it'll slow them down long enough to…"

Lucas

Lucas moved closer to his boss, feeling around for the Colt. For one panicked moment, he thought he might not find it or remember what to do.

"Mr. Kirkland." He touched the rancher's arm. "Where are you hit?"

When Staten didn't answer, Lucas grabbed his boss's shoulder intending to shake him awake, but warm blood met his touch. He had his answer.

Fighting down fear, he moved his hand over the wound. Left shoulder. High. Not close to the heart but too much blood.

Pressing the wound with one hand, Lucas spread his fingers through the dirt near Kirkland's side. One sweep. Two. He touched the butt of the Colt. It took Lucas a few agonizing seconds to grip the gun without decreasing the pressure over the wound. He didn't know if he was doing any good, but it was the only thing he knew to do to possibly stop the bleeding.

Lucas held the gun as far away as he could and fired two shots in the air.

The whole world went silent. He leaned over Staten. "Don't die." His voice came fast and angry. "Don't die on me. I don't know what to do."

Spreading out next to him, Lucas hoped whoever was out there couldn't see them for the weeds and tall grass. He waited, knowing that as soon as it was safe he'd be able to carry Kirkland to the truck, only right now he couldn't seem to stop the tears dripping off his chin.

He went over what Staten had told him to do. If men move in silently, shoot at the ground in front of them. Lucas wasn't sure he could shoot at a man, any man. He'd done target practice, but he'd never shot at a living thing.

The low sound of an engine came again through the silence.

Lucas raised the Colt and fired two more rounds.

The rattle of a truck seemed to turn right toward them. Maybe whoever was out there firing at them planned to run over them both, now that they were down. A hit-and-run right in the middle of a pasture.

Or, maybe the men at the headquarters had heard the two shots.

As the truck light flashed toward him, Lucas raised the Colt and prepared to fire.

Just as he aimed between the headlights he heard shouts and two rounds of gunfire coming from the truck.

They were Kirkland's men. He shook with relief. "They're here, Mr. Kirkland. They're here."

Dropping the gun, Lucas sat up, waving them in with his free hand.

Within seconds the men were out of the truck and surrounding them. One flashed a light over Staten. Blood covered his chest now, as well as the front of Lucas's shirt.

"Give me your shirt, Phil," Jake Longbow ordered. "We'll tie up his shoulder as best as we can."

One of the cowhands ripped the buttons as he yanked off his shirt and dropped to help lift the boss while Jake tied a knot directly over where Lucas's hand had been applying pressure.

"Let's get them to the hospital!" Jake yelled. "Load them in the back of my pickup. A couple of you men crawl in with them to make sure they don't fall out. I'll be driving like I'm running from hell."

Lucas tried to tell them that he wasn't hurt, but no one seemed to hear. They were too busy asking questions and swearing and making threats to whoever did this.

Men pulled rifles and flashlights from Jake's truck, planning to walk the mile-long pasture to make sure no one was on the property.

The smell of hay and leather surrounded Lucas as

he sat in the back of Jake's pickup, back to the cab. His heart was still pounding double-time when he watched the men lift Kirkland in beside him and brace the boss with horse blankets and saddles. Men sat at the four corners while Lucas knelt beside Kirkland. When he lifted Staten's head and used his hat as a pillow, the boss came to.

His deep blue eyes were clear, even though his voice was barely more than a whisper. "Lucas, call Quinn," he said. "Tell her I may be late."

"You got it, boss," Lucas answered. He guessed Kirkland was talking about Quinn O'Grady since she was the only Quinn he knew in town. He'd had no idea that she and Kirkland were even friends, but he'd follow orders.

Lucas fought down a smile. They were a hell of a lot more than friends if she was the one person Kirkland wanted him to call. He thought of asking if one of the men had a cell phone, but decided maybe he should make *this* call in private.

Twenty-One

Quinn

Quinn ran through the hospital doors at full speed. A message had been left on her phone over an hour ago. Some kid saying Staten had been shot and was at the hospital in Lubbock. No details.

When she'd heard it, she had dropped her quilt and grabbed her keys. All the way to the hospital she'd thought of how mad she still was about what he'd said when he found out she was pregnant. How could he think that there would be another man in her life?

Only now, if he died, what did being angry with him matter? She still loved him, still wanted their baby. The thought of facing the years ahead without Staten in her life was too much to bear. She needed him. Wanted him to share the joy of a child with her.

The memory of the touch of his hand across her abdomen almost a week ago returned so strong she could still feel it. One caress he'd made when he thought she was asleep, that was all she needed to know. The last night they'd shared had been about them, whether it was a beginning or an end between them she wasn't sure. But the caress had been about the baby. He wanted the child. That was a beginning. Staten Kirkland was a hard man who rarely showed any emotion, but he wanted the baby that grew inside her, and he wanted her.

Could she be happy with that? Was it enough to build her life around?

If Staten lived, Quinn made up her mind that she wouldn't—couldn't—deny him. He was an honest man who wouldn't offer what he couldn't give. Somehow they'd work it out. Together or apart they'd both raise the child.

"May I help you?" a man in a white coat whom she took to be an orderly asked when she passed her second set of swinging doors.

Quinn didn't take time to look at his name tag. "I'm looking for Staten Kirkland."

The man began shaking his head.

Quinn continued, "He was shot on his ranch earlier tonight. I think it's been about two hours ago since his men brought him in."

"Oh, the rancher. He's in a private room on the third floor. Can't miss it. The men who arrived with him are all still here."

Without another word the orderly hurried off down the hallway while Quinn moved to the nearest set of elevators. When she stepped off on the third floor, she froze. Twenty men, most dressed in chaps, boots and spurs, circled the waiting room. None looked to be waiting patiently. Their shirts were dirty. A few looked bloody, and all seemed a bit lost. Their Western hats sat, crown up, along one wall of the open area.

They all stared at her as if she was a newly arrived

alien. Quinn rarely left her farm, but she knew a few of the men. Marybeth's oldest son—Quinn had decorated the venue for his parents' anniversary party. One tall man who'd been the groom at an outdoor wedding where she'd dressed all the pews with lavender bouquets. A few were volunteer firemen. She'd seen them at the Fourth of July parade. And Jake Longbow, who'd welcomed her when she used to drive out to the Double K to pick up Amalah for their days out. He'd always hollered, "Where you ladies off to?" and they'd name some wild place like the beauty parlor and then ask him to come along.

Jake Longbow had aged since she'd last seen him at Amalah's funeral. Seven years had passed since she lost her best friend. A lot more than Jake Longbow's face had changed over those years.

He gave her a sad smile. "Quinn?" he said slowly, as if not sure she'd know him.

"Yes, Jake. How is he?" When he didn't answer, she added, "How is Staten?"

Jake answered straight out then. No sugarcoating, no lies. "He's in surgery right now. They're taking a bullet out of his shoulder. That's all we know. The emergency room nurse said once he's cleared from the recovery room they'll bring him up here, but since then nobody's told us nothing." Worry dripped from every word.

She nodded. "Is it all right if I wait with you?"

Jake put his bony arm around her and directed her to a row of chairs. "Sure, honey. You wait right next to me."

If anyone thought it strange that a woman living on the opposite side of Crossroads on a lavender farm would be worried about the owner of a huge ranch miles away, they didn't comment.

After a few minutes, a tall, thin kid of about seventeen sat down beside her. The blood on his shirt had dried, leaving Quinn to guess that it wasn't his blood.

If the blood wasn't his, then she knew without asking that it had to be Staten's.

"I was with him when he was shot," the boy whispered. "He asked me to call you and say he'd be late."

She smiled. "I was about to start cooking spaghetti. I'd just moved inside when I noticed you'd called." Even as she said the words she thought how crazy they sounded. Staten was in danger, and she was talking about her plans for dinner.

"I'm Lucas Reyes. I remembered you from a research paper Lauren Brigman did last year. Your farm looks like it should be in a magazine. It's so beautiful in the spring."

"Lauren's a friend of yours?" Quinn was only half following the conversation. Her eyes never left the door to the right.

"Yeah."

"Are you going to her birthday party next week?"

The kid shook his head. "I have to be at freshman orientation that day here in Lubbock. You know, they'll show all upcoming freshmen the campus and probably tell us all about college life. I doubt I'll make it back to town in time for the party."

"So, you're going to Texas Tech." She smiled. Everyone who grew up in Crossroads dreamed of getting away to school or a big city, but in truth most stayed and started families. They farmed, or ranched, or worked for one of the oil companies. Those who did break free often returned to retire. Funny how the very place you can't wait to leave is, in the end, the only place you want to go back to.

Quinn tried to think of something to do besides storming the double doors and making a fool of herself. She wanted to ask Lucas what had happened, but she wasn't sure she could bear to hear the details. If it was bad, and it must have been, she might start crying in front of all Staten's men. She had a feeling he wouldn't like that.

She'd wait. She'd ask Staten as soon as she saw him. As soon as he was out of surgery, as soon as the doors no longer barred her way.

Glancing at Lucas, she asked, "What are you getting Lauren for her birthday?" She had to think of something to say. The men around her were pacing, talking about working night shifts, talking about getting back to the ranch. They were no longer just cowhands. They were guards, soldiers in a war.

One man suggested they do what cattlemen did a hundred years ago during the Remington Blockade. One man, one rifle, one mile. If trouble rode your way, you fired, and all the others came running after they relayed the shot. It had stopped diseased cattle from climbing the caprock a hundred years ago and infecting West Texas ranches.

"I hadn't thought about a present," Lucas said, breaking into her dark thoughts. "I guess I should bring something if I do make it to the party. She'll be sixteen, and for a girl that's a big deal, or so my little sisters tell me. I turn eighteen three days after her birthday, and my folks are buying me a saddle. I'll probably be working every break I get from college, so a good saddle will come in handy. Somehow I don't think that's something a girl would want."

Quinn realized Lucas was doing exactly what she was, trying to keep his mind off what was happening beyond the double doors.

The elevator doors opened, and a mob of men in suits rushed out. Among them was a tall man, looking like an older version of Staten. Quinn recognized Samuel Kirkland, even though she hadn't seen him since she'd been maid-of-honor at Amalah and Staten's wedding. Staten's father had made an appearance that day at the last minute as if the whole affair was about him. A senator from a small town is everyone's friend. When he'd been working the crowd, the bride and groom had seemed nothing more than props. People had stood in the receiving line not to congratulate the young couple, but to shake hands with a senator.

Quinn remembered hearing that Samuel and his second wife stayed the night at the ranch so they could do a photo shoot the next morning. Staten once said that Samuel's third wife looked just like the second so they wouldn't have to redo the photos.

Quinn shook her head. Funny she should think of something so meaningless at a time like this. Thoughts kept drifting in her mind like snapshots in a mixed-up album. Staten had stood behind her for the class picture in the third grade. He'd helped her with her science project in middle school. When her parents died, he'd dropped everything and managed her farm until she could sort through all the paperwork. He'd always been there. She wasn't just the friend of his wife. Quinn was his friend, too.

He'd talked to her about his dad liking to be *from*

the area. When she'd mentioned it to Amalah, she'd said she'd never heard him talk about his dad much. But he'd talked to Quinn.

She knew that Staten still went to Dallas when his dad was back from Washington. But when Samuel came home to see Staten, his father snuck in and out and never stayed overnight at the ranch. His fourth wife said she didn't like the bugs and the wind at the Double K. She claimed the smell of cows made her gag.

Somehow, over the years, Samuel Kirkland's image had outgrown the man. Staten had once laughed and said his many stepmothers married a senator but had to sleep with his dad.

She watched Samuel Kirkland now, still playing to the small crowd of yes-men and reporters.

Jake Longbow rose and went to the senator, filling him in on what little he knew. The suits on either side of Staten's father were all on their cell phones.

"You have a cell?" she asked Lucas. "Your parents might be worried."

"Nope. I borrowed my cousin's office phone to call you. She works down on the first floor." He was silent for a minute before smiling. "I doubt my parents even noticed I wasn't there for supper. My dad always figures if I'm working late at the Double K, someone will make sure I get a meal."

Jake came back to Quinn, looking as if he'd been trying to communicate with a squirrel. "The senator is gettin' ahold of the hospital administrator so he can find out what's goin' on. All he found out was that it'll probably be another hour or more before we know anything."

Quinn watched the room. Cowboys on one side, suits on the other. She knew it would just be a matter of time before someone asked her what she was doing there. The only woman in a room of headstrong men.

"Lucas, would you do me a favor?"

"Of course," he answered. "Anything."

"Come with me downstairs to get something to eat."

The kid stood and offered his arm. "I'd be honored."

With few people noticing, they slipped out the stairway door and walked down two flights of stairs to a small cafeteria. She bought a pizza with the works and French fries on the side. Then, when he hesitated, she ordered him the same and insisted on paying for his.

Half an hour later he laughed, claiming he'd never known such a slender woman could eat so much. "My mom never sits down for a meal. She just nibbles while she cooks, and chases kids, and cleans up. She's round as a butterball. Maybe if I got her to sit down and eat she'd lose weight."

Quinn smiled. "Does her weight matter to you?"

"Not a bit," he answered. "She's huggable size."

The love for his family was obvious. Quinn liked the idea of raising a child who would love her like that.

There was something about the young man that set her at ease. Maybe because she guessed he was one of the shy people in a world of talkers, and she knew he was making a true effort to help her relax.

When they went back to the waiting room, nothing had changed. Still cowboys on one side pacing and suits on the other playing with their cell phones.

Jake limped over to tell them that Staten was doing fine in recovery but no other news. A nurse had let the senator go in for only a moment to see his son. The doctor was with the senator, probably filling him in on the surgery.

Quinn sat in the back by the windows. If she could have managed to be invisible, she would have been. She didn't want to be just waiting, and she couldn't leave.

When Samuel Kirkland walked out of the double doors, he looked shaken. Cameras flashed but his usual bright smile was gone.

All were silent.

He stood in the center of the room and cleared his throat. "Thank you all for coming," Samuel said as if they'd all just dropped by. "My son and I want to thank you for your concern and prayers. He'll be out of recovery in a few minutes. Wants to see all his men, but I'm not sure he doesn't need rest more."

One of the cowhands faced Senator Kirkland, but it was the foreman who spoke. "We all understand how you feel, sir, and we'll keep our visit short, but if Staten wants to see us, we're going in." He hesitated a moment before continuing, "We've got trouble at the Double K, and unless you're planning to take over, we need to be getting our orders from him."

All the cowboys nodded and reached for their hats. One by one the worn Stetsons and Resistols disappeared off the floor, and the low sound of spurs shifting circled through the room as the cowboys moved toward the double doors.

Quinn didn't miss the shocked look on the suits' faces. They were all yes-men who followed whatever the senator said. For a moment Quinn realized she was looking at two different kinds of men, and not one of them would trade sides if they had the chance.

"I would take over," the senator announced, "only, now I know my son is going to be all right, I have urgent business to take care of in Washington. I'm sure he has plenty of help running the ranch. My place is helping to run the country." He straightened to his picture-perfect posture for the cameras.

The cowboys weren't listening; they were disappearing one by one behind the swinging doors.

Quinn looked at Lucas. "I don't want to go in with the others, but I'm not staying here with that man. Could you come down to the cafeteria and get me when everyone's gone?"

"Of course," he answered. "Mr. Kirkland will want to see you. When he told me to call you, it was an order, not a request. I'm guessing he'd rather have seen your face when he woke up from surgery than his father's."

Quinn looked back at the senator. He was preparing to talk to the reporters who'd gotten an anonymous tip that Senator Kirkland was in town on a family emergency. "Staten hates the press. He told me that even when we were kids."

Lucas laughed. "I know he must hate reporters. The first time I was stringing wire for him he told me if I ran out of posts, just hammer in any reporter that stepped on the property."

Quinn smiled and kissed the kid on the check. She could see that he respected his boss, and if he'd been the one Staten told about her, then the feeling went both ways.

Half an hour later Quinn walked into Staten's hospital room. She'd never expected to see him like this. Some people just seemed strong enough to face any storm.

Lucas stood next to the bed. He looked up and saw Quinn at the door. "Miss O'Grady is here, Mr. Kirkland."

Staten's low voice answered, "Thanks for taking care of my lady, kid. I owe you one."

"Anytime, sir." He nodded once to Quinn and picked up his hat. "I'll be outside the door for a few minutes making sure you're not disturbed."

Quinn slowly moved closer to the bed.

Staten's eyes were closed and a bandage wrapped around his chest and shoulder. His left arm was tied into the bandage so he couldn't move it.

She laid her hand over his heart and kissed him gently.

His eyes slowly opened. "I was hoping that was you and not the nurse." His right hand covered hers. "When I was shot, all I could think about was making things right with you, Quinn. I didn't mean what I said, and if I have to apologize every day for the rest of my life, I will. You just got to talk to me. Let me be part of your life. However you want it to be. I'll—"

"You're forgiven, Staten. You don't have to keep apologizing. I figured out what you must have thought when you saw Dan over at my place fixing my tractor. I did a favor for his daughter, and he insisted on paying me back. We're friends, that's all."

She smiled down at him and realized sometime in her forgiveness speech he'd fallen asleep. Maybe all he needed to hear was that he was forgiven.

"I love you, Staten. I think I have all my life." She whispered her words to her sleeping man, knowing that she might never say them when he was awake. "The nurse says you'll be out for the rest of the night, but if you don't mind, I think I'll sit with you awhile."

An hour later she was almost asleep when she heard

him whisper her name. She moved to the side of his bed and brushed her fingers along his jawline.

"Quinn," he said without opening his eyes. "Don't give up on me."

"I'm right here, Staten." It wasn't a promise, but a fact. She'd been close to him always, even when he had no idea she was there.

Twenty-Two

Yancy

Yancy Grey realized something was different the moment he walked into Dorothy's Café. First, most of the tables were full, and it was supposed to be the dead time between lunch and dinner. Second, if he didn't know better, it looked like someone had called a town meeting. Businessmen, farmers, shop owners and cowboys were packing the place like it was Sunday morning after a wild Saturday night, and Dorothy had the only coffee in town.

One look and Yancy started backing away. If there was trouble boiling, he was usually the one it spilled over on. In life's lineup he guessed he was the only one with a Pick Me sign on his forehead, so he'd better be moving on.

"I saved you a place at the counter." Sissy grabbed his arm. "You won't want to miss this."

Yancy thought of screaming that he really, really *did* want to miss this, but by the time he pulled free of the round little waitress, he was halfway across the room.

Looking over the crowd, he saw Cap and Leo right in the middle of the mob. "We got to do something," Cap demanded, slamming his fist on the table so hard spoons jumped.

A man with a badge, the sheriff Yancy had avoided every time he'd seen him, held up his hand as if blocking Cap's suggestion. "This happened outside the city limits. It's a county problem. I've already called in backup, and a Texas Ranger is sitting up in my office as we speak. A man's been hurt. We'll get to the bottom of this."

One cowboy in the back yelled, "Your ranger is a brand inspector, Sheriff Brigman. We're not talking about a cow being shot."

The sheriff corrected. "He's a ranger first. We think Staten Kirkland walked into a crime scene last night. He was shot because he was at the wrong place at the wrong time."

"Crime scene, hell, he was walking across his own land," an old cowboy yelled before spitting a brown stream of tobacco into a cup.

"That better be a paper cup, Jake Longbow, or I swear there's about to be another crime scene right in my café," Dorothy shouted from the pass-through.

"It was, honey-pie," Jake yelled back, not seeming to care that half the town was listening.

Several men fought down laughter. Jake Longbow had been courting Dorothy longer than most of the men in the room had been alive.

"What's going on?" Yancy whispered to Sissy.

"A big-time rancher was shot last night. You've met him, Mrs. Kirkland's grandson? Word is there's not one clue. Could have been drunk hunters, but they'd have to be real drunk to mistake a man like Staten Kirkland for a deer."

The sheriff stood on a chair. "All right, everyone, calm down. I called you all here to help. Someone was on the Double K Ranch last night, and the odds are somebody saw something. We're asking those who can to help us walk over the section of land. We might just get lucky and find a shell casing or something."

"This is starting to sound like an episode of *CSI*." Sissy giggled. "Only I don't think they have a ranch unit. Most folks in America probably think crime only happens in big cities like on TV."

Yancy tried to listen to what was going on, instead of to Sissy, but he smiled at her, so she wouldn't know he was doing his best to ignore her.

Everyone, including Leo and Cap, was willing to go out and help. Yancy didn't want any part of this. Too recently he'd lived on the wrong side of the law and this didn't feel right, but if he didn't volunteer, someone might ask why. He had to think. He had to do what a normal man would do, even if the ex-con jitters were threatening to take over.

"Do we go on horseback?" Jake Longbow asked. "I can have a dozen mounts saddled and ready at the Double K's headquarters in no time."

"No. It's a nice day. We walk. We'll need a few riders to move back and forth, but any man riding needs to stick to the road as much as possible so he doesn't contaminate evidence." Brigman pointed to another man with a badge. "Load up two or three evidence kits we can strap to saddles." He turned to the rest of the men. "We meet at the cattle guard coming on to his ranch from the north in two hours." The sheriff climbed down and began talking to Cap and Leo.

"Evidence kits," Sissy whispered. "We're into big-time crime now."

"Sounds like it," Yancy admitted. The urge to run was strong, but he was too far from the door, and he didn't want to look like a coward.

By the time Yancy worked his way over to Cap and Leo, both were busy taking down names.

"Sheriff left us in charge of keeping up with who goes onto the land. What time they walk on or off. It's an important job, or he wouldn't have taken us out of the field," Cap said after he noticed Yancy standing beside him. "It's a big responsibility, but we can handle it. Leo and me will have to stay at the gate in my car to make sure we don't miss anyone."

"Mind if I ride out and lend a hand with the walking?" Yancy asked, feeling like a fish offering to cut bait.

Mrs. Kirkland's grandson was always polite to him when he stopped by. Even took the time to tell Yancy he thought he was doing a great job around the place. If Yancy was going to step into being normal, now seemed a good place to start.

"No, we don't mind. The sheriff needs all the able-bodied men we can find." Leo shook his head. "This isn't going to be an easy case to crack. Did I tell you that I once thought of being a forensic investigator? I could have done it, too. Read all about blood spatters and beetles aging in dead bodies. They say the average criminal makes a dozen mistakes while he's committing a crime. All we need to find is one."

Yancy was starting to consider this an educational

field trip. If he failed at this normal stuff and went back to a life of crime, he'd know what not to leave behind.

Cap interrupted Leo. "Tell us about it in the car. We need to get up there." He turned and yelled, "Dorothy, load us up a couple of thermoses and some fried pies if you got them."

"Will do." She laughed. "This is just like the days when you were captain of the grass-fire division over at the fire department. You always ordered me around when an emergency came."

As most of the men moved out, a lanky cowboy limped to the counter. "You better not be ordering my Dorothy around, Cap."

Dorothy stepped through the swinging kitchen door with three thermoses. "Oh, hush, Jake, this is official ordering and nothing more." She set two containers in front of Cap and handed one to Jake Longbow. "This one's for you, Jake. Bring it back when all this police business is over."

Jake grinned. "It might be late, sweetie-pie."

"I'll be up waiting." She turned to the others. "You all be careful."

All three men nodded and headed out.

Yancy left a dollar tip, even though he hadn't had time to order anything. There were half-empty cups of coffee everywhere and water glasses spilled across tables in the rush to get out. If Cap would have waited on him, Yancy might have stayed to help Sissy clean up, but the old guys were ready to march.

Two hours later a slow-moving army began to walk across the far pasture of the Double K. The day was warm, but the earth didn't lend itself to straight lines. Mesquite trees, rock formations and ravines where

water flowed every time it rained were all in the way.
Every man walked the mile from fence to fence, with a
stick in his hand and his eyes alert and focused on the
ground. No one knew exactly what they were looking
for. The sheriff just said they'd know it when they saw it.

Yancy saw more piles of manure than anything else.
Weeds and cactus brushed against his jeans. The warm
sunshine brought out a few spiders and bugs he'd never
seen before, but he didn't find anything that looked like
it didn't belong to nature.

It took him over an hour to walk the first mile, and
then he had to move fifty feet over, turn around and
walk back. Only now, the sun was in his eyes and he
couldn't see the next step, much less any evidence. He
almost tumbled to the bottom of a dry creek bed, and
when he managed to climb out, he was relieved to find
a stretch of flat, treeless pasture.

Three quarters of the way back to the road where
Cap's boat of a car was parked, Yancy noticed something shiny next to a cluster of rocks about a foot high.
Beyond the rocks there was a ridge where someone hiding out would have a clear view of the road—a clear
shot at a man standing in the pasture below.

Having been told to call out and not touch anything
unusual, he tried to brush what looked like a spent shell
an inch away from the rock.

It rolled the wrong direction, and the stick was too
thick to fit beneath the rock. He didn't want to shout if
it was nothing. The sheriff or the ranger would simply
rush over and probably yell at him for wasting their
time.

Leaning down, Yancy slipped his hand into the slice

of an opening. Once under the rock, he could wiggle his fingers, so the opening must widen.

He pushed deeper, digging dirt away until his hand was almost completely under the rock. He'd just brush whatever the shiny metal had been out into the sun. He wouldn't pick it up. As soon as he saw it might be a clue, he'd yell.

Pain suddenly shot up his arm, and Yancy jerked his hand away as he yelped in panic and fear.

The men on either side of him came running, asking questions.

"I thought I saw a spent shell, but it rolled under the rock." Yancy stared at blood dripping from his first finger. "When I reached to get it, something bit me."

"We'll get that shell out of the hole," a cowboy smart enough to be wearing gloves said as he slapped Yancy on the back. "You go over to Cap's car. I'm betting he'll have a first-aid kit. Bites are nothing to mess around with."

Yancy did as he was told. All the way to the car, he stared at his finger, dripping blood like the leaky pipe in Mrs. Kirkland's sink. It didn't really hurt that badly, but the thought that something bit him freaked him out. Mosquitos or flies were one thing, but something big enough to take a hunk out of him was serious.

Five minutes later, when he reached the car, Leo and Cap took over as if they were handling a major emergency.

Just as he settled onto the fender of the car to wait for them to find the first-aid kit, a tiny little Volkswagen pulled up. Ellie Emerson, Cap's niece, jumped out, looking all serious in her almost-professional nurse manner.

"Glad you're here, Ellie," Cap yelled from the back

of his car where he and Leo were tossing things out while they searched. "We got us an emergency here."

With her cape flying, she rushed to Yancy.

He tried to smile but must have looked brain-damaged, because she held his chin and stared into his eyes. "Where's he hurt?" she asked as if he wasn't conscious. "Any sign of blurred vision or vomiting?"

Yancy thought about yelling back that his ears hurt, but Cap beat him to the answer. "Figure it out, Ellie. We're busy. I know the kit is in here somewhere."

Lifting his first finger, wrapped with Cap's questionably clean handkerchief, Yancy gave her a hint. "Something bit me."

"Spider, snake, prairie dog?"

"I don't know."

Examining the wound from every angle, she gave her diagnosis. "If it's a snake, we need to get you into the clinic, but this doesn't look like a snake bite."

"You seen a lot of snake bites?" He swallowed hard and fought to keep his eyes from crossing.

She met his gaze. "Two. Both were puncture wounds about half an inch apart. This looks like something was planning to have you for lunch."

"Then you're the expert. I was simply on the menu."

Ellie managed a half smile as if she wasn't sure if he was kidding or not. "If it's a spider, you'll be dead before we can make it to the hospital."

Now he gave a half smile, having no idea if she was joking.

The wind whipped up, circling her cape around her plump little body. "Get in the backseat of this car. We don't want any dust in the wound." She pushed on his shoulder, almost knocking him off the fender. "If you feel faint, let me know. If you pass out, we'll have real trouble getting your long body inside."

He followed orders, thinking she had the worst bedside manner he'd ever seen. But she sure did smell good.

She climbed into the other side with her bag in one hand and a first-aid kit probably older than Yancy in the other.

There wasn't much room in the backseat. She had to put her bag behind her to get close enough to him to work. "I can clean the wound." She captured his forearm between her elbow and her breast as she began wiping the blood off his finger with a square of wet tissue she'd pulled from a sealed packet.

Yancy felt light-headed. Every time she breathed, something very soft pushed against his forearm. He leaned his head back and closed his eyes. He'd never told anyone in prison that he'd never touched a girl. They would have thought it a great joke. But, between age fifteen and twenty he'd been in and out of reform schools or on his own. The few girls in his world weren't the kind he wanted even if they'd been dumb enough to want him. So, when the guys talked about women, he'd played along, retelling stories he'd heard in other places.

"Are you all right?" Ellie pressed closer as she lifted one of his eyelids.

"I think I'm dying," he whispered.

"If a prairie dog bit you, you've probably got rabies. That could kill you if we don't get you to a doctor. I've heard rabies shots are no fun to take."

Cap leaned in the open window. "Give him some water and see if he starts foaming at the mouth."

The rusty voice of Jake Longbow came from somewhere behind Cap. "Looks like he stuck his hand in a prairie-dog hole. Dunk the wound in alcohol and tape it up. He'll be fine."

"But—" Ellie began.

"No buts. Prairie dogs don't carry rabies. Unless he starts running a fever, he's fine."

Cap bristled. "How do you know, Jake? You're not a doctor, and my Ellie is almost a nurse."

"I've been bit or stung by every kind of animal, insect and plant on this place. I finally just started biting them back."

Ellie grinned, and Yancy thought she looked pretty but he wasn't about to say anything. He had a feeling she was only slightly more friendly than the prairie dog.

Five minutes later with his finger professionally bandaged, he stepped from the car and almost collided with the sheriff.

"You Yancy Grey?" the lawman asked.

Yancy almost answered *Yes, boss* like he'd had to answer to the guards. "I am." He straightened and looked at the sheriff. After all, he was just a normal citizen, nothing more.

"Well, Yancy, you did a good job. Besides that mad prairie dog, we found a spent shell the trespassers may have left there last night. We also found several cigarette butts and a few footprints. You've just found us our first evidence."

"Glad I could be of service." Yancy said what he thought he should say. "Where can I help out now?"

The sheriff shook his head. "How about you call it a day? If Ellie can drive you back to town, the rest of us will finish up here."

Yancy thought that sounded good. A moment later, when Ellie told her uncle that she planned to check on

Yancy every two hours to make sure he didn't develop a fever, he thought it sounded great.

Climbing into her little car, he tried to think of something to say as she drove back to town like a maniac. He hadn't driven, even illegally, in five years, but he had no doubt he could do better. At one point he started putting together his obituary. *Man survives wild animal bite only to be killed in car crash.*

He reached over and touched her arm.

"You feeling sick?" she asked without slowing. "All kinds of infections could set in. A few might even kill you."

He slid his fingers along her arm until he reached her fingers. "Would you mind if I held your hand?"

"Of course. Part of nursing is offering comfort."

He thought about asking if comfort extended to other body parts, but he decided he'd never get that lucky. After today he'd probably never get this close to her again.

Ellie insisted on walking him to his one-room place behind the office. "Now, you rest, and I'll check on you in a few hours."

He lay down and let her put a quilt Mrs. K had given him all the way up to his chin.

On one crazy impulse, he rose to his elbow and kissed her cheek, then backed away waiting for the blow.

To his surprise she finished tucking him in and walked away without saying a word.

From the two-inch opening in his door he heard Ellie tell the old folks that he was resting, but they should watch him closely.

"I fear he may be delirious," she said as if giving a medical opinion. Then in a lower tone he barely heard, she added, "And I think I like it."

Twenty-Three

Staten

Dawn still whispered along the horizon as Staten Kirkland stood staring out the window, dressed and ready to leave the hospital. He had about all he wanted of being poked and patted on. He had never been a man who gave or accepted comfort easily, and he didn't want it now.

"If Jake doesn't get here soon, I swear I'll start walking," he said more to his reflection in the glass than the nurse babysitting him.

The woman in green scrubs looked nervous. "We can't do that, Mr. Kirkland."

He thought of reminding her that there was no "we" in the room. She hadn't been shot, she didn't have a ranch to run, and he saw no point in talking to her.

"Like hell I can't." His boots echoed off the tiles. His spurs jingled slightly, a tiny reminder of who he was and what he needed to do. Staten was ready to go back to work. "I wasn't sick when I walked in here, and I'm not sick now." The girl was so thin he could probably blow her out of the way without much effort.

He hated the square room with all the stainless steel and thick glass. He hated the smell of the place. He hated the way things beeped and rang all day and night. He felt as though they'd stuffed his bear of a body into a rabbit cage.

Jake Longbow slipped around the door about the time Staten was thinking he'd simply pick up his parting gifts of a bedpan and small pink water pitcher and leave. Walking home might take days, but it would clear his head. He had a ranch to run and a woman he cared about who needed him, even if she didn't seem to know it. As soon as he figured out what the right thing to do was, he planned to tell Quinn. Problem was, she still didn't want to talk about the baby.

"About time you got here, Jake," Staten snapped when he saw the old ranch hand offering his lopsided grin to the nurse.

Jake didn't take offense. "Doctor said they'd release you about nine o'clock. I figured I'd better get here before seven."

"You were right. I've been waiting since five."

Before Staten could make his escape, the doctor appeared in the doorway. He was young, probably an intern, but he didn't look intimidated. He simply smiled. "Morning, Mr. Kirkland. I figured you'd better be my first patient today. I got a dad who, I swear, could be your twin."

"Does he ranch?"

"No, he runs a law office, but you two would get along." The doctor handed him a packet of papers. "I won't keep you. Here are your discharge forms and instructions on what you can and can't do. That shoulder has to heal, and you can't hurry it no matter how much you try. Only remove that sling to take a shower, and then keep your arm as still as you can. When you come back in two weeks, we'll evaluate your progress."

"I don't need to come back. I'll be well by then," Staten said. "The nurse showed me how to put the sling on. How about I wear it until I don't need it anymore?"

"All right." The doctor didn't argue, obviously seeing any discussion would be pointless. "Try to stay out of the way of any bullets. You were voted the least likely patient we'd ever want to see again."

"Is he being funny, boss?" Jake asked.

Staten walked out the door. "Probably not."

They stopped at the pharmacy and waited in line for pain pills Staten probably wouldn't take. Half an hour later, when they passed through Crossroads, Staten insisted on stopping at the sheriff's office.

Brigman's office was on the main road through town. There was no sign on the front, just a five-point star with a circle around it carved into the door. County offices were downstairs and a courtroom on the second floor.

A reception area in front split off into four offices. One for the sheriff, one reserved for Texas Rangers, one for the coroner and the last one for the justice of the peace. His job must be very peaceful, because no one in town had seen him for months. A receptionist, long past retirement age, was the guard at the gate. She looked old enough to have dated Davy Crockett when he rode into Texas heading for the Alamo.

"Morning," Staten said with a nod. "Sheriff in?"

The woman pointed them to the only open door, then giggled as Jake winked at her.

Jake pointed one finger at the coffeepot. "Mind if I have a cup, Pearly?"

"Not at all," she answered. "I'll make a fresh pot in case you stay around."

Staten tried not to notice the exchange between the two. They might be just being polite, but he swore an undercurrent was weaving through the conversation, and the receptionist was developing bedroom eyes behind her bifocals. He didn't want to know what was going on between the two. In his day, Jake liked to brag that he'd shoved his boots under many a bed and left every lady smiling.

Dan Brigman stood when Staten appeared at his door. The sheriff motioned him over to a table near the window. The entire six-foot surface was covered with maps.

Brigman looked tired, and Staten couldn't help wondering if he'd slept the past two nights. If the bullet that hit Staten had been two inches over, Brigman might be dealing with a murder. It didn't sit well with Staten that he'd be the victim.

"Fill me in, Sheriff." Staten fought from cradling his left arm with his right. There was no use wasting time with small talk. Both men knew why he was there.

With Jake and Staten leaning over a county map, Dan Brigman explained every fact they knew about what had happened the night Staten had been shot. "I have two witnesses who saw an old one-ton truck on the road between your back gate and the county line, but my men watching the main road since your bull got hit said no truck passed them. Since one of the witnesses was sober, I think we'll have to list the sighting as a clue. Only problem is, do you have any idea how many one-ton trucks are registered in this county?"

"There are a few back roads that turn off before the spot where you posted your men. Anyone traveling those would have to know where he was going or they'd be lost for hours driving from one water tank to another."

"Some aren't even on this map," Brigman agreed and moved on. "The shell that Yancy Grey found on your land is pretty common, probably used in half the rifles around. But, if we find the weapon that shot you, we can send it in for testing."

Jake leaned back to spit in his empty coffee cup. "Weapon didn't shoot him, Sheriff, a man did."

The sheriff nodded at Jake and added, "Since you said you heard several shots earlier, we may find where he was standing when he wounded the deer. I'm pretty sure Yancy found the spot where he stood to fire at you. If the same man shot both you and the deer? Probably not, since the slugs we dug out of the deer didn't match the one the doc dug out of you, Staten. There could have been two hunters out there. One looking for game and the other looking for you."

"Hold up a minute. We're talking about a pasture, not the Two Step Bar over in Bailee. What are the chances there would be two men out there at the same time?" Jake thought for a moment, then added, "Or maybe it was a woman firing at you, Staten. You pissed off any stepmothers lately?"

"No," Staten answered. "Me and the latest one gave up talking about two years ago. She told me she was going to have some work done, and I told her to be sure and record it because I'd bet a hundred dollar bill that she's never seen work in her life."

The sheriff choked down a laugh and continued with every detail they'd found that might be a clue. The cigarette butts, the footprints made with shoes, not boots. "From the looks of it, one man climbed out of his car or small truck and waited until you moved out of the shadows, after the truck you saw passed by. He must have guessed you'd want to tail the truck.

"We think the car pulled off the road behind trees, and the shooter found a place where he had cover from three sides. After the shot, he turned around and left through the north gate. That might be why you or Lucas didn't see another vehicle."

Staten didn't like the idea that the shooting had been premeditated. He'd rather have thought it was simply an accident.

He paid attention to every detail as the sheriff continued. "The tracks we found near the spent shell were not that of a truck with any weight. Which explains the two engines you heard. One driving past you, one turning off waiting for you to step out so he could get a clear shot."

"So, you don't think it was just bad luck." Staten took the news cold, without feeling. "If someone was waiting, willing to make a long shot, then the odds were good he knew what he was doing. You think they were out to shoot me."

"You, or one of your men." Brigman scratched his head. "It doesn't make sense. Rustlers don't go after trouble. They want to sneak in and out."

Staten had heard enough. He'd gladly face trouble head-on, but he'd have to think about this. He had no idea if the shot was meant for him, or for anyone who'd driven out to check on the shots fired earlier. All he knew was that at least two people were on his ranch who didn't belong, and apparently both were armed.

By the time Jake got him home, Staten was exhausted and would have even gone back to the hospital to sleep.

He wasn't surprised when Quinn met him at his own front door. She hadn't been over to his place in years, but he knew she'd want to make sure he was all right. In his experience women were like that, even with men they were mad at.

His lady might be quiet and shy, but she had a stubbornness about her that sometimes made him smile.

Jake saw him to the front door and walked away, complaining he should have left his boss in town. "If he keeps complaining, Quinn, just hit him in the head. He's already brain damaged, so I don't see that it would do any harm."

Staten put his good arm over Quinn's shoulders and leaned on her just a bit as she walked him to the couch in his big office. She felt so good against him, he knew she'd be the only medicine he'd ever need.

"I'm guessing you're not going to let me put you to bed." She laughed.

"Not unless you're going with me," he answered.

"But you will rest."

"I will." When he leaned against the pillows she'd already stacked, he relaxed for the first time since he'd been shot. "You going to be here when I wake up?"

She kissed him. "It'll take me all day to pick this place up. Your house is so dark and closed up. Cave dwellers must have built it."

He nodded. "Stepmother number two. She hated the ranch and didn't want a single view interrupting her décor." He didn't add that when Amalah died, he and Randall had taken everything upstairs that they decided they no longer needed, and then they'd lived in the two downstairs bedrooms, the office and the kitchen. When papers and supplies piled up, Staten didn't care. At least he knew where everything was.

After his son died, he stripped away all that had made the house a home. Somehow he wanted a shell to live in. A cell. A hole, where feelings would never find him again.

Five years later, his office was stacked with paperwork. He quit using the cabinets in the kitchen and started just stacking food on the counter. Saved time. He had no idea what was upstairs, where Randall's things had been moved. He rarely climbed the stairs to the four bedrooms on the second floor.

The space that had been Randall's bedroom downstairs was completely bare. He'd go in there now and then and stand thinking that the room reflected his soul, barren and scraped clean.

Only now, when he was weak and exhausted, Quinn had stepped into his colorless world.

"Do whatever you want, Quinn, just be here when I wake up," he whispered, half-asleep. He didn't care if she took a match to the big house. It was no longer a home.

Eight hours later, he woke to the smell of heaven. Quinn had cooked. She was still in his house. He sat up, one pain at a time, and pulled her against him as soon as she came close.

"Feed me," he whispered after he kissed her.

She laughed and helped him to the kitchen table. He was on his third bowl of stew when he noticed that he could see the kitchen counters.

"You cleaned up. You weren't kidding."

"Do you mind?"

"Nope."

She handed him a pill, and he took it without arguing. Then, she walked him to the bedroom and undressed him for a change.

"Stay with me," he asked, wanting her close.

"I can't, but I'll come back tomorrow. When I drive out, I'll tell Jake to send one of the guys over to sleep on the couch in case you need something in the night."

"I won't," Staten said. He thought of arguing about what difference did it make if they slept together here or at her place. But he knew that it did matter to her.

She left before he thought of any words to say. They needed to talk about the change coming, but she wasn't ready yet. He knew he'd have to respect her choices or he'd lose her completely.

In the silent house he thought he should have told her that she'd been his every thought when he was on his way to the hospital.

They both seemed to be fighting for their world, their relationship to remain the same, but it couldn't, it wouldn't.

In less than two weeks Lloyd deBellome would be in town for the concert. She had to make up her mind if she was going to go to the fund-raiser and possibly face him, or run and avoid him. Either way, Staten planned to be by her side.

Thanks to Miss Abernathy's visit at the hospital, he knew more than he ever wanted to know about the master pianist. Lloyd was starting a world tour beginning in Dallas next week and covering the globe. He had agreed to play at Crossroads free, only charging expenses. Of course, this concert would bring him publicity and goodwill for his tour, but that wasn't the reason he agreed.

She quickly mentioned that the expenses included having his classic BMW shipped to Dallas from New York and a first-class plane ticket. But, after all, he needed his car so he could drive to Crossroads. Miss Abernathy explained that he loved the car and needed to drive it one last time before he left for Europe.

Staten didn't care what the guy did as long as he stayed out of Quinn's life.

If he bothered Quinn, he wouldn't have to worry about the tour. He'd be headed back to New York by ambulance.

Twenty-Four

Lauren

"I'm sixteen," Lauren whispered to the mirror in her bedroom. "I'm finally sixteen."

The day was windy and still cloudy, but she didn't care. Tonight was her party. A birthday party on the beach, or it would be if she could call the mud around the lake a beach. Her father had borrowed picnic tables from the Baptist church and ordered a big cake. He'd dug out a pit six inches deep and three feet around and banked it with rocks for a big bonfire.

He'd even offered to decorate the tables, but she decided she'd do that herself. In two hours people would start arriving. It wouldn't be a huge party like Reid Collins had last month, but that didn't matter. Her dad planned to let everyone roast their own hot dog and she'd made sure she'd bought all the toppings.

She'd invited several adults, too, so, hopefully, her father would talk to them and not interrogate her friends. She had simply made a list of all the people who weren't criminals that her father had talked about in the past few months. Lauren wanted him to have a good time, as well.

Her pop sat on the deck blowing up balloons when the doorbell rang. Lauren squealed. She wasn't dressed yet in her new jeans and jacket. The kitchen had no decorations, and the fire wouldn't be started for another hour.

The bell sounded again, and she had no choice but to open the front door.

There, in a business suit, was her mother, looking totally out of place.

"Hello, sweetie," she squealed as if she were the grand prize of the night. "I thought I'd surprise you for your birthday."

Lauren forced a smile. In truth she was surprised Margaret remembered her birthday. Usually a card arrived sometime in March, but never close to the day. "Come on in," she managed, then added, "Please, don't fight with Pop today."

Her mother had the nerve to look hurt. "I'm not here to fight. I'm here to celebrate my baby girl growing up."

Tears welled in Lauren's eyes. All year she'd thought about this day. If her friends saw them fighting, they'd probably feel sorry for her or make fun of her parents. Just this one night she wanted the world to revolve around her.

Margaret looked worried. "I shouldn't have come. This was a bad idea. Just let me get your gift out of the car and I'll go."

Now Mom was making her feel bad. Lauren shouldn't have let her feelings show. She should have just let Mom come in and ruin her party.

Before Lauren could think of what to do, her father

appeared and caught up with his ex-wife halfway to her car. "Stop making this all about you, Margaret. We'll be glad to have your help around here. She's your daughter. You should be here. But, Lauren's right, no fighting today. Whatever you've decided I'm doing wrong this month will just have to wait until the night is over."

Margaret opened her mouth to argue, then snapped it closed.

Lauren watched in shock as Margaret released her trunk and got out a small box and her purse. Pop pulled out a suitcase and said, "Your room's still ready. It may be a little dusty."

"That's fine." Margaret lifted her chin. "I'm not here to be any trouble. I'm not a guest, Dan, I'm here to help with the party."

Pop walked past Lauren and whispered, "That'll be the day. Trouble's walking in, and I'm dumb enough to carry her suitcase."

Lauren grinned. Her father usually let Margaret walk all over him, but today he'd refused to let her do the same to his daughter. She was proud of him for standing up, and she was also proud of Margaret for bending just a little. Maybe the party wouldn't be so bad with both of them here.

An hour later she had to escape. Her parents were trying to kill each other with kindness. Margaret offered to help him do everything, and he praised her for her efforts, though decorating was not her mother's strong suit. Together her parents had managed to make the picnic tables outside look like they'd been taken hostage by clowns.

Lauren walked up the beach toward Tim's house. She wasn't surprised to see him sitting on the deck, his nose in a book. The joker had become a bookworm since he'd broken his leg.

"You coming to my party?" she called.

"Of course. Can't wait. You're my only social life."

She climbed the steps and leaned against the deck railing. "It's no big deal. Just a birthday party. My dad had Dorothy make the cake in the shape of Cookie Monster because I used to love him when I was four. When my mother saw it she freaked out and thought candles would help make it more sixteenth birthday-looking. They didn't help. Other than that, the food will be good."

"I don't care about the cake as long as we can eat it. Yours is the first party I've been to this year," he said.

"Why didn't you go to Reid's last month? Everyone was there."

He shrugged. "I don't know. Reid and I stopped hanging out. Maybe I'm not as funny as I was before the accident. He hasn't dropped by to show off his new car. Guess he's afraid to drive down the hill."

"You're still my friend, Tim."

"Thanks. To tell the truth, I'm in no hurry to see him, either. I'd just as soon sit on the porch and read a book." He frowned at her. "Did you ever have the feeling that we grew up that night at the Gypsy House?"

"Yes," she admitted. "It's like I looked the same the next day, but inside I was different."

"Me, too."

"Promise you'll come tonight," she begged.

"I promise. Mom's driving me over." He looked up and stared at her.

"What?"

Tim seemed to struggle with his thoughts, then said, "Don't go out with Reid if he asks you. Promise me."

"Why?" She hadn't planned to, but it seemed odd of Tim to warn her.

"Just don't. If you mean it that I'm your friend, take my advice."

She smiled, making light of how serious he'd turned all at once. This wasn't the Tim she knew. "All right. I promise."

On the way home along the water's edge, Lauren wondered why Tim felt the need to warn her. Reid was so popular he wouldn't be seen with her anyway. Plus, if they did go out, she could handle him, football player and all. Being a sheriff's daughter had its advantages. She'd been trained.

The shadows had grown long, and she could see the twinkle lights come on at her place. Amazingly, Pop had gotten them up and working. They made the deck look like a fairyland.

She was sixteen. Sixteen, with her whole life in front of her. There was magic in the air tonight. Like she was stepping into a new world, waking up as the cocoon began to crack open.

When she reached the bottom of the deck stairs, Lauren glanced up and saw something that froze her blood.

Her parents were just above her with their lips locked together. They weren't hugging. It looked like somehow their mouths had accidentally touched and stuck together, but their bodies were fighting the attraction.

This could mean nothing but trouble. Lauren whirled around and made it two steps before she slammed into someone.

"Reid!" she managed to say before he pulled her farther down the path, away from the lights.

"What are you so mad about?" he asked, laughing at her. "Your little party not going like you want it to?"

She could smell beer on his breath. "Reid, you've been drinking. Are you drunk?"

"I'm older then you, Lauren. I always will be, so stop talking to me like I'm a kid."

"You're not old enough to drink." She slapped his chest as if he needed waking up.

"What you going to do about it, birthday girl? Tell your daddy?"

Suddenly Lauren felt trapped. If she told Pop, all hell would break loose. Reid had to have driven here. He might not be falling-down drunk, but he was on his way. If he showed up at her party drunk, her father was bound to notice.

"You can't come to my party," she ordered, pushing Reid a few feet farther away from the deck.

"Why not? I brought a bottle to add to the lemonade. You won't even taste it, but you'll feel it. It'll make everyone happy."

"No!" She shoved again.

Reid caught her arm. "Forget the party, Lauren. Go for a ride with me. Just me and you."

"No," she answered, feeling suddenly sorry for him. "Why do you keep asking, Reid? We're not alike. I'm not your type. After the disaster at the Gypsy House, I'm not even sure we're friends."

"Sure you are," Reid insisted as he grabbed her arms and tried to pull her close. "You know you've always been nuts about me." He leaned in to kiss her. "I'll prove it."

Lauren reacted just as Pop had trained her. She jerked her knee up, slamming Reid hard between his legs.

To her surprise, he crumbled.

While he gulped for breath, she said politely, "Thank you for coming to my party, Reid, but I think you'd better go."

She walked away, wishing she could tell her pop how great his lessons had worked. But she never would. She wasn't even mad at Reid. She knew he didn't really like her; he was simply wanting one more girl to join his fan club.

The thought crossed her mind that maybe the reason her parents didn't touch when they kissed was because one would likely hurt the other. It must be a kind of hell to be attracted to someone you hate.

As parties went, Lauren rated hers a B. Nothing bad happened. Everyone laughed and talked. Most of the popular kids didn't show up. Most of her friends did. Reid would have probably been disappointed to know that no one missed him.

Her mother gave her something she might use for once—a diary. Obviously Margaret had lost the argument to give Lauren her old car. All the other gifts were great. Staten Kirkland and Quinn O'Grady, surprisingly, arrived together and gave her a phone with a whole year's worth of usage free.

The rancher and Quinn didn't fit together, but somehow they seemed to be a couple. Lauren decided it must be a full moon or something because strange people seemed to be pairing up. Quinn and Staten. Her mother and Pop. Reid and—no wait a minute. That one was not happening. Not tonight. Not *any* night.

She worried that Pop might think she didn't need a phone, but he said he wished he'd thought of it. Then he listed a few rules. She knew he'd think of more later.

At ten, everyone waved goodbye. Her parents were talking as they did the dishes, so Lauren walked out along the beach. She was sixteen. She had expected to feel different today, but she felt pretty much the same.

Halfway between her house and the O'Grady's place, she noticed Lucas's old pickup parked on the lake road.

When she strode near, he climbed out of the cab. Even in the moonlight he looked different. The boots were still there, but tonight he wore a regular white shirt, black slacks and a red pullover sweater. For a moment, she thought, he looked older.

"I'm sorry I missed your party." He walked slowly toward her. "I just got back from Tech. It's like a whole other world there. In a few months I'll be stepping into this bubble where everything is different."

She laughed. "You sound excited."

"I am."

He took her hand, and they moved to the tailgate where they could sit and watch the night sky. "I wish I could have been here with you. Or better yet, you could have been there with me. The campus is beautiful, and you wouldn't believe the library. There is a bookstore right in the middle, and the place is so big I'll have to hop a bus to get from class to class."

"I wish I'd been there, too. The party was fun. Tim made everyone laugh for the first time since his accident. My folks got along for a change. Mr. Kirkland gave me a phone, and he barely knows me."

"Funny, he gave me one, too. Said it was for my

birthday in three days, but since I was going to be on the road today, he wanted me to have it early."

They pulled their new phones out and clicked them together, then laughed.

Lucas flipped his open. "I haven't used it yet because I didn't have anyone I wanted to call, until now."

"You don't even know my number."

"Tell me," he said.

She ran through the numbers she'd just learned, then said, "Aren't you going to put my number in or at least write it down?"

"I got it," he said. "I won't forget."

The phone suddenly became her favorite gift. "When you leave, we can keep in touch."

"Sounds like a plan. You can tell me what's going on here, and I can tell you about college."

She bumped his shoulder. "You know for three days I'm only a year younger than you, so you'll have to stop treating me like a kid."

He put his arm around her. "Deal. You're no longer a kid." He hopped off the back of the truck and disappeared. Thirty seconds later he stood in front of her with one long-stem yellow rose. "I had to stop at three florists on the way back to find this. Happy birthday. No matter how old you get, *mi cielo*, for three days we'll only be a year apart."

"We're almost the same age." She'd looked up what he'd called her in Spanish and knew it meant *my sky,* but she was too shy to ask him to explain why he called her that.

Laughing, they walked back to her house. Just before they reached the lights, he leaned down and kissed her. Her first real kiss. Not a light touching of lips or a quick peck in greeting, but a long, curl her toes, real kiss. She wrapped her arms around his neck and leaned in, wishing this one kiss could last forever.

When he pulled away so he could see her, Lucas laughed. "You know, we can only do this for three days. After that, you'll be too young for me."

"Do it again," she whispered. "I don't want to forget."

He kissed her again, hugging her so tight she knew he felt as she did. Neither wanted these few minutes to end.

Finally, he pulled away, and without a word he disappeared into the night. If she wasn't still holding the rose, she might have believed she'd dreamed him.

They weren't dating, or falling in love, or promising to be best friends. In August he'd be in college, and she'd be a junior in high school, but they would talk. Mr. Kirkland had no idea what he had started.

Somehow thinking about the next few years didn't seem so bad. Whenever she was alone, she'd think of Lucas, and if he got too rushed at college, maybe he'd remember her and the way they watched the sky.

Lauren walked in the back door and smiled when she didn't hear her parents screaming at each other. The night had turned from good to great with one rose, and nothing, not even their fighting or Reid trying to make a pass or getting a Cookie Monster cake would change that.

"Did you have a good time, sweetie?" Margaret asked.

"I had a great time. It was the perfect party." She kissed them both on the cheek. "Oh, one thing, I've decided I'm going to Tech when I graduate, and I plan to graduate early, so start saving."

Pop looked shocked. He glanced at Margaret. "Man, they sure do grow up fast."

Lauren laughed. "Maybe you two should consider having another kid so you'll still have something to fight about."

To her surprise her pop looked like he was considering the idea. Then, Margaret jabbed him in the ribs with one of the forks for roasting hot dogs.

Lauren backed away as they both tried to out-yell each other on which thought her idea was the worst they'd ever heard.

They were still yelling when Lauren fell asleep.

Twenty-Five

Yancy

The wind howled all Monday morning like a pack of wolves, holding back the spring. Yancy Grey usually liked working outside, but today he'd found one excuse after another to stay indoors.

After a breakfast of leftover donuts, Yancy tackled Miss Bees's to-do list. Like Miss Abernathy, Miss Bees had never married, but unlike Miss Abernathy, she didn't have a kind bone in her body. She'd taught physical education for forty years after playing semi-pro baseball right out of college. She had a wall of trophies and ribbons to prove it. From the looks of her place, she'd played baseball, golf and hockey. Worn sticks and bats and clubs occupied every corner, and she used them as walking canes. Their prominent display was probably her way of burglar-proofing the place.

She limped around her house, pointing with a golf club at every crack in her walls. Most only needed toothpaste stuck in the cracks, left to dry, and one brush of paint to complete the job. But she felt the need to instruct him, to tell him to be careful and inspect everything he did.

"Mind telling me why you're in a bad mood today, Miss Bees?" he finally asked.

"I'm not in a bad mood," she shouted as if he'd suddenly gone deaf. "You don't want to see me in a bad mood, believe me. I'm a woman who keeps her temper under control. I've only lost it a few times in my life and then only with good reason."

He believed her completely. If this was happy, Yancy wasn't sure he would live through mad.

As soon as he finished, he headed back to the office feeling like he needed to be vaccinated to make sure he didn't catch what she had.

The old folks must have heard the wind, too, because Leo was the only one to wander out to sit in the glass office in front of Yancy's rooms. When the mailman walked past, Leo started talking without looking up, like one of them chatty snowmen stores put out around Christmas that were movement activated.

"I've heard tell," Leo began, "that when the wind whines like this, death is riding in. The Apache have a legend about a dark spirit who walks the night in the space between winter and spring. He holds back the warm air for as long as he can. At first he's strong and not even the bravest of the brave can fight him and win, but eventually, he ages and can no longer stand against the changing seasons. When he finally turns his back and rides away, he'll take the breath of whoever stands near."

The few rusty red hairs on Leo's head seemed to stand on end. "So this might be a good day to stay inside, Yancy."

"I don't believe in Apache legends. Plus, you probably made that up, Mr. Leo. In the two months I've been here I've learned not to believe a word you say."

Leo smiled. "You're smart, young man. Only you might want to remember that even an honest man lies now and then, and a liar sometimes accidentally tells the truth."

Yancy just nodded, then decided to skip his usual lunch of soup and head over to Mr. Halls's place. With the wind whipping up dirt, he couldn't paint outside, but he could paint the old principal's living room. It had taken him two days just to move out all the books. Once the walls dried, they'd be putting them back, and no one would notice the paint job. But Mr. Halls wanted it done, so Yancy agreed.

He needed something to keep his mind off Ellie. Cap's niece hadn't been by but once all day, and the last time she'd checked on him, too many people had been around for them to say anything personal to each other, even if he could think of something personal to say.

She had checked his prairie-dog bite and told him he didn't have to wear the bandage anymore. She hadn't even patted his hand or anything. That woman could be downright irritating when she was all professional-like.

Apparently, when he didn't develop rabies, she lost interest in him. If he wanted to keep a girl like her, he needed to come up with some symptoms.

By six that night his back ached from painting and moving books around. He went home planning to clean up and eat at the café. He was too tired to even open a can of soup.

He decided to stretch out on his bed and relax, only

he fell asleep. Dreams of wild prairie dogs chasing him and howling like the wind outside finally woke him. It was almost nine, but Yancy didn't want to go back to sleep.

After pacing the dark glass office, he decided to take a walk. The wind had finally slowed, and it wasn't too cold. Yancy strode out of the side office door and stood in the shadows, thinking about Leo's legend. He'd never really had much he believed in, but he sure didn't believe a dark spirit rode the wind.

Slowly, wishing he'd brought a stick along or one of Miss Bees's bats, he moved to the side of the road. The gas station was still open, but not a single car was parked out front. When he finished his walk, Yancy thought he might go inside and buy one of the burritos. Nothing the gas station sold was worth eating, but it was fast, and this time of night they sometimes had two-for-one sales on the burritos.

As he moved in the shadows, he saw the truck he'd thought might belong to the con called Cowboy pass by. Yancy watched as it turned off the highway and circled around to the back of the gas station where a dozen or more trailer homes were.

The trailer park was blocked from view by a line of storage buildings. Yancy crossed the deserted street and moved behind the station.

It wasn't too hard to find where the truck had parked or the two cons he'd hated in prison. All he had to do was follow the cussing. From his vantage point between two dark mobile homes, he saw the men unloading something from the truck to the trunk of an old car. It looked big enough to be a side of beef or a body. Each claimed he was lifting the heaviest part.

Yancy had no idea what they were doing, but he'd bet it was something illegal. Freddie, the bald one, mentioned something about Arlo not doing his share of the work. Cowboy didn't argue about that but muttered that all this would be over by the end of the month, and he'd never have to look at him or Arlo again.

The wind kicked up, sending old bags and trash whirling through the lot. Yancy didn't think the dark spirit would get him, but he wasn't so sure that the two cons wouldn't track him down if they caught his scent. Somehow they were linked with the recent trouble at the ranches. He could feel it.

Retracing his steps, he noticed the café's open sign was still blinking. Hunger drove him toward the lights.

Several people were in the side room Dorothy had labeled Private Dining as if it were a fancy place that didn't get the same paper napkins the front part did.

When he tried the door it was unlocked, so he thought he'd see if he couldn't get a quick meal.

As soon as he was inside, Sissy stood up from the booth where she'd been sitting and welcomed him. "Dorothy's already shut down the grill, but I could make you a cold sandwich and chips if you're hungry, Yancy. Coffee is left over, but it's free."

"Sounds great." He wasn't particular. "Any kind of sandwich would be fine." He pointed to the back. "What's going on?"

"The chamber of commerce moved over here to eat while they talk about the details for the upcoming event. Ain't you heard? We got us a real big-time fund-raiser. They're talking about making thousands of dollars."

Yancy had heard Miss Abernathy talking about it. A famous pianist was coming to town for one night. She said folks from as far as Abilene and Lubbock would come to hear him. The old piano teacher had talked every one of the residents at Evening Shadows into buying at least one ticket as well as volunteering for the event.

Sissy handed him a coffee cup. "Have a seat with Ellie and I'll bring your plate." She waddled off to the kitchen rubbing her tummy as if it were a crystal ball hidden under her top.

He moved to the last of the booths. "You mind if I sit down?"

Ellie wasn't frowning at him, but she didn't look happy to see him. She seemed to be simply studying him, as though he was the new lab rat.

"I don't mind." To his surprise, she moved over so he could slide in beside her.

Yancy had no idea what to say. She didn't ask about his finger, so he guessed that subject was done.

Finally, she broke the ice. "My uncle Cap bought two tickets for the fund-raiser. You want to go with me? He told me he'd buy two so long as he didn't have to go. He claims he'd rather do parking-lot duty than listen to music that isn't country."

"I've never been to a recital."

"Me, either." She frowned at him. "Do you want to go or not?"

"I'd like to, but I don't have a car. I'm saving up for one."

She had that strange look about her again. As if she were trying to figure out what planet he was from. "I can pick you up, but if we eat anything, you have to pay, because it's a date."

"Do folks eat at recitals?"

"Popcorn maybe," she said.

He'd have to dip into his savings, but he figured it'd be worth it. Smiling, he moved a little closer until his leg brushed against hers. "It's a date."

She grinned. Ellie may not have had many dates, but she'd had more than him. She sat with him while he ate, and Sissy sat across from them talking about how her body was falling apart now that she was pregnant. Yancy barely kept up with the conversation.

When he paid for Ellie's Coke and walked her out to her car, he felt as though he was walking into a normal life with his head up.

He held her car door open, and when she climbed in, he kissed her cheek. "Good night," was all he could manage, though he thought about adding sweetie or honey. Somehow that just didn't fit Ellie.

"Good night," she answered. "See you next Saturday night."

As she drove off he couldn't stop smiling. He had a date.

Yancy had a pure moment of joy before he turned around and saw Freddie and Cowboy staring at him.

His perfectly normal life was about to end. This was worse than Leo's Apache dark spirit.

Twenty-Six

Staten

Staten waited in Quinn's tiny living room for her to finish dressing. A cool spring breeze drifted past her open back door and made the old house smell new. He hated the whole idea of this concert from the beginning, but never as much as he did right now, dressed up in his best suit and boots. With his arm still in the sling, he felt as if he'd be useless to Quinn if trouble came.

"You don't have to go," he yelled at her closed bedroom door. "You've nothing to prove to anyone."

No one around knew what had happened to Quinn when she'd studied under Lloyd deBellome, and Staten knew that was the way she wanted it. They all thought the pianist to be a great and gifted man. If Miss Abernathy called him *special* one more time, Staten swore he'd do his best to choke her with one hand.

Despite the hunger to flatten the guy and break not only his fingers but every bone in his body, Staten wished this night would just be over, and they could all go back to forgetting Lloyd existed. Quinn was the only person who counted. He wanted her safe and happy. Keeping her away from Lloyd seemed the best way to do just that.

Only Quinn had decided she wanted to go to the concert. No, not the concert, he reconsidered. She wanted to face Lloyd. She wanted to be done with the man who'd changed her life, crushed her dreams and sent her into hiding from all strangers for twenty years.

His shy Quinn had something to prove to herself, and Staten planned to stand beside her. He didn't mind that she was shy. Hell, he couldn't think of more than a dozen people he liked to be around, but he didn't want her frightened.

"I have to go," she called from the bedroom. "He's asked Miss Abernathy if I'll be there, and I have to show him I'm no longer afraid of him. He's nothing to me. No more than a rabid dog I once encountered in the woods of Manhattan."

Staten knew she was behind the door giving herself a pep talk. Maybe if she kept talking long enough they'd miss the concert.

His arm and shoulder hurt from doing exactly what the doctor had told him not to do. If she'd just say the word he'd strip off his Sunday clothes and cuddle up in bed with her, but he knew she had made up her mind. He was so proud of her strength.

"Well," he said, "if you're going, I'm going with you. I plan to be right by your side all night, so don't think I'm backing out if you're going."

"I know you will be beside me," she answered. "I'm counting on it. But remember your promise. You will not attack him in any way. This isn't about you, Staten. It's a demon I have to fight on my own."

"What if he attacks *me*?" Staten could only hope.

"He won't. Lloyd would never fight. He is very proud of his appearance. I remember him saying that he was born to perform, blessed with his long aristocratic nose and beautiful hands."

Staten swore under his breath. He had no choice but to go along with what Quinn wanted. Mad as he was that someone had hurt her, if he did the wrong thing, it might hurt their relationship. The possibility of what might be between them had been building inside him since she'd told him she was pregnant. Lloyd deBellome would be here for a few hours, but Staten wanted Quinn in his world for the rest of his life.

They'd been dancing around all the important conversations they needed to have all week. Nothing had been settled about the baby or what either planned to do about it. All he knew was that she wouldn't stay with him at the ranch. If he couldn't get her to spend the night, he didn't have much chance of getting her to move in.

The baby was a Kirkland. He or she should be born on Kirkland land. Only, he wasn't about to say that out loud.

He remembered how his granny used to quote Eleanor Roosevelt. *We must all, at some point, do the one thing that we believe we can not do.* Maybe facing Lloyd was Quinn's one thing, just like letting her make this call about their child was his.

He knew this night was going to be hard for her and he almost claimed he wasn't feeling up to going. Only, Staten guessed she'd just get the sheriff or someone else to go along with her. His shy Quinn was showing the

first signs of having a backbone, and he was so proud
he couldn't, wouldn't rain on her parade.

"I'm ready," she said as she emerged from the bedroom. "And, like it or not, Staten Kirkland, you're my
date."

He watched her walk toward him, more beautiful
than he'd ever seen her. The weight she'd gained with
the pregnancy rounded her slim body to perfection and
the cream-colored silk pantsuit she'd bought to wear tonight hugged her in all the right places. One strand of
midnight pearls hung from her high neckline.

"You're beautiful," he whispered, loving the way her
long hair swayed straight down her back in one shiny
waterfall. How could he have known her all his life and
not seen the full beauty of Quinn until this moment?

"I didn't dress this way because of Lloyd or the fund-
raiser. I want everyone to know tonight that I'm stepping out of hiding. I want them to know I'm with you,
Staten."

"I'd like nothing more," he admitted and realized
just how much he meant every word. "But, Quinn, folks
aren't going to realize we're together tonight because
all anyone is going to see is you."

He offered his arm, and they walked out into the cool
breeze of spring. Staten couldn't stop staring at her.

They drove to the concert both lost in their own
thoughts. Staten couldn't help wishing that the evening
was over, and they were on their way back to her place.
He wanted to hold her.

When they pulled up at the high school, a hundred
cars and trucks were already there. One spot on the
loading dock behind the auditorium was roped off for
Lloyd's classic BMW. Since the spot was empty, Staten

guessed that the guest of honor hadn't arrived yet. All Lloyd had to do was pull up and walk into the back of the auditorium. That way he wouldn't have to mix with the locals. His granny and Miss Bees seemed to be guarding the back door just in case some fan rushed in. Which wasn't likely. Most people in town couldn't name a single famous pianist.

The faculty lot was roped off for valet parking.

Staten pulled into the line and waited his turn. He recognized several men with the volunteer fire department sitting like pigeons on the loading dock beside the back door, waiting for the rush of cars needing to be parked.

Retired Captain Fuller smiled at him from behind a card table. "Five bucks to park your car, Staten. All proceeds go to the fire department."

Staten helped Quinn from the truck, tossed his keys to one of the firemen and handed Cap a twenty.

The old man frowned. "I don't make change."

"I didn't figure you did, Mr. Fuller." Staten might be over twenty years out of high school, but Cap would always be Mr. Fuller to him.

Staten and Quinn walked into the front of the school and along a wide foyer to the open doors of the auditorium. Ransom Canyon High had been built in sections. The main wing and the cafeteria were there when he and Quinn went to school, but the auditorium had been added years later along with the new gym. Both were colorfully walled with a tile mosaic of the canyon.

"You all right, Quinn?" he whispered as they handed over their hundred-dollar tickets. Quinn had a death grip on his good arm, so he wasn't sure.

She nodded slightly, too nervous to speak.

Wanting to help, he pulled one memory of their high school days. "Remember when we had a Howdy Dance down the hall in the cafeteria our senior year? You dressed like Raggedy Ann with your hair up in dog ears."

She smiled. "I turned my head and dipped my hair in your drink, then panicked and slung red soda all over everyone around us." She laughed. "Everyone suddenly had freckles."

He nodded. "I didn't mind. When we danced later I thought of asking if you'd do it again. That was the funniest thing that happened all night."

He looked into her warm, loving eyes, thankful he'd found a memory they alone shared. Leaning close, he whispered, "Ready?"

"Ready," she answered.

They hadn't made it to their seats in the third row before Miss Abernathy waylaid them. "You must come backstage to meet our guest when he arrives. He told me he's been longing to see you again."

Both Staten and Quinn shook their heads, but the dear piano teacher insisted. "Don't worry, we're keeping it very private. I've got Miss Bees at the stage door with orders to let no one in but Master deBellome. She brought a hockey stick and a bat to make sure." Miss Abernathy checked her watch. "I'm afraid you'll only have time for a quick hello. I really thought he'd be here by now. It's almost time to open the curtain."

Staten looked at Quinn and waited. She was calling the shots tonight.

Quinn shook her head slightly just as Miss Abernathy was pulled away by an emergency. It seemed one of the church buses was unloading and blocking the spot for the honored guest.

Once she was out of sight, Quinn let out a long-held breath. "I can do this. I can listen to the music, then leave. If I have to meet him, I'll simply act as if I don't remember him."

"Me, too," Staten whispered. "It won't be too hard a job for me. The sooner the bastard is out of my state, the better."

The crowd began to fill up the auditorium. Staten counted down each minute. In five minutes it would start. In forty minutes it would be over. They'd clap and walk out, and it would all be finished.

He laced Quinn's fingers into his and held on tightly, trying not to think of what the man who was about to step on the stage had done to this woman he cared about. He'd drugged her, then raped her, then beat her, and when she'd refused to allow it to continue, he'd broken her fingers.

Staten felt his breathing quicken and his muscles tighten. Hard as he tried to stop it, hatred rose in his chest.

Hope that the guy wouldn't show up sprang into Staten's thought. It was ten after eight. Maybe he wasn't coming? Even the firemen were in the auditorium in the back row. The only person not here tonight was Lloyd deBellome.

Miss Abernathy showed up again at Staten's side.

"It's past time to start," Staten said, hoping the little piano teacher would suggest calling the whole thing off.

Miss Abernathy looked as if she might start crying. "The master just came in, but he refuses to begin until he sees you, Quinn. He says you were very special to him."

Staten shook his head. He wouldn't put Quinn through that.

Panic rose in Miss Abernathy's voice, and she began to hiccup out in little squeals. People in the audience were getting restless. "Quinn, please come backstage for a moment. I can't deal with this. I had no idea he'd be so temperamental. He…he yelled at me. Called me names no one has ever called me."

To his surprise, Quinn stood. "I'll see him, but Staten is coming with me."

They moved across the front of the stage to where the sheriff stood guarding the entrance to backstage. He pulled the curtain aside and started to speak to Quinn but stopped suddenly as if he'd seen a ghost and not one of his friends.

Miss Abernathy and Quinn moved behind the curtain, but the sheriff gripped Staten's arm when he would have passed.

"Wait a minute, Staten," Dan Brigman whispered. "I don't know what's going on, but I'm not letting you pass. Hell's breaking loose backstage with our guest, and something tells me seeing you won't help."

Staten tried to jerk away but was aware that most of the audience could still see him. "I'm going with Quinn." His words came out fast and hard.

Dan's grip didn't lessen. "If ever a man had murder in his eyes, it's you. I'm not letting you pass until I know what's going on."

Staten knew he only had seconds. He didn't want to fight Dan. The sheriff wasn't the problem.

The truth was all he had time to tell. "Lloyd raped

Quinn when she was in college. He broke her fingers, making her quit any dreams of being a concert pianist, and now the bastard won't play until he sees her."

Dan stared at Staten and seemed to read all he wasn't saying. "If you assault him, I'll have to arrest you. It's my duty."

"I understand."

To his surprise the sheriff released his arm and let Staten pass behind the curtain.

Quinn was standing in the center of the stage. A huge baby grand piano was between her and a tall, thin man with salt and pepper hair streaked back from his high forehead. His features were sharp, like a hawk's. Long nose, lifted eyebrows, hollow cheeks.

"Of course you remember me, Quinn," he said in a harsh whisper as if he'd just been insulted. "I noticed your last name is still O'Grady. Apparently, you never got over me." Lloyd deBellome grinned as if he shared a private joke with her.

Staten looked around. Miss Abernathy was nowhere in sight. Lloyd must have sent her on an errand. Somehow deBellome had planned to get Quinn alone, and he thought he'd won. Only he didn't see Staten to his left ready to storm in if the guy moved one step closer to Quinn. The master couldn't have seen the sheriff behind Staten, either, or the two ladies standing in the open doorway at the back. All his focus was on his prey.

"I'm afraid I don't know you, or want to." Quinn's voice was surprisingly strong. "I recall very little about my time in New York. It was a dark period in my life with nothing worth remembering."

Lloyd deBellome laughed. "I remember you. How you tried to fight at first. How you curled into a ball when I began to discipline you and how you passed out, making the ending to our little mating rather boring. I've looked for you for over twenty years. You were the one that got away. The one I couldn't control. The one I couldn't make scream or beg. I thought I'd lost you forever, but your old piano teacher told me where you were. One call from her and you're in my life again."

Staten took a step, and Dan grabbed him from behind. "I've changed my mind, Staten. I've heard enough. I'll hold him for you if you decide to pound on him."

Staten nodded, knowing he'd honor Quinn's request as long as he could.

"You are nothing to me, not even a memory." Quinn stopped Staten with her strong words. "You're nothing but a sick, mean, old man."

A slow smile twisted Lloyd's face. "How about we talk about this over a drink after the concert? I'm stopping over tonight in Lubbock before I fly out tomorrow. I'll make great money on this tour, and I might be talked into letting you tag along. It could prove very interesting."

Quinn turned away, not even bothering to answer him.

Lloyd did what Staten had been waiting for. He took a step toward her. Almost dragging the sheriff with him, Staten blocked the pianist's path. His right hand doubled into a fist. One blow was all he needed to rearrange the master's face.

Quinn glanced back and raised her hand, silently stopping him for a second. She'd done what she'd come to do. She'd won. There was no need for him to hurt Lloyd because the man could no longer hurt her.

In that one lost moment, Miss Abernathy seemed to

fly in from the wings. The woman who'd told everyone in town how great Lloyd was now looked like an old avenging angel about to rain all hell down on the man.

The curtains began to open as Lloyd snapped, yelling that he was leaving this nothing town and all the crazy hicks who lived in this middle-of-nowhere place. He swore these people wouldn't know great music if they heard it. It would be a waste for him to play. He was meant for the palaces of Europe, not the crossroads to nowhere.

Miss Abernathy told him to get out, but Lloyd kept yelling, telling everyone in the audience what a waste of his valuable time it would be to play for people who were no more than clods on the earth.

Yancy Grey and a few others stood up and started arguing with the master, claiming he looked ridiculous in his monkey suit and long hair.

Miss Abernathy must have become aware of the fact that her concert might develop into a wrestling match at any moment. She ran out the back door crying. She passed Miss Bees, who was waving her hockey stick at the master, calling him every name she could think of.

Staten pulled Quinn backward into the curtains and hugged her tight. "I'm proud of you," he whispered. "I'm so proud of you." He didn't care about the concert or the riot going on.

She smiled up at him. "Do you think we should save Lloyd before this crowd lynches him?"

"No. He's digging his own grave. Give him time."

Staten kissed her gently, then rushed with her to the back door, where a terrible pounding noise had started.

The moment he saw what was happening, Staten froze.

She peeked around him. "What are those ladies doing?"

The pounding was as steady as a heartbeat as Miss Bees swung her golf club against the BMW. "It's good for working off your anger. Try the bat, Beverly. I've already broken the hockey stick."

Miss Abernathy raised a baseball bat and whacked the taillight out, then giggled "You're right. I feel better all ready."

Lloyd must have heard the pounding for he rushed through the open door and started screaming. Apparently the sheriff was already outside in the shadows just watching. Lloyd demanded the officer do something. While the pounding continued, Dan pulled out his notepad to record the complaint.

Staten closed the heavy door to the outside and smiled. The demolition might still be going on, but no one inside would hear it. "We owe these people a concert, Quinn. Play for them the way you played for me the other night. They deserve to hear a real master play."

"I can't," she whispered as he tugged her to the piano.

"Ladies and gentlemen, we don't need to bring someone in to play beautiful music. We have our own gifted pianist." He sat her on the piano bench. "Maybe, just maybe, she'll play tonight."

Quinn didn't move. She just sat perfectly still and stared out at the packed house.

Staten waited for her to start. He knew he was taking a big risk, but it was for her. Nothing would remove the horror of what Lloyd had done to her like proving that he hadn't taken her gift from her.

He waited.

Quinn seemed frozen.

Everyone in the auditorium was silent. They'd all heard Miss Abernathy talk about how Quinn had a great talent. They knew the story about how she'd quit school and returned without giving a reason. They all knew she refused to play in public.

No one in the seats beyond the footlights made a sound.

Taking a deep breath, Staten pulled his arm from the sling and moved to the huge piano. With his big hands on the side, he spun the baby grand around, then he took Quinn's hand, tugged her to her feet and moved the stool so that her back was to the audience.

When he lowered her back to the bench, he whispered, "Play for me, Quinn. Play only for me."

Dragging a folding chair onstage so that Quinn could see him and he could see all the people behind her, he waited.

Finally, she straightened her back and lifted her hands to the ivories.

Complete silence greeted the soft music drifting through the air. Slowly it grew until her melody filled every inch of the huge space, circling around everyone in the room.

Staten crossed his arms and leaned back in his chair. He never stopped smiling as she played.

Deep inside him all the wounds he'd refused to let heal vanished. One shy lady with her gentle ways and magic had coaxed his heart into beating again.

Twenty-Seven

Staten

An hour later, Staten and Quinn sat in the sheriff's office trying to keep their hands off each other while the sheriff tried to sort out everything that had happened at the concert.

All Staten wanted to do was hold Quinn, but the twenty people crammed into the office and the reception area were in his way. She'd stood up to her demons and won. She'd played just for him, leaving no doubt in anyone's mind that she was gifted or that Quinn O'Grady was his woman.

"I need to talk to you," he whispered.

"I know. Me, too, but we can't leave all these people." Quinn grinned. "I'm afraid this is worse than splashing red soda on everyone. The sheriff looks like he's thinking of resigning his post. He keeps glaring at us as if he thinks all these people going crazy is somehow our fault."

"How could it be our fault? We're the only two in the room who didn't want deBellome here in the first place. If Miss Bees and Miss Abernathy hadn't heard what Lloyd said to you, I could have handled him quietly. I would have only broken a few bones."

Quinn nodded. "Everyone knows Miss Bees has a temper. But I've never known of a time where she's actually hurt anyone, or damaged property. With a swing like hers, she should go pro."

Staten grinned. "She sure damaged that little car. It'll have to be towed."

"I was shocked when Miss Abernathy joined her. In a few minutes they turned from two senior citizens into Butch and Sundance."

He glanced over at the piano teacher. Miss Abernathy was in handcuffs and smiling. Everyone who walked by got the whole story about how one of her students was a great pianist. She told everyone she always knew Quinn had it in her. The dear seemed to have forgotten her own criminal activity during Quinn's concert. Miss Abernathy's back was straight and proud, and she didn't seem to mind that her silver bracelets were connected and locked together.

She may have only been able to hear the last few minutes of the concert because she and Miss Bees were busy. But she had no doubt that she'd heard a master play.

"We stopped when the sheriff threatened to lock us up," Miss Bees said to Leo when he passed her a cup of coffee. "I've got a temper, and I didn't like that guy one bit. He seemed to think his car was more important than one of my students, and I won't stand for that."

All the teachers in the room nodded their agreement.

"Leo says we're going up the river," Miss Abernathy whispered loud enough for most of the room to hear. "Oh, Miss Bees, I don't think I'll do well there."

"Well," the former physical education teacher said with her head up, "all I got to say is they'd better have clean sheets. I'm not sleeping on bedbugs."

Yancy Grey and Ellie were down the line of folding chairs from the two delinquents charged with destruction of property. "They don't have bedbugs, Miss Bees. They spray the cells down."

"How do you know that, Yancy?" Miss Bees yelled. "You done a world tour of the prison system, have you?"

"Nope," he said. "I'm just guessing." Yancy tried to go back to talking to Ellie.

Miss Bees wasn't finished. "What are you two doing here anyway? Yancy, you and Ellie haven't done anything wrong. Go home."

"We're witnesses," Yancy said. "I'm just a regular citizen here to do my duty."

Ellie shook her head. "I didn't see anything but that funny-looking guy fall down the stairs."

Staten had been watching them and decided the trip to the sheriff's office was simply part of their first date. Ellie had had to help get deBellome in the ambulance, but Yancy was tagging along. The two could have left the office, but they seemed to think this was an after-the-performance party. All the others who lived at the Evening Shadows Retirement Community must have a pack mentality.

Dan Brigman stood on a chair. "All right, everyone, I need silence."

Everyone agreed to give him the floor.

"First, if Mr. deBellome presses charges, I'm going to have to arrest several of you."

"For what?" Cap yelled from his seat near the door. "All we did is throw out the trash after he tumbled down the stairs."

Everyone laughed except the sheriff.

"Miss Abernathy, did you knowingly and willingly destroy property?"

The old piano teacher smiled. "I did my best."

The sheriff shook his head. "What about you, Miss Bees? Why'd you go along with such a crazy action?"

Miss Bees puffed up. "I didn't go along with anything. I'm the one who started it. I guessed the idiot would hurry out if he thought his car was in danger. Besides, he's the one who gave me the idea. When he strutted in late to his own concert, he pointed one of his long fingers at me and told me to make sure no one touched his car, like I was working for him."

Dan looked as if he was aging by the minute. "Look, ladies, I think we can work this out without charges being filed. I can't imagine the famous Lloyd deBellome wanting it known that two ladies like yourselves got mad enough to do damage. The press would love that story."

He raised his voice and continued, "What I need to know is which one of you tripped the pianist on the back steps leading off the dock? I was trying to stop Miss Bees from taking another swing while he was yelling that a few of you men were standing in his way." The sheriff pointed to Cap, Leo and Mr. Halls. "The next thing I knew he was tumbling down the stairs."

"Where is the bastard anyway?" Cap shouted. "Why don't you ask him?"

Dan glared at Cap. "You know where he is. Ellie and Yancy loaded him in the ambulance. He's on his way to the hospital with a broken nose and a busted knee and who knows what else. I suspect a few of his wounds may have occurred while all of you were rushing in to help him up." The sheriff pointed his finger from one senior citizen to another.

Staten swore that everyone looked guilty, even his granny.

"Now, back to my questions. When the dust cleared, all you folks from the retirement community were standing around. Anyone of you, except Miss Bees, could have tripped him. So, who did it?"

The room was silent for a few seconds, then Mr. Halls shouted, "What'd he say?"

"He wants to know which one of us tripped the bastard," Cap yelled.

The old principal, dressed in one of the suits he'd once walked the hallways in, stood. "I tripped him with my cane," he shouted. "I'm the leader, so I'll do the time."

"No, you didn't," Mrs. Kirkland announced. "I shoved him over with my walker. I was the one closest to him."

Staten would have told his granny to stop lying, but he wasn't too sure.

One by one, each resident stood and confessed. Even Miss Bees claimed she swung her golf club, when the sheriff wasn't looking, and did the deed.

Mrs. Butterfield, who hadn't been following the conversation, stood with the others and said whatever it was, she was sure she was guilty. Mrs. Butterfield never talked much, but apparently she didn't want to be left out. She also offered to bring pies to serve at the trial if someone else would provide the plates, napkins and forks.

Dan gave up. "Yancy, help these folks to their cars and see they all get home. We'll sort this out in the morning."

"But…"

"No buts, Yancy. You're my deputy as of right now. Get all these criminals home."

Yancy didn't look too happy but seemed to cheer up a bit when Ellie offered to help. One by one Staten watched the old folks leave. They were fighters, rabble-rousers and heroes. He could see why his granny had wanted to live with them. Even at twice his age, they were far more fun to be around than he must be.

When they were gone, Dan collapsed in his chair. "I can't arrest any of them."

Staten shook his head. "You going to bring them in one at a time and interrogate them?"

"Nope. It would be a waste of time." The sheriff propped his boots on his desk. "I'll drop by and visit with Lloyd tomorrow. When he finds out we had several witnesses to what he said to Quinn, he'll drop any charges. He can't prove someone actually tripped him, and his insurance will probably pay for his car being vandalized."

"Sounds like he's getting off easy," Staten said.

Quinn shook her head. "There were enough reporters there that word will get out about him refusing to play."

Dan nodded. "I think I even saw one getting tape of them loading him up. He was cussing the town, the state and old folks. I wouldn't be surprised if someone didn't record him shouting at the audience. It'll be all over the news by dawn."

Quinn added matter-of-factly, "He'll have to cancel some, if not all, of his tour to recover. He's so vain I can't see him playing at all until his nose heals. The promoters will probably replace him and sue him for breach of contract."

"So, you're saying his career is over?" the sheriff asked.

She nodded. "Maybe so. If he was young, he might outlive the way he acted, but not now. If the school in New York gets wind of how he yelled and cussed onstage, he'll lose his teaching job, as well. I'll bet Miss Abernathy will make that call first thing in the morning."

Dan looked at Quinn and changed the subject. "I'm sorry I was out back and didn't get to hear you play."

She laughed, suddenly nervous. "If you had been inside, there's no telling what Miss Bees and Miss Abernathy would have done."

Dan leaned forward and took her hand. "If you ever play again, I'd love to hear it."

"I'll invite you." She smiled. "I promise."

Staten felt a shock of pure jealousy for the first time in his life. If it had happened when he'd been a teen he would have been ready to fight, but at forty-three he knew if he said anything, he'd only look like a fool. Dan Brigman was Quinn's friend, and he was just being nice. Or at least he'd better be *just being nice.*

Staten stood, took Quinn's free hand and started toward the door. "If you don't need us, I think Quinn and I will call it a night."

Dan's grin was almost wicked. "I knew you two were a couple when you knocked her door off the frame that day I was in the barn, but I guess everyone in town knows it after tonight."

Staten didn't slow as Quinn said, "What day did you knock my door down?"

"Thanks, Sheriff," Staten yelled back, knowing he'd have to come up with an answer fast.

"Anytime, Kirkland." Dan laughed.

Quinn walked up the steps to her porch, leading Staten into her little house decorated in a style he would never fit into. She couldn't stop smiling, even when she finally turned to him.

Staten puffed up like a bear ready to fight. "If you won't come back to the ranch with me, I'm staying here tonight." Staten stood his ground. "There will be no leaving you alone tonight, Quinn."

She lifted her chin. "You're putting your foot down, are you, Staten?"

"Nope. I'm putting my whole body down next to you. I don't care if we talk or make love or just go to sleep. I'm going to be with you tonight, and that's the way it is."

"I kind of like that idea myself. It won't be easy with your wounded shoulder, but we'll make it work."

Staten looked surprised he won. He didn't seem to know what else to say. "I can't do a very good job of undressing you with this arm in a sling. You may have to do most of that yourself."

"You moved a piano for me. Surely you can remove a few clothes."

Still frowning, he winked at her.

She laughed. "And if you're sleeping in my bed,

we're making love. I'm putting my foot down, Staten, that's the way it is."

Finally he smiled, obviously knowing she was mocking him. Knowing that his rough demand didn't frighten her one bit. "Is that an order, Quinn?"

"Yes. If I'm going to put up with you for the next fifty or sixty years, I need to have some say."

He watched her every move. "How you going to put up with me if you refuse to live in my house? If you won't come to me, I promise you I could never live in this little dollhouse of a place with its tiny bathroom and kitchen so small we keep bumping into each other." He smiled. "Correction, the bumping into part isn't so bad to put up with."

Quinn wanted to bring an end to the discussion that seemed to have no answer. She tugged her top off and Staten seemed to lose the power to speak.

She waited.

Finally, he whispered, "Your breasts are so beautiful. You are so beautiful."

She took his hand and led him to the bedroom. While he studied her, she undressed him. Then she stood very still as he placed his hands on her waist and slid her silk slacks and panties down in one movement.

"Don't hurt your shoulder," she whispered.

"I swear, Quinn, this causes me no pain in my shoulder. I might have to do it as a regular exercise."

They moved under the covers so that she rested on his good shoulder.

"I know most folks say I'm a cold man, Quinn."

"You've never been cold with me, just silent sometimes. You've always been kind. Maybe not so much in words, but in your touch."

"I need to say the words, if only once. You deserve as much and more. I want you in my life. I want you living at the Double K. I want to raise our child together and sleep with you every night. I want to see you in white in front of all our friends so we can promise forever."

"You want a great deal, Staten."

"It's not just a need. I'm not alive if I'm not with you. I have to say it all. I love you, Quinn."

She cuddled against him. "I know, Staten. I love you, too. I have for a long time. You may not know it, but you're my hero. I might have been the one charging the dragon tonight, but you were the one who stood beside me ready to fight."

"All the details can be talked about later, Quinn. Now is the time to show you how much you mean to me."

His big hand moved over her in a gentle embrace. "I don't want just to be in the corners of your world anymore. You've become my entire world."

All night she'd held herself in check. She wouldn't cry. She would not allow herself to break. Only now, as Staten began kissing her, she felt tears bubbling from her eyes.

"What's wrong?" he asked.

"Nothing," she answered. "Absolutely nothing."

The boy who'd always been kind to that shy little girl. The man who opened up to her as he did with no one in his world. The lover who always waited for her to make the first move. The father of her child who wanted her safe and near.

The man who'd just discovered he loved her when she'd loved him all her life. All were with her tonight.

"I love you, Quinn," he whispered against her hair.

"I know," she answered. "I know."

Twenty-Eight

Lauren

Lauren sat on the tailgate of Lucas's old pickup and swung her legs as he draped a blanket over her shoulders. The night really wasn't cold, but she liked the thought of him taking care of her.

He was her first boyfriend. The first guy who liked her, really liked her. It was exciting, newborn and somehow very grown up, all at the same time.

They were back in the pasture where Lucas loved to watch the stars. It was his favorite place, and she knew when he was away at college it would be hers. That is if she ever got a car and could come out here.

She knew it was on the Kirkland ranch and didn't belong to them, but somehow it was their secret spot. Maybe she'd write about tonight in her diary, then when she had a few friends over, she might read about exactly what it was like in the moonlight.

"I can't believe your dad looked at me and ordered me to take you home." Lucas laughed. "Man, did he look mad at all those old folks after the concert. I think if he'd had access to a cattle truck, he would have loaded them all in, walkers and canes included."

Lauren smiled. "He wouldn't have trusted you if he knew you'd bring me here first and not straight home. I'm sure he thinks I'm safe at the house by now."

"I know. If he knew we'd be stopping out here alone, he'd probably be madder than hell." Lucas sat beside her. "This is where you're supposed to say that he'd be all right with it."

She giggled. "I can't lie. If he knew we were here, he'd shoot you. It's nothing to do with you, though. It's just that he hasn't finished lecturing me yet about boys. I think I've got at least another year of lectures before he'll trust me to go out."

"I'll wait," Lucas said. "Now and then, when I'm home, I'll call and we can talk, but, Lauren, we got to do this right. It's too special not to."

She smiled up at him. "You make me feel good when you say stuff like that. Even if you don't mean it."

"What if I did, Lauren? Would it scare you?"

"A little, maybe. I don't think long-term like you do."

He covered her hand with his. "We're going to both change in the next few years. We need to start out as friends. I'd like that."

"Me, too." She'd never had a date. She had a great deal to figure out before she could even talk about what happened after friends.

He must have felt the same way because they talked about the stars and the few months of school that were left. He told her again about what the Texas Tech campus was like and how different life would be for him there.

They talked about the night at the Gypsy House and how she still owed him a blood debt.

Half an hour passed, and she finally said she needed to go home. Even though she loved being with him, Lauren felt like she was lying to Pop. For the second time in her life, she knew she was doing something he wouldn't approve of. Maybe when she was a little older it wouldn't matter, but now she didn't want to lie to him.

Lucas must have felt the same way, because he didn't try to kiss her. He said he'd wait. Maybe he knew that what might be growing between them was more than a few stolen dates. Or, maybe he simply didn't want complications right now.

They were folding up the blanket when she heard the rumble of an engine.

"Someone's on the ranch," he whispered.

They climbed into the truck and listened. After a while Lucas whispered, "It sounds like they are driving the fence lines. Like they're checking for something."

"But what?"

"Maybe a break in the fence. But cowboys do that in daylight, not at night. They wouldn't be checking this fence anyway. There are no cattle here."

Lauren thought for a minute and asked, "When are cattle moved in this pasture?"

"Another week, maybe sooner. Mr. Kirkland is buying calves now." Lucas turned toward her. "That's it! Whoever is driving out here is checking to see if the cattle are on grass yet. Somehow they know a herd is coming. They just don't know when."

"Who sets the date?"

"Kirkland, but there are lots of factors to consider before they're moved. We all know the work is coming, but which pasture, how many cattle, even when the trucks come, all has to be figured out along with a dozen other details like weather and the vet's schedule. Collins has a ranch hand named Arlo who sets his dates and the number of cows moved on the Collins place, but from what I hear, Kirkland makes the call here on the Double K."

"So," Lauren whispered, "if I were a cattle rustler, I might come out every night to check."

Lucas nodded slowly. "And if I wanted to make sure none of the cowhands were wandering around, I'd shoot at the first one I saw." Lucas thumped his head against the back glass. "I heard one of the men say he didn't plan to check this pasture at night, no matter what the foreman said. Some, if not all the men, are leery of the chore."

"Take me home, Lucas, and we'll wait for Pop. I want to tell him our theory."

An hour later they were watching a movie when her dad stepped through the front door. He looked tired, but when he saw Lucas he didn't react like she thought he might.

"You didn't have to stay, Lucas," he said, straightening to his sheriff's stance. Pop was acting like Lucas had stayed to babysit her until an adult got home.

Lucas stood. "I wanted to talk to you, sir. Lauren and I have a theory about what happened on the Kirkland ranch."

"Can't it wait till morning?"

Lauren jumped in. "When Lucas was bringing me home he told me about seeing a car driving the back pasture road late last night."

Together they told her father all the facts, except

that they'd been on the land tonight. To his credit, the sheriff listened.

"Why didn't you go to Kirkland with this?"

Lucas answered. "We tried calling both his house phone at the ranch and his mobile. He didn't answer either."

"I can believe that." Pop smiled as if he knew a secret. "Thanks for telling me. I promise I'll check on it tomorrow morning. Good night, Lucas. Thanks for seeing my daughter home safely."

"You're welcome." Lucas walked to the door. "Good night, Lauren. See you at school Monday."

"See you," Lauren answered.

When the door closed, she expected her pop to start his lecture on never letting anyone into the house when he wasn't home, but Pop just picked up one of the bowls of popcorn and asked what movie was on.

"Aren't you going to lecture me?" she asked.

"Nope. You must have trusted the guy or you wouldn't have let him in. Plus, you two came up with the best theory on why Kirkland got shot that I've heard."

They went over facts of the case in a way that he'd never talked to her about his work. It was as if, now that she was sixteen, she wasn't a kid anymore. Or maybe Margaret had convinced him he was being too hard on her. Who knew, maybe Pop was just getting old and more relaxed.

As they turned out the lights, she asked, "So, Lucas is okay?"

"I wouldn't have asked him to see you home if he wasn't. Kirkland thinks a lot of the kid." Pop reached his bedroom door and turned to say good-night.

"So, it's all right if I go out on a date with him sometime?" She opened her door a few feet down the hall. "That is, if he ever asks me."

"No. He's too old for you."

"But only by a year." She forgot to add that they were only a year apart in age by three days. "He's graduating early."

"We'll talk about it later." Pop closed his door before she could build her defense.

Twenty-Nine

Yancy

Yancy loaded all the old folks into their cars, then walked the few blocks to the retirement community. Ellie had already driven to the other end and promised to make sure each got to their little bungalow safely.

He didn't mind the walk. He needed to clear his head. The only danger might be one of the old folks running over him, and he hoped they were all ahead of him.

When he was in prison, his mind mostly drifted. Every day was about the same. Now that he was out, it was like waking up in a new world every morning. There were things to figure out. Reading hidden meanings in what folks said and what they didn't. Trying to jump into the conversation at the right time. Knowing when to shut up. Part of Yancy wanted to go back to his cell, just for a day or two, to rest his brain.

He straightened and walked faster. The sheriff said he was a deputy tonight. Him, Yancy Grey from nowhere, who didn't have a family, or a driver's license, or a bank account, or much of anything else. He was a deputy, if only for tonight.

Slowly his shoulders slumped as he remembered what the ex-con named Cowboy had told him. Yancy knew he was in trouble the minute he'd seen them, and it hadn't taken the pair long to figure out who he was. Cowboy said he was one of them and always would be. If he didn't go along with them, they'd name him as one of their gang if they got caught, and he'd get the same time they got. So, like it or not, Yancy was a part of their gang. If all went as planned, Cowboy promised he'd get a cut; if it didn't, they'd meet up again in prison.

The first time he'd gone, Yancy had been caught stealing. He really had no one to blame but himself. If Cowboy turned him in just to get back at him, every day of prison would seem ten times as hard. Yancy didn't want to go back. He couldn't.

That night in the shadows of Dorothy's Café, Yancy hadn't said a word. He'd simply listened. Part of what they said had to be true. Both Cowboy and Freddie knew the ropes. They had a man at the Collins ranch helping them, filling them in on details no one in town would know. A guy named Arlo would keep them informed and hide the cattle truck they'd stolen until they made the raid.

The plan was to go in right after Kirkland moved his cattle to the far pasture and round them up the first night. This wasn't going to be a small operation. They planned to pack the truck and be a few hundred miles down the road before dawn.

Cowboy said they'd get rid of what they were driving now, so no one would catch them. The truck they'd stolen to haul eighty head was already hidden on the

Collins place. Cowboy knew someone in New Mexico who'd take the calves off their hands. Freddie promised they only wanted Yancy as a lookout. Someone far enough back from the crime to give them warning.

It crossed Yancy's mind that he should report the cons to the sheriff, but he didn't know any details. Not the man's full name on the Collins ranch or the night it would happen. All they'd told him was that they had a plan in the works, and when it came through, they'd be rolling in money.

Freddie had even hinted that Yancy could make more in one night than most folks around town made in a month.

But, Yancy didn't care about the money. He had enough to take Ellie out on a date, and that seemed enough. But he was too scared to say anything to Cowboy or Freddie. All he'd done was nod as if he was going along with whatever they said.

A few days had passed and, when he didn't hear from them, Yancy figured they'd either changed their plan or moved on. He didn't care as long as they didn't bother him.

Yancy turned into the Evening Shadows Retirement Community trying to figure out what a normal person would do, not that he'd ever be normal with guys like Cowboy and Freddie turning up to remind him how worthless he was.

Plan or no plan, they'd reminded him that the life he was living would never work for long. There'd always be someone who noticed something different about him, or one of the cons showing up to remind him he wasn't like most people.

When he saw Ellie waiting for him on the office

steps, he forgot about being a deputy or worrying what Cowboy had planned. It wouldn't happen for a while, if ever. He had plenty of time to think about how to handle his problem. With luck, he'd have a few more days to be normal. Maybe that's all a guy like him could hope for.

"Did they all find their own little houses?" he asked as he walked up to the steps of the office. She looked so prim and proper in her dress-up clothes, but he kind of missed the cape.

"I think it was a full night for them." She patted the step beside her. "I'm just happy that they made it back home safe and sound. A few of them got so wound up, I got worried."

"Me, too. I'm getting attached to them." He sat down so near they were touching. "The day I got to town someone stole my backpack. I had no money, no clothes, nothing. The guys got together and gave me what I needed, but it was the women who had the idea to hire me to help out around the place. I figured it'd last a month, maybe more, but they're talking about building more bungalows and reopening the pool and getting the city to put in a park over where we burned the tree branches that first day. When that happens they won't just need a handyman, they'll need a manager for this place."

Ellie leaned back with her elbows on the next step. "So you're thinking you might stay? I've lived here all my life, and I think it's a great place to live."

Yancy thought of Cowboy and Freddie. Maybe the best thing to do was run. "I might. I have to see how things work out."

His brain fell off track again when he noticed that without her cape she didn't seem so round. She did have big breasts, though. He had to remind himself not to look at them again, and again, and again.

He decided to step out on a limb. "Ellie, would you mind if I kiss you?"

"No, I wouldn't mind. I've already rubbed my lipstick off."

He decided that was a definite yes. He leaned in, liking the way her breasts cushioned the contact just before his lips hit hers. There were a few things about kissing a chubby woman that made it downright delightful.

Half an hour later, when she left, Yancy figured he'd practiced kissing until he had it down pat. Funny thing about kissing, it pretty much erased every other thought in your mind. He wouldn't be surprised if there wasn't some kind of kissing overload disease that could happen if he got too much of a good thing.

He made it to his room, undressed and fell into bed thinking that if heaven was just reliving one day in your life over and over, he hoped it was this one.

Unfortunately, at dawn the next morning hell came to call. Yancy opened his eyes to see both Cowboy and Freddie perched on the end of his bed like hungry vultures looking for roadkill.

Cowboy started talking before Yancy was fully awake. "We need you to do us a little favor."

"I can't." Yancy sat up. "I have to work today."

"This won't take long." Freddie pushed hard against Yancy's chest. "We need you to be somewhere tonight at exactly midnight. All you have to do is be there as a lookout. If you spot any trouble riding, fire one shot. We'll do the rest."

"I don't have a gun."

Freddie dropped an old dirty .45 beside Yancy. "You

do now. Set up at the county road where it turns off toward the Double K."

When Freddie straightened, Yancy couldn't miss how the man patted the knife at his side.

Both cons backed away, but it was Cowboy who left the parting promise. "Be there at midnight and be armed, or we'll be back, and you and that chubby little girlfriend of yours won't look so pretty when we get through with you. You don't want to see what Freddie can do with a knife faster than you have time to yell."

Yancy didn't breathe until he heard the office door slam behind the men. He was afraid to move. Afraid to touch the gun. Afraid to picture what might happen if he didn't play along with their plan.

The nightmare he'd had for years in prison had come to haunt him. There was no way out. He had to do what they said, and when he did, he'd give up the chance to be a normal man...he'd be a criminal. Again. And, if they got caught, he'd be back in prison.

He no longer had to worry what normal people do. Yancy Grey knew he wasn't normal and never would be. That one night of kissing Ellie would be his last. Even if they didn't get caught on Kirkland's land, Yancy knew he'd have to run. Staying in town would just be asking to get caught.

All morning he worked, swearing he would not take anything from the old folks. Tonight, he'd take Cap's keys and do his midnight watch, then he'd park the car back in the same spot and catch the six o'clock bus out of town. He'd take a few clothes and all the money he'd saved, but he'd leave the leather shaving kit and the warm wool coat and the good gloves.

If he didn't do exactly that, Ellie might get hurt. He

might get killed. It was time for him to wake up from his dream of living a normal life.

He worked until dark trying to get as much done on his lists, then he walked to his room behind the lobby.

Yancy was so tired and worried he almost didn't notice the tray of food on the counter. Pot roast with all the trimmings, and a slice of cherry pie.

A small note had been shoved under the plate. It read: *Enjoy your supper. We don't know what we'd do without you. Miss Bees.*

Thirty

Staten

Staten moved among his men inside the main barn. The sounds of horses stomping and blowing out air surrounded him, along with the rub of leather against leather and spurs jingling as his men saddled up.

Most of the guys had been working all day, but their horses were fresh and ready to run. Even the animals seemed to pick up the excitement circling in the air like a dust devil on freshly plowed ground.

For a moment Staten felt he'd stepped back in time to the wild days of the West. And maybe he had. For miles around they only had one sheriff and one ranger. Not enough lawmen to stop what was about to happen on his land. Even though both lawmen would do the legal thing, the right thing, they didn't truly understand what the land meant to him. It was in his blood, his backbone, his heart.

Smiling, he remembered how his granny used to set the pies on the windowsill to cool. She'd always comment the wind would dust the meringue, so he'd have

Double K mixed in his blood. She'd been right. Staten didn't just own the land, he *was* the ranch.

He moved between two mares and stopped near Dan Brigman. "You going to be able to handle a horse, Sheriff? Jake and a few others are following behind us in pickups. You're welcome to ride with them."

"I can make it fine on horseback." Dan grinned. "I was a Boy Scout."

Staten nodded. He'd given the sheriff a great horse that would run with all the others. As long as Dan held on, he'd be fine.

Staten stood on one of Jake's stools and yelled, "We leave at full dark and ride down into the canyon. It's not the shortest way to the back pasture, but it'll get us there unseen and hopefully, thanks to the wind tonight, unheard.

"Once we get to the arroyo, we form a single line, three or four horse lengths apart. We travel slow and silent. I don't want any of you flushing a covey of quail from a clump of yucca if you can help it."

The men nodded.

"Once you all clear the ridge, stand about six feet apart. When the last man clears, wait for the lead rider's signal. Then, pull your rifles from your scabbards and stand ready. When he makes a sign, I want every rider to lock and load. Those of you with shotguns rack them loud. There is no mistaking that sound."

Dan took over. "Remember. We're not expecting any trouble. We want this arrest to go smooth, without any gunfire. You men will keep the peace simply by standing. These fellows tonight are dangerous. If they thought they had us outnumbered they might try to gun us down.

"Once the ranger and I have them under arrest, the two pickups will come in and back us up. Light should flood the pasture about then, and it may spook a few of the cows."

Staten added, "When the men are handcuffed and safely in custody, I want those rifles put away, and every man on horseback will help take care of the herd. Everything you'll need to fix fences is in Jake's truck. I don't want a man or a calf hurt tonight."

Every cowhand nodded. They'd heard the orders and understood what was said, as well as what wasn't said. No rustler would be getting away. They'd all be in jail before dawn. The trouble the ranches had with rustlers around the area would be over tonight. By using all the men, they were making a stand.

Staten led his horse toward Jake. "You drive one pickup and let Lucas follow in mine. Make sure both are mounted with floodlights."

Jake spit into the darkness. "Lucas is saddled and ready to ride."

Staten shook his head, hating the idea of the kid being involved so closely in this. It was too dangerous, even with the precautions they were taking. Lucas could get hurt. Anyone of his men might be hurt.

Jake stared at Staten. "He knows the canyon as good as you do, boss. He's ridden through it all his life. Plus, he's got a cell phone. He can keep in touch with you." When Staten didn't move, Jake added, "He's a man who rides for the brand, just like all these men. Don't make him less. It wouldn't be the right thing to do."

Staten nodded, knowing that if he pulled Lucas, he'd be saying the kid wasn't as valuable as his other men or as good. "But, who'll drive the other truck?"

"How about that new guy the sheriff brought over tonight? The one that the prairie dog gnawed on. I've been watching him. I may be wrong, but I don't think he knows which end of the horse is which. I asked him if he rode and he said, 'How hard could it be?'"

"You're right. Tell him he's driving the truck and keep tailing you all the way. If he fell off a horse when we cross down into the canyon, we wouldn't find him for a month."

Staten raised his hand and motioned for every man to be ready.

Five minutes later, forty men were riding toward the canyon wall. There was an excitement dancing with the dark shadows of men on horseback racing. Staten could feel it. Breathed it in with the wind. What they were doing tonight would change things.

He only hoped they would change for the better.

Ten minutes later, one by one they pointed their mounts down into the canyon. Lucas took the lead, raising his arm as if about to ride his first wild pony. The kid made the descent look easy.

Staten swore he heard Lucas laugh as he followed the kid down.

All his men had gone down into the canyon before to look for strays. They knew to lean back and let the horse pick his way.

Glancing back at the sheriff, Staten hoped the Boy Scouts taught him well. Dan was wobbling but hanging on. If he took a fall his biggest worry would be the horse rolling over on him. Second worry, he'd roll off a cliff. The fall might only be twenty or thirty feet before he hit rock, but the landing would probably break a few bones.

Once they leveled out on the wide canyon floor, the men rode slowly in groups of two or three. The moon was out and offered enough light to see ahead. The horses needed rest, and Staten knew they had a few hours ride before they circled around to the far pasture.

He thought it strange how all the pastures had a name. He'd heard a few of the huge ranches just used numbers, but as long as he could remember, each of his pastures bore a name not written on any post. The north pasture, the south, timber pasture, Miller pasture, named after the man who'd sold his grandfather the land. And, of course, the far pasture.

Lucas pulled his gray alongside Staten. "It's a good plan," he said. "One that will get the least people hurt. Too bad we couldn't just arrest them at the gate."

"I heard you came up with the reason men were on my land at night. Makes sense." Staten wasn't surprised. Lucas had a way of worrying a problem until he figured it out.

"Lauren and I were just talking about it after the concert." Lucas paused, then added, "The sheriff asked me to take Lauren home. He seemed to have his hands full. We may have thought of the reason men were watching the land, but how'd you know it was going to be tonight?"

"The sheriff told me he had an informant who said there's a man on the Collins place who is working with the rustlers. Said the guy has a stolen truck stashed on the place. This is a crime that has been in the planning stage for at least a month. Have you noticed any extra trucks around the Collins place?"

"Maybe." Lucas shrugged. "There are lots of barns almost empty of hay right now. It wouldn't be that hard to drive an empty cattle truck in the back. Collins men might not question it. But wouldn't someone miss a truck that size?"

"Not if it was stolen across the state lines. It could already be in the barn before state troopers realized it was gone." Staten saw the kid putting together all the facts in his head.

"When we climb out of the canyon, only the sheriff, me, and two other men will ride toward the rustlers. They won't expect anyone coming from the canyon side of the pasture. I want you to stay with the other men and make sure they fall into line. I don't want someone rushing in before we get the bad guys rounded up or, worse, firing to spook the rustlers or the cattle. I'll call your cell and let it ring once when it's time to move the men to the ridge."

"Any advice on how I do that?"

"Start giving calm orders when you ride along the ravine. Repeat exactly what each man is to do. Tell them if they get mixed up, follow your lead."

"Yes, sir." Lucas didn't sound too sure.

"Keep your voice calm and strong. Hard as a rock. They'll follow."

They moved on in silence, and Staten thought of Quinn. She'd be upset if she knew what was going on. In fact she'd be panicked. Even when this was all over, he knew he wouldn't tell her the whole story.

For the hundredth time he tried to picture himself living at her house. Maybe if he knocked out a wall and built a couple of rooms on, or took all the gingerbread trim off, or went up and built a second floor.

Nothing worked. He might hate his dark house on his land, but at least he could live in it without bumping into walls. He could never relax there on Lavender Lane knowing he needed to be here. There wasn't even an extra drawer for him to put his stuff in or a place for his shaving kit on her sink, or enough counter space in the kitchen to keep his supplies.

Funny that he was thinking about such a little problem when he was riding into what might turn out to be the biggest battle of his life.

What did the house matter? It was Quinn and the baby that he wanted. That he *needed*.

As the night aged he worried where they'd put the baby's things in her house. A crib in a bedroom not big enough for a king-size bed. The swing, the high chair, the changing table, the toys. Quinn had never had a kid. She didn't know that they came with a van load of junk.

Only, he couldn't see a child in his house. Not Quinn's child. At one time the house hadn't seemed so bad, but now sadness seemed to hang in the corners like leftover dust.

"You all right?" Lucas broke into his thoughts.

"Yeah, why?" Staten snapped.

"You were mumbling and cussing under your breath."

Staten wasn't surprised. In the five years he'd lived alone, he'd caught himself talking to no one a hundred times. When it happened, he usually took the time to cuss himself out.

"I'm thinking of giving up cussing," he said to Lucas. "Bad habit to get into."

Staten wanted to change the subject. "You got any bad habits, kid?"

"My mom says I'm always planning for the future and sometimes don't see what's going on in the present. She says I might fall over today while I'm dreaming about tomorrow."

Staten smiled. "I guess I do the same thing, except I worry about someday and don't take the time to just walk through today." He laughed. "Hell, kid, we sound like we're damn philosophers."

"You still getting rid of cuss words, Mr. Kirkland?"

"Yep."

They grew quiet and began to watch the side of the canyon. Both didn't want to miss the ribbon of red, sandy mud that would mark the place they'd have to climb.

Staten tasted excitement peppered with a dash of fear. He'd never felt so alive in his life.

He'd never wanted to live forever as much as he did right now.

Thirty-One

Sheriff Brigman pulled his horse to the front beside Staten when they reached the end of the ravine. The far pasture spread out before them like a midnight blanket of grass barely starting to green.

Lucas dropped back, raised his hand, and all the men behind stopped to wait for their order to ride. They'd stay behind in the shadows just below the ridge until it was time.

Staten pulled his rifle and laid it over his arm. The sheriff and the ranger did the same.

Slowly, like a thundercloud moving low over the land, Staten and the two lawmen rode their horses toward the shadow of a cattle truck backed up against the loading chutes at the corner of the pasture. Two men were running the cattle in one at a time while a third man loaded them onto the truck.

Staten heard the quick jerking movements of the cattle, their hooves clicking against the rock and metal, their low cries of complaint at being bothered. He could have been blindfolded and still known what was happening.

This was no haphazard operation. Seventy or eighty head of yearlings would be a substantial loss. These men weren't some small-time farmer feeding his family with one stolen cow. This was an organized crime.

Staten circled in the shadows until he was behind a tall man who almost looked like a real cowboy, but his movements were too impatient. He might be accustomed to riding, but he wasn't skilled at working cattle.

The sheriff and the ranger moved toward the truck, coming up on the back side, so the one loading wouldn't see them until they were a few feet away.

The other two men who'd followed Staten out of the ravine took the rustler closest to the road. He was shorter, less skilled than his partners.

The click of Brigman racking a round into the chamber sounded almost as loud as a gunshot in the silent night. Staten touched his phone so it dialed Lucas. The glow of the phone drew the cowboy's attention.

Staten wasn't surprised when the rustler in the Stetson pulled his gun.

"Aim that weapon and you're dead." Staten's voice came hard and clear as the barrel of his rifle leveled on his target.

The tall cowboy hesitated, as did the bald guy near the fence.

For a few seconds he saw the tall man's head turn, as if he might try something. Then, like a whisper, came the sounds of rifles being racked along the ridge. Forty weapons were pointed directly at the three men in the pasture.

A line of shadows, rifles raised to take aim, stood as silent guardians.

All three of the rustlers raised their hands. They

might have had a chance with the men before them, but they knew they'd be sitting ducks for the men on the ridge.

One by one they climbed from their horses. The cowboy and the man at the truck didn't protest, but the bald guy jerked as if he thought he might pull free and run.

Dan Brigman fought him to the ground.

In a single flash of light from the pickup pulling up, Staten saw a knife reflect. Without hesitation, he slammed his boot against the hand that held the knife.

The rustler yelped in pain as Brigman pulled the outlaw's injured hand behind his back and cuffed him.

"Thanks," the sheriff said as he pulled the man up. "I appreciate the help."

"Anytime," Staten answered, suddenly feeling like laughing. It was over. They'd done it. The plan had worked.

Staten didn't take a deep breath until all three men were crammed into the back of the cruiser. A tall rustler known as Cowboy, his friend who went by Freddie and a third man who worked for the Collins ranch who only gave a first name of Arlo.

When Cowboy saw Yancy talking to the sheriff, he yelled that Yancy was one of his gang.

The sheriff leaned down by the window and said, "Wrong. He's one of *our* gang."

The men moved like ghosts in the night repairing the fence, removing the cattle truck and making sure none of the cows were hurt. They'd be checked again in the morning. Every man was back to doing his regular work, but this night would be talked about for years.

Staten tossed his saddle and bridle into Jake's pickup. He turned his horse loose, climbed into the cab of his truck and looked back at the handyman from his granny's retirement home. "How about I give you a ride home, Yancy?"

"Okay," he yelled, just seeming to realize there was not any room in the cruiser with three prisoners in the back and a ranger riding shotgun.

As they drove back to town, they went over every detail of the night. Finally, Staten admitted, "None of this would have happened if you hadn't tipped us off."

"I had to," Yancy said. "I didn't want anyone in this community to get hurt. You know, I don't have a family, but if I did, I think it would feel like this."

"You're one of this community now, Yancy, for as long as you want to be. If the job disappears where you are, you're always welcome at headquarters. I can always use a good man."

"Would I have to ride a horse?"

"Yep, but how hard could it be?"

Thirty-Two

Staten drove back to headquarters, feeling as if he hadn't slept in weeks. His shoulder and arm ached, but he refused to put the sling back on. He could handle the pain. First, he needed to check on his men.

He found most of them in the bunkhouse having breakfast, as if they hadn't been up all night. After half a pot of coffee and half an hour of talk, he told them all to sleep in shifts and run a lean crew for what had to be done.

The foreman and Jake took over, making assignments, and the cowhands groaned as they moved away from the table.

Staten headed back to his truck. He had one more errand to do before calling it a night. Dan Brigman had been by his side all night, and the sheriff's work probably wouldn't be done for hours. Staten wanted to help any way he could.

He wasn't surprised to find Dan toiling in his office. Without wasting time with small talk, they went to work putting down every detail for the report. The three men who'd tried to rob him needed to go to jail for a long time. No telling how many times they'd attempted smaller operations.

Two hours later Dan offered to buy Staten breakfast, and they walked down to Dorothy's Café.

Once they were settled and the specials were ordered, Staten said, "You mind if I ask you something, Sheriff?"

"Go ahead."

"Well—" he'd talked to the guy most of the past twenty-four hours, but this was hard to say "—I was wondering if you'd consider being my best man. I'm thinking of getting married."

Brigman laughed. "To who?"

"Damn it, who do you think?" Now, after he'd risked his life beside Dan Brigman, Staten found out the man was a nitwit. "Hell, forget I asked."

The sheriff simply laughed. "Of course I'll be your best man, but Quinn's not going to say yes to you. Not even if you ask her real nice like you just did me."

Staten grumbled over his coffee. "You're probably right. But she sees a better me than I am, so I can always hope."

"Most women do. Except my wife. I think a wife sees the worst every chance she gets or at least mine does."

As Sissy set the platters on the table, both men gave up talking in favor of eating.

"When you going to deliver, Sissy?" Dan asked as she refilled their coffee.

"Ellie says I'm two weeks overdue. So who knows." The little waitress laughed. "Half the retirement home is eating either breakfast or lunch here every day. Mrs. Ollie said she's seen the birthing film they show in Child Development a hundred times. She thinks she can deliver in a pinch."

Dan shook his head. "When you get that first contraction, call me. I'll be here before you get your apron off."

"Thanks, Sheriff. I'll consider the offer."

Staten just kept eating as if he wasn't listening to the conversation.

Finally, when most of the six-inch stack of pancakes was gone, Dan said, "Ask Quinn to marry you, Staten. The worst she can say is no, and I'm guessing, saying no to you won't be an easy job."

Staten stood and grabbed his hat. "I think I'll go home and clean up. You're right, maybe it's time I went courtin'."

As he walked out the door, he heard Dan yell, "Long past time, Kirkland!"

Ten minutes later as headquarters came into view, the first thing he noticed was his grandparents' old place setting back in the breaks of trees. It always shone in the dawn light. For a moment he wished they were still there. They'd built their place exactly like a ranch house should be, blending into the landscape, not perched on a rise, cutting the view up.

Every time he looked that direction, he smiled. They'd been happy in the house that had birthed generations.

As he watched, his granny stepped out on the front porch and began sweeping.

For a second Staten thought he must be dreaming. Granny was in town at the retirement community. She'd never even mentioned coming back to the old place.

But there she was. Older, thinner, but standing look-

ing at him just like she'd been all those years while he'd
grown up.

Staten turned his pickup toward the old house. If this
was a mirage, he might as well find out now. It had been
more than twenty-four hours since he'd slept. Seemed
right he could be losing his mind.

By the time he reached the front porch she'd gone
inside, but he could smell pies baking.

Impossible. No one had lived in the place in twenty
years. Three months after his grandpa died, his grandmother had moved to town. She'd said the place had
too many memories.

His spurs jingled as he stomped up the steps, waiting for his granny to come out. The windows on the
old place were clean, and a few were even open to the
sweet spring air.

The old screen door creaked as Quinn stepped out,
wearing jeans and an old flannel shirt. "About time you
came home," she said.

Staten thought his heart might explode. "You're moving in with me?"

"No," she answered. "I'm moving in here. Granny
told me I could have the place." She smiled. "I was kind
of hoping you might move in here with me."

He fought from grabbing her and holding her so tight
she'd never leave, but he had to do this right. "I can't
do that, Quinn, not unless you'll marry me. This is no
fling or affair between us. This is forever. If you live
in this house, you'll take my name."

She smiled. "I could agree to those terms."

He pulled her close, lifted her off the ground and
began swinging her around and around.

Granny leaned out one of the windows. "Put her down, Staten, you'll make the baby dizzy."

He stopped but didn't turn loose of her. "You know about the baby?"

"Hell," Granny Kirkland, who'd never cussed in her life, said. "Half the town knows about the baby. Several of us have been planning the wedding and the baby shower for a month or more. Do you two really think anything happens in this town without me knowing about it?"

He kissed the top of Granny's head. "You know, I don't think I ever need to sleep again. I'm dreaming right now."

Then he turned, and right in front of his grandmother, he asked Quinn to marry him.

And as he knew she would, Quinn said yes to the man she'd always loved.

Thirty-Three

Lauren

"Hello, Lauren. Did you hear the news?"

"About the capture of the rustlers?" she whispered into her new phone. "Everyone is talking about it. Are you all right, Lucas? I heard you were in on the fight, and you weren't at school today."

He laughed. "I slept all day, and it wasn't much of a fight. We kind of walked softly and carried a big stick."

She giggled into the phone. "You sound like Reid quoting Teddy Roosevelt."

"I felt like a Rough Rider last night." He was silent. "I've decided what I'm going to major in."

"What?"

"Law."

"Me, too," she said.

Lucas laughed then whispered, "Good night, *mi cielo*."

Yancy

A few miles away, Yancy Grey stepped from his room to the office. All the aging dwarves were gone from their usual spots in the sunny area. Mr. Halls had forgotten to wash the coffee cup he always drank cocoa from, and Miss Bees had left one of her bats by the door.

He felt like the den mother picking up after a meeting. Despite being tired, they'd all been talkative tonight. Several said the sheriff told everyone at the café that Yancy had been a hero during the capture of criminals last night.

He smiled. The sheriff had kept his secret. No one would find out how he'd known that the crime was about to be committed. When he'd gone to the sheriff's office yesterday morning, he wasn't sure if he would live to see another day. Cowboy and Freddie had been his nightmare for years. But, sometimes a man has to face his fears before he can have any hope of living a normal life.

As he walked back to his room, Yancy noticed something propped against his bedroom door.

An old backpack. The one he'd carried with him from prison.

Slowly he picked up the pack that had been missing for almost three months.

It felt heavier than it had the day he arrived in Crossroads.

Yancy dumped out all he'd owned a few months ago on the bed.

Then for a long while Yancy just stared at the contents. Brand-new underwear and socks. The bloody shirt he'd worn when he'd been arrested more than five years ago had been washed and folded neatly. His initials had been embossed onto the leather shaving kit. A brand-new wool coat and gloves, the tags still on them. The three hundred dollars he'd lied about having was in a wallet.

Who, he wondered. Someone had stolen his pack and then returned it with all he'd dreamed of having in it.

A tear ran down his cheek. He'd achieved his goal. He was rich.

Walking out into the night he smiled out at the midnight sky and knew there was only one thing left to do in his life.

Set himself some new goals.

* * * * *

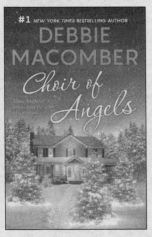

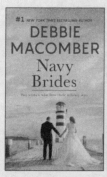
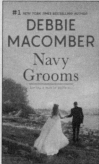
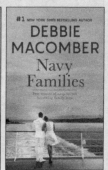

Get 4 FREE REWARDS!

We'll send you 2 FREE Books plus 2 FREE Mystery Gifts.

FREE Value Over **$20**

Both the **Romance** and **Suspense** collections feature compelling novels written by many of today's best-selling authors.

DEBBIE MACOMBER

33019	ALASKA HOME	___	$7.99 U.S.	___	$9.99 CAN.
32918	AN ENGAGEMENT IN SEATTLE	___	$7.99 U.S.	___	$9.99 CAN.
32798	ORCHARD VALLEY GROOMS	___	$7.99 U.S.	___	$9.99 CAN.
31894	ALWAYS DAKOTA	___	$7.99 U.S.	___	$9.99 CAN.
31888	DAKOTA HOME	___	$7.99 U.S.	___	$9.99 CAN.
31883	DAKOTA BORN	___	$7.99 U.S.	___	$9.99 CAN.
31868	COUNTRY BRIDE	___	$7.99 U.S.	___	$9.99 CAN.
31864	THE MANNING GROOMS	___	$7.99 U.S.	___	$9.99 CAN.
31860	THE MANNING BRIDES	___	$7.99 U.S.	___	$9.99 CAN.
31829	TRADING CHRISTMAS	___	$7.99 U.S.	___	$9.99 CAN.
31580	MARRIAGE BETWEEN FRIENDS	___	$7.99 U.S.	___	$8.99 CAN.
31551	A REAL PRINCE	___	$7.99 U.S.	___	$8.99 CAN.
31441	HEART OF TEXAS VOLUME 2	___	$7.99 U.S.	___	$8.99 CAN.
31413	LOVE IN PLAIN SIGHT	___	$7.99 U.S.	___	$9.99 CAN.
31341	THE UNEXPECTED HUSBAND	___	$7.99 U.S.	___	$9.99 CAN.
31325	A TURN IN THE ROAD	___	$7.99 U.S.	___	$9.99 CAN.
31917	BECAUSE IT'S CHRISTMAS	___	$7.99 U.S.	___	$9.99 CAN.
31535	PROMISE TEXAS	___	$7.99 U.S.	___	$8.99 CAN.
33018	ALASKA NIGHTS	___	$7.99 U.S.	___	$9.99 CAN.
31624	ON A CLEAR DAY	___	$7.99 U.S.	___	$8.99 CAN.
31903	WEDDING DREAMS	___	$7.99 U.S.	___	$9.99 CAN.
31907	THE KNITTING DIARIES	___	$7.99 U.S.	___	$9.99 CAN.
31926	THE SOONER THE BETTER	___	$7.99 U.S.	___	$9.99 CAN

(limited quantities available)

TOTAL AMOUNT	$ _____
POSTAGE & HANDLING	$ _____
($1.00 for 1 book, 50¢ for each additional)	
APPLICABLE TAXES*	$ _____
TOTAL PAYABLE	$ _____

(check or money order—please do not send cash)

To order, complete this form and send it, along with a check or money order for the total above, payable to MIRA Books, to: **In the U.S.:** 3010 Walden Avenue, P.O. Box 9077, Buffalo, NY 14269-9077; **In Canada:** P.O. Box 636, Fort Erie, Ontario, L2A 5X3.

Name: _____

Address: _____ City: _____

State/Prov.: _____ Zip/Postal Code: _____

Account Number (if applicable): _____

075 CSAS

mira

Harlequin.com

MDM1217BL

*New York residents remit applicable sales taxes.
*Canadian residents remit applicable GST and provincial taxes.